From Dream to Dream

From Dream to Dream

❧

Arlene Golds

FROM DREAM TO DREAM

This is a work of fiction. All the characters and events portrayed in this book are fictional, and any resemblance to real people or incidents is purely coincidental.

A Baen Books Original

Baen Publishing Enterprises
P.O. Box 1403
Riverdale, NY 10471
www.baen.com

ISBN 10: 1-4165-2066-X
ISBN 13: 978-1-4165-2066-5

Cover art by Tom Kidd

First printing, June 2006

Distributed by Simon & Schuster
1230 Avenue of the Americas
New York, NY 10020

Library of Congress Cataloging-in-Publication Data

Golds, Arlene.
  From dream to dream / Arlene Golds.
      p. cm.
  ISBN 1-4165-2066-X (hc)
  I. Title.

  PS3607.O475F76 2006
  813'.6—dc22

                                                        2006003142

10 9 8 7 6 5 4 3 2 1

Pages by Joy Freeman (www.pagesbyjoy.com)
Printed in the United States of America

This book is dedicated to my husband and children,

who only complained a little about all of the time

I spent pecking away at my computer.

ɔѵɔ

Chapter 1

Pausing to tear a shuddering yet strangely silent breath from her uncooperative lungs, she glanced hurriedly at the hazy outlines of her surroundings. No longer did she retain any sense of direction, and from the first she had lacked any concept of how she had found herself darting through this maze of buildings that rose above her and pressed in from all sides. There was no trail of bread crumbs or even tears to lead her back through the twists and turns of this night, but for all her inability to retrace a single step or to work her way free to the end of this labyrinth, she knew exactly where she was. She was trapped in the murky pathways of a nightmare, and the route she had wound through the suffocating dark was oddly familiar, as was the oppressive sensation of pursuit that had clung to her heels from the moment her feet had wrenched her unwillingly from the safety of her home and out into a dream world where she somehow still felt fully and undeniably awake.

Whimpering soundlessly she plunged forward once more, her limbs heavy as if they had been exchanged for the leaden arms and legs of a massive corpse and now wanted to return to their quiet grave. She struggled against this deadweight, dragging it through a landscape that was itself as chilling and close as a tomb. The back of her neck prickled and sharp jabs of pain streaked down her spine, so she knew that her pursuers were directly behind her now, and that her strangely thick and unresponsive

1

body would never outrun them. She hurled herself at a nearby door, pounding furiously at its rough wood face, but the sound was immediately swallowed as if it had been some tasty morsel that must be guzzled whole. Truly frightened now, she opened her mouth to scream, but the dry crackle that surfaced was sucked away by the swelling silence even before the feeble sound could reach her ears. Panting noiselessly, she turned back toward the night, but the path had closed before her as if the buildings had all stepped forward to witness what would happen next. As in so many dreams that had haunted her life, there was nothing she could do, nowhere she could run, and nowhere to hide from whatever menace stalked her.

The scrape of a foot on pavement finally sundered the silence that had enclosed her, and then she could hear the harsh rasp of voices. With a sense of futility that she had known in countless dreams, she pressed her back against the unyielding door and tried to lose herself in its shadow. As she huddled in the meager darkness, the grate of footsteps and voices grew louder, echoing back and forth off of walls that leaned dangerously forward in their eagerness to watch what transpired on the ground far below. From the swirling gray fog that was the eternal landscape of nightmares, two figures emerged, looming both monstrous and indistinct.

The squeal of teeth grinding against teeth pierced her eardrums, and she winced at the abrasive sound. From a profile that momentarily boasted a snout above a fang-filled, jutting jaw, a voice rasped, "Why the sudden orders to actually catch this one? She seems no different from the others." As he spoke, the snout faded into a large but otherwise human nose, and the fangs and jaw both melted as if into a mist.

The hunched and shaggy form shambling beside the other raised a hulking head, and an unexpected and inexplicable shaft of light reflected off eyes that glowed yellow, but as she watched from her precarious hiding place, the form of this pursuer also wavered, appearing human one second and monstrous the next, and then once again human, or maybe something in between. "I don't know," his voice grumbled, "but he must sense something unusual in this one, or he wouldn't have sent us for the kill."

A wave of dizziness struck her, almost knocking her from her feet and pulling her into the dark, airless depths that surged around her, but her eyes clung stubbornly to the wavering forms of her stalkers as if seeing them clearly was the only thing that could save her from drowning, the only thing that could somehow keep her from being seen. The two had passed her now, but had yet to turn their faces in the direction of the shallow recess where she stood unmoving, eyes stinging as the beasts floated in and out of her vision. On they walked, away from her, as if they truly couldn't see her where she stood so near, as if her silent plea for invisibility wouldn't let them. Yet that was impossible; such a thing only happened in her dreams, and whatever nightmare held her, she still couldn't believe that this was one of her dreams. Another dizzying wave swelled around her, and this time she was afraid that nothing could stop her from being swept away, not even seeing the beasts clearly, for suddenly it seemed that seeing them would be the surest way to reveal herself.

Abruptly the beast with the vacillating form of a snout stopped and turned, and she could hear the whistling sound of air sucked into his grotesquely wide nostrils. "Do you smell that?" he asked brusquely.

The other turned, his face pointed directly toward where she cowered against the door, hopelessly begging for invisibility. She could discern no features other than the gleaming yellow eyes that swept over her without the least glimmer of recognition. "I smell nothing," he growled. "You're the hound. What do you think you smell?"

Again the first one sniffed loudly, his face still lost from view except for the twitching of the flaring snout and the glint of saliva dripping from fangs as yellow as his companion's eyes. "Fear," he rumbled. "Sweat. Tears. Dreamer."

"She must have just passed this way. I see nothing," was the curt reply.

"The smell is strong. Getting stronger," the first one whined, his voice both shrill and guttural, and she was reminded briefly of a dog thrashing at the end of a leash.

"Very well," muttered the voice attached to the eyes, and as one the two massive shapes stepped a single step in her direction, their nightmare faces coming sharply into view, their eyes finally meeting hers.

Seeing her death in their eyes, she jerked backward, desperately willing the wood of the door to absorb her as effortlessly as it had earlier absorbed the sound of her panicked knock, and then she found herself suddenly and miraculously on the other side of the door. For a moment too brief to measure, she stared at the blank back of the door, and then as a gruff shout sounded from the other side, she turned and scurried away into the waiting darkness. She was not, as she would have expected, inside a house with ill-lit hallways and gloomy landings, but still outside in the corridors of night. She once more ran through the eerie and blurred landscape of a nightmare, but this time there was one crucial difference. She had finally been released from the heavy encumbrance of a bad dream. Her limbs were no longer weighed down as if by premature death, but were once more her own limbs, tired but tenacious, and prepared to race through the dark with renewed determination.

Yet despite the resurrection of her strength and energy, her situation had only grown more perilous. As she gained speed, so did her stalkers, until she could hear the pounding of their feet as one with the pounding of her heart. They were closer now than they had been since the beginning of this strange chase, and growing closer with each surge of her pulse, so close that it seemed as if their eager grunts were inside her very head. She was clearly running out of time, and unlike the many occasions she had been here before, she was certain that the death that pursued her was real and could not be evaded by forcing her eyes to open on her bedroom walls.

Before her a towering fence sprouted from the ground, and with the abrupt thrust of its appearance she once again had nowhere left to run. Directly behind her a howl of triumph ripped through the fabric of the illusory night, but she refused to turn and submissively face her mortality. There was so much in this frenzied chase through the dark that seemed stolen from some vivid dream, from threats like the beasts that hunted her to marvels like the closed door she had seeped through like water through a sponge, that when faced with no better options, she would throw herself into the arms of the seeming hallucination and hope for the best. It no longer mattered whose dream enclosed her; she would make it her own. There were limits that often bound her in her dreams, but there were also freedoms she could never possess in real life: she could render herself invisible, she could fight with the fury of a hero in some exploitation action movie, and she could fly.

In dreams she could lift herself off of the ground in an illogical defiance of gravity and soar over obstacles in her path, and with the shadowy fence looming before her, she fervently wished her feet away from the indistinct earth that held them.

For a brief moment it felt as if two hands with flaming claws had exploded from the soil to grasp her ankles, but with the same burst of will she sometimes wielded in dreams, she broke free and began to rise slowly through the air. Ponderously she rose with that heart-stopping sluggishness that too could only exist in a dream, until she was hovering a few feet above the swirling gray ground. It was too slow, she knew it was too slow, and although she willed herself to rise faster, she continued to inch upward so slowly, so painfully slowly. And it was too slow, far too slow, for suddenly the gray was broken by two glowing yellow eyes, and then two dripping fangs were ripping through the calf of one dangling leg. A bubble of pain ruptured within her, and at long last a scream broke free, the type of scream that only came with the terror of being fully awake. The scream leapt higher than the fence, vaulting toward the black sky where hazy stars vaguely twinkled like luminescent fish feeding just beneath the surface of a scum-choked pond. And attached to her scream like one of those fish hooked on a line, she was reeled into the dense heavens, torn free from the familiar pull of gravity and cast farther than the worst nightmare had ever carried her before.

Heat seeped through her lids and she opened her eyes to see specks of golden light swirling like fragments of dust in the cool morning air. Shuddering slightly, she lifted a hand to her head, shielding her eyes against the intrusion of the sun. Never since she had been a child had she had a nightmare so real, so uncanny, and yet so persistent. It had seemed so believable, the overriding urge to escape the smothering walls of her apartment, the sensation of almost immediate pursuit, the emergence of strange and murky streets to block the path back to safety. Even her stalkers, shading from beast to man and back again, had seemed as substantial as the bed in which she once again found herself. It had all been so vivid, and the fear and pain so intense, that despite all the trademarks that clearly marked it as nothing but another bad dream, the experience felt impossible to shake, more impossible than even the worst of her previous nightmares.

Only moments before she had plunged through a black sky, past dimly flashing stars, with a foreign landscape laid out beneath her like an unfinished jigsaw puzzle. Now she was herself laid out beneath the bright morning light, feeling as if more than a few of her pieces were also missing.

With a groan, she stretched her aching muscles, but as she shifted her left leg, a searing pain seized her from heel to knee, and she sat up abruptly, eyes on the offending calf. Two ragged gashes marred the smooth surface of her leg, oozing with a strange greenish fluid as well as with the bright red of her blood. She blinked in momentary confusion, for not only was her leg sluggishly bleeding, but she was also and most definitely not at home within the sheltering walls of her room. She was outside, surrounded by stunted, gnarled trees and cushioned by a thick mattress of grass.

"Just great," griped a voice from nearby. "It looks like we've got another one. I don't know what in their world is going on, but that's the eighth one this month."

Her head jerked up and her eyes focused on a scowling face with golden brown eyes and a disheveled head of rusty hair that shimmered in the sunlight like a heat mirage.

Another voice laughed, and then remarked teasingly, "I don't know why you're complaining. It's not as if they've been difficult to return. In fact, just the opposite. This one's probably no different, and we'll have her back home before she can blink." A richly golden head and sparkling blue eyes joined the glowering man, and the young woman attached to these features dropped a smile as light as the man's frown was heavy.

"Where am I, and who are you?" she croaked from where she still hunched in the grass.

"Oh, so you can talk, can you?" responded the woman, her eyes widening in surprise. "Well, that doesn't happen often, but it will certainly make things more interesting for my bored friend here."

"You're not answering my questions," she snapped irritably, fingers fisting the grass as she frowned at the faces hovering above her.

In response the woman's sunny expression was eclipsed by an uncertain frown, and she turned her eyes to the man beside her. His eyes, however, stayed firmly fixed on the face glaring up at him from the ground. "Her eyes are unnaturally focused, especially for a Dreamer," he observed, his voice impassive but his eyes a bit wild.

"That's because I'm not dreaming, at least not at this moment," she snarled from her place on the ground.

"Of course you are," responded the man, "or you wouldn't be here at all. You must just be a far more lucid Dreamer than most." He reached out a golden arm, offering her his hand. "Here, let me help you up," he ordered in a voice that precluded any possible objection. Still frowning, she slipped her fingers into his, and his hand closed over hers with a jolt of electricity, as if they both had been rubbing stockinged feet on carpeting. Without the slightest change in expression, he hauled her to her feet, but he pulled his fingers away from hers so quickly that for a fleeting second she wondered if she had somehow burned him. Then her injured leg was buckling beneath her, and all she could wonder was why the ground was rising toward her so slowly.

Two hands quickly caught her beneath her armpits as she toppled over, and she was trapped in the snare of golden brown eyes. From somewhere below her, the woman's voice gasped, and then as if from an insurmountable distance, announced, "She's hurt. Her leg is bleeding. I think . . ."

"What?" demanded the man.

The woman's voice scampered out in a breathless rush. "I think she's been bitten. By a Figment."

"Impossible!" thundered the man. "No one can sleep through a Figment bite!"

"See for yourself," the woman replied, her voice shaking as fiercely as the wounded leg she was probing.

There was an explosion of light in the eyes that held her, and then suddenly she was on her stomach, with two sets of fingers prodding the festering gashes on her leg. Just as she had when the fangs had first raked her, she screamed in a release of unbearable pain. Almost immediately the prying hands pulled away, and then cutting through the lingering echoes of her scream, she could hear the voices of the rusty-haired man and the fair young woman.

"She screamed," whispered the woman.

The man answered dryly, "I noticed."

Clutching back the blanket of nausea that threatened to smother her, she pulled herself to her knees and scrambled around to face the two who had found her. "And I'll scream again if you jab your fingers into my leg," she informed them hoarsely.

Golden brown eyes ensnared hers once again. "What happened to your leg?" demanded the man, his snarl more pronounced than it had been when he had first stumbled upon her.

"I'll answer your questions when you answer mine," she responded defiantly. "Where am I and who are you?"

The two before her exchanged a silent glance, and some indecipherable message seemed to pass between them. Then the man gave an almost imperceptible shrug of his shoulders, and in response the fair woman turned to where the other knelt on the ground, glaring back at the two who had found her with eyes as shockingly clear as a shallow mountain stream rushing over the submerged pebbles of her pain and fear.

"We'll tell you because it really doesn't matter what we say; you'll either completely forget it, or just think it was part of your dream anyway," the woman remarked.

"So then tell me, and we'll see whether or not I remember," was the terse reply. "Let's start with who you are."

"I'm Mischa, and this is Gyfree. We're guards and guides between your world and our own. For some reason our two worlds are unusually close to each other, and the partitions dividing them are not exactly foolproof, specifically in those places where people from your world enter the realm of dreams. So sometimes when someone like you is journeying through your dream universe, you accidentally slip through the partition, and your mind ends up here, instead of back in your own world, where your body is tucked snugly into bed. When this happens it is our job to return you to where you belong. In a sense, we guide you safely through the rest of your dream, which just happens to take place in our world, so that you can finally wake up back in your own bed, happily unaware that you've ever been gone."

Her eyes had widened with the other's words. "Are you telling me that my dreams are more than imaginary experiences inside my head? That a dream can actually carry me somewhere else? Somewhere other than the world I know when I'm awake?"

Mischa smiled crookedly, her eyes twinkling as if there was a humor hidden in this exchange that only she could appreciate. "That's what I'm telling you, more or less. Your mind is here, and since your mind is still connected to your body, you are here, body and mind. But since you are actually asleep in your own world, you are also back there at the same time, body and mind. You see, a powerful dream can create a second reality, and it is that second reality that can, among other things, transport a Dreamer into another world like ours. The more powerful the dream, the more powerful the presence of the Dreamer in our world."

"Wait a second. You're asking me to believe that someone from my world, supposedly still dreaming securely in bed, can also physically end up somewhere else? I don't care how you explain it; I just don't see how that could be possible."

"Call it sleepwalking on a grand scale," Gyfree interjected impatiently. "Now your turn. What happened to your leg, and how much of the dream that has brought you here do you still remember?"

"I remember everything. That is, everything except ever going to bed or falling asleep."

"Then tell us what happened," drawled Gyfree, his eyes sparkling dangerously.

Shrugging her shoulders, she complied. "I felt an urgent need to be outside. Almost immediately I could sense that I was being followed, but suddenly the streets around me were not the familiar streets I walk every day, but the sort of streets that always spring up around me in a nightmare. So I ran, and when I could run no more, I hid in the shadow of a door. It was there I saw my pursuers, saw their forms waver back and forth between beasts and ordinary men. I ran again until a giant fence sprang up before me. I tried to fly over the fence, but as my body slowly rose off the ground, one of the beasts sank his fangs into the back of my leg. I screamed, something I've never been able to do before in a dream, and the scream sent me plunging into the sky and all the way here." A grim smile cracked her face. "And by the way, my name is Drew."

There was no answering smile from either Mischa or Gyfree. Instead, the two turned troubled eyes to each other, and Gyfree growled. "I still say it's impossible. The first touch of a Figment should have brought more than enough pain to snap her awake. Any Figment able to hold her long enough to actually draw blood would have also had ample strength and opportunity to kill her."

"What if she wasn't asleep when she was bitten?" Mischa demanded.

"That still wouldn't explain either how she escaped the Figment, assuming there even was a Figment, or more importantly, how she ended up here," retorted Gyfree.

With a shrug of her shoulders that clearly indicated she had no answer, Mischa turned back toward Drew and asked, "You don't really think you're dreaming now, do you?"

"I don't think so, but everything continues to be so strange, maybe I am. It wouldn't be the first time in my life when I've thought myself awake while dreaming. It may not happen to me often anymore, but it was fairly common when I was a child."

"What were your dreams like as a child?" Mischa questioned quickly.

"Almost inseparable from my waking. Sometimes when I think back, I'm not sure which memories are dreams, and which are real."

"This is ridiculous," snapped Gyfree. "She has to be dreaming, because she couldn't be here otherwise."

"What about her leg?" Mischa demanded.

"Probably some injury she suffered before her dream, and she's simply incorporated it into the dream itself."

"But it shows all the signs of a Figment bite. There's even evidence of Figment saliva."

"It's just a normal infection," Gyfree stubbornly disagreed.

"What makes you so sure? She's clearly not a normal Dreamer. She can even talk, and coherently at that."

"Talking is rare, but not unheard of," Gyfree insisted.

"Dreaming or not," Drew drawled, "I am still here, and I don't appreciate being talked about as if I'm not. Would someone please explain to me what a Figment is?"

"No more explanations," Gyfree returned. "This is a dream, as far as you're concerned. You are a Dreamer, and Dreamers don't ask questions, and they certainly don't get answers. They do as they're told, and that's what you're going to do. Exactly what you're told."

Drew's eyes narrowed menacingly. "I'll do as I'm told when I understand what I'm being told, and why. If you want cooperation, you will have to gain it first."

Gyfree turned away, ignoring the undeniable challenge in both Drew's expression and pronouncement. "She must have come through around here. It should only take a moment to find the exact spot and send her back," he observed.

"You felt her break through only moments before we got here. Considering how little time has passed since then, not to mention the condition of her leg, I would say she came through right here. But I think you're wasting your time. Her presence here is too strong. I think she needs to be taken to the Source."

Without warning, Gyfree lifted Drew into his arms and turned her around to face a bright blue sky that seemed to spring high overhead directly from the ground itself. Then stepping forward, he pressed her up against the surprisingly slick surface of the sky, and without pausing, slid her sideways across its curved surface.

"What are you doing?" Drew demanded in a muffled voice, her face crushed against the seeming sky.

Rather than respond, Gyfree slid her back in the other direction.

"What are you doing?" demanded Mischa. "If she could pass through, she would already have done it easily, and without you shoving her against the Barrier face-first. What has gotten into you?"

Even from behind, Drew could feel Gyfree's shoulders slump, and then she was sliding to the ground as he once more turned away to address Mischa. "You'll be in charge here while I take her to the Source," he instructed. "If any other Dreamers come through, let the better students deal with them. And keep an extra close watch on this section of the Barrier while I'm gone. Considering the way things have been going lately, I want to make sure nothing unusual slips through." He returned his attention to Drew. Sharp points of light darting from his eyes once again pinned her in place. "Up on your feet," he told her. "You're coming with me."

"No," Drew resisted.

Gyfree reached out and ruthlessly hauled her to her feet. "You're a Dreamer, and Dreamers never refuse to do as they're told. And I'm telling you to come with me."

Pain again clawed its way up Drew's calf with long ragged fingers and she gasped as her leg inevitably crumpled beneath her.

"Gyfree, you idiot," Mischa scolded. "She's not going anywhere on that leg unless you do something to help her. Whether or not you're willing to admit she has a Figment bite, she still can't walk with blood and whatever else leaking from those gashes."

"She's dreaming," Gyfree stubbornly insisted, "so she shouldn't really be able to feel any pain. If she did, it would wake her up, and if she was awake, she couldn't be here."

Mischa shook her head. "You have always been the most obstinate man. There may be no easy answers to explain what's happening, but that doesn't matter. The only thing that matters is that you clearly must take her to the Source, and you'll never get her there if she can't walk. So stop fretting about whether or not she should feel pain, and simply fix her leg!"

Gyfree shifted his glare to Mischa, who first winked, then smiled sweetly in return. Without warning, and with even less ceremony, he then threw Drew over his shoulder and stomped off with her through the stunted trees, where she was sure she could see, in the gray wrinkled bark, hidden faces grimacing in either fear or amusement, or perhaps somehow an equal dose of both.

Even they were uneasy coming into his presence. They knew their own value, and their skills were rarely questioned, yet still they were uneasy. And for once they had a reason, for he had given them a task they should have easily accomplished, and for the first time in their experience, they had failed. So they were uneasy, as they were always uneasy, but now they were also afraid, for he was not a forgiving man. In fact, he was not even a man, or at least not exactly, but then of course, neither were they.

On their knees they approached, for even from them, his most effective tools, he demanded no less. From others he actually demanded more, but they had a position of stature in his eyes that they would kill, and had killed often, to preserve. With heads low and eyes on the swirling gray ground, they groveled before him, trying to hide, although from him it was impossible to hide, the shaking in their limbs. He would not only know that they were shaking; he would already know the reason.

"Well?" His voice exploded above them, and as always the sound was like burning shrapnel ripping into their ears and through their skulls.

"We found her," answered one, his monstrous snout emerging into sharp focus, quivering nervously and dripping a thin stream of blood.

"We followed her," the other added, his yellow eyes squeezed tightly shut as if the lids had been weighed down by the heavy silence following his partner's words. "It was easy to herd her into the trap you had set."

"Well?" he persisted blandly, although even this sound was like white-hot nails driving through their brains.

"She had powers," the first one tried to explain, sniveling loudly, the nostrils of his large but human nose flaring wildly then constricting to tiny pinpoints.

"Well?" he whispered, and now the sound was like a splinter of fiery steel scraping along their spines, lacerating nerves until they collapsed, whimpering in their agony.

"She escaped," the second one gasped, blood red tears leaking from beneath his clenched lids.

A ragged claw lifted the second one's bowed head by the chin, forcing it back until it could go no further without snapping his neck. Then the claw stabbed through the bottom of his jaw, slicing through the leathery tissue until his mouth was filled with the acrid taste of his blood.

"How is that possible?" demanded the voice, its razor sharpness flooding the punctured mouth with more blood than the claw had drawn. Another clawed hand snaked out, seizing a fistful of the first one's hair and wrenching up his head until more blood trickled down his forehead than from his nose, and he was forced to meet the slitted eyes in his master's writhing face. "Well?" gouged the voice.

The snout convulsed, dark blood now streaming down the quaking chin beneath, then words poured from the first one's mouth more thickly than the gushing blood. "She could do things she should never have been able to do. She slipped through a door as if she knew it truly wasn't there. She ran, and ran so quickly we could hardly keep up, when the climate of the dream should have weighed her down so she couldn't run at all. And she flew, just as if she was the one dreaming, as if the dream was hers and hers alone. But we did catch up with her as she rose off the ground. I bit her, ripping her leg open from just below the knee all the way down to her ankle. That should have brought her down so we could kill her. But it didn't, because she screamed. She shouldn't have been able to scream, but she did. And that scream tore her out of my grasp and sent her soaring right through the Barrier."

"It must have been her," gurgled the second through a mouth

dripping blood, yellow eyes full of not just fear, but also sudden wonder.

"That is no excuse," hissed the voice, the sound so sharp that more blood filled the second one's mouth, and trickled from the corners of his eyes. "She gave up her hold on you years ago." The clawed hands withdrew, and the two minions collapsed, sides heaving as they sprawled on the ground and struggled for breath. In time they grappled back up to their knees, but as soon as they had regained some small measure of composure, the voice detonated, shattering the very air and sending them reeling back to the ground, facedown in the puddles of blood each had left. "You will find her!" the voice howled, so that new blood gushed from their ears, from their noses, and from their mouths. "You will find her wherever she may be, and this time you will either kill her or suffer the consequences. If you fail, you will wish for death, but death is a gift I will never grant. Now go!"

Yellow eyes snapped open. "Through the Barrier?" the second one gurgled through a mouth filled with blood.

"Through the Barrier and beyond if necessary!" blasted the voice. "Now go, unless you'd rather stay and deal with me!"

Their heads lifted, expressions awash with horror, and then their features wavered, and once again they simply appeared to be two men with blood-streaked faces and eyes full of fear. Without another word they backed away on their knees, across a path suddenly strewn with jagged fragments of burning glass and through air that dripped acid, until blood seeped from every pore on their hands and legs and the flesh peeled from their backs and skulls like bark shucked from a dead tree. When they were finally engulfed by a wave of black, they cried out in gratitude.

He stood where they had left him, motionless in the center of a fiery maelstrom, sparking sheets of wind whipping around his silent hub, the skin writhing across his face a sure sign that there was no calm in the eye of this storm. The winds about him thrashed and screamed in ever-increasing fury until the world in which he stood must surely be eradicated. Nothing and no one could survive the rage that radiated outward to burn everything in its path. Yet within the whirling chaos, a calm form coalesced, silver flecks merging together like iron filaments beneath a magnet to slowly but inexorably shape an inhumanly beautiful face, and then a woman stepped out of the tempest to meet him.

"If you're serious about killing her, you will probably have to send me," she murmured, and her voice was capable of gripping even his spine with icy fingers.

He glowered at her exquisite face, but the winds encasing him subsided as quickly as they had arisen. "I don't trust you," he snapped. "And I will never pay whatever price you demand."

Her laughter tinkled, but he heard the crack of ice streaking like lightning across a frozen lake, and he could briefly feel the suddenly frigid surface beneath his feet shift away from him, leaving him stranded and adrift. "Yet I would ask nothing of you that you wouldn't be more than willing to do. Nothing you haven't done many times before."

"What I do, I do only because I choose. Never because I'm asked. I will never be obligated to another being, especially not to you."

"So you think you can kill this Dreamer without my help?" she asked, a fine sheet of frost billowing from her lips until her entire form wavered beneath a veil of ice.

The slits in his eyes narrowed, cleaving his red irises with a razor-thin line. His smile was as cruel and biting as the one beneath the ice. "So where is the Dreamer who created you?" he asked suddenly.

She sighed, and the icy fog of her breath further obscured her face. "Dead, long dead," she answered.

"How did you manage to get close enough for the kill?" he demanded, unable to disguise the feverish urgency in his question.

She laughed again, and again the world beneath his feet shifted. "So that's your problem, is it?" Her face and body dimmed beneath the thickening layer of ice that enveloped her. "She was more clever than she knew when she dreamed you. Well, I can assure you, if you ever send me, I will have no problem getting very, very close." The surface of the ice trembled, and a delicate mist rose like drops of mercury floating in space. When the mist cleared, a man even more breathtaking than the woman stood in the exact same spot in the storm-lashed void. "Death is a simple thing to achieve when your victim isn't trying to run, but is instead eager to feel your embrace," remarked the alluring vision. "Which is a satisfaction, I'm sorry to say, you'll never know as long as you reject my offer."

"This time my minions won't fail."

"Well, if they do, you know how to call me. I'll be expecting to hear from you." With a final chilling laugh, the ravishing face rippled and dissolved into swirling silver flecks that slowly dissipated in the heavy gloom.

Alone in the gulf between dreams and waking, he stood, blood red skin blazing over the sharply protruding bones of his face, his demonic features the only fixed and unalterable realities in this vast place where he reigned supreme.

They floated in the blackness, freed from all sensation, released from the overwhelming pain. Here the skin readhered to their skulls and spines, and the gashes riddling their arms and legs shrank back into their mottled skin. The shards of their master's voice that had lodged in their brains were extracted one by one, as if by a loving hand, although neither had ever known the touch of any hand that did not stab holes through their jaws or rip the hair from their heads. Immersed in the darkness they again found themselves, and in repose their features vacillated slowly from man to beast and back again. If possible they would have remained suspended here forever, cradled by eternal night, but the choice was no more theirs than the night was real. Even the welcoming dark was a cruel trick of their master's, a trick that lulled them, that made them forget what pain he could inflict so that they could feel its full intensity when he brought them to its brink again. Even now they were at the mercy of their master's whims, and too soon for their comfort they could feel his red glare slicing through the blackness and pinning them like wriggling insects to a felt board, the sharp needles of his attention rendering them incapable of serving any purpose other than the one he intended. There in the dark he pulled them apart, ripping away their limbs, tearing out their hearts and lungs, subjecting them to the smallest sample of what he could do if they failed him this time; then as they hung to themselves by the most tenuous of threads, he rebuilt them, stronger, more lethal, more suited to the task he had allotted them. Finished with his reconstruction, he wrapped his clawed hands around his finely honed weapons, and wresting them from the sheath of the dark, hurled them in the direction of their unsuspecting target.

They landed panting on the other side of the Barrier, sprawled on their hands and knees like the irreversible beasts they now were, tongues lolling and eyes scanning the line of stunted trees that stretched before them. A quivering snout was lowered to the ground, and then there was the loud sound of sniffing, followed by a piercing whine.

"Well, Hund, can you smell her?" growled the one whose intense yellow eyes continued to dart across the trees.

"Yes, Auge, her scent is strong. And there is the stench of blood as well. But she is not alone. There are Sentries," sniveled Hund.

Auge's voice rumbled ominously in his throat until Hund's ears flattened against his head and his lips curled back from his dripping fangs. "Then I will kill them all," Auge snarled, slitted yellow eyes venomous. "Just lead and when we find them, I'll rip out their throats while you watch."

"You are no more eager for the kill than I am, and no better skilled," barked Hund.

"Then stop mewling like a puppy, and we will go kill them together."

Together the two hunters loped in the direction of the shriveled trees, which seemed to shrink away from the touch of a danger far more formidable than fire.

Drew bounced on Gyfree's shoulder until her brain reeled and her stomach lurched, and the grinning face of Mischa bobbing in and out of view behind her did nothing to calm either the churning of her head or the heaving of her gut. She felt like a bag stuffed with the refuse of her own memories and beliefs, memories and beliefs that had once been familiar and meaning-ful to her but were no longer relevant, so had been packed up and thrown away, then picked up and jostled by an impatient garbage man. And like the trash bag crammed too full, she was ready to burst at the seams and spew her contents across the indifferent ground. When Gyfree plunged precipitously down a steep slope, jolting her carelessly against his rigid shoulder and back, the bag did indeed finally rupture, and it seemed to Drew as she watched from a detached distance that she lost not only the lining of her stomach, but all the bits and pieces of her once comprehensible life.

"Now look what you've done," Mischa snapped irritably as she caught up to the spot where Gyfree had suddenly halted to drop his retching burden to the ground. "You threw her over your shoulder as if she was a mindless bundle, and then bounced her around until you made her sick. It serves you right that she's vomited all over you." Glaring angrily at Gyfree, she knelt down beside Drew, and presented her with the open mouth of a canteen. "Rinse out your mouth and you'll feel better," she advised. When Drew silently did as she was instructed, rinsing her mouth with a swish from the canteen and then spitting into the grass, Mischa asked in a crisp voice, "So have you ever vomited during a dream before?"

Wiping her mouth with the back of a shaking hand, Drew moaned, "Never. I always wake up to vomit if I feel the need." She glanced up at Gyfree's expressionless face and added, "I'm sorry about that. Now you're going to stink as badly as I probably do." Then a weak grin abruptly lit her face. "But don't worry about it, because it's not real vomit, only dream vomit, so neither of us really stinks at all. I'm just dreaming that we do."

Mischa squealed with surprised laughter, then grinned impishly up at Gyfree. "Just a standard Dreamer, right? A Dreamer who can converse, be injured, throw up, and even joke. Just an ordinary, everyday Dreamer."

"Be quiet," Gyfree grunted, a perplexed frown darkening his expression. Turning a face as ominous as a stormy sky toward Drew, he asked, "How did you vomit?"

"The usual way, I suppose," Drew quipped. "The muscles in my esophagus contracted and brought up the rebellious contents of my stomach."

Mischa laughed again, but Gyfree's countenance suggested that the storm, and his temper, were both about to be unleashed. "That doesn't answer my question," he blazed.

"I guess you could say I'm not only a lucid Dreamer, but also a queasy Dreamer," Drew remarked blandly.

"What you are," Gyfree growled, although his eyes had mysteriously softened, "is a highly troublesome Dreamer. I should have known something like you would eventually happen to me." With those cryptic words he once more swept her into his arms, although this time he was careful to cradle her gently against his chest as he charged through a twisted forest where the wind in the leaves above strangely echoed the mocking snicker of the woman who trailed directly behind him.

Chapter 2

The sun had only inched forward a fraction in the sky when Gyfree, with Drew in his arms and Mischa tripping directly behind, stumbled into a clearing populated by several small dwellings and filled with a chattering group of people, all relatively young except for a single gray-haired man standing silently in their midst like a lone candle surrounded by a flock of eager, flittering moths. Gyfree stopped abruptly at the sight of the older man, unconsciously tightening his grip on Drew until she felt obligated to protest, "If you squeeze any harder I'm almost certain to wake up!"

The older man, who had been smiling ruefully at Gyfree, shifted startled eyes to Drew's flushed and very alert face. "What exactly do we have here?" he inquired.

When neither Gyfree nor Mischa responded, and the silence seemed to be sucking the breath from all those surrounding her, Drew spoke up, "I'm a Dreamer, or so I've been told. Repeatedly, I might add."

The young people gasped loudly and collectively, as if they had in fact been long denied the right to breathe and had finally been granted the most fleeting of moments to gulp a lungful of sorely needed air. The gray-haired man, however, simply smiled, and lifting a single questioning eyebrow at Gyfree, remarked, "And I suppose your dream involves being carried around in the arms of a handsome young man?"

"Not really. Carrying me was Gyfree's idea, but he didn't really have many other options because of the injury to my leg."

Now even the man looked startled, and the young people all seemed to have completely forgotten how to breathe. His mouth opened, then closed, then opened again, and finally the man looked at Gyfree, this time his expression far more helpless than rueful or amused. "I have a strange feeling that I was compelled to come here ahead of schedule for a good reason," he admitted. "Although I'm not certain that I'm fully prepared to cope with whatever that reason might be."

"She's just a remarkably lucid Dreamer," Gyfree insisted, glowering at the older man.

"See what I mean?" chimed in Drew, a grin struggling to emerge at the corners of her mouth. "No matter what I say or what happens, Gyfree keeps telling me that I'm just a Dreamer."

"Sir," Mischa interjected, stepping forward. "Would you please look at her leg?"

Although Gyfree's daunting glare was directed her way, he remained silent and Mischa was free to ignore him.

"Her leg?" repeated the older man.

Gyfree and the man locked eyes, and Drew could almost see the insistent questions and hesitant answers streaking through the air like electricity on a power line. Then the man stepped forward and squatted on the ground, taking the arch of her foot in a gentle grasp and rotating her leg carefully so he could examine the injured calf. As if they had no choice, Gyfree and Mischa dropped their eyes to again gauge the extent of the wound, and twisting her neck and glancing down the length of her body, Drew also once more contemplated her mangled flesh. The bleeding had stopped, and a blotchy brown and yellow crust had formed around the edges of the wound, but the ragged gashes still oozed a thick green slime and the skin bordering the lacerations was now laced with fine green strands that traced the pattern of a spiderweb across the back of her leg. Whether it was caused by the sight of her festering wound, or the man's sharp intake of breath, or Mischa's quickly suppressed shriek, Drew's head suddenly reeled and she clutched convulsively at the warm shirt beneath her hand. A jolt skated up her arm as the frantically pumping heart below her palm seemed to catch and match the rhythm of her own.

"Gyfree! What were you thinking?" the man blared. "You should have dealt with this immediately! Why did you carry her all the way back here?"

"I thought it was a normal wound, and just needed to be cleaned and bandaged," Gyfree apologized.

While the man visibly struggled to find a suitable response, Drew watched in horror as a thrashing green thread snaked out from the web to encircle the front of her leg. Yet before she could utter a word herself, Mischa, her eyes still glued to Drew's calf, again shrieked, and this time she made no attempt to stifle her shrill cry. "Now, Gyfree!" she shouted.

Instantly Gyfree dropped to the ground, twisting Drew in his arms so that she suddenly found herself sprawling facedown across his legs. Then his hand was clasping the back of her calf, and his fingers were freezing through her skin, down through her muscles with a coldness so intense it turned her bones to brittle ice. This time when she screamed she called the blackness to her, and when it arrived with open arms, she gladly threw herself into its numbing embrace.

Darkness had no stench, but death did, and it was the stench of death they had carried with them ever since their master had reached through the darkness to twist them irreversibly to his purpose. There had been a time, long ago, when they had served him out of choice, out of pride that they could serve one so powerful, that they were dangerous enough to merit his attention, that they were treacherous enough to suffice as his tools. Now there was no choice; they were his, had been his from the very first without even realizing that to accept such a master was to surrender completely all aspirations of freedom or choice. They were his, so completely his that their forms were finally as fixed and inescapable as his had always been. And the stench of death, of his hand upon them, was now so much a part of them that the grass beneath their clawed feet withered and the trees they passed shed shriveled leaves to mark their passage, leaving across the body of the land the unmistakable slash of a mortal wound.

Snout flaring, Hund unerringly followed their quarry's trail, while Auge dutifully followed him. It was only a short time before Hund scurried down a sharp incline and dropped to his haunches, muzzle quivering in eagerness as he crouched with his head bare inches from something sticky and foul on the ground. "She is sick as well as hurt," he whined excitedly. "She will be easy to kill if we catch her soon."

Auge's slitted yellow eyes gleamed with an insatiable hunger, and it was solely the lingering touch of his master that restrained him from howling thunderously for all of this world, and perhaps even several neighboring worlds, to hear. Instead he growled low in his throat, until his entire body and the scorched ground beneath his feet thrummed with his overpowering appetite for blood. In his heightened state of anticipation, he could already taste the sweet salty tang on his lips, could feel the warm flow trickling down the back of his throat, could see the Dreamer dead at his feet, her throat ripped out and spilling ever more of her bright red blood. "The kill awaits," he snarled, his ravenous need stripping the flesh from all the words he might have said and leaving only a few dry bones for Hund to gnaw. Yet they were enough to whet Hund's appetite, and with a whine as replete with yearning as Auge's growl, he loped ahead through the woods, again following the heady scent of the coveted kill.

Black arms pulled inexorably away despite her best efforts to cling to their comforting emptiness, and as the fingers of dark brushed hers fleetingly in farewell, a finger of light poked into the crease at the corner of one eye, wriggling between her lids and prying them apart. More light seeped through the cracked lid, pulsing like the blip on a heart monitor, and her eye fluttered fitfully as if trying to trace the peaks and valleys flashing across her vision. When a strand of light spiked higher than any preceding peak, her eyelid withdrew so her eye could follow, and she suddenly found herself staring with bemusement into a pair of blazing, golden brown eyes.

"I just had the strangest dream," she mumbled before her mind reluctantly released its hold on the last receding remnants of darkness. Then, as memory returned and she recognized those brown eyes, she sat up abruptly, one shaking hand unconsciously gripping Gyfree's arm as he held her in his lap. "And it's not over yet, is it?" she added hoarsely.

"It's only just beginning," he admitted uneasily. For the first time since he and Mischa had found her, he actually smiled, but his lips were pulled as thin as a rubber band ready to snap, and

Drew could clearly see the tautness of his facial muscles and the tension in his eyes. And buried beneath both, a dreadful hope.

In a voice as full of strain as Gyfree's face, Mischa asked, "Not to belabor the obvious, but have you ever before dreamed that you had fainted, and then returned to your original dream after you dreamed that you had regained consciousness?"

Turning her head toward the source of the other woman's voice, Drew smiled weakly. "Dreams within dreams," she murmured.

"Pardon me?" Mischa queried, a frown forming delicate ridges across the bridge of her nose.

"Do you dream here, in your world?" Drew questioned.

Before Mischa could answer, Gyfree, his voice as rough as sandpaper, rasped, "I do."

Returning her eyes to his smoldering brown gaze, Drew continued, "Do you ever find yourself trapped in a nightmare that you know, even as you dream, is a nightmare? And because you know you are dreaming, you also know all you need to do to escape is wake up? That waking up is your only chance to escape? So you will yourself awake, forcing your eyes open even though they feel as heavy as death. You get out of your bed, trying to shake off the clinging grasp of the nightmare, but the nightmare refuses to be shaken and suddenly it is there with you, leaping across your bedroom floor, and you realize that you are not awake after all, that you only dreamed that you had opened your eyes and climbed out of bed. So again you try to will yourself awake, and again you think you have succeeded, only to find that once more you have only dreamed yourself safe when you are still as trapped as before. You do this again and again, all through the night, dream within dream within dream, until somehow, finally, you really do wake up. Yet even though you've succeeded at last, and you know without a doubt that you are awake, you still feel as you wend your way through the day that the nightmare is only a step away, quietly stalking you, until you wonder which world is the real one, the one you dream when you're asleep or the one you dream when you're awake."

Gyfree closed his eyes and shuddered, and as she watched, Drew could see his throat convulse as if he was trying to swallow something impossible to swallow. When he opened his eyes again, she recognized the phantoms in his eyes for she had often seen the same phantoms in her own. "We have to get you out of here," he announced tersely.

"Yes you do, and quickly," interrupted an authoritative voice, and Drew turned her head toward the older man, the lines of age more clearly etched in a face more pale than she recalled. "But this is too hazardous and too important for you to do alone. Like it or not, this woman is not an ordinary Dreamer, and whether she is dreaming now makes no difference. Awake or asleep, the nightmare will follow her here, as you, my son, are well aware. Mischa will go with you. I can take her place until you both return, or until your replacements arrive." He smiled wanly. "Now I know why I felt this overwhelming urge to cut short my inspection of the rest of the Barrier and come straight here. Right now, this is the most important place for me to be." His eyes swept across the young people still gathered at his back, and they too seemed only pale reflections of the lively group Drew had first seen when Gyfree had stalked into the clearing with her in his arms. "I would like one or two others to go with Gyfree and Mischa. Considering the risks, I will not send anyone who is unwilling to go. Are any of you willing to volunteer?"

A young woman even more pallid than the others stepped forward, wringing her hands together as if they were two sopping rags. "I will go," she offered hesitantly.

Gyfree's eyes narrowed and his mouth hardened into a thin, implacable line. "You're too young and inexperienced," he snapped.

The young woman raised her chin and dropped her hands to her sides, clenching her fingers into two tiny fists. "I want to go."

Before Gyfree could refuse, the older man interrupted. "Timi," he asked gently, "why do you want to go?"

Timi's forehead creased. "I don't know," she admitted, "but I feel an overwhelming need, as if I must go or something terrible will happen. Please, sir, I know I probably don't have much to offer, and I know there will be dangers, but I still feel as if I have to go."

"Very well," the man responded. "Then you will go. Now the four of you must be on your way while there's still time." He turned and faced the group at his back. "Hurry and prepare them some packs!" he ordered, and several of the young people turned and rushed into the scattered dwellings. Then returning his attention to Gyfree, he said, "You know what to do. You must travel quickly."

"What about my leg?" Drew protested. "We won't be able to move quickly if Gyfree has to carry me the entire way."

"Take a look," Mischa advised with a quirk of her lips.

Casting a nervous glance down the length of her leg, Drew was shocked to see the previously mangled flesh replaced by skin that stretched smoothly over the taut muscle of her calf, unmarked except for the faint outline of a man's open palm. "Now I know I'm dreaming," she breathed.

Mischa laughed, the glint in her eyes reflecting the sun that seeped through the tops of the encircling trees. "Gyfree has a magical touch, when he chooses to use it," she remarked, casting a suggestively sly smile in his direction.

A moment earlier Drew might have responded, but a strangeness was now tugging at her, tugging with a nearly irresistible persistence, much like the strangeness that had tugged her away from the familiar yet foreign walls of her apartment. Suddenly it felt as if she was on the edge of a chasm she knew all too well, ready to plunge once again into the darkness that she never could fully escape. One step and she would be there, one step in the direction that only her dreams could lead, down where the monsters would surely give chase, down where a man with golden brown eyes and flaming hair and hands that could freeze with a single touch must somehow also belong. One step, and she would take it while standing still.

The shafts of light gracing the forest floor vanished as if a giant hand had eclipsed the sun, and where trees had stood only a moment before, there was nothing but a roiling gray mist that reached out with clammy fingers to raise the hairs on her arms and across the back of her neck. Pain shot up her spine, the gnawing pain that always informed her in her dreams that something sinister was not only in pursuit, but drawing near. Then out of the gray she could see two forms coalesce, slowly and uncertainly at first, as if the gray swirls were being stirred like clouds in a restless wind, whipped into the illusion of meaningful shape and then torn into meaningless shreds again, but then the forms solidified, and out of the gray sprang two beasts with wild eyes and dripping fangs. They were larger than men, much larger, and they loped on all fours, curved talons churning the gray through which they lunged. They raised their heads as if they could see her as clearly as she saw them, and she caught the glint of yellow eyes and a glimpse of a monstrous, quivering snout before the beasts threw back their heads and howled a silent howl. They seemed so distant, and at the same time so near, that she knew she could only be in a nightmare, that she had not actually escaped the nightmare even though she had believed herself awake, and with the return of the nightmare, the dream she had mistaken for reality, the dream that had seemed unmistakably real, was gone. The clearing was gone, and gone were Mischa, Timi, the old man, and all the others who had stood there only seconds before. Yet for once she was not alone in the nightmare; she was still sitting in a warm lap, clutching a dusty shirt, and above her were two brown eyes awash with golden flecks.

Gyfree surged to his feet, roughly hauling Drew up by the arm that a heartbeat ago had clung to his shirt. "Scream!" he ordered brusquely, opening his own mouth wide to unleash a roar that echoed with the crack of thunder. As the storm of his shout crashed over her, she flung her own scream at the encroaching nightmare, and when the shrill blast hurtled after his, it was like lightning chasing his thunder to rip through the gray beasts, dissolving them back into wispy tatters of cloud, and returning a flash of brilliant light to the world. In the light was the clearing, and in the clearing was a cluster of faces with sharp bones and hollow cheeks starkly revealed in the merciless glare.

Grabbing Drew urgently by her free arm, Mischa demanded, "How much time do we have before it gets here?"

As clearly as she could see the earnest face before her, she could still see the answer loping through the woods in her direction. "There are two, and they will be here in a little while. They have just passed the place where I was sick, so we still have some time."

Another arm whirled Drew around, and this time she was snared by the eyes of the old man, and by her own reflection swirling in their incredible depths. There was something inexplicably vast about the eyes that held her, something more than human. Those eyes possessed her for a brief moment that lasted an eternity, and she knew that the old man had seen far more of her than she had ever willingly exposed to another, and perhaps far more than she had ever seen herself. Somehow in that fleeting instant she had been stripped of all barricades, but she had not been found lacking. "Well, Dreamer, time is a funny thing," he told her with a smile full of more sorrow than any single man could carry. "It has brought your nightmares back to you, and so has finally brought you here, to me and my world. And although it took so long for you to arrive, you and I are already almost out of time together. So no arguing; like Gyfree, you must do as you're told. Into that cabin; go change into some other clothes." His other arm whipped out to seize the nearest young woman. "Hurry," he ordered her. "Find different clothes for the Dreamer." Eyes wide with quick understanding, the young woman grabbed Drew by the arm and whisked her away.

Moments later Drew was back in the clearing, clad in a shirt and pants so soft that she felt like a snake that had finally shed its old skin and could stop, at least for a while, the constant chafing. Gyfree, Mischa, and Timi were all waiting, packs slung across their backs, expressions grim as they watched the path that had brought Drew to them, and that was now bringing something far more menacing than any Dreamer. Gyfree, also in clean clothing, was the first to turn as she neared, as if he could sense her just as she could sense the approaching beasts. As he stepped toward her, so did the old man, reaching out a hand to grasp one of hers and another to grasp Gyfree's. "Take care of one another," he told them, and lifting his eyes to include Mischa and Timi, then added, "all of you." Dropping the hands he clasped as if they were a burden too heavy for him to continue holding, he ordered, "Now go, and go swiftly. We will do what we can to delay them."

"Be careful, Father," Gyfree implored, and then turning on his heel, he plunged into the restlessly whispering forest, the Dreamer and the others following directly in his wake.

Gyfree's father watched the four companions until the trees obscured them with twitching branches, and then with eyes still fastened on the shadowy path, he shouted over his shoulder, "Bring me the Dreamer's clothes, and bring them quickly!"

Hund and Auge careened into the clearing, howling in triumph as well as in insatiable hunger, but their exultant howls were arrested as their slitted eyes swept over the deserted site. In the center of the vacant space, Auge stood motionless, and then a growl rumbled through him, building in intensity until his entire body quaked and the ground beneath his feet heaved like waves on the ocean. "I thought you said she would be here!" he roared, shaking the shriveling leafs from the surrounding trees so that all of their branches stretched like skeletal arms against the gray, lightless sky. "Where is she?"

Snout quivering violently, nostrils wide and streaked with pulsing black veins, Hund prowled the area, his piercing whine redolent of unappeased appetite and a mounting frustration. "She should be here," he lamented. "The scent is so strong, so sickly, so full of her pain. This place smells of so much of her pain, so much hurt that she should never have been able to leave here. The odor is strong, so strong, so sweetly pungent, how could she not be here?" Plummeting to his knees and raking the soil with his razor-sharp claws, he loosed a shriek of inarticulate chagrin and yearning that set the air churning until the graveyard of dead leafs swirled off the ground and capered around the clearing like the ghosts of the gaunt and despoiled trees.

Lunging in a burst of animal rage, Auge battered Hund to the ground, but the hand of his master reached across the chasm of space to restrain him, and instead of ripping out his partner's throat and sating himself on the viscous blood that pulsed sluggishly just beneath the surface of the leathery skin exposed to his fangs, he snarled, "Well, she isn't here, and you will find where her scent leads so we can track her wherever she has gone!"

Hund's lips curled away from his own honed fangs, and a growl reverberated in the back of his bared throat, but he too felt the grip of his master, and instead of shredding Auge's fleshy belly with his flexing claws, he snapped, "I will find the trail of her scent when you get off of me!"

The two snarled at each other, fangs dripping and eyes flashing red, and then Auge uncoiled, rolling back onto his taloned feet and dragging himself away from the desired kill. With Auge's withdrawal, Hund bounded onto his feet, and stooping with his muzzle only inches from the ground, circled and recircled the vacated camp. Finally he paused at the edge of the clearing, and dropping down to all fours, snuffled loudly, first creeping forward and back, and then to the far side and back. A whine again built in the back of his throat, escalating to a piercing wail that elicited another thunderous growl from the restlessly teetering Auge. "So where is she?" Auge finally bellowed.

"There are two possible trails," Hund sniveled noisily. "Her scent leaves in two different directions."

"So which is the strongest?" Auge rumbled ominously, his

clawed hands flexing and contracting and his taloned feet digging trenches into the dirt beneath the shriveled leafs.

The nostrils of his snout gaped wide as he sniffed the potential paths they might follow, until at last Hund rasped, "One way there is also the scent of many Sentries, a dozen or more. Her scent is less strong in this direction, and most likely is only there because the Sentries touched her and carried her scent away with them. In the other direction there is also the scent of at least one Sentry, but her smell is stronger. We will try that direction first."

"Very well," Auge grunted, a drop of thick saliva dripping from one fang and spilling onto the ground, where dry leafs erupted into flame and a tendril of acrid smoke spiraled upward, its ghostly fingers eventually clasping the bony fingers of the nearby treetops. When the remaining leafs were sucked into the roaring blaze, and fire licked the peeling skin from the trunks of the nearest trees, the predators were already away, chasing their elusive prey.

They tore through the trees, unaware of the devastation they left in their wake, and even more uncaring. Nor did they question the absence of obstructions in their path, as impervious to the trees that leaned away from their passage as they were to the complete lack of any lives other than their own. Where they touched this world there could be no life: no animals, no birds, not even the tiniest insects that burrowed beneath the ground. Their master had shaped them well, had shaped them to scatter death with every breath they exhaled and every step they tramped. Death shadowed them, seizing everything they touched and everything they passed, yet the certain death they brought had been created for a reason, and that reason still fled somewhere on the path ahead.

Snout filled with the heady scent of their quarry, Hund dashed through the nightmare wasteland that they carried with them, heedless of everything but the hunger that rode across his back and sank claws into his belly. A step behind trailed Auge, savage hunger whipping him forward with a brutality no less than his own. When Hund abruptly checked his headlong progress, Auge careened into his back, sending them both sprawling. In an instant they had both bounded to their feet and turned to face each other, each growling viciously, each crouched as if ready to spring and rip the other to shreds. And yet again the hand of their master stretched across the barrier of space and pulled them away from the brink of mutual destruction so that they might fulfill their appointed task.

"Why have we stopped?" Auge demanded, standing slowly and retracting his claws.

Hund's claws also withdrew as he, too, painstakingly straightened his spine. "The scent leads here, to this spot. She must be hiding nearby, very near."

"Then use your nose and find her now!" roared Auge, even the hand of his master unable to hold back his escalating rage.

Hund snarled, baring his fangs and unleashing his claws once more, but he still lowered his muzzle to the ground and, snuffling noisily, laboriously tracked the tantalizing scent to the base of a tree, which immediately shed its now withered leafs. Standing in the flurry of falling leafs, he howled, the sound echoing through the forest to shake the leafs from trees so distant they should have still been immune to the touch of the beasts. Then bending to the forest floor, he swept one large paw, claws fully extended, across the ground, and when he heaved his massive bulk back up, a woman's clothes hung limply from his talons. "Her clothing!" he shrieked. "The only thing here is her clothing!"

Throwing back his head, Auge also howled, his shriek soaring upward as if to tear a hole in the sky. "Where is she?" he roared, lunging forward to grab Hund by the neck, his claws peeking out to extract glistening drops of blood from the other's throat.

Jerking his head down, Hund grazed Auge's paw with his fangs, drawing fine stripes of blood across the clutching fingers, and the two fell apart, lips curling and chests heaving as they confronted each other, their master's distant hand hastily erecting an impassable barrier between them. "She must have gone the other way," Hund finally admitted, the rumble in his throat both ominous and grudging. "The Sentries must have gone along to diffuse her scent so we would be sidetracked. We must go back and find her scent before it is lost."

They had no choice but to backtrack, but first Auge's frustrated bloodthirstiness must be appeased. He could not kill Hund; his master would not permit it. Yet he needed a release of his pent-up passions, and with a swipe of his paw he reached across the chasm dividing them, and swept the offending clothes from Hund's grasp. Plunging to the ground, he shredded the clothes as if the Dreamer's body was still within their fragile folds, tearing with his fangs, rending with his claws, leaving nothing behind except tatters of cloth that lay on his tongue like bitter scraps of skin.

From the shelter of a tree distant enough for safety but near enough for observation, Gyfree's father surveyed the two creatures as one mutilated the Dreamer's clothes and the other hungrily watched. Even pressed against the rough bark his hands weakly trembled, partially in weariness but mostly in relief, for his ruse had succeeded, and the hunters had followed the wrong scent. As a decoy the clothes alone would not have been enough to lure the beasts, but by sending all of the apprentice Sentries to trail behind Gyfree and the others, he had been able to help successfully obscure the true scent of the Dreamer, and the four who needed to escape had gained at least some small measure of desperately needed time. He had in fact accomplished all he had hoped to accomplish; he had diverted and delayed the beasts. Yet as he continued to watch from the relative safety of his hiding place, and as his hands continued to tremble, he realized that what shook him still was neither exhaustion nor relief, but fear. He knew, now that he could see them, see them clearly and feel the full force of their presence, that simply delaying the beasts would not be enough, as much as he had secretly hoped that it might be enough. He could not pretend, even to himself, that they were too weak to do more than minimal harm, that there would be plenty of time to deal with them when Gyfree returned.

Only once before had he seen Figments so solid, so substantial, and so menacing. Their forms never wavered, but remained as immutable as his own. They were here, palpably here, their essence so undiluted and so debased that his world was being ravaged before his eyes. This world could not tolerate the strain of such corruption, not even for a moment, for even from his vantage point he could see the trees shrink away and then succumb to inevitable death, could see the grass knot up and crumble, could even feel the soil parch and the air itself sink with the weight of pollution. Death surely stalked wherever those Figments stalked, and soon they would be back on Gyfree's trail, threatening both him and the Dreamer and wreaking additional havoc on his defenseless land. The pain of that land would be his pain, as the pain surrounding him was already his, for this was his land, his as it was no other's, his ultimate care and responsibility. He could not allow the carriers of such pain to wander unchecked here any more than he could allow them to kill Gyfree and the Dreamer. Substantial or insubstantial, the beasts before him were only Figments, and there had been a time when banishing two such Figments would have been effortless for him; he had eliminated hundreds of Figments in his years, his bond with the land granting him the authority to dispel Figments as thoughtlessly as the sun dispelled fog. Even now, when age had brought the waning of his powers as surely and steadily as the end of day brought the setting of the sun, exiling two Figments should not be an impossible task. And impossible or not, it was a task he must accept, for it was a task that no one else could perform, at least not yet.

Stretching out his once formidable senses, he merged his awareness into that of the land; with painful abruptness he felt a distantly raging fire as if its flames licked his feeble arms and legs instead of the trunks and branches of so many trees, and for a brief moment all he knew was an agony that overwhelmed any desire for life. Yet even as he and the trees shrieked silently in shock and the throes of death, he detected the touch of rain on the flames, and then the heat was slowly dissipating from his skin, dribbling in flickers down his torso as if sponged away by gentle fingers. With the extinction of the fire, he felt himself standing among the smoking trees, feet entrenched in mud as stagnant as his body, his limbs heavy and lifeless, mere charred remainders through which blood had once flowed like sap through his veins as he was fed by the soil and nourished by the sun.

Whimpering with the death of so much of himself, so much of his land, he extended his senses farther, to land yet untouched by the presence of the beasts, and from this fertile land he drew what strength he could handle, until the blood again pumped through his veins and his limbs tingled both with the renewal of sensation and with the swelling of his power. All of the strength of the land was his, strength that lay in the richness of the soil, strength that hummed in the knee-high grasses, strength that cascaded from the rivers and crashed with each waterfall, strength that burrowed deep with the roots of every tree, strength that was there for the asking, as much as he could hold. Once he had been able to hold it all as easily as he held a single leaf in the palm of his hand, but he was older now, and not as robust, so even a leaf could at times seem more heavy than he could bear, but when there was great need, as there was now, he would bear the weight of so much strength because that was his charge and there was no choice. So he pulled everything he could to himself until he was certain his skin would burst like an old, cracked canteen that had been overfilled with water. Then, the flickering shadow of distant leafs playing across his face and the rush and tumble of a waterfall beating in his chest, he stepped away from his hiding place to confront the beasts. When he raised his hands, wind spilled from his fingertips, and with the rush of wind came the aroma of burgeoning earth, so that Hund's nostrils flared and he tore his eyes away from Auge's ravening contortions.

"You will leave this place!" boomed the old man with the breath of the wind. Specks of green light, the very spirit and essence of every living plant he had called, spurted from his fingers, carried like summer's seeds by the wind to encircle the monstrous trespassers. As the specks of light sailed through the air they lengthened into thin green blades that pierced the leathery armor that fleshed the beasts, but when these spears of grass drew blood, the old man trembled in fear. Hurting them was not what he had intended. The Figments should not be bleeding; they should be dissipating, their skin dissolving like shadows in the direct light of the sun. They should not be able to maintain a hold on the land that had risen to expel them.

The beast on the ground heaved to his feet, tattered clothing hanging from his fangs like dead skin, and together he and the other beast faced the old man, lips and claws curling, slitted eyes webbed with tendrils of blood, massive shoulders hunched and jagged spines tensed, seemingly oblivious to the blood seeping from dozens of gashes spattered across their skin. "Who do you think you are, old man?" rumbled Hund, his snout quivering as if in anticipation.

The old man didn't answer, but instead spread his fingers wide, and this time iridescent beads flowed from his fingers, angling through the air, the tiny droplets merging into bigger and then even bigger teardrops that transformed into blue spears before raining down on the Figments. These too drew blood as they sliced through the leathery hides, yet the figures of the beasts never wavered. Instead the Figments advanced, razored paws swiping aside the plunging spears as if they were only harmless drops of rain, and as they drew near, the old man faltered and his hands fell, the strength of the land draining away from him just as the life had drained from trees that had felt the beasts' approach.

The Figments halted a few feet away, fangs glistening with saliva and eyes dark with hunger. "Who do you think you are, old man?" repeated Hund with a snarl.

Straightening his shoulders and lifting his chin defiantly, the old man declared, "I am Keeper of this land, and you Figments have no place here. I order you to leave immediately."

Auge threw back his head and laughed, the tatters caught on his fangs dancing a macabre dance of the dead. "Well, Keeper, it seems you have no power over us. Either you are too old and weak, or we are stronger than even we realized. What do you think, Hund?"

Eyes glinting and snout twitching, Hund growled, "I think this Keeper brought the Dreamer's scent here, and that he is the one who tricked us. His smell was also on the clothes we found."

Auge's roar reverberated through the forest, felling not just the leafs, but the trees themselves, until the entire area echoed with the screams of roots torn free and with toppling crashes, and soaring above all, the shrill shriek of his bestial cries. When Hund's bellow joined in, the ground beneath the Keeper's feet split apart, cracks snaking out like a spiderweb trying to escape from the poisonous killer in its own center. There was no need for either Figment to touch the old man, for he fell as the forest around him fell, the skin on his face fracturing like the earth on which he sprawled. Yet such an easy kill could not satisfy their rage or their hunger, and the Figments fell upon his body, shredding with the same frenzy that Auge had slashed the Dreamer's clothes. When at long last their fury had partly subsided, and they had been jerked away by two faraway hands to resume their master's pursuit, there was real skin dangling from their fangs and claws, and their bellies were gorged with blood. Behind them, cast aside in the crimson stained dust, was a body too mauled to recognize, but the land knew who rested there and would have reached out to absorb him back into its folds, just as he had so often absorbed it, if the ground directly beneath his silent form, and the ground for miles around, had not been as inert and plundered as his corpse. The Keeper had died and the land could only mourn from afar, mourn for all that had already passed away and for all that might still come to pass.

Chapter 3

Sunshine speckled the forest floor as if marking a path for the Dreamer and her escorts, but though his feet followed dutifully, Gyfree's eyes and mind were far from the helpful light. The darkness of a scowl shadowed his face as he brooded over the events that had already marked this day and set it aside from all of the days that had gone before. First and most importantly there was the Dreamer, whose vivid presence unsettled him in ways he'd rather not admit. At first he had been unwilling to even acknowledge that she was no ordinary Dreamer, for he had been shaken by everything her presence might mean, especially to himself. But now he had no choice but to accept her for what she was, what he had both hoped and feared she was from the moment she had first locked her luminous eyes on his face, and he had felt that spark of recognition, and something even deeper. Involuntarily he glanced back over his shoulder, and there she was, clear eyes canvassing the forest like an artist storing details for a future painting. No, not an ordinary Dreamer by any stretch of the imagination, not even by the distortions of his own wildest dreams.

Walking directly behind the Dreamer was Timi, whose presence marked yet another unforeseen circumstance that caused him as much unease as the Dreamer's arrival, but this time untouched by the secret twinges of excitement and the hidden thrill he felt with Drew. As First Sentry for this world, it was his job to occasionally assist in the training of new recruits, and his job to oust

anyone he deemed unfit. For several weeks he and Mischa had
been busy preparing the most recent batch of would-be Barrier
guards, teaching them the easiest and swiftest methods for finding
and removing Dreamers. They had even had several opportunities
to expose the recruits to real Dreamers, since for some unknown
reason, the frequency of Dreamers slipping through the Barrier
had been steadily increasing, especially in the general region
surrounding the point where Drew had broken through. Overall
the group had progressed well, and had successfully handled the
Dreamers when awarded the chance; that is with the exception
of Timi. For some inexplicable reason, Timi seemed incapable of
dealing with the Dreamers, recoiling from them with a fear that left
her almost completely paralyzed. The more bemused and distant
the Dreamer, the greater and the more debilitating her fear. Even
when training exercises were conducted without the presence of a
Dreamer, she was timid and indecisive, incapable of remembering
from day to day the skills her instructors had already covered.
Initiative was as foreign to her nature as aggression, and it was
clear to both himself and Mischa that she was totally unsuited
for the position. Just that morning he and Mischa had wandered
away from the Sentries' encampment to discuss whether to grant
Timi any more chances, or whether it was time to send her on
her way. They had finally decided to expel her when he had felt
the jolt of Drew's arrival, and the last thing he had expected when
he had carried a truly unnerving Dreamer into camp was that
Timi would volunteer to accompany them to the Source, and that
his father would be there to foist her upon them. Given a choice,
Timi would have been the last person he would have permitted
on such a potentially perilous venture.

Then of course there was Mischa. They had worked together
before this time, and effectively. There was no questioning Mischa's
competence, or her devotion to duty, no matter how irreverent she
might sometimes be. Yet something in her attitude had changed
recently, either toward him or toward the office they performed.
Before she had been brisk and businesslike, sometimes sardonic,
but always professional. Now she was playful, teasing, baiting him
constantly with an impish gleam in her eyes, like a child who
believes she deserves to be spoiled and is just waiting for the adults
to catch on. She too made him uneasy, but it was an uneasiness
devoid of any other emotions and so simple to shrug off.

Some distance behind him he could sense the novice Sentries treading the same path he and his companions had already traversed, and he understood that his father had sent them along this trail, and why. In some ways this fact concerned him more than anything else that had transpired during this pivotal day. The Sentries were there to obscure the Dreamer's presence, but he knew, just as his father knew, that it would take far more to divert the beasts who stalked her, and he knew this was why his father had taken the Dreamer's clothes. The Figments most successful at following a Dreamer often had a keen sense of smell, although there were always those rare few who simply had an uncannily accurate sense of their Dreamer's whereabouts without the need to resort to any tracking skills at all. If the Figments trailing Drew were relying on the usual skills, the clothes would provide a decoy that would hopefully divert the Figments from the true trail, at least for a while. The farther the Figments might track the scent of the clothes, the more time Gyfree and the three women would have to escape. Gyfree's father would carry those clothes into the farthest recesses of the forest, would carry them until he could feel the Figments directly behind him, their proximity like the stench of decay filling his nose. Then, and only then, would he drop the clothes and hide. He would take this risk, stake everything on the hope that the Figments would follow him, rather than wait in the clearing to confront the creatures, because he knew, just as his son knew, that this was his best chance to buy time for those who fled. There had been a time when he would never have needed to rely on such subterfuge, but that time was long past, as only he and Gyfree truly realized. So to save the others, he would not stay to fight, but instead would run, and would hide. To increase the chance of success, he would also rouse the land shielding the traveling companions to release as much scent as possible to further confuse the Figments, but this was the only power he possessed as Keeper that he would be able to employ. It was really the only power he had left to employ.

Gyfree knew all of this, but he knew his father as well, and what concerned him, what gripped him by the lungs until his chest burned with trapped air, what squeezed his heart until the blood was forced upward into his eyes and ears to darken the world and drum inside his head, what terrified him more than the reality of the Dreamer, was the possibility that, even if the ruse worked and those fleeing had been bought valuable time, his father would not be content with accomplishing nothing more, would not be content to merely hide. Yes, he knew his father well; understood too well this man who had taken him in when his true son had died and had treated Gyfree as if he had never been a substitute for what had been lost. Long had the man he called father been a dynamic force, for he was Keeper of this world. But age had accomplished what no Figment could, and in the past years he had felt his father's powers waning, had felt his connection to the land fading, just as his own sense of the land had grown. And now he, not his father, could sense the entire land as if he carried it both on and beneath his skin, as if the ridges of his spine were hills and mountains and the hair sprouting from his head was a forest of disheveled rusty trees. At the back of his mind he felt the tickling trace of the land's whispering voice, and although this voice never competed with those of the people around him, it was still always there, ready to snatch his attention if a pressing need arose.

Today the whisper had risen to a moan, as if the land was in pain or in mourning for itself, and this was the final thing that had contributed to his gnawing unease, for there was something terribly wrong, and there had been something terribly wrong from the moment he had walked into the clearing with the Dreamer in his arms. He could feel the nagging ache of the land like a toothache stabbing away at his jaw, an ache that had been throbbing with increasing intensity until he was forced to clench his teeth to stop himself from groaning. And still the pain grew, reaching up fingers to scrape at his skull, piercing the thick bone and scratching his brain, growing more insistent and demanding until suddenly the whispering moan of the land dissolved into a shriek, shrill with the crackle and bursts of fire bombarding grass and detonating trees.

Wheeling around he grabbed the hands of the Dreamer, his eyes filling with something intangible, something that pulled her eyes far away, and immediately the trees around them vanished; they stood alone inside the vast gray field of an unsettling dream, nothing beneath or above them, until out of this emptiness a shimmering landscape emerged, populated by skeletal grass and the wavering ghosts of barren trees. With the jerkiness of time-lapse photography, the phantom landscape burst into ethereal flames, gray shadows licking and consuming gray shadows in absolute silence. As the shadow fire fitfully toppled the translucent trees, tears leaked from Gyfree's eyes, and in a voice that demanded instant response, he shouted, "Cry! You must cry if we are to stop the fire!"

With Gyfree's shout of fire, Drew could suddenly smell acrid smoke as it reached out to burn her nose and sear her eyes, its nettling touch drawing the tears Gyfree required. Scalding tears spilled down her cheeks just as they spilled down his, a torrent of tears tumbling from their jaws to vanish into the gray vapor that was slowly climbing up their legs. Where the tears fell somewhere unseen far below there was a thunderous hiss, while before Drew's eyes streaks of gray angled across the phantom trees like a driving rain. Slowly the shadowy flames receded, as if caught in a film rolling backward in stilted motion, and then the skeletal grass and branches stood alone once more, starkly black against the background of gray, and Drew could actually hear the murmur of raindrops as they splattered somewhere far away on ground untouched by her and Gyfree's feet. As the last whiff of smoke dissipated, and the shadowy trees dissolved, Gyfree dropped her hands, and Drew blinked to see trees that were no longer ghosts, but green and vibrant with life, leap into view around her, and she understood that the land springing beneath her feet was the same land visited by the rain, although an unknown distance stretched between the scorched earth and where she and Gyfree faced each other, their faces unmarked by the paths of recent tears.

"What happened?" Mischa demanded before Drew could draw breath and finally give name to the expression she recognized in Gyfree's eyes, the expression that had shaken her from the moment she had first looked up and met his gaze. He too was a Dreamer, she thought to herself. A Dreamer no more asleep than she felt herself.

"There was a fire back in the clearing," Gyfree answered tersely. "The Figments caused it, and we put it out."

Mischa nodded curtly, eyes expressionless as they swept from Gyfree's face to Drew's and back again. Timi, however, stared unblinking at Drew, then stepped forward and tentatively touched the other's arm. Not recoiling from the Dreamer as both Gyfree and Mischa would have expected, Timi smiled tremulously and said, "You're really here, aren't you?"

"Let's move," Gyfree interrupted brusquely. "The Figments might already be on our trail."

The four rushed onward, Timi walking as close as she possibly could to Drew without stepping on the other woman's feet or bumping her off the path. Yet the group had only covered a short distance when Gyfree suddenly collapsed, his knees buckling as if some immense foot had kicked his legs out from under him. Sprawled on the ground his body convulsed and his hands grasped at the grass as if there was a sturdy rope hidden there that would save him from falling into an invisible chasm that had opened beneath his feet. Drew rushed forward, her eyes suddenly distant, and with the strength she knew only in dreams, yanked his fists from the grass and pulled him to his feet, then held him there as the tremors haltingly abated. When the nightmare in his eyes cleared, she released him despite the continued trembling in his limbs, and the new trembling in her own.

"What in the dreamworld was that?" Mischa demanded, her face pale and rigid.

All traces of gold had been swallowed by the black center of Gyfree's eyes. "The Keeper is dead," he announced hoarsely. "The Figments killed him."

As impossible as it seemed, even more color drained from Mischa's face. "Figments do not possess enough power to kill a Keeper," she protested.

"These do," Gyfree rebutted shortly.

"I'm sorry," Mischa whispered. "I can only guess how you must feel."

"What happens now?" asked Timi in a small, shaking voice.

"The land will choose a new Keeper to guard it," Mischa responded, turning away so she could avoid the black anguish that had swallowed Gyfree's eyes.

"It already has," rasped Gyfree as if the words would scrape his throat raw. "Me."

Whirling around in surprise so intense she forgot to dodge his eyes, Mischa blurted, "You? How is that possible?"

"I don't know, but I could feel the land even before this happened. I felt the fire in the clearing as if it had been ignited inside me. Now my feelings are even stronger than before." He fell silent, but there were unspoken words pouring through his eyes. "I feel as if the heart of the land has lodged in my heart," he thought, but the thought wasn't his alone, for he could feel the land slipping through his consciousness to shape the words he would not say, "and that the blood pumping in my veins flows through each river and stream. I feel as if my breath is the air that encloses us all, and without my lungs there would be no breath for anyone. I can feel the land inside me and surrounding me, and I know its pain and the darkness that trespasses here leaving that pain in its tracks." He cleared his throat as if to break away the rawness, but his voice was more raw, not less, as he spoke aloud again. "I can feel the Figments just as the land feels their footsteps, and I even know where they now range. They are on their way back toward the clearing. And as Keeper my first task is still to remove the Dreamer from their grasp, so let's go."

The new Keeper did not wait for them to acquiesce; spinning on his heel, he plunged back through the trees, his own pain and sorrow blinding him to the look of anguish and guilt that had finally clouded the Dreamer's clear eyes.

Watching from the isolation of his own private nightmare theater, he stretched out a hand to once again direct the course of events unfolding like a scene from some low-budget horror movie in which the leads romped around foolishly as the film flickered in and out of focus and certain death lurked just out of the camera's range. It was certain death that he was trying to bring to the screen, but so far his characters had bungled their parts, and death had only struck behind the real action scenes. In growing frustration he watched and listened, the image before him flat and the sound filling his ears tinny, as if he was trapped at a neighborhood drive-in, but when the villains he had cast stumbled back into the clearing that was thus far at the center of the movie, he leaned forward in anticipation, willing them toward the film's bloody climax.

Hund orbited the clearing, snout flaring only inches from the ground, his usual whine swelling like badly composed background music. As the whining melody reached its crescendo, Auge, trailing behind as impatiently as an ambitious supporting actor, sank his claws into Hund's snarled mane and yanked his head away from the sodden ground.

"So?" snarled Auge.

"Her scent is gone," Hund whimpered. "Rain must have washed it away, for it is wet here now."

Auge howled, as did the distant director. She had slipped through his grasp, as she always slipped through his grasp. Not since that first night, when she had dreamed him into existence, had he been able to zoom in close enough for the kill. New to his own creation, not yet knowing what part he had been cast to play, he had stood at the edge of her bed and watched her sleep, watched in awe the tossing and turning of her childish form, watched and waited for her eyes to open so he could meet his producer face to face. When finally her eyelids had been raised like the curtain on the stage of her face, and the light in her eyes had spilled across the room, and she had seen him where he stood patiently awaiting her notice, she had frozen in bed, as if she was trying to convince both him and herself that he wasn't really part of the picture. So he had just stood there, watching her with his slitted demon eyes, seeing himself as she envisioned him, reflected indelibly in the lens of her eyes, a hideous horned, fanged, and clawed creature with fiery skin that writhed in an ongoing, grotesque dance of death across the protruding bones of his face. He had stood there so close, unable to move just as she seemed unable to move, frozen with her in some classic frame of time. Then finally her lips had parted, and her voice rang out through the darkened setting, "Mommy!" A spotlight blazed down the hall, and suddenly he realized what his part had been, and that he had missed all his cues. He should have made her burn, made her burn as he burned because that was the role she had dreamed for him, and he would never be all she had expected him to be until he fulfilled his part. Yet it had been too late by then, for he had heard the approach of the player she had chosen to delete him from the scene, and he had fled because that was all he could do.

It was only later, when he had encountered others of his kind, others whose lives had sprouted from the mind of a Dreamer, that he fully understood just what his own Dreamer had done. Dreams were tenuous things, fluid things, and the Figments whose lives were conceived in dreams were as fluid as the nightmare landscape that had been unable to completely hold them. Powerful Dreamers could give life to the beasts they created to haunt them, but once these Figments had broken free, Dreamers no longer had complete control. The newly born Figments could assume whatever shape they chose, including human, although few possessed the strength to maintain any single shape for long, and almost none could avoid slipping back frequently into the form chosen by their Dreamer. Watching a Figment stalk through the shady world between dreams and waking that most of them inhabited was like watching a kaleidoscope of wispy shapes. It was this incorporeality that limited most Figments to either the void or the dreamworld, but it was also what granted them the freedom to continually recreate themselves. A few Figments even had the strength to enter a waking world and to hold the shape they wore there, at least for a while. Yet all Figments, weak or strong, still held in common that versatility of shape, all except him. He was the only Figment without the power to change, the only Figment whose Dreamer had dreamed him so irrevocably that he could not alter a single detail of his hideous appearance. In the realm of dreams, in the realm of the void, he was the one and only thing of permanence. He was also the strongest, a Figment that almost all others soon called master, a Figment created with a swelling size and presence that subjugated all others, but for all his ominous strength, all his towering might, he could not shed the face and form of a child's nightmare, could not free himself from the horror he had seen in his Dreamer's eyes.

It was within his power to change others, to grant them the appearance of permanence if it suited his own purposes, to give them a lethal substance they could not otherwise possess, but he could not transfer their malleability to himself. His Dreamer had unwittingly dreamed him far too inescapably within her control, and his best hope for breaking free, for transforming the shape of his face, for becoming even more than she had dreamed him to be, was to kill her. Perhaps when the uncompromising vision that had brought him into the picture had been eliminated, and the Dreamer lay dead at his feet, then the repulsiveness that costumed him could be left like unwanted footage on the editing floor. And the power he longed for, the power to be completely free, the power to recreate himself, would finally be his.

Yet disconcertingly, his Dreamer proved most difficult to kill. Not long after that first night, but long enough for him to learn and truly understand just what she had done, he had returned to her house and had stood once more at the foot of her bed, willing her to awaken so he could see her with her own death in her eyes. Then her eyes had slid open, but before he could lunge forward for the kill, those eyes had ensnared him. He could see himself once more reflected in her eyes, but for the first time since he had sprung to life, he was changed. Her eyes had accomplished the one thing impossible; with a single glance she had transformed him, but the new shape she had wrapped him in was like a straitjacket slipped over his head to render him harmless. Held in her eyes he could not move as wavering Figments echoing his new shape sprang to life all around him. When the newborn Figments began to dance, so did he, his limbs pulled up and down without his volition as he and the other pirates capered about her bed. Around and around they cavorted, her slowly swelling eyes following every graceless jerk, until her mouth gaped open and she screamed just as she had the time before, "Mommy!" When he fled back into the night, the pirate facade had fallen away and he was again his inescapable self.

That had been the last time she had permitted him to approach near enough for the kill. The next time he seeped through the walls of her house he could feel her immediately rouse, could sense her sitting up abruptly in her bed, and he knew his presence was as palpable to her as her presence was to him. Even without her eyes to ensnare him, he could feel the transformation seize him, could feel himself swelling to immensity, could feel his arms stretch and his legs thicken until he was standing on four limbs as heavy as tree trunks. He moved awkwardly as the walls of the house seemed to press down on him, and a giant tail moved with him. Trying to turn his head and look behind him, he discovered that his neck had grown unbelievably long, and although the ceiling would not permit him to elevate this extended neck, he could still swing it around to parallel his equally enormous tail. His breath rumbled up the stairway to her room, but his dinosaur body was too immense to budge within the confines of the house. Once more she had immobilized him, and it wasn't until the first spears of morning light had sliced through his amazing bulk that her hold on him had been relinquished and he could return to himself and slip away, back into the welcome void where nothing and no one held the power to oppose him.

After that he was never even permitted to enter her home; of all the places in her world, it was the only one with walls suddenly impenetrable to him. The next time he had drawn near she had awakened before he could even reach her house, and he had found himself not inside as he had expected, but stranded directly beneath her bedroom window. This time when she seized him with the power of her waking dream, he felt the blood evaporate from his body, felt his skin chill and dampen, felt himself die and return to life all in a single second. He was empty, shockingly empty, and he needed to find blood, preferably a woman's blood, to fill the aching hole he now carried within. With the realization that she had transformed him into a vampire, he finally knew fear, for if she held him until dawn cracked the sky, he might actually die. With a wrench of will that left him shaking, he fled back into the void, back to himself.

From that night on he was completely barred from the waking world that harbored her; however he tried, he could not hold himself there for more than a gasp, and so he was reduced to trying to reach her in the realm of dreams. His power was diminished there, for in dreams the Dreamers held sway, even though they themselves seemed to have no concept of their strength. Yet it was not unheard of, however rare, for vengeful Figments to actually catch and kill a Dreamer during a nightmare. When this happened, and the Dreamer actually met death in a dream, there was no waking up. So he waited and watched from his height in the void, and when a promising nightmare filled her sleep, he slipped into the dream world to chase her. The walls of a house rose up around him, blocking him at every turn, but still he sped through the shifting corridors and misleading rooms, knowing she was just ahead, exulting because she was mindlessly fleeing him as he had hoped she might, recognizing that he must catch her before she woke up. Then suddenly he found himself in a deserted room without windows or doors, and howling with fury, he hurled himself against the nearest wall, slamming into the impossibly solid barrier over and over to no avail. He could feel her too, feel her in the very next room as she slipped behind a door to hide from him, and he understood that even if he could break free from the walls that restrained him, he would never be able to open the door she had closed because she would never allow it. His howls shook the walls, shook the entire house of her dream, and then suddenly the walls around him dissolved like smoke in the wind, and he was back in the void, far away from where she had bounded awake.

Every nightmare she breathed life into after that might as well have been off limits to him. Try as he might to slip in unnoticed, the moment she felt his slightest touch, she would slip into another nightmare, then another, always keeping a dream ahead of him until the moment she once again jolted awake. Nor could he send his minions to accomplish what he could not, for if she felt even the slightest trace of his touch upon them, she slipped away just as surely as if he himself had intruded upon her dreams. He could not even send them into the waking world to kill her as she slept, for only those completely transformed by his touch had the strength to enter and stay, and they throbbed with his taint so completely that they were barred from her presence as surely as he would have been. Finally he had no choice but to yield to the inevitable, and to hope that as she grew older she would leave her childhood dreams behind, and that her forgotten nightmares would fade away completely until her hold on him had vanished.

So he watched and waited while the years passed by, and although her nightmares came far less often, she still slipped away every time he disturbed them. Day and night he watched, night and day he waited, and through empty days and dream-filled nights she moved from adolescence to adulthood, transforming from child to woman with a grace that he resented since he could still not change at all. And still he watched and still he waited as she moved through dreams and through waking. Her life in the waking world was one of restless shifting, for she never stayed anywhere or with anyone for long, and he knew as she did not the reason: her dreamworld was still the real and powerful one, the world where she truly lived and belonged. And because of this he knew at last that his waiting had been for nothing, that her grip on him would never weaken and really could only be loosened with death. And he also knew that waiting was no longer an option, for she was young, with a lengthy life stretching before her, and he had already waited long enough.

Unapproachable in the waking world, inaccessible in the dreamworld, she had eluded him for long, but no more, for at last he knew what he must do. She was strongest in her world, strongest in her dreams, but he was strongest in the void, in that space that was neither waking nor dreaming, and somehow he must either transport her there or bring the void to her for the kill. At last he had a purpose, and slowly at first, he began to give that purpose the substance and force that infused his own being. He began watching for strong nightmares, it no longer mattered whose, as long as they were created by Dreamers powerful enough to bestow the slightest touch of reality to the places they dreamed. The moment he detected such a nightmare, he would rush to the source and slip undetected into the dream. Once there he would latch onto a piece of the nightmare—an endless stairway, a locked and unbreakable door, a towering fence, a hazy street in a maze of hazy streets—and holding the nightmare feature in hands that could grant permanence at will, he snatched it away into the void. There he assembled the bits and pieces, the wisps and tatters of stolen dreams, until he had created a full nightmare landscape of his own, a landscape he could manipulate and control, a landscape that was now just one more part of the void, but which he could send into the waking world whenever he chose. Then he selected two of his minions, the most lethal and vicious, two minions who also bore the mark of her creation but whom she had completely forgotten, and he taught them the pathways of the nightmare's streets, shielding their presence, and his touch upon them, with the very essence of the void itself.

At last the trap was ready, and he thrilled with the knowledge that soon she would be his, that it was almost time. Yet he would not be hasty because there would only be one chance; he knew she would only allow one chance, so he could not afford to fail. Her world was full of Dreamers, so first he would test his nightmare trap on some of them. Moving his nightmare directly outside the house of a Dreamer, he waited and watched from afar just as he had instructed his minions to wait and watch from quite near. Just as he had hoped, the proximity of such a substantial nightmare was too tantalizing for a true Dreamer to ignore. It made this one restless, like an almost inaudible scratch at the door that demanded immediate attention, although the hapless hearer could not explain why. Out into the night the Dreamer rushed, straight into the waiting arms of the nightmare, and directly behind followed the minions, giving chase through the twisted streets until, just as they reached out for the kill, their master pulled the nightmare out from under them, yanking them fully back into the void, and although they knew not to question, they soon came to understand that this game they played night after night was no more than a chase, and that there would be no killing until he told them so. Held back from the kill, they even chased several of the snared Dreamers through the Barrier between worlds, forcing them up against weak spots in the dividing wall, pushing their practice victims farther than most nightmares. These Dreamers had been too feeble to exist beyond the Barrier, and had soon returned as if their bodies and minds had actually been divided between two different realities, despite the fact that something entirely different had happened to them. But this was no concern of his minions, and certainly no concern of his. Each Dreamer was forgotten as soon as the next one was ambushed.

Over and over again he set his baited trap and his minions played their stalking game, and then one night, finally convinced he could not fail, he informed them that it was time to catch and kill. His only fear had been that she would avoid the nightmare because his touch was upon everything there; he knew she would feel the familiarity of his presence, but he had been fairly certain that the trace left by so many different nightmares would diffuse his taint, and he had been right. She had plunged into the nightmare as quickly and thoughtlessly as all the other Dreamers who had felt it before, and in that moment, he had tasted triumph, for even if she felt him with the approach of his minions, she would have no strength to resist him here. He would use his entire being to control the nightmare that held her, use all his vast power to wrap it around her, and she would finally be his. But then somehow, despite all the patient planning and painstaking care, despite what should have been her powerlessness, he had still failed; she had eluded him again, and this time she had transformed the very nightmare he had created, transformed it as if she alone had dreamed it into existence, and then she had used its potency to propel her beyond the void and through the Barrier that few Figments dared now pass, into a new world that confused even his senses. And she had been strong enough, more than strong enough, to accept her strange surroundings as more than just another dream, strong enough to grasp hold of this new world and stay. This Dreamer, unlike the others who had gone before, did not slip back.

Eyes enthralled with the distant spectacle of his minions floundering through the lifeless clearing, he was still unsurprised to feel a chill hand on his shoulder and icy breath on his neck. He didn't bother to turn, but simply shrugged the hand away. "What do you want?" he snarled.

"My, my. Temper, temper," a cool voice chided. "I just wanted to check in and see how well your minions were doing. Not very well, it appears. Have they done anything yet other than run around in circles?"

Whirling around to face her, he growled, "They have killed the Barrier's Keeper."

For a moment the surface of her expression fractured, and he thought he could almost detect turbulent depths churning underneath, but then her cool mockery rose and he wondered if he had been mistaken. "Who would have thought that possible, especially considering the number of Figments he has defeated in the years since the Barrier was first breached? So who is the new Keeper?" she asked nonchalantly.

His expression darkened, the turmoil in his depths unmasked by the writhing skin of his face. "From what I could sense, his son, who is accompanying my Dreamer."

"His son?" she repeated, and despite her habitual cold drawl, he thought he detected a flicker of shock, perhaps even anticipation, in her ice-chip eyes. Then her lids fell with the swift violence of an avalanche, and if possible a mantle of ice even more cold and treacherous slid down her face. "If you send me I could easily destroy both him and your precious Dreamer," she offered with a smile of frosty indifference.

"My minions will still find them and take care of them," he growled.

"Perhaps," she sighed, her eyelashes tinkling against her frigid cheeks. "Perhaps not. Nothing is certain except that I will succeed if they fail."

"You will not be given the chance," he snarled. "I don't trust you, for you are as deceptive as your beauty."

Reaching up a slender hand with long, frosty blue nails, she stroked his restless face. Then placing her wintry blue lips to his, she kissed him briefly, exhaling ice-laden air down into the furnace of his lungs. "Yes," she breathed, "yet you still need me, just as you have always needed me, however reluctantly." With a chilling laugh she stepped back, to be swallowed by a sudden flurry of sparkling snow. For a moment he watched a few, swirling silvery flecks as they slowly winked out, and then he turned back toward the monotonous scene of his minions circling and recircling the clearing. Reaching his hand across the darkened theater of space, he once more provided direction to his aspiring players, casting all his formidable skills into the picture in the hope that he could salvage the entire production without needing to meet the price of an equally talented, unpredictable, and ambitious leading lady.

Chapter 4

A new world more vivid and alive than any she had ever known burgeoned around Drew, but she no longer saw the curiously alert trees with watchful faces hidden in the whorls and gnarls of their trunks. Nor could she still hear the electric thrum that raced overhead as if messages were whizzing back and forth just out of range of her comprehension. She had stopped feeling the ground beneath her as it attentively cushioned her feet and briskly bounced back to lend a spring to each step she took, had stopped smelling the hint of spice that hung so heavy and intoxicating in the air that breathing left a sweet taste on her tongue. None of these things existed for her anymore; now nothing existed except a bloody corpse cast aside in a graveyard of lost grass and earth and trees.

The old man who had helped her, the one Gyfree had called Father and both Mischa and Timi had addressed as Sir, the one all three of her companions had referred to as the Keeper: that old man was dead only because of her intrusion into his land. When she had wrenched Gyfree to his feet, she had somehow seen everything he had seen, and ever since she had been unable to see anything else. She recognized the beasts who had ravaged the Keeper; she even knew the burn of those fangs ripping through flesh, and she knew without a doubt that she had brought devastation to this world. She had brought pain and death to the Keeper, and carnage to the land. She had finally found her dreamworld, and then had tainted it with a nightmare.

51

The air hummed soothingly in her ears and the trees breathed sighs of comfort, faces in the bark gentle and reassuring. Even the ground reached up to massage her feet and caress her ankles with consoling fingers of grass, but Drew remained oblivious to every sight and sound and sensation that lived outside the confines of her mind. Her inner vision burned with blood; apart yet immersed she watched intently as the dark and viscous crimson blaze rose from the forest floor, long sticky tongues licking the trunks of trees with an all-consuming hunger, heat rising with the bloody flames to scorch her eyebrows and lashes, sickly smoke mounting to blister the lining of her nose. The ghostly forest dropped away as she was consumed in flame, baptized by blood and fire so that she might hope for a different life, a life that beckoned to her now if she would only continue wading through the bloody blaze.

With the same will she used to evade the beasts who haunted her dreams, the will she sometimes even wielded to change the course of unpleasant dreams, she now plunged through her mind, throwing her entire being into the nightmare of fiery death. Grimly she plowed across white-hot coals as the raging flames peeled away her old layers of self, until she was nothing but a skeleton drifting through this infernal world in search of skin. Somewhere ahead that promise of skin, of a new identity to wrap around and heal her, beckoned with increasing intensity, and without pause she obeyed. Stepping through the flames toward the insistent call, she found herself on the verge of a vast desert, heat rippling in waves across an endless stretch of burning white sand. Overhead a sun that dominated over half of the sky swamped the sand and its lone visitor with light so intense that everything here, including the small ridge of sky outlining the sun, was bleached the same blinding white. Drew didn't hesitate as she lunged forward into the shimmering light of this desert, the sand shifting and sliding beneath her feet.

The heat of the fire she had passed through was nothing compared to the heat that blasted into her here. The coals she had earlier braved were no more than warm kisses on the soles of her feet; now jaws with teeth of gnawing flame clamped down around her ankles so that every step was like stumbling directly into the mouth of hell itself. Away from the fire her old skin had reappeared, only to burst into thousands of blisters that popped and then shriveled in the blink of an eye, until her skin was once more peeling away, this time leaving her deeper self raw and exposed to the bleaching sun. The glare of this place paralyzed her eyes, and after the first few steps she could see nothing, but it made little difference in this inferno where there was nothing to see except endless sand and even more endless sun. Onward she staggered, the treacherous sand pulling and gnashing at her feet until she toppled to her hands and knees and started crawling, her entire body now crunched by the mouth of hell. Breathing had become an effort, each gulp of air turning her lungs into a furnace that sent not oxygen, but more heat to course through her body and scorch her veins. She tried to swallow, to find moisture to temper her flaming tongue, but her mouth was as dry as the desert. Water was only a distant dream, faint and tenuous, and she knew she could survive without it for she already had, and after all, in life you survived only if you didn't cling to foolish dreams that bore no relation to reality. For her reality was this consuming heat, this creeping progress through merciless sand, and the voice that promised to heal the deeper pain that even the heat couldn't touch. Time had no place in this reality. Each moment contained all moments, equally full of pain and promise, so her hands and feet channeled through the sand in one eternal moment that no longer had either a beginning or an end.

Then something cool, or at least less hot than the heat, touched her tattered face, and time regained its footing in this timeless place. Her hands and then her knees and finally her legs and feet broke free from the grip of the sand, and something that felt suspiciously like mud gently sucked the heat from what was once more skin. Shafts of brown and blue flitted across the field of white that still filled her vision and she blinked, sudden tears welling in the corners and spilling out to wash away the film of grit that rimmed her eyes. She blinked again, and through her tears saw the clouded image of a stream with muddy banks take shape. The memory of water as more than a distant dream returned and she clambered on her hands and knees to the water's edge, lowering her still hot face into cool shallows and gingerly taking a few precious sips. As she lifted her head, a loud buzz sounded in one ear, and she turned her swimming eyes to find the largest bee she had ever seen as it hovered bare inches from her face, its wings a blur of heart-racing motion that reminded her forcibly of a hummingbird. Its fuzzy striped body ended with a barbed stinger longer than her longest finger, and its head boasted what could only be described as an equally long beak. It buzzed again over the whirring sound of its wings, then circling her head once, darted off through the trees lining the bank of the stream. She watched in bemusement as it disappeared through branches heavy with a rainbow of blossoms, and then she turned back toward the welcome coolness of the stream. Yet as she turned her head something flickered in the corner of her eye, and instead of lowering her face back into the water, she swivelled around to face whatever was there.

Stretched across the nearby forest and even across the tinkling stream was a shimmering white wall, and as she reached out a shaking hand, she could feel the unbearable heat radiating from what appeared to be its impenetrable surface. She swallowed a sudden lump of fire in her throat, feeling it burn a path to her stomach and down into her gut. A barrier. She had come through a barrier. Another barrier.

Memory slammed into her with a force that sent her reeling onto her back. Everything was there again, and as disastrously clear as ever. The first dream that somehow was not a dream, and had unexpectedly sent her catapulting through the sky to another world. Gyfree's world, the world she had been absorbing with delight until she had caused the Keeper's death. The blood and fire she had summoned and succumbed to. The call that had promised new life out of death, a promise that she could rise from the ashes that she had herself created. The searing heat of the desert. The endless trek. The loss and now the return of memory.

Dreams within dreams. It had happened again. She had vaulted from one dream to another, and then another. Chased by her own nightmares from dream to dream. And this time there might not even be a way to get back.

For as long as he recalled he had been here, and for just as long he had known that he was simply waiting to leave for the place he truly belonged, wherever that place might be. It was pleasant enough here, he supposed, but it was strangely empty. It wasn't that he was lonely, or at least not exactly, for he had the hummeybees to keep him company. It was just that everything here felt indistinct and remote, as if he was watching his own life unfold from a distance and that everything he witnessed occurred underwater. Somewhere else it all might seem colorful and sharp, but for him it was muted and smudged.

Daily he walked to the shimmering wall that held him here and stretched a hand toward its blistering surface, but he was always careful not to step too close. Once when he had felt a particularly strong need to feel something that was real and intense, he had stepped to within a foot of the wall, but the flash of pain had been transitory and unsatisfying. The most intense things derived from the experience were a persistent itch that lasted weeks as his blisters healed, and the gritty film that covered his eyes for almost a month, fogging his vision even more than it was usually fogged. Undergoing that one pure second of sensation had definitely not been worth the lengthy period of irritation that followed, yet despite the flat flavor of anticlimax he always tasted thereafter, he still went every day and stood cautiously away from the wall, his arm extended in front of his body so that his hand might safely bathe in the vaguely rippling current of heat. He went not for this meager sensation, for his life was pieced together by so many meager sensations that the loss of one meant nothing. He went because he felt compelled to go, because some obscure fascination returned him daily to the one thing in his world that existed with an intensity he could recognize but not share. He didn't know how, but he knew that the wall was the one thing in his world that meant something, the only thing that could ever make a difference. And he knew that someday someone would come through that wall, however inconceivable such an event might be, and that he would then be delivered to the place where his real life, a life rich with sensations, would begin. There was even a face connected with this dream of freedom, a pale face with light eyes and wispy hair, and a smile as distant as a star. When that face found him, he would find life. Until then he would float here on the surface of being and watch the muted colors and shapes swimming by far below, and with each breath he would call into the depths so that face could find him and bring him everything he needed.

Hands heedlessly busy knotting and unknotting a length of vine he had found in the forest, he sat on a rock in the sun and let his mind drift aimlessly through the trees as his eyes inched shut. Spread out below his mind's eye were blossoming trees and buzzing hummeybees, a carelessly brushed watercolor with pastel hues blending into muddy hues. Weaving through this hazy canvas was the smeared thread of the stream, its banks bleeding into the surrounding landscape so that its boundaries remained indistinct. And there, cutting trees in half and cleaving through the stream so that water seemed to flow from its hard face, was the sharply focused line of the wall.

A flutter of movement near the intersection of stream and wall created a sudden blot in the lower corner of the picture, but before he could filter through the other layers of washed out colors to identify the blot, a loud buzz reverberated in his ear. "There'z zomeone at the ztream."

The pigments of his vision swirled together into a random blotch of grays and browns as he blinked his eyes open. As always he tried but failed to focus on the hummeybee's pulsating wings. "The stream?" he echoed blankly. "Someone at the stream?"

"Like you," the hummeybee replied, "but zmaller and zofter. Body not zo flat and hard."

"Someone at the stream?" he repeated.

"Yez," the hummeybee droned excitedly, darting around his head so swiftly that his eyes could not follow. "Come zee, come zee."

Rising reflexively to his feet he turned in the direction of the mysterious blot that still lingered as a dingy smear in the corner of his mind. The hummeybee streaked eagerly ahead, spiraling in circles before zipping back to orbit him, then speeding away again. Ignoring the antics of the hummeybee, he plodded slowly ahead with steps so halting that he knew he could shut his eyes and see himself from afar as just another splotch of color melted into the other browns and grays. Yet when he did close his eyes all he could see was the wistful and pale face with its wisps of silvery white hair.

"Juzt ahead, juzt ahead," whirred the hummeybee, its wingbeats emphasizing each word.

His eyes slid open and shifted forward, but his feet faltered and he knew he could move no farther, so he just stood still, waiting as he always had waited, waiting because that was all he knew how to do.

Ahead there was a faint rustle, and the sucking sound of something pulling free from mud. Then footsteps, the first footsteps he had ever heard beside his own, the sound sharp and musical to his ears. He held his breath, afraid to miss a single note, and even over the steady drone of the hummeybee he could hear the footsteps grow louder and closer and ever more distinct. From around a bend in the path a face suddenly appeared, but it was not the face of his vision. This one was darker, smoky hair glinting with a profusion of color, skin flushed and eyes gleaming with a green more green than the surrounding trees. She stopped and stared at him as he stood staring back, and it crossed his mind that she seemed to be waiting, just as he was waiting. Neither spoke, but both raised their eyes to the nearby wall looming high overhead when a surge of heat washed over them and the white expanse began to pulsate and shiver.

They would have floundered forever through the clearing, or have turned to rend each other to shreds in their hunger and frustration, but their task was farther from fulfillment than before and their master had once again stretched his razored claws across the abyss to not only intervene, but to also punish their latest failure. He had seized them in his invisible yet massive hand, stabbing his venomous talons into their flesh, slicing through leathery skin and muscle until his claws clacked against bone. For a time that seemingly spanned the entire length of existence, he did nothing else but hold them there, the poison in his touch seeping like acid through their quivering forms, atrophying their muscles, dissolving their bones, melting their minds until they were once more reduced to malleable clay. Once again they were his to recreate however he chose. Retracting his claws the merest fraction, he brought them back from the depths of agony, steeling their bodies, sharpening their deadliness, hardening their resolve. Yet even as he reshaped them, he restored the core of their memories and identities just as he always did, not from any fondness or compassion, but because if they were nothing but extensions of him, they would most likely be doomed to fail. As tools they had been and would always be flawed, as all tools were inevitably flawed, but he still believed that they would be the most effective and deadly as themselves, for only if they stayed predominantly themselves could there be any chance that his Dreamer would remain oblivious to the identity of her real enemy, at least until their claws were tearing through her throat, and it was too late for her to do anything other than recognize that it was actually his fiery touch bringing death.

Loosening his grip on them, he turned his minions to face the path that the Dreamer had traveled when she had left the clearing, for although she continued even now to bar him from her presence, he could see her just as he could always see her, and since he had finally gained his bearings in this new world, he could at last place her precise location. He had felt her enter this world, felt her just as he always felt her, but until now his feelings had been confused by the Barrier, and he had been frustrated in his attempts to integrate sight and sensation. He could see her; he could feel her, but he could not feel the direction he could see her take. Yet he was too powerful to be limited for long; it had taken time to adjust, but at last he could not only see her clearly in the center of his private screen, he could also feel her with the same intensity he had known standing that first night at the foot of her bed, could again see and feel her as if she lay directly before him, so close he could follow every movement she made. And now that he could both see and feel where she was, he could herd his minions in the right direction and bring them near enough to their goal that their tracking skills could again be employed. Since she had long ago surrendered her memory and her power over them, and even now did not know or understand what pursued her, they could still follow where he could not.

So he drove them down the path, bypassing the point where the fledgling Sentries had turned aside to circle back, but just as Hund's snout trembled and nostrils flared to life, the Dreamer's presence in this world suddenly vanished. Only a second before she had been there, a short distance ahead, lost in one of her waking dreams, and then she had not been there at all. Yet he hadn't lost her completely, for even now he could see her stumbling blindly, could feel her as she staggered and then crawled through a nightmare between worlds, a nightmare filled with infinite desolation and what should have been unbearable pain. She should not have been able to move through such a fierce and fiery nightmare, but she was moving, and moving steadily, through an agony that made his searing touch seem like a lover's gentle caress. With the full weight of the nightmare bearing down on her, she continued to creep forward until at last he could see her break through a burning barrier and plunge into the cool pocket of a small, isolated world.

The hand he had started to withdraw from his minions again tightened its hold, this time hauling them back to the void where he watched and waited. Brought into the trap of his actual presence, the minions groveled and whined, pressing their faces into the still-fresh bloodstains at his feet. His lips split open as a razor-sharp smile sliced his face apart, and if they had seen this edged smile, new blood would have spurted from their eyes and noses and mouths. They were spared because they cowered, and watching them wallow in the blood and tears they had previously shed, he felt himself swell as he had many times before, swell with unbridled pleasure, swell to immensity, the void swelling around him to contain his expanding magnitude. Then he contracted into himself again, still immense, but not so immense that he made demands on the void's unceasing capacity to adapt.

Many waking worlds believed the void was just an empty place, devoid of substance and life, but it wasn't a vacuum; it was infinite space filled with unending potential, space so infinite that it could hold him however immense he became, potential so unending that even a Figment with an inescapable face could dream. Floating free from the worlds of waking and dreaming, the void thrived in an in-between place that bordered both but was limited by neither. And although it was vast, comprised of thousands, perhaps even millions, of separate pockets, none of the places in the void were truly separate from one another. All places in the void existed together, folding in upon each other in an infinite number of layers. These layers of supposed emptiness that he and countless other Figments inhabited were not all that different from the world of dreams, which might be why he and the others were so comfortable here. The void was in many ways a mirror of the dreamworld, a place of infinite possibilities where nightmares were the reality, a place where Figments were as real as the nightmares they had been born to inhabit. And just as all places in the void were folded together, all dreams and nightmares in the dreamworld also existed as one, eternally there whenever a Dreamer chose to pay a visit. These dreams were also folded in layers, dream within dream within dream into infinity, and it was easier than waking for a true Dreamer to slip from one of these dreamworlds to another and on until the end. Yet for both the realms of dream and void there was really no end to the layers, and even if there had been, the last would have simply folded over onto the first and back into every previous layer, so that slipping into one was almost like slipping into them all. Only the lack of vision could erect nonexistent walls.

So Dreamers could travel dream to dream, visualizing each destination whether or not they realized it, and Figments could travel from one pocket in the void to another as long as they too could picture their destination. It was in fact easy to travel anywhere from the void, whether it was a waking world or dream world or just another space in the void; in the realm of infinite possibilities, all the traveler had to do was envision a destination, although only the strongest Figments had the substance to fully enter a waking world, and to therefore stay. And it was almost as easy for Figments and Dreamers both to travel anywhere from a dream, although few Dreamers had the strength to carry themselves fully into the dreamworld, and thus beyond into the void or a waking world other than their own. The only thing that was impossible, impossible for even the most powerful Dreamers and Figments, was moving directly from one waking world to another; jumping from world to world, in fact, was possible only by way of a dream or the void. That was why he had brought his minions here. The dream path his Dreamer had taken to the nightmare was too difficult and elusive for them to envision and follow on their own, and he was too impatient to usher them through it. And even he could not speed them directly to their goal, carrying them straight from one world to another. From here, though, he could send his hunters directly after his prey, right through the nightmare to the tiny quiet space where his Dreamer now stood. It would be just as easy as delivering them to the nightmare itself, and far more efficient. When he had pulled them back, that had been his intention, but as they groveled at his feet, he knew he could not take so simple a course. If he sent them straight to his Dreamer, he would spare them the pain she had suffered, but that was not his way; it was not in his nature to ever show mercy, however inadvertently, not even if his own best interests were served by foregoing one act of cruelty.

Closing his minions once more in his grasp, he hurled them directly toward the blazing sand and dropped them beneath the immense and merciless sun. But he did not leave them there. He watched from the safety of the void as their skin shriveled and split apart, then his unseen but ruthless hand goaded them forward with quick jabs from his claws, stabbing and slashing whenever they faltered. Across the vast desert he never relented, driving them through sand as hot as his hidden core, beneath a sun as blinding as death. They had known agony before, known agony so many times that its embrace was as warm and comforting as a friend's, although neither had ever known what warmth or comfort or even a friend might be. They had known agony that removed them from themselves, that left them hovering somewhere in the air their master breathed, that left them dangling above their mangled bodies as if the bloody wrecks they saw belonged to their own hapless victims, for there was a limit to the scope of pain even they could know and still know themselves. They had known agony that burned, that blazed through skin and muscle and bone and kept burning until the old self was ashes, and then burned even more as the ashes were fused into a new skeleton, new muscles, new skin, a new self. They had known agony, were familiar with all its tricks and ways, but they had never known agony like this. And this time there was no escape, no cessation, no release; they were bound to their bodies, bound to the agony, bound because they couldn't lie still in their master's hands or sprawl senseless at his feet, bound because they had to keep moving, bound because he wouldn't let them stop, wouldn't let them drift away, wouldn't let them die.

On and on the agony drove them, for agony and their master had always been one, and were more so now than ever. And whenever they thought that agony had driven them as far as they could go, that there was nothing else the agony could do that it hadn't done before, that succumbing to the fierce sand and sun would be a relief, then the agony reawakened whatever had numbed, reattaching severed nerves solely to unravel them once more, fiber by ragged fiber. Now they knew agony that would not end, yet would never grow familiar, and for the first time since they had been born from the mind of their Dreamer, they knew not just pain; they knew boundless fear, a fear that overwhelmed them because their suffering was no longer limited to the cruel-ties of their master. With the birth of this all-encompassing fear they scurried without prodding, trying to jettison their drum-ming hearts and the choking lumps in their throats, thinking to leave these unwanted things behind as sacrifices on the altar of panic. Now at long last their master withdrew to his fold of the void, gnawing on his own lips until the blood gushed down his throat, gulping the salty flow so he wouldn't howl his need and hunger as he watched his minions finally dive through the shimmering expanse of the barrier that divided them and him from the Dreamer.

Gyfree stomped ahead as if he could release all his sorrow through the soles of his feet and trample it into the ground, but even though he knew the ground would gladly accept any burden he asked, he could not let loose of his pain. He carried it in the back of his throat in a bitter lump he could not swallow, in his chest where his heart and lungs had solidified to stone, in his arms so heavy that his fingers dangled like lead weights at his sides; he carried it everywhere except his legs, for all the pain there emptied into his feet so that he could haul his burdens forward. The only real father he had known was dead, and he was filled with grief, but the weight of what he had lost was nothing compared to the weight of all he had gained. For the land, with its miles-deep layers of soil and rock, and all the life clinging to its rich surface, was a heavy load to carry, and the added bulk of its sorrow and pain and fear made it heavier still. If the land had laid quiet, as it usually did, he could have borne the weight its presence added to his own sorrow, but the land was no more at peace than its new Keeper. The land mourned as he mourned, but it also bucked and writhed in a way only he could feel, like a giant frantically trying to shake loose the small yet vicious creatures climbing with jagged claws up its mountainous spine. And now he could feel those deadly claws as if they ripped through his own spine, and the scourge of their passage across the land was an open wound spreading over his skin. It was almost too much to bear, though bear it he must, and this necessity also weighed him down.

His thoughts were too cumbersome, too entangled with the land, for him to notice anything outside himself. He didn't notice the troubled frown that creased Mischa's usually smooth forehead or the consternation that shaded her habitually sunny eyes. He didn't notice the sudden and uncharacteristic intensity in Timi's face as she studied the Dreamer. Most importantly, he didn't notice the distance in Drew's eyes or the silence that enfolded her like an impenetrable shield as tears ran unchecked down her cheeks. He did notice, however, when she suddenly winked out of existence, for he felt her loss even before Timi had time to scream.

"She's gone!" wailed Timi. "I could see it happen. I could see in her eyes that she was dreaming." Tears now streaked her pale cheeks, blurring the angles and lines of her face until she seemed, if possible, even less distinct than before. "She was still with us, still walking, but with each step she seemed to grow more distant. She didn't shrink or dissipate like some Dreamers do before they leave. She somehow just seemed farther and farther away. And then she was gone."

Mischa's frown deepened, but she shrugged her shoulders with her usual light playfulness. "Well, if she's gone, our job is done. I guess she was just a particularly lucid Dreamer after all."

"She didn't return to her own world," Gyfree announced, and the trees around the three shivered.

"Then where is she?" demanded Mischa.

"She's not anywhere in this world, for I can feel no sense of her presence from the land."

"Your unprecedented promotion to Keeper hasn't destroyed your other skills, has it?" Mischa grilled sharply.

Gyfree didn't answer, but he knew Mischa didn't expect him to. She knew what he was and knew what he could do, and he finally recognized that it troubled her now as it never had before. He even agreed that she might have good reason to be troubled. She was right that his selection as Keeper was disquieting, and certain to cause an upheaval in this quiet world. She was also right in assuming, as she clearly did, that his previous skills were completely unchanged. Becoming Keeper could add to his powers, but it couldn't alter who he was. The growing distance in his eyes would quickly confirm the suspicion in hers.

Still facing her across the trail, he mentally stepped away to test the current of the dreamworld, the sensation of Drew vivid in his mind. It took only a fraction of a moment to locate her trace. As clearly as he could feel the land still beneath his feet, he could feel the path she had taken away from him, a dream path that led directly to the clearing where his father sprawled dead, his limbs twisted in grotesque imitation of the nearest trees' gnarled branches. Yet the path didn't end there, and it wasn't her journey here that had taken her completely away. She had come to this death-filled place just as he had, for the strongest Dreamers could walk through the waking and dream worlds at the same time. It was the path from here, the path he could sense but not follow with only his dreaming mind, that had snatched her from him. If he was to find her he must follow that path just as she had, and with a wrench that tore the ground from beneath his feet, he threw his entire being in pursuit. Mischa wouldn't be happy when he disappeared from view, but she would understand what had happened and would know what to do.

For the first time since he was a child, he found his complete self in a place other than his world. He could still feel his connection to the land he had left, stretched behind him like a safety rope that would not only keep him from falling to his death, but would lead him back home. Even without this security he would have plunged forward without hesitation, but now he could do so with an untroubled mind. Unlike Drew, he would not be stranded in a strange world with no idea how to return. She would be as lost as she could have been in his world if he hadn't found her, but he wouldn't allow her to stay lost for long.

The path opened before him, and he teetered on the edge of a blistering white desert beneath a sun-bloated sky. The air around him exploded, heat blasting him apart, but the cool touch of the land at his back was enough to bring him to himself again. He could not conceive how Drew could have survived this place, how she could have found the strength to venture forward, but as he stood in the same spot she had stood, he could clearly feel her path unrolling at his feet. To follow her he would have to dive into the waiting inferno, but he would do everything within his power to protect himself first. Dreams within dreams. That was how Drew had described the seamless layers, although it was clear to him that she didn't yet understand how deep or far the layers reached. Nor did she really comprehend the implications, or see what dreams could shape even from within other dreams. But he did.

His earliest dreams had been filled with ice, his nightmares stocked with ice maidens whose cold fingers could drain him of life, but in a place like this ice was the promise rather than the defeat of life. From the depths of his mind he raised the dream of ice, and his breath frosted into the molten air, the tiny crystals hovering before his face like multifaceted diamonds that twinkled then melted away. That was his first breath of ice, and the only one he lost. With his next exhalation, a thin coat of ice spread across his face, and the next breath thickened and extended the ice. Silvery blue veins branched over his head and down his back, icy threads racing down his neck and chest, crisscrossing his arms and cascading down his legs. Every breath brought more ice, layer upon layer just like the dreams that had brought the ice, and soon he felt like a pond in winter, his surface frozen enough to bear almost any weight, while all the life he contained retreated to the warmth of the muddy bottom, swimming freely far outside the range of winter's grasp. His shape was the shape of a pillar of ice, and his vision was as obscured as his features beneath the thickening blue, but deep within all this ice he was completely unrestricted. With his dream eyes he could see Drew's trail, and with his dream strength he could haul the heavy ice as effortlessly as he could haul the blood in his veins and the air in his lungs.

Shielded in his suit of glistening ice, he strode into the mouth of hell. The heat immediately swallowed him, licking his shield with a fiery tongue, gnashing at the ice with fangs of flame. The surface of the ice chipped and melted, but this was to be expected, and he was already breathing more ice to replace what he lost. From his hidden core new ice formed, rising from the bottom up, lower layers pushed upward by each new layer below, emerging finally to perish beneath the onslaught of the heat. In the depths of the ice he was sweating, for he was working furiously now to not lose more ice than he could restore. Time stalled as he rushed forward, as if it was holding him back from his destination, intent on delivering him as a prize to the heat. And yet time also seemed to race against him, helping the heat melt the layers of ice more quickly than he could ever hope to replenish them. Soon he was sweating from more than exertion; he was sweating from the nearness of the heat, his shield reduced to the thinnest of veneers. And still the shield kept thinning, until finally each layer melted as soon as it formed and he was drenched in water rather than encased in ice. The heat dragged at him now, tugging at his feet to pull him down, flicking the water from his body with a careless slap, but still he persevered, breathing ice that instantly melted, but even in melting, kept him just cool enough that he could push on. He had long lost count of how many times water had splashed down his face and temporarily soaked his body, and had long lost hope that this nightmare would ever end, when he stumbled into an unexpected pocket of coolness, and the most recent gush of melted ice didn't evaporate, but instead left him sodden and shivering.

Blinking away the icy water and the salty sweat from his eyes, he saw a new green world, strangely washed out and fuzzed around the edges, slowly come into focus. Sharper than his view of this new world, however, was his perception of Drew. He could feel her clearly now, could even feel the sudden fear that quickened her heart, and he knew she was directly ahead. Without waiting for his eyes to finish readjusting to a world with dim rather than blinding light, he stumbled down the path in her direction.

Around a bend in the path there were two faces, both immobilized by surprise, turned in his direction. The first, as he already knew, was Drew's, the flush in her cheeks the only sign of the hellfire through which she had waded. The other face was a man's, and even Gyfree could not help but recognize the absolute perfection of the other's features. He was like a breathing statue carved from the purest white stone by an artist obsessed with the slightest possibility that his work might be flawed. The man was pale where Gyfree was golden, but instead of looking sickly, his polished fairness made Gyfree's darker, sun-touched skin seem sallow and harsh. Next to him Gyfree knew his nose would be too crooked, his hair too unruly, his eyes too muddy, his frame too bulky. These were things he would never have considered only a short time ago, but he saw himself now reflected in Drew's eyes, face streaked with water and sweat, and his lungs constricted until he thought the inferno must have stolen his breath away after all.

"Gyfree!" exclaimed Drew, breaking the brittle silence. "How did you get here?"

"I followed you," he answered colorlessly.

"Followed me?" she repeated. "How? To tell the truth, I'm not even sure how I got here."

From behind the pale man's head there darted a black and yellow striped body with iridescent wings beating too rapidly for eyes to follow. "They zpeak, they zpeak!" it buzzed.

"I can hear that," the man responded in a voice as smooth and polished as his face. Ignoring Gyfree he smiled at Drew and murmured, "You're not the one I was expecting. Your hair is darker.

Your skin is richer. Your eyes are more vibrant. You are not a watercolor, and she is. I will leave with you instead."

Somewhere between the world he had left and the world he had entered, something tugged violently on the invisible rope securing Gyfree. Ignoring the other man just as he had been ignored, he grabbed Drew by the arm and declared urgently, "We have to leave this place, and soon."

Drew didn't resist the pull on her arm, but her eyes moved from Gyfree's face to the stranger's. "Where are we?" she asked.

A puzzled frown turned down the corners of the man's mouth, but not a single crease marred his brow. "Where I have lived while I waited," he answered slowly. "It is simply a place. There is nothing special about it. Except for the hummeybees, it lacks color."

"Hummeybees?" Drew repeated blankly.

"Like me," droned the hovering creature. "We are hiz friendz."

Both Drew and Gyfree stared at the wickedly barbed stinger protruding from a body as large as a man's fist, and neither said a word.

The stranger whistled loudly, and another hummeybee hurtled through the trees to hover next to the first. "These two will come with me," the man announced calmly. "We are ready to go now."

Another savage jerk on the invisible rope made Gyfree stagger. There was definitely something following the same path he and Drew had already followed, and he was afraid he knew exactly what that something must be. "There are Figments on the way," he blurted. "Drew, we must leave before they arrive!"

The pale stranger stepped forward, a hummeybee on each shoulder, and seized Drew's other arm. "You are not leaving without me," he insisted. "I have waited too long already, and now that you have come, I will wait no more. I will not stay a prisoner here."

"You can't come," Gyfree growled. "It will be difficult enough for us to escape. We can't carry you along as well."

The hummeybees buzzed dangerously, their stingers twitching as the man's eyes narrowed. "If you refuse to take me, then I will refuse to let you leave. The sting of a hummeybee is poisonous, you see."

Gyfree's eyes narrowed as well, and the shadow of a nightmare flitted across his face. Yet before he could summon his own lethal threat, Drew intervened. "There is no time to argue if the beasts that killed the Keeper are coming. And if they are coming, we can't leave this man here, defenseless and alone."

"Not defenzelezz. Not alone," objected the second hummeybee in a buzz that was softer than the first's.

"We have to take him," Drew continued as if the hummeybee hadn't spoken. "It would be wrong to abandon him here."

Gyfree's eyes darkened as if somewhere behind them the lights had all blown out. "Very well," he conceded, his voice as flat and lifeless as his eyes. Holding Drew's eyes with his own, he told her, "Ice. You have to dream of ice." Releasing her arm, he clasped her warm hands in his. "Just do as I do. We are going to dream that we are buried under a mountain of ice."

Comprehension widened Drew's eyes. "So that's why you are soaking wet," she murmured. A smile trembled on her lips. "I have no idea how to intentionally do this. You'll have to show me."

Gyfree's eyes lightened ever so slightly as he smiled back. "We've done this sort of thing before; you just haven't been given enough time to think about it before now. So watch the dream fill my eyes, and just follow."

Slipping into the cool light in Gyfree's eyes, Drew suddenly found herself floating within an icy blue bubble. She could still feel the touch of the stranger's hand on her arm, and still hear the drone of the hummeybees, but the only thing she could see other than silvery blue was the luminous brown of Gyfree's eyes. The blue evoked the image of ice in her mind; not just a little ice, but a field of ice that towered above her and fell below her and stretched across the horizon as far as she could see. She was encircled by ice, growing colder by the second, with veins of ice webbing her skin, thickening until she had grown a second skin, a crystalline skin of ice. Her skin of ice was a fragile creation, beautiful and delicate, like a clinging gown of snowflakes. She could see each individual crystal, unique and sculptured, a work of art more intricate than anything she had ever seen in the dusty corridors of a museum. She squeezed the hands in hers to share the wonder of it all, but as the hands squeezed hers in return, a shock of heat blasted through the ice to leave both her and Gyfree dazed and drenched.

The wall above them was swaying, trembling as if some unbearable pain had recently ripped through its frame. Their feet back on relatively solid ground, Gyfree and Drew blinked, their eyes drawn toward the rocking and bucking barricade, and as they watched through the foggy remnants of their dream, the wall shuddered and a crack snaked upward to split it apart. Another wave of heat spilled over them, but this time it was countered by a burst of cool air, as if this slumbering land had been aroused by the sudden danger and had hastily armed itself with its only weapon. Or at least the first weapon at hand.

A howl replete with pain and hunger echoed off the damaged wall, and then a howl even more wracked and ravenous than the first tore the leafs from the trees. The ground trembled as if recoiling from insupportable weight, and then the beasts charged into view, lips curled back, saliva dripping from bared fangs to sizzle and smoke in the dirt, bloodstained claws fully extended, red-veined eyes focused unwaveringly on Drew. Together they threw back their heads to howl once more in triumph, and the sound shattered the air and drove away the last few wisps of Gyfree's and Drew's ice-filled dream.

"At last," growled Auge, creeping forward steadily, eyes glowing in anticipation, shoulders hunching and thighs bunching in preparation for his inevitable lunge. "We know who you are now, and you must be ours."

"Ours at last," Hund agreed hungrily, snout flaring and nostrils pulsing wildly as he too inched forward, clawed hands clenching and unclenching as if already shredding his prey.

Before Drew could open her mouth to scream, before Gyfree could react or the stranger could flee, the two hummeybees darted forward, whirring behind the heads of the impervious beasts, their wings flashing sparks and their stingers quivering as they aimed directly at the backs of the leathery necks. With a grace that was balletic, the two swooped down in perfect unison and drove their jagged stingers home.

Auge and Hund jerked to a stop, their eyes filming over and their limbs twitching as they struggled vainly for control of their own bodies. Drool dribbled from the corners of their mouths and their eyes rattled in their sockets as the color drained from their hides, leaving them as washed out and indistinct as the surrounding land. Then in a unison as sickening as the hummeybees' had been breathtaking, their legs buckled beneath them and they toppled to the ground, rousing a storm of dust and dead leafs as they fell.

In a flicker of motion too fast for eyes to follow, the hummey-bees zoomed back to hover above the strange man's shoulders. "Quick!" buzzed the larger of the two. "They will not ztay down for long. We muzt be gone when they awake!"

The smaller hummeybee flitted across to Drew, hovering directly before her face. "You two will dream of the ize again. Thiz time dream uz into the ize az well. Now hurry!"

Even through the swirling debris that obscured them, Drew could detect the darkening of the beasts' skin and the progressively wild thrashing of their limbs. Tearing her eyes away from both her stalkers and the insistently buzzing hummeybee, she found herself held once more by Gyfree's eyes, her hands clasped in his. Within the brown depths his eyes flickered with the silvery blue of ice, and once more he carried her with him, but this time the ice didn't drift gently across her skin; it crashed down like a mountain, burying them both, along with the hummeybees and the other man. Everything was cold, more cold than she could have ever dreamed, too cold for any nightmare of hers. She was lost in the cold, too cold to try to jolt free from the dream that held her, too cold to ever dream again. Cold, all she knew was cold, and the only warmth she had ever known had been in another dream, a dream she could not quite recall although she could still feel its touch slipping through the cold to clasp her fingers.

Heat rushed up her arms and wrapped around her shoulders as Gyfree squeezed her freezing hands and enfolded her in his hidden dream of warmth, a warmth that somehow could survive in the very heart of the incredible cold. Brown eyes smiled into hers and she basked for a second in their light, but then the weight of the ice pressed down, and the rumble of the stirring beasts reverberated through the ice, and Drew awoke to herself. Gyfree's hands still clutched hers, fingers curling between fingers, while the stranger gripped her arm with the chill hand of death, two hummeybees poised with frozen wings on his shoulders. They were all encased in ice, and except for the hands embracing her hands, they were all completely immobilized. With Gyfree she had dreamed that ice, dreamed enough ice to withstand even the inferno, and she could see in his eyes that he was dreaming it still, but she had no idea how the ice could save them when its weight was almost too heavy to bear, and certainly too heavy to allow them to move. As if he could see the question floating behind her eyes, Gyfree squeezed her hands so tightly that she would have winced if her face wasn't ice, so tightly that his hands seemed to tell her hands to just hold on.

Gyfree was surprised by the outpouring of ice that he and Drew had dreamed together, surprised once again by how quickly they had been able to fuse their visions, surprised by the overwhelming power that had burst from their combined dreams. Even in his worst nightmares there had never been so much ice, but despite the mass pressing down, he knew no fear. Together he and Drew could clearly accomplish amazing things, but this time he didn't even need her help. He could see the uncertainty in her eyes, could see the strain of the ice in the tense lines of her face, and he squeezed her hands again, once more to reassure her rather than to pull her back from the brink of the dream before it could claim her. Then he mentally took hold of the rope that stretched tautly between him and his world, and gave it a sharp tug. As he had anticipated, the rope rebounded, and a fraction of a second later, the mountain of ice was being hauled through the blasting inferno as if it had no more weight than a clump of frozen dirt. Heat slid over the speeding ice, and water trickled from its surface, but the world to which they were all now tethered reeled in its catch with ever increasing velocity as the excess bulk melted away. At first, and for a long while, Drew could not even sense the heat around them, but gradually she could feel the slightest hint of warmth whisking by, and could even feel the nameless man's fingers finally stir against her arm. She could hear the buzz of the thawing hummeybees, and could feel her own limbs tingle back to life, but the sensation at the center of her awareness, a sensation more intense than any other she could recall, was the sensation of Gyfree's hands clutching her own, his fingers weaving a pattern through her fingers more complex than any dream.

Chapter 5

The moment Gyfree had winked out of existence to follow the vanished Dreamer, Mischa was left with her hands not just full, but overflowing. With two Figments potentially on their trail and no real means to defend themselves without Gyfree, the last thing Mischa needed to contend with was Timi's sudden onslaught of hysteria. Instead of diffusing the indelible traces of their scent with some well-placed pepper as Gyfree had taught her, and then searching out a secluded place to hide, Mischa was forced to wrestle the screaming and thrashing Timi to the ground, and to hold her there while the younger woman drummed her heels in the dirt as if even now she was running away. As Mischa pressed the other woman's flailing arms to the ground, Timi tossed her head wildly from side to side in some furious denial, although her inarticulate sobs and mind-scraping moans failed to explain what she so fiercely wanted to deny. Tears raced across her pale cheeks, wiping away what little color she had possessed, and Mischa wondered, as she had countless times before, what haunted this young woman's peace. Whatever possessed her now certainly held her in an unshakeable grip, for nothing Mischa could say seemed able to break her free. A shield of delirium surrounded Timi, and all of Mischa's words, whether comforting or bracing or threatening, simply bounced off to land harmlessly in the restlessly swaying grass that bordered the trail. Despite all of her efforts, Mischa couldn't convince Timi to calm down, or more importantly, get up and move. She even failed in an attempt to drag the younger woman away from the exposed path, for Timi dug her heels into the ground and twisted so frantically that it was beyond even Mischa's ability to budge her. If anyone other than Mischa had been left there, jeopardized by Timi's inexplicable tirade, Timi would have been deserted, but leaving a companion, however frustrating and irrational, was not Mischa's way. Time dragged by dangerously, and she could almost feel the beasts slathering as they lunged at her exposed back, but still she cajoled and bullied, and still Timi screeched and writhed.

Then the crunch of footsteps directly behind her induced Mischa to release Timi and spin around, but instead of the Figments she feared, Gyfree and Drew wobbled before her, both stupidly smiling and soaking wet. But they were not alone. Behind Drew, and leaning against her, was the most incredibly handsome man Mischa had ever seen. And behind the man were two bees as large as a man's fist, both graced with pulsing, rainbow-colored wings.

"What took you so long?" Mischa asked Gyfree with a crooked smile, although her eyes were unabashedly absorbed by the stranger's face.

From where she sprawled in the dirt, Timi screeched so piercingly that even Mischa, inured to her shrieks, was forced to wince. Then flopping over like a fish on dry land, Timi wriggled across the ground and threw herself behind the nearest tree.

Gyfree raised a questioning brow that Mischa more sensed than saw since her eyes had yet to break free from the stranger's face. "Don't ask me," she responded. "Since the moment you left in pursuit of Drew, she's been completely out of control."

Gyfree stomped over to where Timi cringed, her face pressed into the rough bark of the tree and her arms looped around its trunk. Grasping her by her armpits he pulled as she dug her nails into the soft bark, and although she wrestled wildly to free herself, even in her desperation she could never match his strength. He lifted her effortlessly from the ground, and despite her frenzied kicking, carried her back to the others as she covered her face with shaking hands and sobbed loudly. Gyfree dumped her unceremoniously, and roughly wrenched her hands from her face before grabbing her by the arms and shaking her so that her head snapped back and light glistened across her tearstained skin.

"You're the one!" gasped a voice, and three additional pairs of eyes, including Timi's, turned toward the nameless man. "You're the face I've seen as long as I can remember," the man continued. "The one I've been waiting for. You were supposed to set me free, but these others did instead."

Timi stared at him as tears continued to course down her stricken face. "You look exactly as I remember," she finally whispered. "Exactly as I dreamed you."

"Timi!" exclaimed Mischa in a voice so filled with horror that Drew shuddered.

"Timi!" Gyfree echoed, dropping his hands and rolling back on his heels. "Is there something you need to tell us?" he asked quietly.

Timi closed her eyes and a shudder traveled down her body, starting with a mere twitch of the head, then a tremor of the shoulders, growing as it plummeted downward to shake her body and rock her legs. "Dreamers frighten me. You've seen how they make me react, you and Mischa, but you never thought to question why. You never even asked why I volunteered to become a Sentry in the first place, especially since I seemed so unsuited to the task. You see, I was hoping to learn something about myself, but I was unprepared for what I did learn. All of the Dreamers I've seen come through the Barrier have been so insubstantial, and their hold on this world has been so weak, that it made me feel as if my own grip was slipping, as if I was in danger of losing the only life I've ever known. How could I continue to exist in this world if Dreamers held such a feeble hold? Ever since joining the Sentries, I've felt myself slowly fading away, as if every frail Dreamer was still more real than me. Then when Drew showed up, so alive, so aware, so vital, I suddenly felt not less alive, but more. Finally there was a Dreamer other than Gyfree who could see this world, could feel this world, could taste and smell and live in this world. Maybe if she saw me, talked to me, touched me, then I was just as real as she seemed to be. Maybe by understanding her I could even learn to understand myself. When she vanished, I felt as if the ground had vanished beneath my feet. If she couldn't hold to this world, then I knew I couldn't either. When Gyfree vanished, Gyfree of all people, I knew I had to be next."

"Just say it, Timi. If you're here at all, then say it," urged Gyfree.

Timi looked him in the eyes, her most recent tears trembling on her lashes as if they were suddenly uncertain of what path to take. "I'm a Dreamer," she whispered.

"How is that possible?" Mischa questioned, her voice brittle with fear although her eyes were still absorbed by the stranger's handsome face.

"I don't know," admitted Timi, her eyes flitting to the same face that held Mischa in thrall. "If I understood it myself, then I wouldn't be as frightened as you are now. Maybe I stumbled through the Barrier years ago, and was somehow overlooked, left to wander here. Allowed to live here. I don't remember that happening. I don't remember a time when I wasn't here. I have memories of this world from the time I was a child, but maybe I've dreamed those memories, dreamed everything I think I know, everything I seem to remember."

"And maybe you've always been here," Gyfree remarked, "and still been a Dreamer."

"Do you understand what you're saying?" Mischa demanded, her voice harsh although her trapped eyes had grown progressively softer and softer. "You of all people should understand what this could mean."

Drew had been listening with an increasingly perplexed frown gathering between her eyes. "I don't understand," she interjected into the silence that, following Mischa's last words, had thickened like quicksand in the air, and now threatened to smother them all.

"There are no Dreamers from this world," Timi finally muttered.

"But Gyfree's a Dreamer," objected Drew.

"He's not from this world," replied Timi grudgingly, as if the words had some hidden power to harm.

Drew turned her head and found herself once again tumbling into Gyfree's eyes, floundering through the flecks of brown and gold to touch the darkness at the center. When he smiled, Drew, and only Drew, could see the shape of something familiar springing to life behind the smile and inside his eyes. When his lips parted, she already knew what he would say, and what she would answer.

Gyfree whispered, "I'm from yours."

And Drew whispered back, "What nightmare follows you?"

For a long moment they stood in a different place, locked in each other's eyes, both aware of the dark shapes hovering in the corners of their shared vision, dark shapes that only they could see. Then in unspoken agreement they lowered their eyes and returned to the world to which Gyfree was safely tethered. "We need to get moving," mumbled Gyfree.

"What about him?" Mischa asked, and everyone else returned their eyes to the nameless man. He had wandered away from the others and now knelt near a patch of bright blue wildflowers, his hands cupped around the brilliant blossoms, his nose inhaling the rich perfume, tears trickling down his perfect face, a hummeybee buzzing contentedly on each shoulder. "Is there any reason he can't come along?"

Timi turned startled eyes toward the other woman. "Don't you understand?" she blurted. "I dreamed him. That makes him a Figment."

"Well," mused Mischa, "he seems harmless enough, and solid enough, to me. He hasn't altered even once. If he's a Figment, he's the most amazing one I've ever seen. I guess if this is what you dream, we may not be facing the end of the world after all."

The Figment raised his eyes to Mischa's and smiled. "This world is so beautiful," he breathed, "so full of life and color. Like you." His eyes shifted to Drew's face as he added, "And like her. You are both so vivid, more vivid than the one who should have set me free."

Timi stumbled to her feet, face drained of what little color she had possessed, the tear tracks on her cheeks leaving smudges that made her appear slightly out of focus. "I dreamed him, and I don't want him here," she announced, the hurt in her voice more distinct than her face. "I banished him once, and even if I don't have the strength to banish him a second time, I know Gyfree does."

The hummeybees buzzed dangerously as they darted over to hover directly in front of Timi's face, their stingers pulsing and wings scattering light. "He will ztay here. We will ztay here. There will be no going back," whirred the larger hummeybee.

"You heard the bugs," laughed Mischa as she offered the Figment her hand and pulled him to his feet.

"Not bugz," buzzed the smaller of the two. "Hummeybeez."

"Fine. Hummeybees, I'm on your side," Mischa replied. Without a backward glance, or any glance that would have removed her eyes from the Figment, she set off down the path, the Figment at her side and the hummeybees flying close behind. With the possibility of other and quite different Figments soon rediscovering their trail, first Timi, then Drew, and finally Gyfree, fell in behind the besotted and suddenly, disconcertingly, carefree Mischa.

His blood ran bitter down his throat as he watched his minions twitch and writhe in the grip of the poison that had felled them, the poison of creatures armored in a menace even greater than the beasts themselves. And because of these fierce and seemingly impenetrable creatures, the Dreamer had already returned safely to her new world, and even now was slipping farther from his clutch, while the worthless beasts continued to convulse in the dust, in a world that slithered through his talons whenever he tried to take hold. From here he could reach the damaged Barrier through which his minions had passed, but whenever he attempted to move beyond, he felt as if he was trying to grasp a fistful of water. There was something about this world that eluded him just as his Dreamer eluded him, so there was nothing he could do but watch, nothing he could do but wait for the beasts to revive, nothing he could do but anticipate the feel of their bones snapping in his grasp, their blood dripping off his skin, their minds dangling from his ragged claws. He would have them again, would punish them for their latest failure, would give them yet another chance because the alternative was one he still refused to confront.

Despite the intensity of his attention on the untouchable distance, he sensed the cold of her approach, just as he always sensed her approach. Fingers like icicles bit into his shoulder, and frost ringed his ear. "Not a very impressive picture," she murmured. "Definitely flat and out of focus. Perhaps even a bit grainy. Lacking in plot and character development as well."

"Be quiet," he snarled. "They're waking up."

A chill laugh misted the air, but she said nothing, watching with him as the eyes of the two beasts slitted open and the creatures struggled to their knees.

Memory flooded first into Hund's dirt- and blood-streaked face, submerging the confusion in his eyes. His snout quivered frantically as he swept his head from side to side in search of their escaped prey, and when not a single trace led away from the path, he gnashed his fangs and slashed his claws through the bark of the nearest tree, then threw back his head and howled in unappeased hunger and uncontrollable fear, the fear slowly superceding the hunger and shaking his limbs, for he knew that they had failed again and the consequences would be unimaginably severe.

Hund's wracked howls returned Auge fully to himself, awakening his own anguished hunger and staggering fear, and he too howled until every tree surrounding them stood barren. "We had her!" he wailed, punctuating every word with a swipe of his extended claws through the bare branches of a leafless tree while a shower of splintered wood rained at his feet. "How could we lose her? Now we will pay!"

"We will pay," echoed Hund, his own fury abruptly extinguished. He collapsed to the ground, curling his long hairy arms around his legs and huddling in a quivering ball, face pressed against his knees as if he could hide from his fate if he just refused to look up. "We will pay," he moaned over and over while Auge paced furiously back and forth, digging trenches in the dirt with his restless talons.

For a time neither Figment knew how to measure, the only sounds in this world were Hund's despairing moans and Auge's gouging steps. Then suddenly Auge stopped, his yellow eyes narrowed on Hund's cringing and shaking mass, and with a vicious swipe from the back of one paw, knocked his partner flat. "Why aren't we paying yet?" he growled. "Why are we still here, waiting? It is not like our master to delay punishment."

Hund didn't answer, but instead buried his head even further into the knees he still firmly clasped.

"I'll tell you why," Auge continued. "He must not be able to reach us here. Even he has his limits, or he would never have needed us in the first place, and we must have finally reached a place beyond the end of his limits."

"We will pay," moaned Hund. "There can be no escape. We will pay."

Auge lunged at the prostrate Hund, fangs bared inches from the back of the other's neck. "We will pay," he rumbled, "only if we go back. And I for one have no intention of returning. Not through that fiery hell. And not for the sake of experiencing an even more harrowing hell. This may not be a large world, but it is big enough for us." His paw cupped the tender spot on the back of his own neck before he added, "And there is prey here worthy of the kill."

Hund loosened the grip on his knees and tentatively lifted his head. There was no dark retribution waiting there, no demon smile slicing through his skin, no razor-sharp claws reaching out to rip through his body; nothing but dirt and grass and stripped trees. His nostrils flared, but there was no smell of blood, no trace of the rotten stench that preceded his master's touch, no acid air to burn a path through his veins; nothing but the rich smell of a suddenly decaying land. "We will stay," he murmured in wonder. "We will be free."

Neither could hear their master roar as he unleashed his unfathomable fury. Neither could feel the distant void shake with a force that would have flattened any waking world. Neither could see the murderous tempest that lashed through the inferno to pound against the damaged Barrier with fists of darkness. Nor could they hear or feel the ice-hard laugh, or see the beautiful cold face that jeered at their master. "You left them just a little too much mind of their own. A brain is a dangerous thing when it's not completely under your control. It reminds me of one of the sleepers' silly sayings. No pain, no gain. No endless pain for them, no gain for you."

She didn't flinch as he rounded on her, face writhing as wild flames roared across his crimson skin, fangs bared and already dripping blood, eyes impossibly insane. She didn't flinch, but the layer of ice shielding her thickened until her face was a distant blur, its mockery softened. "Quiet!" he howled, and although the ice fractured, tiny cracks adorning its surface like delicate lace, she still didn't flinch.

Through the ice she watched him rage, his features as clear and cutting as if there existed no barrier between them, as clear and cutting as they always were for her. In all the dreamworlds, in all of the void, even in all the waking realms, he was for her the one being the most real, the most desirable. She wanted everything he was, his unquenchable fierceness, his hot cruelty, his unchangeable presence. She was a creature of shifting ice, a treacherous surface with countless hazards hidden beneath, but for all her menace, and all her unplumbed depths, she was nothing but ice at the core, uncertain, fragile, impermanent ice, as changeable as the water from which ice was formed. She desired his quickness rather than her glacial slowness, his passion rather than her cool distance, his fire instead of her ice, for whether it roared to immensity or quieted to a single flame, fire was never anything other than itself, and his was a fire that nothing and no one could ever extinguish. But to have those things, to seize hold of something more enduring than she could ever be, she must first have him, and not as she had already had him countless times before. She needed to not just touch him, to not just be touched by him, but to possess him, utterly and completely, to carry his entire being to her icy inner core so that his essence could ignite her from the inside out. Then she would be as complete, as vibrant, as alive as he was now. But first she would have to trick him, for he was strongly independent and would never agree to surrender even a fraction of himself to another, and she needed far more than a fraction. She needed him whole. And she would have him, she would catch him with her glacial patience, for she knew what drove him, and he never guessed the hidden things that drove her. He didn't trust her, but even so, he trusted her far too much.

His rage seemed as alive and unchanging as he did, but she knew his emotions were the only changeable aspect of his character, and she could sense the perfect moment to interrupt. "I can help you," she murmured.

"I still refuse your help!" he stormed. "I will travel to that world myself and tear those two apart. Then I'll put them together again to suit my purposes better than before, and when I bring them back, they will be too lethal for anything or anyone to stop."

"And what if that world still eludes you? You can't grasp it in your claws, so why do you think you'll be able to slip inside?"

The flames in his eyes leapt wildly, but his only answer was a growl.

"Even if you could ultimately force your way in," she continued coolly, seemingly impervious to the threat blazing in his eyes and rumbling in his throat, "how do you know you can afford the time such an effort will take? Where will your precious Dreamer be by the time you have gained an entry and your minions are once more ready?"

"Wherever she is, I will find her. It doesn't matter how far she goes, I will always be able to detect her as surely as I can detect the raging of my own heart."

"And what if she finds some other pocket world, some other place closed to not just you, but also to your minions? After all, you and I are living proof that far more is possible than anyone imagines. Or should I say that anything imaginable is possible, perhaps even probable?" she breathed with a sigh of ice.

"I will not send you for the kill," he growled. "I welcome any risk that doesn't involve you, even if it means my Dreamer slips forever from my grasp."

"I wasn't suggesting that you send me anywhere at all," she chided. "I've decided that I'm not really interested in providing that level of help, not when you don't really need it yet. When I offer those services, it will only be when you are so desperate that you will meet any price. That is obviously not now, and may actually be never."

"What do you have in mind then?" he demanded, his breath hot enough to melt the ice from her face.

In answer she trailed an icy finger across his cheek, seemingly entranced by the thread of steam that spiraled into the air. "There's a trail of ice that leads straight through the wall, right up to your uncooperative servants," she purred. "Alone you don't have the ability to reach them, but I do; the feel of the ice will take me straight to them. I could bring them to you here, or drop them in that inferno, directly into your waiting hand. It would be such a simple thing to do that the price would be quite small."

"You're playing games," he accused, sinking his claws through thick ice to prick her arm, raising bright blue drops that immediately melted and diffused into the surrounding ice.

"Not at all," she replied coolly, careful to hide her pleasure in the pain he had given, for she knew he would only be drawn in, at least at this point, if she maintained the icy indifference that had always fired his desires. "In fact, I'm in a whimsical mood which makes me far too honest. It simply takes too much energy to lie to you, and right now I don't feel like making the effort."

"So what is the price?" he rumbled, tightening his grip so that a thrill of pure sensual delight shot through her and it took all of her strength not to moan in abandon.

"A kiss," she whispered. "Just a kiss. Payable on delivery."

"Since when is a kiss worth so much?"

"Since you stopped giving them freely," she replied with a frosty smile.

"What trick are you playing?"

"No trick. Not this time. Your minions for a kiss. A simple task for a simple price. But decide soon. I'm growing bored. You know how quickly I can change, especially my mind."

His eyes burned into hers, burned through the ice, through her nerves, through her brain, igniting that spark of fire deep within that only he could ignite. "Very well," he growled, his breath as quick and hot as hers was quick and cold.

Closing her eyes she reached through the dark, clinging with spectral fingers to the long arm that was already stretched across space to mark the way. Through the void she sped, and through the inferno, its heat unable to penetrate her cold, for even here only he could penetrate her cold. When she finally gained his twitching hand, and slipped her own fingers across his, she could feel his fist close around her, squeezing sharply to remind her of his power. Far from her body and far from his keen eyes she could unabashedly glory in the heat of his hold, could glory in the power that he wielded, the power he didn't know would someday be hers. For her the pain came fiercely not when he tightened his grip on her, but when he once more set her free.

The path cut by the ice opened before her, its scent and texture hauntingly familiar. Ice was her element, and where it had passed, she easily followed. It led her that last step up to the wall and through, a distance that was a short footfall for her, but an impassable chasm for him. She thrilled with pleasure to know that for once he had to rely on her power, and back where she stood motionless and silent by his side, the ice obscuring her face cracked apart in the shape of a smile.

Just a short distance along the route of the ice and she was there, her phantom eyes watching as his minions romped through piles of dead leafs like children who had never felt the grasp of a nightmare. With the patience of a glacier devouring the land one small bite at a time, she watched and waited. Eventually the beasts felt something cold at their backs and their wild reveling ceased. Hund turned toward the cold and his nostrils flared, but all he could smell was winter as the dark veins in his snout slowly froze. Auge focused yellow eyes on the empty path, his shoulders tensing in anticipation of some pending attack, but there was nothing stalking them other than the sudden cold. He started to turn slowly away when a flicker of silvery blue caught his eye, and there on the ground was a web of frost expanding rapidly as if a giant invisible spider was busily at work. It took him only a moment to realize that he and Hund were the intended flies, but it was a moment too long. The web was already racing toward their feet, the blue strands heavy and thick as ropes. Auge howled a warning, but it was too late, for Hund had been snared by the thrashing blue cords, his feet bound by ropes of ice that his frenzied claws couldn't sever. Auge tried to run, but his feet were far too heavy to outrace the swelling web of ice. Intense cold grabbed him by the ankles and yanked him from his feet, and as he fell the cold shackled his wrists and coiled around his neck, slicing through his skin to freeze the blood in his veins. "It's her," he tried to gasp. "He sent her."

The two beasts futilely dug their claws into the ground, but the web of ice encircled them and hauled them away as if they were fish caught in a net. Inexorably they were tugged over the rough ground, but they didn't even notice the rocks that bruised and cut them, and they were indifferent to the cords of ice that sliced into their skin. All of their awareness was focused on the wall looming above them, and on the certain anguish that awaited them on the other side. The lattice of ice absorbed the flash of heat near the wall, and repelled the blistering fire that pounced when they passed through, but they would have been grateful to vanish in the heat if burning alive could have spared them from the approaching moment of judgment.

He was waiting just beyond the wall, his shadowy hand open before her to let her know he would not wait another heartbeat for the gift she brought. Sliding her fingers in a cold caress against his open palm, she released the ensnared beasts within range of his twitching claws. As his heat melted the web of ice that had trapped them, the creatures shrieked, shrilly and briefly, and then his fist closed around them, and his claws sliced through their throats to silence them in midscream. She lingered long enough to watch from up close, to bask in the pain he inflicted, to wallow in the blood he spilled, to revel in his presence while he was too preoccupied to maintain his defenses against her. She shivered with pleasure as he ripped his minions open from chin to groin, nailing them to the fiery sand with fragments of their own broken bones. She moaned in ecstasy as he poured smoking sand into their open wounds, but as she felt the torrid excitement melting ice from her body as she stood at his side so far away, she knew that she would expose too much of herself if she stayed. Racing back along the path of his arm, she returned to her body with a shudder, and shutting her eyes against the distant and arousing spectacle, she once more armored herself in a thick layer of ice to patiently await the return of his attention.

When at long last she could sense his eyes burning into her, she raised the icy lids from her own eyes and gazed back glassily. "Since when are you so squeamish?" he growled.

"Not squeamish," she answered coolly. "Just tired. That little excursion was more tiring than I expected."

"We already agreed to the price," he rumbled dangerously. "Don't try to extort more from me now."

"There's nothing else I want," she sighed. "At least not yet. But I would appreciate that kiss so I can be on my way."

His eyes drilled into hers as if he could unearth her deepest secrets, but as far as he could see, there was nothing but ice. He was still suspicious, for he knew she could not be trusted, but a bargain was a bargain, even for creatures such as they, and a kiss was little enough to pay for the service she had rendered. After all, there had even been a time when he would have kissed her freely. For there had been a time when she had fooled him completely, had made him believe that she too had been created immutable, had convinced him that they were the only two of their kind. He knew better now, but she still had the power to tempt him, and it was sometimes difficult to guard against her when he secretly longed to be tempted.

His lips crashed down, dissolving the ice around her mouth, splitting her pale lips apart as his forked tongue darted between her teeth and his fangs pressed down to bruise her flawless face. Where his mouth met hers he felt a welcome coolness, an icy tingle that thrilled along his spine. This was the price he had agreed to pay, but he was careful, very careful, to not let her draw him in too far. With a shiver of pleasure he tried, but failed, to suppress, he lifted his head and glared down at her now blood red lips.

"Thank you," she whispered, her breath still faintly warm from his touch. "Good luck with your latest installment of new and improved servants." It was difficult to keep her voice cool, difficult to rein in her breath so it would not race away from her, difficult to disguise her exultation, but difficulty had never hampered her before. He might be suspicious, as he was always suspicious, but he still thought he had the upper hand, and so had no idea what she had truly accomplished. This time the price had seemed like nothing, for she had made sure that it was nothing other than what it seemed. Yet it was also more than it seemed, for next time, or perhaps the time after that, when she asked him to pay the real price, the price she needed him to pay, it would seem no more significant than that single kiss. And he would pay that price gladly as well, for now it would be the price he secretly longed for and expected, and it would be too late when he finally recognized that her price was far more than he could easily afford. No, she thought as she dissolved into a silvery mist, he didn't trust her, but he still trusted her far, far too much.

Drew's perplexed frown was focused on the tense lines of Timi's back just as Timi's eyes were focused on the carefree forms of Mischa and her new companion. There was more happening here than Drew could readily understand, and many questions that she needed to have answered. For reasons she was unprepared to pinpoint, she felt self-conscious approaching Gyfree, and Mischa was far too engrossed in the handsome Figment to notice anyone else. That left Timi, and despite the stiff and unpromising set of her shoulders, Drew slipped up beside the pale young woman and fell into the rhythm of her steps. For a while her presence went either unnoticed or unacknowledged, but when Drew carefully brushed the other's arm, Timi turned dull eyes in her direction.

"I'm sorry to bother you," Drew apologized, "but—"

"You're feeling lost and confused, right?" Timi interrupted. "Well, you're not alone." Her eyes turned back toward the laughing pair leading the way.

Choosing to ignore the obvious rebuff, Drew asked, "What is it about him that bothers you so much?"

"Him?" Timi repeated, pretending not to understand.

"Yes, him," responded Drew, gesturing ahead.

Timi turned back, eyes stricken, what little color she possessed draining from her face. "You're so powerful, like Gyfree, that it's easy to forget that you're new to all of this."

"Well, I am, and as you've already noted, I'm feeling more than a little lost and confused. There are just so many things I can't quite grasp."

"Such as?"

"Where are you taking me? And why do you seem to be doing something different with me than you do with other Dreamers who find their way here?"

"Other Dreamers have such a weak hold on this world that the most a Sentry usually has to do is retrace whatever path they have followed, and return them to the fracture in the Barrier they slipped through. Once there, the Dreamers just slip back through without any help, back to where they still lie sleeping. And sometimes it's not even necessary to find where they broke through. Their presence here is so weak that one moment they'll be here, and the next moment they'll just wink out, for their minds and bodies will flit away on their own, back through the Barrier and all the way to their homes. Their presence in their own world is still so strong that they pull themselves back without any help from us. There are Dreamers who arrive and disappear again so quickly that we don't even know they've been here," Timi answered flatly, as if mindlessly repeating a lesson that had been drummed relentlessly into her head.

"So what makes me different?" persisted Drew.

"You're a very strong Dreamer," Timi answered with a shudder. "Your hold is so strong that you can withstand the pull of the Barrier itself, even withstand the pull of your own dreaming self because you are more here than you are back in your own bed. Unlike you, most Dreamers aren't even aware that they are here. They just barely slip through, and to them this place is as hazy and indistinct as the places which do exist only in dreams, as hazy and indistinct as they themselves are to us. They don't truly see this world; they can't touch it, not like you. It's been a long time since a Dreamer like you has entered here, but it's that possibility more than anything else that has long made us keep a close watch on the Barrier."

"And now that I am here?" queried Drew.

"We must take you to the one place in the Barrier that has the power to draw you back into your own world."

"The Source?"

"Yes, the Source."

"How far is this Source?"

"A long way. A very long way," sighed Timi, her voice trailing away into the faintest whisper.

"There's no simpler way to send me back?"

Timi shook her head. "There is no simpler way. And because you are being followed by a couple of impressively frightening Figments, our task will be all the more difficult."

"So what exactly are Figments, and why are two of them trying to kill me?" Drew pressed, her eyes suddenly intent on Timi's face.

Timi dropped her eyes to the ground, hunching her shoulders as if she wanted to curl into herself. "Sometimes a Dreamer dreams of something, or more accurately someone, who seems, at least for a moment, so real that what started as just a dream is granted life. We call such a being a Figment."

"So you're telling me that Figments are living, walking nightmares? That the monsters haunting my dreams are more than just bad dreams?"

"Yes, although most Figments never leave their own world, a world that exists somewhere between the world of dreams and what we call a waking world. They can slip in and out of dreams, but where they truly belong is their own world, the world of the void."

"Then what are Figments doing here, in your world?"

"Although it is far more common among the strongest Figments, even a weak one can sometimes slip into a waking world. A world like yours, or mine. These Figments are usually drawn to the Dreamer who brought them into existence. That's how most of them find the strength, as well as the resolve, to enter a waking world. Sometimes they are just following their Dreamer, longing to be near the source of their own power. Sometimes they even try to approach their Dreamer, looking for love or acceptance, or something we can't even begin to comprehend. And sometimes they seek to kill their Dreamer, for the one thing that limits them, the one thing that can exert at least some control over them, whether consciously or unconsciously, is the Dreamer who brought them to life," explained Timi, agony spilling from her eyes as she gazed once more at the Figment she had claimed as her own.

Drew felt first her eyes and then her thoughts dragged away toward the handsome Figment. "So you dreamed him," she questioned with another gesture at Mischa's escort, sight and mind suddenly filled with nothing but the graceful line of his shoulders, "and in the process created life?"

Timi's shoulders hunched even lower as her eyes sought the safety of the ground. "Yes."

"And that bothers you?"

Timi's eyes darted furtively ahead before once more clinging to the ground. "Only in part. What bothers me the most is that he's not normal. Watch him. His form never wavers. Figments, no matter how strong they may be in other ways, cannot hold the same form for more than a few minutes. That means my Figment's unusually powerful, and someone like me should never have been able to dream him at all. Not only are there no Dreamers from this world, but Dreamers who can live here, like Gyfree and maybe even you, are so vibrant and full of life. Not like me at all."

Drew shook her head as if to break free from an invisible fist entangled in her hair, and as the ghostly fingers loosened, she found herself once again watching the Figment, but this time dispassionately. Timi was right; his form never wavered. Yet there was still something ethereal, something insubstantial in his softly glowing eyes and hazy smile. In her opinion, the hummeybees on his shoulders were far more vivid and felt far more alive, although there was something in his bearing, in the turn of his head, that was evocative of Timi, and that was the one elusive quality that gave him the life he did possess. "Maybe you're just underestimating yourself," she suggested.

Instead of responding, Timi continued as if Drew hadn't spoken. "And that's not all. I dreamed him. I'm not imagining that. I dreamed him. And then I was so frightened of what had happened that I locked him away. I found a secluded world and I dreamed him there. He should never have been able to find a way out. I'm still not sure how he got here."

Now it was Drew whose eyes sought the ground. "After the Keeper died, I started dreaming. What we call in my world daydreaming. It was a horrible dream, full of pain and fire, but through my dream I seemed to hear a voice calling me, promising that everything would be fine if I just followed wherever that voice might lead. And in my dream I followed. And shortly after I came to myself again, there he was. It may sound ridiculous, but somehow, when I looked into his eyes, I could see that he had been the one calling."

Timi's hand clasped Drew's arm as if in search of support. "That shouldn't have been possible. He should never have been able to call anyone but me. And look at him now. He's interested in everything around him, everything but me. I dreamed him! I should be the center of his attention. He should love me, or he should hate me, but this indifference isn't normal. None of this should be happening, not like this. Figments don't act this way. Yours certainly don't."

"Mine?" Drew echoed hollowly.

"The Figments that are chasing you. Don't you understand what I've been trying to tell you? Figments don't just randomly chase anyone."

Drew gulped as a lump formed in her throat, threatening to choke her. "So the beasts that are chasing me . . ."

"Are probably your own creation," Timi finished when Drew couldn't.

For a brief second, Drew closed her eyes, only opening them again when she tripped over a rock in the path. "Then I killed the Keeper," she whispered.

"You didn't kill the Keeper any more than I'm seducing Mischa. Figments may spring from the mind of a Dreamer, but they are their own creatures," Timi replied, her eyes again fixed on the couple leading the way.

Drew stubbornly shook her head. "If I created the Figments who killed the Keeper, then I am ultimately responsible for his death."

"Perhaps, but perhaps not. Things aren't quite that simple. Let's say you had a son, but you were too young to raise him, too young to even understand what had happened, so someone came and took him away. And then you grew up, not even remembering that you had ever had a child at all. Then someday he murders someone, and only then do you learn that he was your child. Are you to blame for his acts, or is he to blame for what he became between the time he left you and the time he chose to kill?"

"What are you talking about?" asked Drew irritably, her annoyance temporarily superceding her renewed anguish.

"Most Figments, especially powerful Figments, are created by children," Timi replied, her attention finally diverted from the Figment who strolled just ahead. "Children are far more apt to dream vividly, and far more apt to populate their dreams with real horrors. And far less likely to exert control over the creatures they dream to life."

Drew shook her head, and a frown darkened her eyes until they were bleaker than any nightmare riddled mind. "But monsters don't learn to be monsters, do they? If I dreamed something as a monster, then I must be the one responsible for whatever it is and does. Even if I was a child at the time. Even if I didn't realize what I was doing. Even if years pass before it causes harm. The horror was still born because of me."

"I meant it when I told you that it's not that simple," Timi persisted. "Dreams are not an easy thing to control. Especially when you're small and frightened and you must face each night alone, with nothing but your fears to keep you company. And when your dreams do slip free, and everyone tells you that those dreams couldn't possibly be real, how are you supposed to gain control over what supposedly doesn't exist? That is the experience of most children who are Dreamers. Their nightmares are at their most powerful when they are at their weakest and most insecure. Nightmares change as most people grow up. Even though most Dreamers may never realize it, and may still feel enough of the old terror to be frightened awake, adult minds learn to diffuse the power inherent in dreams, and to safely neutralize what they accidently create, at least most of the time. Especially strong Dreamers like you may still dream a Figment to life, but I doubt it would have the power of any Figment you dreamed as a child. Even among children the creation of a truly potent Figment is rare."

For reasons that reached deeper than she could understand, Drew shivered. The Figments stalking her were truly frightening, but there was still something about them that made her feel as if, with a little effort, she could master them. They might be frightening, but somehow she knew they weren't frightening enough. Her nightmares as a child had been vivid indeed. A few in particular. Those dreams were as real to her now as they had ever been. She shivered again, thrusting her remembered dreams away. "So what do you do when a Figment invades your world?"

With a quick glance over her shoulder, Timi answered, "Either the Figments follow when their Dreamer leaves, or if they show a tendency to stay, the Keeper of this world expels them. It is of the first importance, though, to keep a Figment away from its Dreamer."

"Why? All of you clearly feel some urgent need to get rid of me, and although I appreciate not being left to fend for myself, I still can't help thinking, as horribly callous as it sounds, that if you left me to the mercy of those beasts, at least one of your problems would be solved for you."

Timi shuddered. "That's the worst thing that can happen. If a Figment kills its Dreamer here, that Figment is empowered and gains so strong a hold on this world that it is almost impossible to expel. There was a Dreamer killed here once, before our Sentries could reach her, and it took the Keeper weeks to rid this land of her Figment. Needless to say, in the meantime there were countless Figment bites for Gyfree to heal, and several fatalities. A Figment freed from its Dreamer is the most dangerous kind of all."

The memory of a terrifying dream that seemed more real than ever before again forced its way into Drew's mind, and again she deliberately pushed it away. "Since there are supposedly no Dreamers in your world, how do you know so much?" she asked. "From all I've heard, my world must be full of Dreamers, and there we know nothing of Figments at all."

"Dreamers are more rare than you realize even in your world."

"Is that why we know so little?"

"Only in part. You see, most people in your world ignore a child's nightmare visions, even when they're real," Gyfree stated from behind, so that Drew started guiltily.

"But in this world," Timi added quietly, "they can't be ignored."

"Why?"

"Different rules apply here," Gyfree answered curtly.

"I still don't understand," Drew admitted plaintively.

Timi turned around, facing Drew and Gyfree as they paused side by side, sudden and uncharacteristic anger enlivening her face. "Haven't you figured it out yet? What do you think you and Gyfree have done several times already? Dreams aren't just dreams here. They are power. For Dreamers like the two of you, dreams are the power to change things, the power to alter reality. Whatever a true Dreamer dreams here is reality. Don't you see? Everything a Dreamer dreams, waking or sleeping, has the power to change this world. Everything. Look what has already happened here because of you and your dreams. In your world a daydream may seem like nothing, but here you were able to throw your mind and body into such a dream, and now a Figment who was banished years ago is back walking this world. For good or bad, you changed something, and you changed it without thinking about or understanding what you were doing. One little daydream, and who knows how much damage has been done."

"That's enough, Timi," Gyfree warned, voice hard and eyes narrowed forbiddingly.

"No, it's not," Timi insisted, her eyes stubborn even though her hands were shaking as she clenched them at her sides. "There are dangers here she needs to understand."

"It's okay," Drew interjected before Gyfree could respond. Meeting Timi's eyes, she smiled weakly. "What else do I need to know?"

Some of the anger drained from Timi's face, but she still addressed Drew with unusual intensity. "Even if you are only here in a dream, you will still be able to sleep in this world. Consider it just one more part of your dream, a part that only the strongest of Dreamers is able to experience. Dreams within dreams, remember? A dream of sleep within a dream of this world. And within the dream of sleep, there may come other dreams. So it's important, when you do sleep, to be as careful as you can with whatever other dreams may come to you. Whenever a Dreamer like you sleeps, your dreams divide your mind and body between two realities, but there is still sufficient force even behind these diffused dreams to cause serious trouble. It doesn't even make a difference if you're dreaming from within countless other dreams; whatever dream occupies you at any given moment is the only dream that matters. Especially when the Dreamer is as powerful as you. No matter what, your sleeping dreams will still retain their power and, most importantly, their potential for danger."

"So are these sleeping dreams more dangerous than daydreams?" queried Drew.

"With experience a Dreamer can learn to control daydreams, but sleeping dreams can be tricky. These are the dreams that can slip beyond any Dreamer's conscious control. These are the dreams that usually create Figments." Timi's eyes turned abruptly up the path toward where Mischa and the handsome Figment strolled side by side, oblivious to the fact that their companions had stopped. Once more her pale face filled with anger, and her voice was harsh as she continued. "As far as we know, most Figments born into your world slip almost immediately into the void, and even if they manage to slip back into your world, only a few can maintain a hold for more than a short time, or become more than one of the insubstantial ghosts that you fear as children but ignore as adults. They flit in and they flit back out, unable to stay for any longer than they can hold a single shape. Yet it is not the same in this world." With a wrench that Drew could feel, Timi pulled her eyes away from her Figment, and again fixed them on her. "As Gyfree could tell you, when a Figment is born here, it does not slip away. It must be consciously and immediately dreamed away, and somehow kept away, or it will wreak havoc. And as anyone in this world can tell you, all Figments finding their way here gain the strength denied to them almost everywhere else, enough strength to cause real trouble; it doesn't matter how insubstantial and weak they may still appear, or how inconstant a form they take. Just as Dreamers like you can somehow realize your fullest potential here, so can all Figments. And once here, once they learn their own power, once they see the damage they can do, they rarely choose to leave. That is why this world would never have survived without a Keeper who was stronger than even the strongest Figments. Yet even for the Keeper there are limits. And that's why this world has no Dreamers of its own, why I am such an aberration. If this world was full of Dreamers with only a fraction of your strength, the result would be a living nightmare, a realm of total chaos. This world would collapse under the weight of so many realized dreams. Why do you think we are so quick when it comes to sending Dreamers back to your world? Someone like you could destroy us. Even I could destroy us. In this world, there is nothing as dangerous as a Dreamer."

"What about Gyfree?" Drew inquired, not even fully aware that his fingers had closed around hers.

"I've always been the greatest danger of all," he stated in a voice that darkened the sky and shook the leafs on the trees.

Without another word, Timi turned to trail behind her Figment and Mischa, and hand in hand, the two most dangerous Dreamers to survive childhood silently followed.

Chapter 6

Staked out beneath the scorching sun, scoured by the white-hot sand, the beasts yearned for nothing more than death, but death was one gift their master would never grant. He had left them here, their bodies torn, their blood pumped into the sand, their eyes blinded and their tongues shriveled, their guts and their backs and their brains on fire. He had left them here, and left them fully aware of where they were and who they were and why they were here. They had failed him, and worse, had thought to escape him, and now they would never even be able to escape themselves. They would forevermore be his creatures, shaped by agony and filled with fear. It mattered little whether he returned for them or left them here indefinitely, for the pain and terror would always remain the same.

Time had no meaning in this hell where the sun never set, never even inched away from its subjugation of the sky. They were here, had always been here, would always be here. An eternity, or perhaps several eternities passed, and then he was there, looming above them, blocking out the blaze of the sun, burning them more fiercely with his presence than they had ever been burned before. With a flick of one claw he fused their open bellies closed, sealing the fiery sand inside to rage within them forever. Time resumed as his hand closed around them and wrenched them away from the inferno, back to the void where the full force of his being brought the blood seeping through their skin. At long last he released them, and they crumpled to the ground, faces pressed to their clawed fists as if in prayer.

"Well?" his voice sawed through their minds like a ragged scalpel amputating a limb.

"We failed," sniveled Hund, his snout trembling against his paws.

A fist of talons slammed into the side of Hund's head, hurling him across the void. "Well?" their master asked again, voice hammering through their minds.

"We tried to betray you, master. We were fools," Auge confessed in a whining rush, his paws wrapping around his head as if such a futile gesture could actually provide some protection.

"It was his idea," whimpered Hund from the distant spot where he still sprawled, blood oozing from his ears and nose.

"Yes, it was," drawled their master, and Auge screamed, blood bursting from his open mouth even though he had not been touched by anything other than that lethal voice. "And after we have spent a little more time together, I am certain you will never betray or fail me again."

When Auge and Hund opened their mouths this time, no screams could slip past the choking pain.

Vivid streaks of red and purple stained the sky as the tired group stumbled into a small clearing that boasted a ring of stones in its center. Whoever had paused here, whether long ago or recently, had left no other marks of their visit, but had quietly been on their way, perhaps leaving the stones as a sign that in this vast, empty forest, they at least were alive. Considering that this was the first sign of human life she had seen since setting out with her traveling companions, the sight of the ash-filled fire pit was both welcome and troubling to Drew.

Turning to Gyfree as he stood at her side, Drew asked, "Where are all the people in this world?"

His eyes were shadowy, not unfocused but focused on something far away, as he replied, "Although there is one exception, there are no towns on the borders of this world, for the nearness of the Barrier makes most people uneasy. And the possibility that a Dreamer might slip through makes even those immune to the presence of the Barrier itself fearful. Most people in this world live clustered in the center, either in cities or the nearby countryside."

"So no one comes here except for those who guard the Barrier?"

"Sentries, or would-be Sentries. Dreamers. And the Keeper. No one else ventures into this forest. The fire pit was probably left by someone guarding this section of the Barrier."

Drew shivered as if something icy had reached through the ashes to chill her to the bone, as if the purpose of the fire pit was to repel people rather than draw them to its potential for warmth. "So what is the one exception?" she asked.

"There is a town next to the Source, so next to the Barrier as well."

"And people live there, but refuse to live near the Barrier otherwise?"

"Yes, for it's the section of the Barrier that is the most secure, despite some problems it had several years ago," Gyfree answered, but his eyes were cold, and there were lines etching his mouth that were decidedly grim.

Drew shuddered again, but this time at the iciness in Gyfree's face, an iciness that froze the next question on her tongue.

As the two Dreamers stood silently facing each other, Timi collapsed to the ground nearby, curling over to rub her feet. "Are we going to be able to stop here and get some rest?" she moaned.

Gyfree nodded. "I haven't felt the Figments return, so for the time being, we are safe. I'll know the second they do reappear. As soon as the land feels them, so will I."

For the first time since they had resumed their trek through the woods, Mischa's attention was at least partially diverted from the perfect features of Timi's Figment. Frowning in Gyfree's general direction, she sniped, "I don't understand how you could possibly be Keeper. You're not really one of us."

Before Gyfree could respond, a slight flush flooded Timi's cheeks, and she actually snapped, "That didn't seem to bother you before, and it certainly didn't stop you from trying to captivate him until my Figment showed up."

Both Mischa and the Figment flicked a contemptuous glance Timi's way, and then, her eyes flickering back and forth between her past interest and her current obsession, Mischa persisted, "I still would like an explanation. Having a Dreamer as the Keeper may pose dangers to this world beyond any we have known before."

"The world picked him," Timi insisted as she glared challeng-
ingly across at her creation. "I doubt that the world would pick
someone who posed a threat."

Mischa continued to ignore Timi, although the Figment watched
her coldly as the two hummeybees buzzed loudly, their drone
holding a distinct menace, their barbed stingers quivering as they
pointed in her direction.

"What changed in this world that caused the first Keeper to be
selected?" Gyfree asked wearily, his eyes haunted by ghosts that,
at least for the moment, only he could see.

The color drained from Mischa's face until she looked like the
pale reflection of her former self. "The Barrier was broken," she
answered huskily, her eyes pausing in their restless shifting and
settling on Gyfree's face.

"And then what happened?" pursued Gyfree harshly, his voice
scraping raw everyone's nerves.

"Chaos," whispered Mischa. "The Dreamer who broke through
was followed by a Figment who killed everyone in its path.
Including the Keeper's son. Then the land rose up and infused
the Keeper with the power to banish the Figment, as well as
any future Figments that might follow a Dreamer through the
weakened Barrier."

"Other than banishing them, could the Keeper exert any power
over Figments?"

"No," Mischa breathed, "only a Dreamer can have any real
power over a Figment."

"So," returned Gyfree, his hand painfully gripping Drew's as he
once again held it unconsciously in his grasp, "perhaps a Dreamer
as Keeper is the only possibility left to this land. Perhaps banishing
Figments is no longer enough, and a Keeper is needed who can
actually control or maybe even destroy them instead. You know
as well as I that the Barrier has grown progressively weaker over
the last few years. What do you think an ordinary Keeper could
do if the Barrier gave way completely? As a Dreamer I may still
pose a threat to this world, but it's just possible that just as I've
always represented the biggest danger, I may now represent the
biggest hope." As she looked at him, Mischa's eyes slowly filled
with fear. "Don't think about it," he told her softly. "Just go back
to your Figment friend and let him help you forget the risks this
world itself is courting." As she backed away he added bluntly,

"And be grateful I'm saving my powers for Figments who are different from him."

Mischa backed into the Figment's embrace, and as his arms closed around her, new color as vibrant as the sunset flooded her cheeks and the fear drained from her eyes like sunlight from the sky. Turning in his clasp, she smiled, and as he murmured something in her ear, she even laughed, the sound ringing through the forest as if she had no cares in the world, or at least none she could remember. Wrapped in each other's arms, they tripped farther into the woods, disappearing among the trees, although the treble of Mischa's laughter and the answering bass of the Figment's murmurs echoed through the clearing, the soft drone of the hummeybees providing background music for the staccato gasps and moans that soon infused the melody and gradually climbed to an ear-shattering crescendo.

The atmosphere in the clearing was decidedly awkward, and as the sounds from the forest escalated, Timi in particular became increasingly agitated. Her hands visibly shook as she helped roll out blankets around the fire pit, and after one especially shrill squeal, she collapsed to the ground with a jerk. Casting a look of appeal at Gyfree, she finally blurted, "If you have the power to banish or even destroy him, you must. He may not be hideous, but in his own way he's as dangerous as Drew's Figments."

"What makes you think he's dangerous?" Gyfree inquired with a puzzled smile. "It may sound like he's hurting Mischa, but I'm relatively sure that he's not."

Something dark flashed in Timi's eyes, as if some secret pain had escaped from where she had hidden it deep inside, and suddenly surfaced like a livid scar. "I can't explain, but I do know he's a menace."

Gyfree shook his head slowly, his eyes and mouth setting like cement in the sun, and then retorted, "I've been called a menace too many times myself, and I will not destroy anyone or anything simply on a hunch, or because of feelings that might have their source in something as untrustworthy as jealousy. If and when your Figment does something that merits retribution, I will take whatever steps seem appropriate at the time. But I will not destroy him simply because you want me to."

Timi dropped her head and stared at the hands in her lap as if they had been discarded there by some incomprehensible source, and then biting her lower lip, she watched the alien hands twisting and writhing in a strange dance. After a long moment punctuated by the continued moans and sighs emanating from the woods, she said, "I'll go gather some firewood. It will be getting cold soon."

Night was settling over the small group like a blanket, and although the edges were still fringed with the violet tinge of the setting sun, Mischa, the Figment, and Timi had all snuggled into its folds to snatch what sleep they could. Even the hummeybees were still, their wings completely motionless, their incessant buzzing reduced to a quiet murmur.

A fire crackled within the stone circle, casting light and shadow over the faces of Gyfree and Drew as they stared at the flames, their eyes so intent on the heart of the blaze that it seemed as if all of the answers to every possible question must be hidden there. Yet the only truths concealed deep in the fire were the secrets of fire itself: the ecstasy of burning, the drive to consume the very thing that granted life, the need to forever find something new to embrace and destroy. Drew's eyes grew dark with the fire's consuming needs, and after a long while, when the others had succumbed to gentle snoring and the occasional sigh of sleep, she tore her attention from the fire and transferred it to Gyfree's face. "How long have you been here, in this world?" she asked softly.

Eyes as dark as her own turned toward Drew. "I don't know exactly," Gyfree replied. "Since I was a child."

"A child!" exclaimed Drew, her voice stirring the quiet so that the hummeybees emitted a single sharp buzz. "Why did you never return?"

Gyfree's head turned back to the fire, but there was ice, not flame, reflected in his eyes. "It wasn't safe. The Figment that had chased me here was banished by the Keeper, but only after killing a large number of people, including the Keeper's son."

Drew sucked in a breath so harshly that the fire flickered, leaning into the current of air that had pulled it away from its own center. "So you're the Dreamer who first broke the Barrier," she gasped.

"Yes. Before I came, this world had never known the danger of a Dreamer or the death brought by a Figment."

Without thought, Drew reached out and lightly brushed her

hand down Gyfree's arm. "I still don't understand why you have remained here so long. All other Dreamers are sent back, so why weren't you?"

Gyfree's voice was so low it seemed to melt into the flames, but Drew heard each word as clearly as if it had been shouted. "I was at first, but it happened again, almost immediately. She chased me here, followed after me, and although she was banished again, it was only with great difficulty, so the Keeper decided it was safer to keep me here. Safer than risking me ripping another hole in the Barrier that she could follow me through. And even if he had wanted to send me back, it would have been a difficult task to accomplish, because somehow, the second time she chased me, I managed to dream myself here completely. Mind and body both fully here, and not in the old world at all."

"Couldn't she still pursue you?"

"She tried, but failed. Not only could the Keeper feel her coming each time, so could I. Between the power he held through the land, and my dream power, we were able to keep her out. It took both of us, but it worked. And even though I can remember her clearly, can still see her whenever I close my eyes, even though her memory haunts me to this day, she has not tried to enter here in several years now. There came a point when she simply stopped trying." His eyes once more lifted, and his hand grasped hers with sudden fervor. "But in your world, the world that used to be my world, she would have killed me long ago. It was easily within her power, for she was a very strong Figment."

Drew squeezed back as his hand squeezed hers. "But there must have been other Dreamers since you, Dreamers followed by other bloodthirsty Figments, and those Dreamers were sent back."

"Yes," he whispered, his eyes flooding with a dark so pure they turned pitch black.

"Did you ever have to take any of those Dreamers to the place you're taking me?"

"A few. But of those only one seemed unusually aware. He's the one who taught us much of what we know of your world. Since I left that world when I was still a small child, all I could remember clearly were my own dreams. But he was older, much older than you and I are now, and even when he was less lucid, there were many things about that world he was able to explain, however inadvertently. He had spent his entire life as a Dreamer trapped in a world where, to most people, dreams were only the fantasies of their unconscious minds, even though dreams were something else entirely different to him. He had clearly given much thought to what his dreams could accomplish, so there were many things he seemed to understand that most Dreamers never comprehend. He understood what Figments were, even understood the delicate balance of power between Dreamers and those they had dreamed into existence. Most importantly, he understood where he was, and what was happening. He understood the possibilities offered here, and had actually sought out this world so he could destroy his own Figment. Yet in the end, he too was sent back, for even he lacked the strength to stay."

"Would it have made a difference if he had possessed the strength to stay?"

"He was eager to return home once he had rid himself of his Figment."

"But if he had wanted to stay, and had been strong enough, would it have mattered?"

"It would have been impossible. His body and mind were divided between two worlds, and he could not remain in two separate places forever."

"Why not?"

"It placed stresses on him that were apparent even to me, and I was still just a child at the time. There were times he seemed almost as alive and present as you, but the times when he would become vague and uncertain, the times when his sleeping body and mind would try to pull him back, were far more frequent. One second he would be alert, the next confused and disoriented. He came here with a purpose, but once his purpose was fulfilled and his Figment was dead, there was nothing to hold him here, and he grew increasingly befuddled and withdrawn. Once we reached our destination, nothing and no one could have held him back. He rushed toward the Source, and then, in a blink, he was gone."

"But what if he had been here fully, as fully as you? Then would he have been able to stay?"

"No. The people in this world would have never allowed it. There are many on this world who would even have sent me away. But the Keeper had adopted me as his son after his real son was lost, and no one here would openly challenge his decision."

Drew studied the shadows flit across his face, shadows that no longer had anything to do with the fire. "There's more bothering you than your position as a Dreamer in this world, isn't there? More even than your father's death, or people considering you a menace?" she asked.

For a long moment the only voice in the clearing was the crackling one of the fire. Then, as slowly as if his words had to surface from some long-forgotten and deeply buried dream, Gyfree answered, "Every time other Dreamers have broken through the Barrier, I've felt no qualms sending them back. I never felt as if any of them were like me; most were vague, disoriented, seemingly half asleep. It was easy to send them back because most of them never even knew they were here. Even the stronger ones seemed tenuous and unreal much of the time. And never since the day the Keeper asked me to stay has there been a Figment even half as strong as the one that followed me. The Figments have usually been like the Dreamers they followed, weak and flimsy wisps of ghosts. Despite the strength they gained here, they were easy to expel. Even the ones who were truly dangerous seemed too weak to enter their Dreamers' waking world. The only harm any of these Figments could have ever brought to their Dreamers was here, in this world. So I never worried about sending away Dreamers followed by such weak Figments. And over the years I never questioned whether or not I truly belonged here, because compared to every other Dreamer, even the strongest Dreamer of them all, I clearly did."

"So what's wrong?" Drew insisted. "If you feel that it's right for you to be here, what has you looking so bleak?"

"You."

"Me?" Drew questioned, startled into a loud squeak that made the hummeybees buzz a drowsy warning. "Why me?"

Gyfree's eyes seemed to swallow his entire face, and then reached out to swallow her, and everything surrounding her as well. "You are the first Dreamer who has ever been real, as substantial and alive as I am. More substantial and alive than the people in this world, at least to me. So now I wonder if I do belong here. If you don't, perhaps neither do I. And if I still do, I wonder if somehow you belong here too. If there is a way for us both to stay, it could destroy this world, and if we both leave, that could destroy this world too. What is worse, no Dreamer or Keeper to protect the land and sustain the Barrier, or two Dreamers potentially wreaking havoc on reality? I just don't know anymore."

"Would you want me to stay?" Drew asked faintly.

In a flash the darkness drained and the ice melted from Gyfree's eyes, and in the brown depths tiny flames leapt higher than those in the fire pit. "Yes," he answered briefly, then as quickly as the flames had flared, they were extinguished by the dark and the ice. "Among other things," he breathed roughly, "the Figments that follow you are as solid and substantial as we are, and pose a real threat. If we don't destroy them here, and you still return home, they may actually possess the strength to hunt you down in your own world, where your powers are severely limited, and if they catch you there, they will be able to kill you. After all, they have already come close to killing you once."

The Dreamers sat hand in hand, their eyes once more immersed in the fire because it was the safest place to be. Then finally Drew asked in a voice as crackling as the blaze, "Do you miss anything from the other world?"

"Not really," Gyfree responded. "Even when I lived there, everything seemed unreal, more like a dream than my dreams actually were. I never stayed anywhere long, but moved from place to place, and it seems to me that even the faces of the people I lived with were constantly changing, although even that may have been a dream. Sometimes it's hard to be sure what were the dreams back then, and what were the realities."

"I remember seeing a swingset topple over when I was a child," mused Drew. "I can still envision it clearly, see it tilt slowly backward, almost like in a slow-motion film, the faces of the children blank with surprise as they were carried into a cloud of dust. That memory is so vivid, so real, and I have no idea whether it was a dream, or whether it actually happened. And I never asked my parents if they recalled such a thing, because in the end I didn't really want to know if it happened in a dream or outside a dream. It would have ruined the memory if it was clarified in any way."

Again Gyfree squeezed the hand that still nested in his own. "What are your parents like?" he asked, as if in wonder that she had parents to describe.

Drew shrugged, the gesture as uncertain as her memory of the tumbling swingset. "I don't really know," she admitted. "I spent an entire childhood with them, but at times it seemed as if I inhabited one world and they inhabited another. We moved around a lot, so I never had friends, and as early as I can remember, I relied solely on myself. I even had a sister, but she was so different from me that living with her was like living with a stranger. She loved people, loved attention, and people loved to give her all of their attention. I felt like the invisible child, the one always watching from outside, the one who was there, but at the same time, not there enough to merit notice. As soon as I could move out on my own, I did. I went to college, and studied, and still made no close friends although I stayed in the same place for more than a year. Ever since, I have moved from place to place, job to job, as if moving is all I know how to do, as if I will find someplace familiar, someplace that feels like a home, if I just keep moving enough. And I haven't heard from my parents, or my sister, in years. As soon as I was gone, they didn't even remember my birthday."

Gyfree sighed, and for Drew it was the sound of all those lonely nights she had huddled in her bed, watching demons looming over her or pirates bounding around her room, wondering if calling out for her mother would bring safety or give life to the most terrifying nightmare of all. She didn't explain to Gyfree, although she was certain he would understand, that in some ways her worst nightmare, the nightmare that had frightened her above all others, was not the one that boasted the fiercest of monsters stalking her night after night; instead it had been of her mother with that cold, distant look that was always on her face, raising a hand with a loaded gun clenched in her fingers to shoot a bullet directly between Drew's eyes. She always awoke as the bullet grazed her skin, but afterward, as she burrowed beneath her covers, shivering and alert, she knew better than to call her mother's name.

"How would you feel if you could never go back?" Gyfree questioned, dispelling the nightmare memory that had momentarily dragged Drew away.

She could feel him waiting for her answer, could sense the tension traveling down his arm and into her hand, and could tell that, despite his suspense, that he already knew what her response would be. "Relieved," she whispered. "I would be relieved."

The night stretched over them, enclosing them in consoling

arms as the fire flickered and dwindled, its never-ending hunger once again left unappeased. When the ring of stones was finally filled only with the dull glow of embers, Gyfree announced, "It's late. We have a long way to go, and who knows how much time to sleep."

"What about my Figments?"

"I'll know the moment they reenter this world, and the land itself will make sure I wake up."

"What if we dream?"

"As long as you remember what you dream, then you can deal with it when you wake up."

"And if I don't remember?"

"Then the dream will probably not have enough strength to survive." His hand squeezed hers one final time before releasing it to the embrace of the night. "Trust me. I've been doing this a long time now, and there's always a way to untangle the webs you dream. Or almost always."

Beneath the stairs there was a door, but most people ignored it. Maybe they didn't see it, or maybe they thought it was the typical tiny broom closet often tucked beneath stairways, but for whatever reason, no one but she ever opened the door, and no one but she knew that a room was nestled there, a room that stretched back farther than the eye could accept, a room much larger and cozier than it should have been. This was her refuge, the place she retreated to whenever she needed a moment to think things through, whenever she needed to be alone. Strangers might march back and forth on the other side of the door, and the sound of feet might be heard rushing up and down the stairs, but in here she was safe, warm, apart.

There was a bed in the room, just big enough for her, and she would rest there for hours listening to the world pass by, pass her by. She sat there now, eyes on the door, suddenly and inexplicably frightened that there was no lock on the handle, for the first time in her memory afraid that this place might not be the safe refuge she had always imagined it to be. Then there was sound on the other side, more sound than she had experienced before, and the doorknob rattled, then started to turn. She held her breath and backed into the farthest corner, hoping that whoever was there would just go away, or not notice her hiding there and leave, or would see her immediately and seize hold of her before she could slip away.

The door disappeared and he was there, and with him came so much light that now she understood why no one but she had ever bothered with this room; it was dark, impossibly dark. She looked at him, afraid that he would not see her, would not notice her at all, would turn back through the door and shut her inside forever, alone in the dark forever. So she stepped forward, and as she moved, so did he, a step, and then another step, and then they were standing face to face, breathing each other's breath, feeling each other's heat. His arms closed around her and his body pressed into hers, and she came alive as his mouth crashed down, parting her lips with an urgency she had never known. An ache rose within her, from deep within, an ache she had never felt before, as if a long-unheeded hunger had been buried inside and had finally been released to rise to the surface. His lips moved eagerly to her face, to her neck, and back to her lips, until every nerve in her body burned and her knees started to buckle. She would have crumpled to the ground but he held her up, held her tight, held her as if both their lives depended on how close he could hold her. Every part of her body tingled and throbbed, just like a foot that had been sat on too long and was now feeling all of the pain of waking up, all the intensity of returned sensation. She felt aware as never before, alive as never before, awake as never before.

With the thought of waking came the realization that she wasn't awake at all. Despite the keenness of all she was feeling, she was asleep, sound asleep and dreaming. Dreaming that she and Gyfree were pressed together in a rather intimate embrace, their lips firmly attached, and their hearts thumping wildly in unison. Dreaming a very vivid dream in a world where such dreams became a reality.

Every muscle in Drew's body tensed, and as her lips froze and her body went rigid, Gyfree's hold on her slackened. For another moment they still stood close, the heat of their bodies unabated, and then he stepped away, his hands falling to his sides like deadweights as bright color rushed to his face.

"I . . . I'm sorry," Gyfree faltered.

"I'm so sorry," rushed Drew before the final word had escaped Gyfree's mouth. "I just started dreaming; I couldn't help it."

A frown creased Gyfree's brow. "I am the one dreaming," he responded. "I started dreaming that you had disappeared from this world and I couldn't find you anywhere. I could feel you, but I couldn't find you, and then my feelings led me to a door beneath some stairs, and when I opened it, there you were." The color in his face deepened. "I'm sorry I dreamed us, I dreamed you . . ."

Hesitantly Drew reached out and touched his arm. "You may be dreaming," she whispered, "but you're not the only one. I started dreaming too, a dream I've dreamed countless times before, so I know you didn't dream me there. I was hiding, fearing that the Figments would find me, but at the same time hoping you would. If anyone should be sorry, it's me." Color as deep as Gyfree's stained her face. "I don't usually dream those sorts of dreams," she muttered apologetically.

Silence filled the dream-born room beneath the stairs, and then Gyfree whispered, "Have you ever dreamed about someone you don't really know, but in your dream it seems you've known them forever, that they have always been a part of your life, an important part, perhaps even the most important part? Then you wake up, and you've lost this important person, lost them so completely that you can't even remember what they looked like or who they were or why they mattered to you."

When Drew nodded her head, Gyfree continued. "That's how I felt when I found you this morning, and you looked up at me with your clear green eyes; I felt as if we had always known each other, had always been close. I was angry that you were a Dreamer, angry that my dream come to life was really just a dream after all, and not one that I could transform into reality since I wasn't the one dreaming you here. I even tried to convince myself that you were no different from any other Dreamer, that I was just imagining things, because that was the only way I could deal with the fact that you could disappear at any time. But you are different, and I can't stop myself from feeling that you are that someone who has always eluded me in my dreams, that someone I've both known and waited for forever. And now I'm not just afraid of that someone important slipping away from me when I wake up; I'm afraid that at any moment, waking or sleeping, you will suddenly slip back into the world you came from, and this time I will remember exactly what you looked like and who you were and why you mattered. That was why I dreamed this dream. Because I'm afraid; because if you don't truly belong here, if you are only here in a dream, there is nothing I can do to keep you from slipping away when the time does come."

Drew stepped close, back into the circle of his heat. "We're still dreaming now, aren't we?" she asked huskily.

He nodded, stepping so close to her that their bodies brushed together, their clothes whispering against each other. "The best kind of dreaming," he murmured.

"Then we have every excuse in the world," she breathed, "since it's only a dream."

This time his arms folded around her tentatively, and the lips on hers plied gently, but as the fever of the kiss mounted, they felt carried beyond themselves once more, until their two bodies again trembled with the intensity of their shared dream. Then just as the kiss deepened into something more, and Drew was reduced to clinging to his chest, he ended it, lifting his head sharply as if a distant screech had pierced his ears. "Time to wake up," he stated hoarsely. "Your Figments just got back."

A moment later Drew found herself blinking the sleep from her eyes as she stared at the first rays of light sifting down through the high branches of the trees and streaking the forest floor.

"Good morning," a voice whispered behind her, and she turned to see Gyfree smiling uncertainly in her direction.

The color rose to her cheeks as she smiled back. "Good morning," she responded, a glimmer of mischief abruptly sparking to life in her eyes. "Have any interesting dreams?"

Laughter lit his eyes and his smile gained confidence. "Only a rather nasty nightmare," he teased.

Drew wrinkled her nose at him, but before she could retaliate, Timi's sleepy voice mumbled, "What's going on?"

The laughter ebbed from Gyfree's face as he answered, "The Figments are back, and they're headed straight toward us." His eyes sought Drew's again, but this time they were stony with emotions he had quickly buried. "I think it best if we stop running and wait here for them to arrive. At the rate they're moving, it won't take much time, but at least we'll have a few minutes to prepare."

"Prepare for what?" yawned Mischa as she sat up across the clearing, the arms of Timi's Figment wrapped around her waist, his perfect face buried in her lap.

"Drew's Figments," Gyfree replied shortly. "They'll be here soon."

"Are you crazy, or just suicidal?" Mischa demanded, the sensually sleepy fog clearing from her eyes.

"If we run, they'll catch us. If a confrontation is inevitable, better we choose the time and place," Gyfree responded shortly.

"Well, leave us out of your plans," Mischa returned, her hand convulsively gripping the Figment's arm. "We'll be hiding. I'm not letting you risk his life." With a toss of her head she scrambled to her feet, pulling the Figment up behind her. The hummeybees darted around the remaining three, buzzing harshly and menacing them with their jagged stingers before trailing behind the couple who plunged into the sheltering arms of the forest as if they were the only two people in the world whose lives had value.

Timi stood uncertainly, back pressed against the nearest tree, her eyes darting back and forth between the spot where Mischa and the Figment had vanished and the space where Gyfree and Drew stood, their bodies as coiled as snakes ready to strike.

"You can go if you want," Gyfree informed her tersely.

Timi shook her head so slightly that it seemed she hadn't moved at all. "I'll stay," she answered quietly. She shook her head again, and this time markedly. "It's not like Mischa to run away. It's not like her at all."

Gyfree stared into the shadows that had closed behind Mischa and the Figment. "No," he mused, "it's definitely not like the Mischa I've always known. But there's no time to worry about that right now." He reached out and clasped both of Drew's hands in his own, transferring his eyes to her face. "As Keeper I should attempt to banish your Figments, but instead I'm going to try something that's never been tried before. As far as I know, no one has ever been able to destroy another's Figments, but if I only banish these, they might attack you in your world if you return. Stay close because I may need you, but don't expose yourself either. You and Timi should be safe if you hide in the trees behind me."

"No," Drew replied bluntly.

Gyfree's forehead creased and his eyes hardened. "What do you mean, no?"

Drew squeezed his hands as she gazed up into his glittering eyes. "I've had this feeling," she explained, "ever since we came face to face with the two Figments chasing me. I can deal with them. I have power over them, I know it. It is not your task to handle these Figments, it is mine. You have to let me try."

Gyfree shook his head stubbornly. "You have been here so little time. You don't have the experience yet to manage this."

"Time isn't the issue because so much has happened so quickly, and I've already learned more than I could have ever imagined. Trust me. I know exactly what to do." With his hands in hers she hurled both of them into the dreamworld, just as he had previously carried her. Around them the gray landscape once more materialized, but this time there was a ghostly ring of stones beside them, and the translucent form of Timi clinging to a phantom tree. They were still in the clearing, but they were equally inside a dream. "They'll follow me here, won't they?" she asked. When he nodded his head, she stated, "Good. This time we'll meet on my terms, not theirs."

Long it had been, long and full of unendurable pain that they had no choice but to endure, long in the embrace of their master, long breathing the same hot breath that coursed through his lungs, long pumping the same acid blood through their veins that scorched through his, long gnawing on the same bitter morsels that only fueled his insatiable hunger for her dead flesh, long becoming the creatures he finally wanted them to be, long losing themselves until all they knew was what he wanted them to know, all they felt was what he wanted them to feel, all they desired was the death he had long desired. Long it had been, long until their only care was his, their only drive was his, their only identity was his.

Satisfied at last he had peeled them away like old skin and, closing them in his claws, thrust them once more through the void to that world where even now his Dreamer dreamed a powerful dream. He dropped them nearby, near enough that she would not have the time to dream herself completely away, but not so near that she would immediately recognize the hand that carried them to her and by instinct somehow hold them at bay. He dropped them nearby, at just the right distance, so that she would be forced to prepare, so that she would have committed to her defense, cast herself into whatever dream she foolishly thought could save her, before she realized what she truly had to face. He dropped them nearby, and then he waited, flames leaping from his skin as if he would reduce the entire void to ashes, face writhing in the painful pleasure of anticipation. Finally she would be his; finally she would be dead and he would be free.

Auge and Hund dropped to all fours, talons rasping against the ground like steel against stone. Neither glanced at the other; neither made the slightest sound as they loped in pursuit of their quarry. There was no hesitation, no stumbling, no fighting; there was no hunger of their own, only the hunger of the master who had set them this task. Through the forest they rushed, carrying with them a nightmare from which no one could ever possibly awaken. When their prey slipped into a dreamworld, they followed, feet and hands sprinting over the gray ground as easily as if it were solid rather than woven from the flimsy wisps of dreams. Their speed intensified, for she was directly ahead now, and they could feel her with the wrenching clarity their master had always felt her, and could have found her without Hund's keen nose or Auge's discerning eyes, if they had still cared about the strengths two creatures once known as Hund and Auge had long ago possessed. The old Hund and Auge had been given their last chance and had failed, but the new Hund and Auge would not.

The hunters broke into the clearing, the grayness of their attendant nightmare shimmering as it merged with the gray of her dream, and there where gray met gray stood their intended victim, eyeing them coolly as she urged a man to step away from her. There was no delay, no need to relish the moment, as the beasts lunged toward her, fangs exposed and claws extended. The time had come at last for the Dreamer to die, and for them to kill. So forward they rushed, and she did not try to flee from them, did not even try to scream. Instead she stepped into their charge, and with surprising speed and impossible strength, seized Hund by the arm and threw him over her shoulder and into the ground with a force that shattered bones even though he impacted against supposedly insubstantial mist.

For Drew the advance of the Figments felt like a scene from some long-ago but shockingly recognizable dream. Perhaps when she was a child she would have turned to run, bolting awake as the monsters' breath seared her neck and fangs scraped her spine. But she was no longer a child, and it had been a long time since she had felt herself rendered helpless by each and every stray nightmare that haunted her nights. She was rarely the victim of her own dreams anymore; could not, in fact, recall the last dream in which she had played the defenseless sacrifice. She was not always brave in her dreams, was not always strong, but there were times she knew she was dreaming and could choose to be both. Like now, when she had sought out a dream for the very power she knew she might find there.

Gyfree had been reluctant to allow her to face the Figments, but perhaps he had finally seen the potency of the dream pouring through her eyes, for he had eventually acquiesced with the understanding that he could help if she seemed in danger of being overwhelmed. He had stepped away when the beasts had attacked, just as she had requested, and even though she felt no need for his assistance, it was a comfort to feel him there, a relief to know that he would sustain the fabric of the dream so she might turn her entire focus onto her own tasks. Without the slightest hesitation, she stepped forward to meet the forgotten yet hauntingly familiar monsters of her childhood nightmares, and with the power she had dreamed of only as an adult, grabbed the snouted one and hurled him to the ground, dreaming that the force would shatter every bone in his body.

She had no time to listen for the crunch of shattered bones, no time to look for a sign that she had actually hurt him, for the other beast was already upon her. As he reached for her with razor-sharp claws she dreamed that she was impossible to touch, and his talons changed their course to swipe at empty air. He roared with frustration, hurling himself at her, but it was if an invisible barrier had sprung up between them, and try as he might, all he could do was strike and gnash at the air. He could not pass the unseen barrier to touch her, but there was nothing to stop her from touching him. With a force she dreamed was deadly, she kicked the beast in the chest, knocking him across the clearing and into the impaling branches of a wraithlike tree she had dreamed into existence. There he hung, bleeding from his mouth and from countless oozing holes where tree branches poked through his skin.

She looked behind her, but there was no movement on the ground, not even the slight rise and fall of a body still breathing. She turned back toward the impaled beast whose eyes kept burning into her, and as Gyfree stepped up beside her, walked over to where his bloody bulk dangled from the tree. Her eyes met his fierce ones, and as she watched, the dark crimson drained from his eyes just as the blood was draining from his body, until he was staring at her with eyes as yellow as she must have first dreamed them, eyes that looked back with an expression as clear and seeing as her own. "I realized you were our Dreamer the very first time you escaped," gasped the Figment. "But there should have been no escape this time. What did you do?"

Drew swallowed the sudden pain in her throat as she looked into the clear, clear eyes of the Figment she had unknowingly given birth to so many years ago. "I dreamed you dead," she answered huskily.

The dying beast nodded as he held her in place with his clear, clear yellow eyes. The corners of his mouth turned up ever so slightly as he breathed out his last words and the last of his life, "Thank you." Then his clear, clear eyes clouded over, and for the first time since he had opened them in a long ago dream he saw nothing to hurt him, nothing to fear, nothing to enslave him; clearly, quite clearly, he saw nothing at all.

The gray swirled around them, surging through and dissolving the dead Figments before fading away, and Drew found herself back in a clearing lit by daylight rather than by the hazy atmosphere of a dream; shaking uncontrollably, she clung to Gyfree, tears leaking down her cheeks like the crimson draining from her Figment's eyes. Timi stood a few feet away, her face devoid of all color, her eyes more frightened as she looked at Drew than when she had seen the murderous Figments.

"How did you kill those things?" Timi asked faintly, her voice as pale and lifeless as her face.

Drew squeezed her eyes shut as if that could remove her vision of the dying Figment, his eyes so beautiful and so clear and so full of gratitude. "Remember what you told me?" she whispered back. "Dreams are power here, so all I had to do was dream."

Gyfree's arms folded around her as if he could shelter her from her nightmares as easily as he might shelter her from the cold.

"Yet those were the most solid, powerful Figments I have ever seen. They seemed as substantial as either of you, more substantial than me. They were no longer limited by whatever dream brought them to life. How could you defeat them so easily?" persisted Timi.

For a long moment Drew stood motionless, her face pressed against Gyfree as if she was a child in bed, his chest her pillow and his arms the blankets she had pulled over her head to hide from the visions that haunted her nights. Yet finally, just like the child compelled to peek from beneath the protection of her blankets to see whether or not the monsters were still there, Drew lifted her head to look directly at the one thing that haunted her most. "It was easy to kill them," she breathed, her eyes full of the dark and all its phantoms, "because they were nothing. The only thing that made them dangerous was that they bore the mark of another's touch. As soon as they entered the clearing, I could feel his taint on them, and when I touched them, I could feel nothing but him, and though it's been a very long time since I have so distinctly felt his presence, I recognized it immediately. He was the most potent, terrifying, deadly demon to ever stalk my dreams. As much as I would like to dream otherwise, it is he who stalks me even now." Drew's eyes slowly returned from the terrors of the dark to focus once more on Timi's face. "You think you've seen powerful Figments. You've seen nothing. You've felt nothing. You know nothing of what awaits me, nothing of how truly lethal a Figment can be, nothing of him. The Figments I just killed were nothing but his tools, his helpless slaves. I saw it all as the second Figment died; his eyes told me more than you could ever tolerate. Now that his servants are destroyed, I know that he's the Figment I need to worry about, that he's always been the one seeking my death. Of all the monsters ever to haunt my dreams, he's the one most worthy of fear. And I can assure you, as frightened as you may be, you cannot be nearly as frightened as me."

Chapter 7

Everything crumbled around him, but he made no sound, no movement, did not even spit out the foul ashes in his mouth. His Dreamer had accomplished the one thing he had never expected, perhaps the one thing he should have expected. She had not only defeated his deadliest minions, she had released them from his power forever. He could find other servants, but he had searched long for those two, and had chosen them not only because they seemed to be the best, but because he had wanted, desperately wanted, her death to come at the hands of creatures she had herself created. If he could not kill her himself, at least something she had given birth to, something else she had spurned and deserted could.

There had been a risk, a risk he had readily accepted, that she would remember them if they weren't quick enough with their kill, and in remembering, would gain some small power over them. Yet there had been just as great a risk that she would recognize his touch on any minions he sent, and in recognizing, hold them at bay. As long as he was banned from killing her himself, such risks were inevitable. That was why he had tried to strike so quickly, why he had lured her into a place where he and his minions would be the only powerful ones, a place where she should have been stripped of all the powers she had ever known dreaming, all the powers she unknowingly possessed as long as she remained in her own waking world. And when that place had failed to hold her, at least she had entered a world where Figments, once allowed in, were stronger than they could have ever been even in the void itself. A place where they might even be stronger than the Dreamer who had given them life, perhaps even strong enough to break through all those protections she had unconsciously dreamed for herself, especially if he made them even stronger, made them stronger than every other beast he had ever touched. And although she too was in many ways stronger in this new world, he was certain that even the power to realize her dreams should not be enough to help her shake the stalkers whom he had made strong enough to follow, strong enough to dog her heels, more than strong enough to look in her eyes and still kill.

Yet they still had not been strong enough, had still seemed doomed to fail, and at last there had been no other choice, so he had made his minions even stronger yet, made them mindlessly and inescapably lethal, and had then delivered them almost directly to their prey, so that once again they would have the unmistakable advantage, just as they should have had the advantage in the nightmare trap he had set to ensnare her. Knowing just what his minions were capable of, he had had no real fear of actual defeat; never in his wildest moments had he ever expected her capable of so much more.

So it would be a waste seeking and shaping others, a true exercise in futility, for she had always had the ability to keep one step ahead of him, just beyond his grasp; each time he had thought he felt his fingers closing around her, she had evaded him again. And now that she had been reminded of his true existence, she would be more alert than she had been in years, and he would have no chance to gain the freedom he so craved. In fact, her reawakened awareness would probably restrict him far more than he had been restricted since he had been created, for at last she knew he was more than just a dream, knew that he was as alive and real as she was, and far more dangerous than she could ever be. And she knew, knew without a doubt, that he sought her death. He had been born strong, and had grown stronger because she had been taught doubt and disbelief in her own dreams; he had gained even more strength when she had at least partially abandoned him to the memories of her childhood, but now she would never abandon any part of his memory again.

The icy breath on his neck came just as he had expected, as did the icy voice mocking in his ear. "Such a shame, really. Two such promising beasts, and they never had a chance against one little Dreamer. Quite an impressive display on her part, actually. Perhaps you need to reconsider your tactics for dealing with this one. Where the beasts seem doomed to fail, maybe beauty could succeed."

Still he did not move, did not respond to the cruel gibes in any way. He simply stood, eyes fixed unblinkingly on nothing. Already he could feel the change, for he could no longer see the Dreamer however he might try, and although he could sense she was still alive, the sharpness of her presence had dulled for him perceptibly. She was withdrawing, now that she knew he was truly there, setting up a barrier she didn't even realize existed but that would shut him away from her forever. She would be completely lost to him soon, lost not only to his sight, but also lost to his sensations, and as long as she remembered, as long as he remained trapped within her thoughts, pinned down by her attention, he would be bound here in the dark, weaker than he had ever been, until the distant day she died.

He had been the strongest in the realm of the void, but that had not been enough; he had felt chafed by the constraints his Dreamer had unknowingly placed upon him just by the fact of her continued existence, had wanted more than anything to escape from the face that had brought such disgust and horror to her eyes, so he had gambled everything, had gambled all by finally consuming his minions so that they reeked of him, had gambled all and lost all. Either he must accept his fate, or accept the one alternative he had steadfastly avoided. There were risks if he took advantage of the one desperate chance still available, but there were also opportunities that only he fully understood. He had gambled before, and given the choice, he would gamble again, would eagerly gamble away the last of his freedom if it gave him that one last hope of winning everything after all.

"So," he demanded harshly without turning to face the coldness at his back, "what do you want?"

"Why, just to commiserate with you on your unfortunate loss," she breathed with a billow of frost that briefly numbed his ear.

"And to perhaps watch me languish here in the dark?"

A freezing finger trailed along his spine. "There is that too, of course, but as enjoyable as that may be, there are things that could be far more enjoyable for both of us."

She could hear the quickening of his lungs, but she could not see the speculative narrowing of his slitted eyes. "So what do you have in mind?" he rumbled.

Two frigid arms encircled his waist as she leaned into his heat. "I give you want you want, and you give me what I want."

"We both know what I want," he growled. "What is it you want?"

Since he refused to move, she circled around his massive body, her arms still entwined about his waist, and looked up into his fiery eyes with her frosty ones. "I want the one thing you are no longer willing to give me. You." She pressed against him until steam seeped from all of the places their bodies touched. "I want you to touch me the way you touched me so many times before. One more time is all I ask. One more time for you to take me however you wish. I just want to feel you, and then I will ask nothing more ever again."

His arms shot up and claws sank through the ice to pierce her shoulders, drawing blue-streaked drops of blood, but unlike the last time, it served her better to reveal her intense pleasure; she had drawn him in with her frosty indifference, and now it was time to drive him to distraction with her biting desire, so she groaned longingly without reservation. Blue lids drooped heavily over her eyes, masking her entire face in unfeigned physical desire, hiding those less sensual yearnings which lurked a bit deeper. As the heat in his hands tore through her body she shuddered, and then her quivering lips fell apart in invitation as the ice melting from her skin sizzled and splattered against the ground. The heat of his desire exploded against her, scattering sharp slivers of ice through the void, but still he refused to lower his head and glut himself with the sweet and icy taste of her blood on his tongue. Despite his arousal, and despite her mounting desire, he restrained himself; even now he did not trust her, for there were good reasons not to trust her however badly he wanted to plunge himself into her icy core.

"What game are you playing?" he demanded roughly, the words flaming off his tongue and scorching her cheeks.

"No game," she whispered, voice raspy and uneven as if she had inhaled too much smoke. "A fair exchange. You want your Dreamer and I want you. A death for a last fling. With your Dreamer dead there will never again be anything else I could ask, or any service I could possibly provide. Her death is your freedom even from me, but in return I get to savor you for one small space of time." She leaned forward and with teeth as cold and keen as icicles bit through the skin of his chest, lapping his scalding blood with her wintry tongue as he shivered ecstatically beneath her touch. "It's your choice," she murmured, pulling away, his blood trickling from the corners of her lips. "You can have her dead, and have me as you choose, or you can have nothing at all."

With a howl he dropped his mouth to hers, his tongue lashing out to lick his own blood from her face, his fangs splitting open her swollen lips. For a moment they clung together, shaken like trees in a storm by the passion they usually held tightly in check, and then with a strength greater than anything in nature, they wrenched themselves away from each other and stood panting, sparkling ice and raging fire in both their eyes, acrid smoke and frosty mist rising from both their bodies.

"If you kill her all I must do is take you," he gasped, his mind equally ablaze from her nearness and the memory of the kiss they had shared the last time they had met, "and there are no other conditions."

This was the moment she had been preparing for, the moment when everything would hang in the balance. "There is just one small thing," she said nonchalantly.

His roar rocked the void and would have shattered any Figment less powerful, but she stood closest to him in strength, and where others would have crumbled, she did not even quail. "Tricks, all you do is play tricks! I knew better than to listen to you!"

Despite the fierce writhing of his skin and the dangerous flexing of his claws, she stepped closer, veins of blue branching across her skin, shards of ice heavy in her voice. "You must take me in your hand and carry me to the world where she hides," she said coldly, as if he had never interrupted, as if she had never felt the explosive heat of his anger, or even known his scorching passion. "If I am to kill her, you must take me to her first."

The slits in his eyes expanded and contracted, and his mouth compressed into a slashing line as he reined in his anger to gaze at her expressionless face as if it hid a secret that he must solve. "Why would you need such help?" he demanded harshly.

Careful to hold her frozen facade in place, she shrugged. "I made the mistake of entering there once before, and I've never been able to return."

"Why were you there?" he rasped, the sound sending a thrill of pleasure through the ice.

"To kill my Dreamer."

His talons closed around one icy arm, honed edges again extracting glossy pearls of blood. "So why is that world still closed to you?"

Frozen lashes hooded her eyes. "The Keeper banished me and his defenses would never let me return."

"The Keeper is dead."

"Perhaps his defenses are still in place. Or perhaps it is the new Keeper still keeping me out," she replied with seeming indifference.

He glowered at her with eyes that could dissolve flesh and bone, but the ice shielding her flawless face remained as unyielding as the surface of a frozen lake clutched in winter's hand, and as treacherous in its lustrous beauty. "Very well," he finally growled. "I will send you, and if you succeed I will pay your price, but then you will never enter my presence again."

"Agreed," she answered, the crack of her smile opening a chasm beneath his feet that would be difficult, if not impossible, to avoid tumbling into.

The vision of the dying Figment shone clearly in Drew's eyes: the gleaming yellow left behind as the blood red drained from his eyes, the receding of his jagged fangs, the sagging of his face into something softer, something almost human. Yet the image that clung more tenaciously than any other was his expression the moment he realized that he was indeed going to die, for in that instant his entire face was transformed not just by a relief that nearly buckled Drew's knees, but by a joy so overwhelming that the very sight of it pinched her lungs and constricted the veins webbing her heart. More than anything, that fleeting look of incredulous joy proclaimed to Drew the true nature of her real enemy, and she was left shaken to her core.

With an arm around her waist, Gyfree lowered Drew gently to the ground, while Timi, her face awash with contrition, rustled through her pack to scrounge up a hasty breakfast. Drew accepted everything she was given without even glancing at the proffered food, for everything tasted like ashes, and she only ate because eating was something she must do to stay alive. And at the moment the suddenly difficult task of staying alive was the one thing that fully occupied her mind.

Breakfast was long over and the sun sifting through the trees far more intense by the time Drew lifted her eyes to Gyfree's and murmured, "They were killers, but they were victims first. He made them what they were and sent them after me."

Gyfree shook his head, shadows of his own nightmare memories saturating his eyes. "Why didn't he come after you himself?" he asked.

"I don't know," she admitted. "Maybe I didn't seem worth the effort. Maybe now he'll change his mind."

"It doesn't feel right," mused Gyfree as a frown stalked across his face. "You must have dreamed him as a child, and it doesn't make sense that he would wait so long."

A phantom of random memories flitted through Drew's eyes. "I don't think he did. I think he tried more than once when I was small, but for some reason, he could never get close enough to kill me."

"It still makes little sense," Gyfree objected. "My own Figment hasn't tried to reach me for years. I think there comes a point when we no longer are that important to them. A time, I suppose, when they grow up and move on to other things."

"Or perhaps," Timi interrupted, her eyes as intense as the sunlight baking the forest floor, "they are both infinitely patient and have simply been biding their time until a likely opportunity presented itself. There is a reason you've stayed here all these years, Gyfree, and it's not just because this is your home. This world became your home in the first place because you would never have survived in your own world. For all you know, that's as true now as it ever was."

Gyfree shifted troubled eyes to Timi's flushed face. "You're full of surprises, aren't you?" he remarked. "One minute you're incapacitated by fright, and the next you're seeing straight to the possible heart of things. You're as . . ."

"Changeable as a Figment," Timi finished, her face as suddenly pale as it had been rosy only a moment before.

"You're nothing like a Figment," Gyfree retorted, "but there is more to you than I ever realized." Then, as if an unwelcome visitor had suddenly intruded within the confines of his mind to startle him, Gyfree jumped, twisting his head from side to side, his eyes sweeping the clearing. "Where is Mischa?" he demanded. "And where is your Figment?"

Timi's own eyes widened in alarm. "They should have come back by now. Even if Mischa expected us all to be killed, she would never have just gone on without checking on us first."

Gyfree leaned over and grabbed the pale young woman by the shoulders. "Timi, you must tell me everything you know, or even just suspect, about your Figment. I have a feeling there is more happening here than you're willing to explain."

A painful pink erupted in Timi's cheeks, and she immediately dropped her eyes.

A look of startled comprehension burst from Gyfree's eyes, and he rocked back on his heels. "How long can you clearly recall being a Dreamer, Timi?" he demanded in a voice that could not be ignored.

The color in Timi's cheeks deepened, although the effect was to render the rest of her more pale rather than more vibrant, as if the bloom in her face was separate from her, and there to only draw attention to her true lack of color. "A couple of years," she admitted in a threadbare whisper.

Gyfree's own face had grown so pale that he seemed no more present than Timi, and his hands had started to visibly shake. "You don't remember dreaming before that?" he asked hoarsely.

"No, never."

"You never dreamed as a child?"

Timi shook her head.

"So your Figment is a creation of your adult mind," Gyfree stated in a voice as unsteady as his hands, "and the product of the only strong dream you've ever had."

Timi only nodded.

"Your dream came on a hot summer night when even the trees seemed to restlessly protest the heat."

Timi's eyes finally rose from the ground, and she gazed at Gyfree like a child who realizes her most painful secret has never been a secret at all. "How do you know?" she whispered.

"Because I finally realize that it was my dream that made you dream in the first place," rasped Gyfree.

Timi neither flinched nor gasped, and for the first time since

Mischa's absence had been noted, the color in her face made her seem more, not less alive. "Maybe your explanation should come before mine," she remarked.

Gyfree sat back with a thump, his fingers unconsciously weaving an intricate pattern through Drew's as his body settled close to hers. His eyes filled with the distance of a long-ago dream as he began, "It hasn't been easy being the only Dreamer in this world. I've always felt set apart; perhaps less set apart than I would have been in my old world, but still different from everyone surrounding me. A couple of years ago I went through a short period of time when I even considered trying to go back. Yet this was my home, and I couldn't find the will to leave. So one summer night, a night just like the one I described to you, I dreamed that I was not really alone, that there was somewhere another Dreamer in this world dreaming at that very moment just as I was dreaming."

"So I am a Figment!" blurted Timi.

"No," Gyfree responded, "because I dreamed that someone already living in this world would become a Dreamer, not that a Dreamer would suddenly spring into existence. I didn't create you, but I did change you."

"Why didn't you tell me this sooner? If what you're saying is true, it must have occurred to you who I really was, once you discovered that I was a Dreamer."

Gyfree shook his head in bemusement. "I don't have a good answer for that. Maybe it's because I always assumed I would recognize you immediately, that somehow that secret bond we shared would be impossible to miss. And because I never felt particularly drawn to you, I overlooked what should have been obvious. Like it or not, we Dreamers can be amazingly blind when it comes to recognizing the truth about our own dreams."

"Yet you knew what you had dreamed. So you must have known what your dream had done to someone, whether or not you recognized that someone as me," insisted Timi.

"Yes, I knew," conceded Gyfree, eyes dark with memory. "It was a very powerful dream, and even while I still slept, I was horrified at what had happened. I could feel you out there somewhere, could feel your Figment slip from your dream, and I knew that I must help you banish him, although even in my dreaming, I feared that simply banishing him would not be enough. So I cast myself through the dream universe, seeking a nightmare so fierce that no one could ever survive it, hoping that if your Figment could be sent there and destroyed, my offense and your transformation would never be discovered. Perhaps it was because of the heat of that night, but I envisioned a vast, fiery desert, and then in my dream I was there, standing just outside, feeling all the searing fear and pain that had given birth to such a devastating dream. And knowing what unbearable pain awaited, I still dreamed that you would send your Figment there, for I was truly afraid that I had finally dreamed something dangerous enough to force my exile from this world, and I knew that, however apart I might be, I wanted to stay here as fiercely as I had wanted to stay when I had first arrived so many years ago. I could feel when your Figment vanished from this world, and I knew a moment of intense remorse for inflicting such pain on any creature, but then I could feel that you had not sent him into the nightmare after all; somehow you had sent him through it, beyond into a small, pocket world uninhabited by people, a world somehow connected to the nightmare, a world that felt as if it had been created as a refuge from the unbearable heat. And I was content to leave him there, for suddenly I was sure that no one could ever again pass through the nightmare as you had done."

"I was still dreaming when the nightmare you found unfolded below me," whispered Timi, her voice and eyes full of a distant pain. "I could feel the heat rising from it so intensely that I was almost certain that I would awaken to find my eyebrows scorched and my face blistered, but I would have still dropped my Figment there if I hadn't heard his voice in my head, begging me not to let him burn, begging me to let him stay with me. I couldn't let him stay, whether because of your dreaming or my own fears I still don't know, but I couldn't destroy him either. Yet even as I hovered above the merciless heat, dreaming that there must be another way, it seemed as if a path opened before me, and at the end of that path was another world, and I dreamed that the world I glimpsed would hold him, and that the path I had found would never open again."

"Not bad for a first-time Dreamer," Gyfree remarked. "Especially for one who had grown up never knowing a dream."

Timi looked at him with eyes finally free from the ghosts that had been haunting her. "So I didn't accidentally dream myself here. I am really here, completely here. A Dreamer, perhaps, but not a lost Dreamer, wandering far from my body and far from my real home."

"You belong here as much as you did before you ever knew a dream," Gyfree informed her.

A faint smile crooked Timi's lips. "You know, I've never again dreamed like I did that first time. Ever since my dreams are as airy as the Dreamers who usually arrive here. I still dream, but nothing is strong enough to slip beyond my control."

"I dreamed that for you too," admitted Gyfree, his voice raw. "I knew it was dangerous to place another Dreamer in this world, especially a new one, but I couldn't dream you back to the way you had been before. I felt less lonely knowing you were some-where in this world, as if I had a little sister or brother whom I had never met. So I dreamed you less power, but I did not dream your dreams away."

A preoccupied silence filled the clearing like a luminescent mist, only to be dissipated by Drew's sudden sharp words. "What kind of power exists in dreaming that it can change another person?"

Gyfree shrugged his shoulders, but his eyes darkened with uncertainty. "I don't know," he admitted. "I'd never done such a thing before, and I've never done anything like that since. I don't know how I could have possibly done what I did."

Drew met his puzzled eyes with her own, feeling as if, buried somewhere deep inside, they each held the missing jigsaw pieces that would make the other whole. "And what of Timi's Figment?" she finally asked. "How did he call me to him? Because he did call, and I was compelled to come."

Gyfree nodded, and with a visible effort, returned his attention to Timi. "What exactly did you dream?"

This time when excess color surged through her face, it was as if a vibrant flower had bloomed within her to stain her cheeks with hidden life. "I felt so alone, so undesirable, that when I did dream, I dreamed of someone completely different from me, someone who could be and do more than I could ever be and do. You've seen what I dreamed," she mumbled. "And you've seen what he can do."

"I'm not sure of exactly what I've seen," Gyfree said softly. "I've had my mind on a number of things, and your Figment wasn't even one of my more pressing concerns."

Timi's eyes flashed. "Why didn't you banish him when I asked? He is, after all, a Figment, and Figments are always banished from this world," she countered.

Gyfree opened his mouth, but before he could answer, Drew interrupted, "Because your Figment wouldn't let him."

"What do you mean?" demanded Gyfree, his eyes back on Drew.

Drew's intense green eyes, however, had turned to Timi. "That's what he does, isn't it?" she continued. "He insinuates himself into your mind and imposes his will on you. He's an ultimate seducer. If he can, he makes you forget yourself and your concerns, makes you want to forget yourself and your concerns. He makes you feel that there are no real concerns other than his. That's how he trapped me. He caught me in a moment of weakness when I longed to escape myself, and he promised that if I would just come to him, he would give me a new life. A life free from everything that bothered me about myself. A life devoted solely to him. He might not have known exactly what he was doing, but he did it regardless. He was created to seduce everyone around him so they would devote themselves to fulfilling his needs."

"Wait a second," protested Gyfree, his face now as flushed as Timi's was once more pale. "I may not have agreed to banish him, but I have felt very little interest in him or his needs. My attention has been focused on much more than him." The color in his face deepened as he looked accusingly at Drew. "And you seemed to have your mind on other things as well."

"He doesn't have the same hold on everyone," Timi interceded. "His influence on the two of you has been minimal. As Drew said, he was able to call her in a moment of weakness, and probably to prevail upon her feelings of sympathy so she would agree to rescue him. He was also able to convince you, Gyfree, to overlook him, to treat him as if he was indeed harmless. It's even possible, now that I think about it, that when he persuaded you that he wasn't worthy of your attention, he encouraged you to miss what you should have recognized immediately: that he was a Figment you had already helped banish, a Figment whose creation you were partially responsible for. But he must have realized almost immediately how tenuous his hold was on each of you, so he used his much more intense hold on Mischa to convince her to run away as soon as an opportunity offered itself."

"What makes us different from Mischa?" questioned Gyfree.

Timi actually snickered, a sly look adding a sparkle to her once dull eyes. "As you remarked, you both had other things on your minds, and those other things were impossible for him to dislodge. For all Mischa's flirtatiousness—and yes, Gyfree, she has been known to try flirting with you however impervious you might have been—there was no one else with a strong enough hold on her mind and interests to keep him out. For him, she was a perfect victim. Unattached, yet ripe for attention."

"And what of you?" questioned Drew, as flushed and self-conscious as Gyfree.

"I've had time to think about that," Timi admitted. "At first I couldn't understand why my own Figment should show so little interest in me. I finally realized that it was because his power, the power to completely seduce an unattached mind, could never be used on me. I am his Dreamer, so I have at least some small power over him, and that keeps him from being able to exert full control over me. What he desires is total domination, but the relationship between Figment and Dreamer is far too complex for him to ever be able to completely dominate me." She flushed again, ever so slightly, like the faintest touch of dawn as the sun first tipped the sky. "And of course, he had no interest in seducing me. I could serve no useful purpose, like Gyfree, and he preferred the vibrant beauty of Mischa and Drew. He tried to seduce Drew, and quite successfully seduced Mischa, but even if I had not been his Dreamer, he would never have made the effort with me."

The corner of Drew's mouth quirked although she was still careful to avoid the intensity of Gyfree's eyes as they rested on her face. "If it hadn't clearly already happened, I would say your lack of self-esteem was going to land you in serious trouble one of these days."

Timi shrugged nonchalantly, but the intense color suffusing her cheeks gave her away. "Instead it may have landed all of us in trouble," she confessed. "I don't think we can continue to the Source until we find Mischa, and do something about my Figment."

"Agreed," Gyfree declared.

"So for the time being you're allowing me to stay?" Drew questioned, her eyes finally braving Gyfree's, her face as pale as Timi's had once been.

"Yes," he tersely replied.

"Is the presence of Timi's Figment really more dangerous than the presence of a Dreamer like me?"

"I don't know," answered Gyfree as he scrambled to his feet, pulling Drew up behind him. "But I do know which of the two of you I'm willing to lose."

As Gyfree moved toward the crumpled blankets beside the ash-filled fire pit, Drew followed, but before she could think of a suitable response to his words, a shimmering spear of silver-flecked light crashed into the clearing, causing her and Gyfree to both recoil as if they had either been licked by flames or bitten by ice. When a form coalesced within the silver light, however, only Timi took the time to scream.

She stood before him in all her deceptive beauty, silver flecks sparkling from her skin, her smile as frozen and deep as a snow drift over a chasm. She stood and she waited, her icy eyes as impenetrable and unyielding as winter itself. This was how he had first desired her, how he so often desired her still, for he yearned for the moment when she seemed as implacable and hard as a snowstorm. There had even been a time when he had possessed her in winter's guise, believing she would always be so cold and severe, just as he would always be fiery and unrestrained. Yet just as spring followed winter in the waking world, in time she had changed on him, slowly at first, but then with a rush, as if all the seeds of lost summer had embedded deep within her to blossom in one foul assault. Desire had melted the ice from her eyes and blood had banished the blue from her lips, but it was not until her passion had suddenly uncovered a completely transformed face that he had known he had been betrayed, and would be betrayed again if it suited whatever purposes she still held hidden inside.

He desired her still. Perhaps even more than before, for her own unbridled desire ignited even a greater fire within him than had her icy facade. But the total abandon he had known throwing himself into winter's unforgiving grasp would never come again. He wanted her, as he had always and would always want her, but now he knew what treachery winter hid beneath her smile. Undeniably he wanted her, could not stop wanting her, and even though he had resisted, he knew that it was inevitable that he would succumb to her once again. That was why he had agreed to pay her price, why he had agreed despite the fact that there was clearly more to her price than she acknowledged, much more than he could probably afford. But he would finally have his Dreamer killed, for he knew just how deadly his wintry lover could be, and he would have his ice queen once more, would plunge into her freezing depths until she melted in his arms. He would have her, but he would not trust her.

She stood before him, as ruthless in her patience as an advancing glacier, and for a moment he almost took her, almost threw her to the ground, almost gnawed through the ice to draw blood from that immaculate face, but he restrained himself. She might not realize, as he did, that his power would be far greater the moment his Dreamer was killed, and any tricks his lover might intend to play would have considerably less of a chance at success. So he would be patient as she was patient. He would burn with patience, burn with the suppression of his desire.

She stood before him, and finally he reached out his hand, reached as if he was extending himself through the farthest folds of the void, and wrapped his invisible claws around her shimmering form. She shuddered in his grasp, and once again he had to rein in his desire. "You must enclose me completely," she moaned, her voice muffled, as if she had already been carried far away. "Your presence must smother mine."

His hand expanded until he seemed to see her wavering form through a fine red mist. Her eyelids drooped sensually and an indecipherable smile played across her lips. "Whenever you are ready," she called. "Take me straight to her."

A growl built deep in his chest until his hand clenched and his claws itched to pierce through her icy facade. "I will drop you where I last sensed her," he finally rumbled. "You will have to find her yourself."

Within his fist, she was careful not to show her elation, but within herself, she squirmed with pleasure. Once again she had maneuvered her lover into doing exactly what she wanted, precisely when she wanted it done. He had submitted to her price, but only after she had driven him so ruthlessly that he had finally blundered, driven him until he had left his mark on his minions so unmistakably that they could not afford another failure. Yet fail they had, just as she had expected they would, and now the

Dreamer truly remembered, and in remembering had closed herself away from her creation's sight and senses. Yes, everything was happening just as she wished, just as she had envisioned in her icy scheming. And as her demon lover hurled her through the void and past the Barrier she could never have crossed on her own, her inner ice tinkled and chimed with delight, for everything she wanted would soon be hers.

She could feel the ground of a waking world solidify beneath her feet, could hear the shrill sound of a scream, could smell fear, but not just any fear. She smelled the fear she had waited so long to smell, so close, and this time she made no attempt to hide her gleeful smile.

Drew felt frozen in place as she watched the exquisite face unfolding from within the silver flecks. It took a moment for her to realize that she was cold, unbelievably cold, and that her body was frozen to the ground as if she had stepped on a frigid metal rail with wet, bare feet. She tore her eyes from the inhumanly beautiful face and looked down to see thick blue threads zigzagging up her legs, and a quick glance toward Gyfree revealed that heavy cords of blue were also binding him in place. She could sense the faintest touch of her demon Figment upon this beautiful, ice-cold apparition, and she suddenly was more afraid than she had been since that long-ago night when she had opened her dream-filled eyes to see him standing hungrily at the foot of her bed. Yet her own fear was forgotten even more quickly than it had been remembered, for when she raised her eyes to Gyfree's face, his eyes were filled with flinty ice crystals and his skin was as blue as a corpse.

The stunning vision stepped gracefully across the frozen ground, her feet gliding through the chunks of ice strewn across her path as if she was a bride wading through rose petals. A veil of ice even seemed to drift across her face like the most delicate veil of fine lace, and the icicles that dangled from her clasped fingers were more lovely than the freshest wedding bouquet. She moved slowly, as if in time to the stately march that brought all women to their intended grooms, her eyes on the man who had brought her to this long-anticipated, glorious moment when she would proclaim her final conquest to an audience held in thrall by her unearthly beauty. He had tried to run, her smile said, but no man could resist a woman like her forever, and now his running days were over. Permanently.

As she reached Gyfree's side she raised a blue-fingered hand to stroke his cheek, leaving five streaks of frost like a brand frozen into his skin. "Well, little boy," she murmured in a voice that sent chills down the spine and thickened blood in the veins until the very heart felt clogged with slush. "You've grown up rather nicely, haven't you? You were such a scruffy, skinny child, but you're actually a rather attractive man." She pulled his head down with one hand and pressed her lips to his. When she released him and stepped back, Drew could see that his mouth and chin were white, as was the back of his head where the vision had touched him. His eyes, however, were so black it seemed that the icy slivers within them had melted away. The vision smiled again, and to Drew it was as horrible as if winter itself had smiled at the same moment that it had unleashed an earth-shattering blizzard. "We have so much to catch up on, don't we?" the vision purred. "I hear you've done fairly well for yourself. You're even Keeper here now. I was worried about that. You have kept me away from the Barrier all these years, but you never dreamed of what would happen if I found a different way in. That was quite foolish of you, but as Keeper you might, just might, have still been able to cause me the slightest bit of trouble. Lucky for me that you and your foolish companions hadn't budged from this spot before I dropped in. I hate having a good surprise ruined. Don't you? Which reminds me. As the saying goes in your old world, business before pleasure. Where is the Dreamer he sent me here to kill?"

"I'm here," chimed in a shaky voice, and Drew turned startled eyes toward the place where Timi stood, the shadow of a dream flitting through her eyes, her chin lifted defiantly as if daring the exquisite Figment to touch her with an icy hand.

The Figment's glorious eyes narrowed as she surveyed the young woman whose face was so drained of color that she almost appeared like a pillar of ice herself. She stepped away from Gyfree and the nearby Drew and toward Timi, cold eyes so intently drilling into the young woman that she did not see the ghostly shape of a hummeybee materialize directly behind her frost-rimed head. Unlike the real hummeybees, Timi's dream version sped on silent wings, its razored stinger as long and glowing as a poker that had rested continually deep in the heart of a fire. Timi was careful to avoid looking at her lethal creation as it dove toward the back of the beautiful ice queen, stinger aimed directly between the frost-covered shoulder blades, but her caution was wasted. The spectral hummeybee plunged into the ice queen's back, only to instantly vanish, the hissing sound of burning metal doused in water the sole evidence that it had ever been given birth.

The ice queen paused, her delicate brows raised above frost-filled eyes. "No, I think not," she mused. "If that is the best you can do, you are definitely not the one I seek. Your dreams are too tenuous to pose any threat. Dealing with you wouldn't even offer sport; you're not worth the effort it would take to kill you. So stop bothering me." With the airy gesture of someone blowing a kiss, the Figment exhaled a silver-flecked breath in the direction of Timi's face, and the young woman crumpled soundlessly to the ground.

The interruption provided by Timi, however, had afforded enough time for the frozen heaviness in Drew's mind to melt away, and a dream now filled her eyes with all of the heat and rage of a wildfire. If ice was the weapon she must fight, at least her dreams had often seethed with the perfect counterweapon. The heat of her dream spread rapidly within her mind and through her body, until she could feel the life flowing once more through her limbs, could even see the ice binding her melt and then evaporate into the air. She flexed her toes against the thawing ground, and flexed her fingers in the warming air, and as the last grip of the ice fell away, stepped closer to Gyfree and took his stiff, icy hand in her own. The heat traveled from her palm into his, and she could feel his fingers twitching as he weakly tried to return her clasp. Yet there was not enough time to accomplish more.

"You, on the other hand," the cold voice whispered in Drew's ear, "are definitely of interest. In fact, of all Dreamers alive or dead, you may be the most interesting of all." The beautiful woman moved from behind Drew to stand directly before her, exquisite face coldly amused. "Yes, very interesting indeed," she murmured, and as Drew watched, the lovely face shimmered and dissolved, silver flecks swirling as if caught in a turbulent storm. When the storm settled a man as breathtaking as the woman, but with eyes equally biting, stood before her on the frozen ground. The man reached out a hand to cup Drew's face, but where his skin met hers, a thin stream of steam drifted into the air. For a brief moment the eyes in the flawless face widened as if in surprise, but the moment was fleeting, and as she looked into the ice-hard face, Drew wasn't certain whether or not that single moment had existed only in her dream.

A smile curled the man's sensuous lips, but it reminded Drew of jagged lightning as it skated across his face. "Do you even know what makes you special?" asked the man. "You created the most powerful Figment of all. You created the one Figment so alive that his form is as permanent and fixed as yours. More permanent, in fact, because where you change over time, he remains forever the same. He is the one who makes all other Figments bow down and call him master. All Figments, that is, except me." The cold eyes traveled down Drew's body to the hand she held clasped in Gyfree's. Another smile streaked across his face, splitting apart the icy stillness. "Very touching, but I'm afraid this one is mine," he murmured, reaching out a hand with fingers as long and pointed as icicles to touch Gyfree's arm. Within the heat of Drew's grasp, Gyfree's fingers again stiffened with cold, and his warm palm hardened beneath a layer of ice. Pain shot through Drew's fingers, as if she clutched freezing metal in her bare hand, but still she held on. "Too bad for you, really. Considering how much you have in common, you would have probably made a perfect pair. Unfortunately, neither of you bothered to destroy your creations when we were still weak enough to kill. Through all the passing years, we've grown far stronger than even the two of you could ever dream. And now it's no longer within your power to destroy us. The most you could ever accomplish these days is simply keeping us at arms' length. And as you see," the cold voice pressed, the inhuman face wavering back and forth between the perfect features of a woman and a man, "even that ability will ultimately fail."

Drew's eyes sparked, red flames licking at the black centers focused on the wavering face. "So why isn't my Figment here if he's so strong?" she demanded. "Why isn't he here to kill me himself? Why did he send you instead?"

The vacillating face laughed, and despite the fluid changeability of the features, the voice was still as hard and unforgiving as the heart of winter. "I told you that you were special. You have a particularly strong ability to keep him at arms' length. Even before he blundered, you managed to keep him away without even consciously trying. That's why he sent me to kill you. No other Dreamer could have kept him away for so long, but then, no other Dreamer could have dreamed him in the first place. You may be special, but he's also very, very special. Especially to me."

"Is that why you agreed to kill me? To please him?"

This time it was the woman's face that threw back her frost-filled hair and laughed, the sound rumbling through the trees like a distant avalanche. "I didn't agree to kill you. I begged for the opportunity, although actually pleasing him was the last thing I had in mind. That is one way he and I are exactly alike. Everything he does, he does for himself. Everything I do is for myself and only myself. I needed his help to get here, and I used his craving for your death to get him to unwittingly help me. I did come here to kill, but not to kill you. I would prefer you to stay alive, at least for a while. As long as you live, and as long as you remember him, you will limit his power. And by limiting him, you will strengthen me. You will give him and all of his power to me, and then I will have the force, the vitality, the substance that he alone now claims. No, I have no intention of killing you."

The fire leapt in Drew's eyes, but as much as she filled her daydream vision with flames, she still could not return warmth to the frozen hand held immobile in her grip. "You're Gyfree's Figment," she stated. "You came to kill him."

The man's face answered. "Of course. He kept me away for years, but I watched and waited until an opportunity to slip past his precautions offered itself. Let that be a lesson to you, Dreamer. I hope it's a lesson you learn well. Never drop your vigilance, or he'll descend upon you, and you'll have no more warning than my Dreamer here. To warn you is to empower you, and that is something neither he nor I are foolish enough to allow." The face shifted again, the eyes ringed with tiny crystals of ice that sparkled like precious jewels against the flawless skin. "Although if I have my way, he will no longer be around to haunt you. In fact, you should wish me success, and surrender my Dreamer to me freely. This one's death will make me stronger, and the stronger I am, the better my chances of defeating my demon lover, and the only chance you'll ever have of living life without needing to keep one eye always open."

"And if I refuse?"

The man's face smiled cruelly as he answered, "I'll kill him regardless, but I might accidentally hurt you in the process." The lovely face solidified once more, and the woman of ice stood calmly before Drew. "Don't consider it a loss when he dies," she sighed, her breath redolent with the stench of all the decay and death buried deep beneath the pristine surface of fresh snow. "Passion can only make you weak, will distract you from what is truly important. I lost my hold on your demon in a moment of passion, for I forgot to keep hidden my changeable nature. Men, even demon men, are so obsessed with what they want us to be, that they are very unforgiving if we expose something more. It has taken me a long time to regain at least part of the position I lost in one moment of passion, to get close enough to my former lover to finally lure him into my trap. Don't let passion expose you to disappointments, or even dangers, it would be much better to avoid. Just like me, you'll be stronger when my Dreamer is dead."

Freezing eyes locked on burning eyes, and Drew knew, knew without question, that in any direct confrontation, she would lose. Ice would conquer fire, and Gyfree would be dead. There was nothing she could do to stop it, not if she played the ice queen's game. Instead she dropped her head, smoky hair falling across her face to hide the new dream pouring through her eyes, her shoulders stooped as if in defeat even though defeat was not something she intended to accept.

The ice queen suddenly seemed far away as Drew cast her mind fully into her dream. She was hidden beneath the stairs again, lying on the bed, but she wasn't alone. Gyfree was with her, wrapped in her arms, her mouth above his breathing hot air into his lungs, her smoldering body pressing insistently against his. In her dream he was as impatient and inflamed as she was, and his lips devoured hers eagerly as his hands slid up her back, crushing her against him until she felt her flesh melting into his flesh, felt the blaze of a fire that threatened to consume them both. And still they kissed, their breath quick and urgent, their hearts raging against each other, their bodies clinging together, burning with the abandon of a wildfire.

In the frozen clearing the ice queen smiled in triumph as she laid a blue-tipped hand over her Dreamer's heart, and her eyes glittered as she felt his blood thicken, felt his veins harden, felt his heartbeat falter, and then felt the last feeble contraction of his heart, and finally, after years of waiting and yearning for this moment, felt him die. His lifeless body crumpled to the ground, and as he fell, so did the other Dreamer, his hand still clutched in hers. The beautiful face fell away, and something truly hideous laughed raucously, but Drew paid no attention, for she was far away, Gyfree's lips devouring hers, just as fire seemed to devour their two bodies. "Poor Dreamer," the icy nightmare mocked. "For all you know, I will devour his cravings when I devour your demon, and I'll soon be back seeking your death. In the meantime, however, I will need to take him something to convince him you are already dead. I'm sure you won't mind, but he's going to demand at least some of your blood." Reaching out a jagged blue claw, the Figment ripped through the sleeve of Drew's borrowed clothes, slicing through her skin from shoulder to wrist, catching the blood that gushed forth in the palms of her icy hands before vanishing into a swirl of silver flecks.

Locked in Gyfree's embrace, Drew could still feel the sharp pain tear through her arm, as if a blade of ice had sliced her open all the way to the bone. And almost inseparable from that distant pain was the sensation of Gyfree's hand lying motionless and icy in hers. But here two insistent hands gripped her back, and just beneath her body was his responsive body, and where their two bodies touched she could feel the rush of heat through his veins, could feel his lungs gulping the same fiery air she breathed, could feel his heart surging wildly against hers, could even feel him suddenly shudder violently. Opening her eyes, she stared down into his. "She's gone," he whispered, breath warm against her face. "Now what?"

"Now we dream, as vividly as we can, that I knew what I was doing."

Drew remembered few stories from her childhood, perhaps because few stories had seemed as relevant or as real as her dreams. There had been one story, though, that had somehow clung to her memory as tenaciously as any dream, and that had been the story of Snow White. There had always been something about the idea that everyone thought she was dead; they had even encased her body in a coffin. But it had been clear to Drew that Snow White couldn't be dead, because a kiss could not bring a dead person back to life. Yet a kiss might very well wake someone from a dream, so it seemed obvious that Snow White was alive and well, living happily in a dream while the waking world wailed and wept around her. Prince Charming had not brought her back to life. He had disturbed her dream and awakened her, and whether that would guarantee a happily ever after for the two of them remained to be seen. If he forced her awake every time she was in the middle of a pleasant dream, he certainly wasn't going to be around for long.

Like Snow White, Drew dreamed a pleasant dream, and in her dream Gyfree was no more dead than Snow White had been; he was happily alive in a dream somewhere. In fact, he was alive in the same dream she inhabited, and all it would take would be a kiss in the waking world to rouse him from his deathlike slumber. Here in the room beneath the stairs she hugged Gyfree close, her lips pressed firmly against his, and at the same time, back in the clearing her lips moved as if they had a life of their own, trailing across the still, cold face that lay on the ground beside her dreaming body. There was no breath drifting across the icy lips when her mouth found his, but she still parted his lips with her own, kissing him as deeply as she kissed him in her dream. At first nothing happened, and despair seized her, threatening to drag her into a nightmare in which Gyfree's ghost would haunt her forever, but then the cold lips quivered, and the burning lips in her dream stilled. The heat rushed back into her deserted body, and she found herself laying on the cold, hard ground, kissing Gyfree as he lay beside her, his body pressing against hers with a force that finally rolled her over onto her back. After a few minutes that left her breathless, the lips on hers lifted, and she cracked her eyes open to stare at the golden brown eyes glowing down at her. Then Gyfree smiled, and it was the most wonderful thing she had ever seen; so wonderful that she doubted Prince Charming could have been more stunned than she felt when the cold corpse he had touched with his lips was transformed into his dream princess.

"Do you two want to be alone?" a voice teased weakly from across the clearing, and both Gyfree and Drew turned their heads to see Timi wobbling unsteadily on her feet. "I can just go hide behind a tree."

"That won't be necessary," Gyfree answered lightly. "There's a little hideaway we can get to as quick as a dream if we want to be alone. And no one except the two of us will even know we're gone."

Whether it was the strain left by the ice queen's visit, the fear she had known with Gyfree's death and the even greater fear that preceded his return to life, or simply the sense of anticlimax that followed a dream so passionate it had brightened her room beneath the stairs, Drew's emotions required some release, and she laughed until the tears ran down her cheeks and her sides ached as much as her arm. When the laughter and tears had finally subsided, Gyfree pulled her gently up to sit beside where he now knelt on the ground, but even his slight tug sent a bolt of unbearable pain down her arm. The world around her swirled with a gray that had nothing to do with any dream, and from a distance even farther than the room beneath the stairs, she could hear Timi's shrill shriek. As if from an insurmountable height she gazed down at her arm. The long gash left by the Figment was filled with tiny crystals of ice that swarmed like maggots in rotten meat, and the blood that seeped from the wound was blue, just as the surrounding skin was blue, the unhealthy blue of a corpse. Then Gyfree's hands were on her, were covering her festering wound, and the pain was being sponged away; the gray receded from the world and Timi's voice sounded directly in her ear. "Is she going to be okay?"

"She'll be fine," Gyfree answered, his voice as unsteady as his hands were calm.

"I'm already fine," Drew informed them both. "What's one more Figment wound to a Dreamer? Especially a Dreamer who has someone nearby who can heal even the nastiest bite or gash."

Although it wasn't the first time, it was still a very nice feeling to have Gyfree take her in his arms and hold her close despite the fact that they both seemed to be fully awake.

Chapter 8

She had little time. The blood would need to be fresh to convince him. But first she needed to regain her composure, to fit her facade carefully back in place. The elation that had overtaken her with her Dreamer's death had rocked her usual calm, and it was vital that he not see the truth she had painstakingly kept hidden. She had been as circumscribed by a powerful Dreamer as he was, but now she was free as he would never be free, free and strong, free and fated to be stronger yet, but only if he never understood what she had done. So she delved within her inner ice, immersing herself in the frigid depths, thrilling to the feel of her veins filling with slush, her lungs filling with frost, her muscles and her bones and every nerve in her body transforming to crystalline, lovely ice. Ice made her impenetrable, gave her the illusion of permanence, granted her the power to deceive. That was the power her Dreamer had endowed her with, a power that he could no longer limit with each breath he took.

The cool smile again curled her lips and her eyes looked like miniature oceans in which countless ice floes drifted. Yet just as she was lifting her foot to take that one last step into his territory within the void, something shifted, as if a crack had marred the smooth surface of her facade in a spot where the ice should have been thickest, but was suddenly thinnest instead. From that one crack thousands others generated, tiny fissures streaking across the silvery ice one after the other until her facade was as shattered as a smashed mirror. Her carefully constructed self scattered in jagged fragments at her feet, leaving her more stripped and vulnerable than she had been since that never-to-be-forgotten moment when she had first stood shivering beside a small boy's bed as he screamed in horror. It had taken so many years, but she had finally killed that boy, had frozen his heart, frozen every drop of blood in his veins and air in his lungs, and had left him dead on the ground, had left him beside that other Dreamer who must not have surrendered after all, for somehow he was alive again, and she could feel the hot blood soaring through his veins and thundering in his heart, could feel his entire body aflame with more life than she had ever felt from him before. She had tried to convince that other Dreamer that she possessed less power than she thought, but she had clearly possessed even more than the ice queen herself had ever suspected, for only she could have returned life that a Figment had stolen.

So she stood shivering a step away from where he waited, his Dreamer's blood cooling in her hands, and for the first time in a very long time, she felt the bite of the cold. Her Dreamer was alive, his presence shaking her with an intensity she could not escape, and then he was gone from her senses, like a light that had been switched off, just as the demon's Dreamer was gone for him. Gone, but still palatably alive, alive even though she could feel nothing of him now, nothing at all. He was still alive, and she was weaker, not stronger than before. Yet like her lover's Dreamer, she would not surrender; she would use her weakness as a weapon, make it part of her well-stocked arsenal of deception. Pulling from her last reserves of ice, she again replaced her ravaged face with her beautiful facade, and still trembling, stepped into her lover and rival's presence.

There were furrows in the gray where he had stormed through, pacing restlessly as he awaited her return. The skin of his face writhed with barely suppressed fury as his eyes blazed with barely suppressed fear. He was accustomed to being in complete command, the master in every situation, and she could see that his need to rely on her, to even trust her, had chafed him almost beyond his ability to endure. He would be difficult to handle, almost impossible in her weakened state, but handle him she must.

He whirled around to face her as she slipped noiselessly into his realm, his eyes immediately riveted on her empty arms.

"Where is she?" he roared. "Why didn't you bring me her dead body?"

She stepped closer, her cupped palms extended before her, the Dreamer's blood heavy in her hands. She made no attempt to hide the shaking of her limbs or steady the wavering of her face. "It was more than I could do," she whispered. "More of a burden than I had the strength to bear. So I brought you this instead."

His eyes narrowed to honed edges as he examined her face, but the smell of the blood distracted him, set him on fire so that he howled, burying his face in her hands to lap hungrily at the precious fluid. It was sweet on his tongue, sweeter than anything he had known before, and he glutted himself on its sweetness. He had no doubt that this was his Dreamer's blood; he could feel it just as he had once felt her, alive and vibrant on his tongue. He could smell her, taste her in the blood; could smell her fear, taste her pain, could even see her in his mind's eye as she somehow grappled with death. It was all in the blood, the sweet, intoxicating blood.

Yet there was so little blood, not nearly enough to sate his appetite, and as he licked away the last elusive drop from the shaking hands, he looked up and growled, "Why did you not bring more?"

She did not try to hide the quiver in her voice. "I brought what I could." It helped that she didn't really have to lie, that she could deceive him with a portion of truth. "She was stronger than you imagine. Almost too strong for me. Even though I surprised her, I couldn't hold her frozen. I couldn't soothe her with my man's face. I had to resort to the most basic form of bloodshed, and even then I only succeeded because she was distracted by the death of one of her companions." She drew a shuddering breath. "My confrontation with her left me weaker than I've been since I was first created. Bringing you a handful of her blood was all I could do."

He glared at her for a time, and then with a flash of motion she expected but could not anticipate, swiped his claws across her body and knocked her from her feet. "You have never been weak," he snarled as he loomed over her. "What trick are you playing now?"

She sprawled where she had fallen, making no effort to regain her feet, the full extent of her weakness only partially feigned.

"Does it really come as a surprise to you," she gasped, "that the most powerful Figment ever created should possess a Dreamer with abilities far beyond the average Dreamer? Is it really so amazing that the Dreamer who so easily defeated your deadliest servants could cause problems for even me?"

He lunged forward and pulled her to her feet, his claws drawing thick drops of blood as they easily pierced her skin. "I feel no different," he boomed. "How do I even know she's dead? If she was as strong as you claim, how can I be certain you were able to succeed?"

"When my Dreamer died," she lied, "all I felt was a blank, as if he had vanished outside the range of my senses. What did you expect to feel? Did you expect to feel her heart stop, her breath freeze, her mind drift away?" I felt it with my Dreamer, she thought, but it meant nothing, nothing at all. It was a trick more devious than any I have ever played. It is your Dreamer who is deceptive, much more deceptive than me. "She's gone, so there is nothing for you to feel but her absence."

He shook her, and she swayed in his grasp as if she was water rather than ice at the core. "I don't trust you," he thundered, his eyes agleam with malice, lips curled back from his bloody fangs. "But I am ready to fulfill my end of the bargain regardless."

Real panic shot through her eyes, shattering the hard crystals that he could never before see beyond. "If you take me now," she panted, "I will not have the strength to survive. You will destroy me."

"So you are at my mercy," he gloated.

"Yes," she breathed. "Even a kiss of yours would make me vanish now. If you refuse me the chance to recover then I will perish. But if you wait," she added, her voice tinged with a seductive edge, "I will bow down and call you master. What Figment will dare question you when all see that you have finally vanquished me? You will gain greater power in my defeat than in my destruction. There is nothing as glorious as having a true opponent submit to your will. With me at your feet you shall truly reign supreme."

His hands on her tightened, his claws leaving jagged tears in her unprotected skin. "What trick are you trying to play now?" he thundered.

It was difficult to say, more difficult than she had anticipated, but it was a long game she played, and a seeming loss now would guarantee that the game was far from over. "There are no tricks left me," she whimpered. "I'm simply begging for my life."

"And what of our bargain?" he demanded, eyes full of undisguised lust now that she seemed to pose no threat.

"Let me recover," she answered, allowing her own desire to spark in her eyes. "I still want you, just as I have always wanted you. But I also want to live."

"And you will call me master?"

"Yes."

"And do my bidding?"

"Yes."

The slits in his eyes expanded, darkness reaching out to swallow everything he saw, and in that moment she feared herself lost, but then the slits contracted to a mere knife edge, and she knew that he had reined himself in, that he had allowed himself to be tempted by those promises she would never keep. "Very well," he rumbled, pulling her face against his until his fangs grazed her cheeks and she could smell the sweet blood on his breath. "As soon as you are yourself again, I will expect you to return to me." A smile sharper than the slits in his eyes split his face. "But don't take too long. I can already feel my power growing, and soon I may be so powerful that I will overwhelm you even at your full strength."

It was all to her advantage that her weakness had encouraged his delusions of increasing strength, but at the moment he could still crush her between his hands if he chose. It would be best if she didn't wait for him to change his mind. His claws continued to dig into her lacerated arms, but she simply closed her eyes and let her skin dissolve into fine crystals of ice that slipped through his fingers and swirled through the air before carrying her away to at least temporary safety.

This time when he began to pace, his clawed feet tearing chunks from the void, he was just as impatient for her return as he had been before, just as greedy for what she might bring, just as frenzied although this time not fearful at all, for when she reappeared, he would devour more than a handful of blood.

Even being wrapped in Gyfree's arms was not enough to distract Drew for long from the disconcerting problems she and her companions faced. After a few minutes of resting her head in the niche beneath his shoulder, she raised troubled eyes to the miraculously lively brown ones smiling down at her. "Exactly what are we supposed to do now?" she questioned. "You supposedly have a dangerous Dreamer on your hands—"

"In my hands, actually," Gyfree interrupted.

Drew wrinkled her nose at him but continued on as if he hadn't spoken, "Who must be returned to someplace that you people call the Source. Mischa and Timi's Figment are missing. Timi's Figment may have the power to ensnare anyone they meet, and it is probably up to us, or at least the two of you, to stop him before that happens. And we're being pursued by two incredibly powerful, murderous Figments. And we may have no warning before one or both of them descend on us again." She took a deep breath. "In other words, we couldn't dream up this much trouble even if we tried."

Gyfree's expression had grown more somber, but there was nothing at that point in time that could have banished the joy of simply being alive from his eyes. "What do you think, Timi?" he asked, turning his head toward the young woman.

Startled, Timi asked blankly, "What do I think?"

A flash of understanding passed between Gyfree and Drew, and then Gyfree repeated, "Yes, what do you think, Timi?"

"Why are you asking me?"

"Because you've already shown some remarkable insights, and have proven yourself an invaluable companion. So what do you think?"

"You heard what your Figment said," Timi answered, the color draining from her face until it seemed she would disappear as dramatically as the ice queen had appeared. "I'm not even worth the effort to kill. I'm useless."

"And you believe a Figment who tricked her own lover into sending her here so she could kill Gyfree, and planned to trick him again with the lie that she had killed me?" Drew retorted. "For all you know, she lied about why she didn't kill you. Maybe she would have exhausted enough strength on you that she would have never been able to kill Gyfree. It doesn't matter what she said. All that matters is that you had enough presence of mind to distract her attention at the moment that could make the most difference. Without you, we would have lost."

Timi blinked, her eyes as full of doubt as a child who expects to be punished and is instead given a coveted treat, but when she spoke her voice was decisive. "To begin with, you both need to make sure your dreams ban your Figments from this world, although that may no longer be enough to keep them away. Especially if they are combining their powers in any way that you cannot envision. And because of something Gyfree's Figment said, I think we need to get away from this clearing as quickly as possible. We've been surprised by a Figment once, and I think it best if we avoid another similar surprise. Things might not end as well next time." The smile that twitched her lips was suggestively sly. "And I still think we should go after Mischa rather than rush Drew to the Source. Considering the things chasing both of you, I think it would be best if you stay close together for the time being. Your best chance of survival may be as a team, and the worst thing we could do right now is send Drew back to the other world. I hope the two of you don't mind working together," Timi said with mock sorrow even as her smile grew, "but I honestly feel that it's best for both worlds if you do."

Drew was surprised when Gyfree actually chuckled. Despite the dangers they faced, he was laughing. And a smile came to her own face, for she realized not only had she never heard Gyfree laugh before, but that it was one of the most wonderful sounds she had ever heard. Their lives were all in danger, the living world beneath their feet was in peril, and yet Drew and her companions plunged into the woods to follow Mischa's trail with grinning faces and light-filled eyes.

Alone she knew cold as no other being could ever know it. She was immobilized by the cold, her limbs stiff and heavy at her sides, the blood in her veins thick as syrup, the breath in her lungs a solid block. Her skin was so cold that it had hardened, and was now as thick and unyielding as her dense, frozen bones. She could no more change the expression on her face than she could close her eyes, for her lashes were frozen to her skin and she had no choice but to watch the cold radiating outward from where she rested, freezing the swirls of gray into grotesque shapes that teased her with hidden meanings. The cold reached through her and beyond her, tempering her like heat tempered steel. As the cold grew, so did her strength, until like water enclosed in a glass bottle and crammed inside a freezer, she had expanded to the point where she knew she must burst, shattering the very thing that had once given her shape. Yet like the water turned ice, the only true shape was the one she had now become, and she no longer required anything beyond herself and beyond the cold that gave her life, that was her life, that was her. For her there was no sensation beyond the cold: no pain, no hunger, no fear. She was simply cold; nothing more and nothing less than completely cold. This was, after all, how she had been dreamed, and how she would remain if she could not prevail against her lover. Nothing and no one except him could touch her without becoming what she was herself. And maybe now not even he could withstand the terrible, terrible cold. With that thought, the thought of his heat captured by her cold, transforming her cold, she knew that despite her previous denial, there still remained other sensations, sensations that not even the cold could freeze away: there was greed and there was desire, just as there were always greed and desire where he was concerned.

She had arrived here so weak, unexpectedly drained by her Dreamer's miraculous resurrection and by the brutal hand of her lover. She had not even been certain that the cold would return to salvage her, and she had sprawled nearly lifeless on the ground, cold enough to shiver, but not nearly cold enough. It had been slow, had taken so long, as if she had been gripped by the ruthless hands of summer and would never again be released to winter's loving embrace. Summer could not thaw her, but it still would not free her, and she shuddered uncontrollably because she knew she would never be cold enough again. Then finally autumn had come to run kind fingers through her hair until she could feel the faintest touch of frost. As if she had been a tree in one of multiple worlds, autumn had stripped away all her color, stripped her and left her barren, exposed to the coming of the cold. For a long time she had shivered in anticipation, longing for the first breath of ice to caress her skin, and when at last it had come, she had wept tears of joy and relief, wept until the tears were frozen on her cheeks and across the film of her eyes.

Now at last she was herself again, perhaps even more than herself, for she had given herself to the cold with an abandon she had never known before, an abandon that had never seemed necessary before. She had always been ice at her core, but now she was filled with ice as hard and exquisite as diamonds. She could meet her lover, and meet him as an equal, for she felt stronger than she had before, strong enough to have a chance. And despite all her setbacks, she knew she could win, for she had an advantage in the upcoming struggle that he didn't even know was a struggle. He thought he was stronger because of his Dreamer's death, but she knew he was weaker than ever before, and it was her knowledge of the truth that she could use as a weapon to deceive and to conquer. As he would soon learn, there was no greater weakness than a mistaken belief in power.

From the surrounding void she pulled every last degree of cold into herself until her skin actually tingled and her eyes sparked frost. The gray swirled around her once more, the grotesque shapes dissolving back to mist. She was ready at last, armored in ice and armed with her deviousness and her desire. And whatever might befall, when it was over, she would be free as never before, free from her lifelong reliance on the cold.

When she stepped into his presence, the silver flecks dropping around her ankles like a discarded gown, his eyes were already burning into her. Then he was upon her, claws reaching out to seize hold, fangs on her throat, and she threw herself into battle with all the abandon with which she had thrown herself into the cold.

The trail left by Mischa and the Figment was easy to follow; they might have fled from their companions, but there was no evidence that they had given the least thought to the possibility that they might actually be followed. Neither Timi nor Gyfree needed to comment that such negligence was unlike Mischa, for the glances they exchanged and the growing crease between Gyfree's eyes said it clearly enough. Whatever was happening, it seemed obvious that Mischa was far too absorbed in her new lover to pay much heed to anything else, and the occasional signs of amorous rest stops only further confirmed that Mischa truly wasn't herself.

At first the trail through the woods was meandering and unsure, but then suddenly it altered, shifting away from the Barrier toward the interior of Gyfree's world. As the three stood at the apparent turning point in Mischa's travels, Gyfree's eyes glazed out of focus, as if he was conversing with someone or something distant. When his gaze returned, the light in his eyes had noticeably dimmed. "According to the land," he announced, "they're heading toward the nearest town. And quickly." His eyes shifted to Timi's face. "Why the sudden change in course and speed?" he asked curtly.

"People," she whispered. "He wants to gain control over more people. Maybe he's growing tired of just Mischa. Or maybe she inadvertently mentioned that there were more people in this world than he's ever imagined. Either way, it's people he wants, and people he'll soon get in abundance if we can't catch up with him first."

"He won't really be able to enslave just anybody, will he?" Drew interjected. "His powers are limited, aren't they? After all, his control over the three of us was minimal."

Timi shook her head gently, as if correcting a small child. "The three of us were protected in ways he couldn't overcome. But there are many people in this world who will fall easy prey to his wiles. Look how easily he seduced Mischa. She is a strong-minded woman, and she thought she was in love with Gyfree, but her attachment was far too weak to make a difference. Only those with the most ardent and intimate sort of bonds will be immune. He can lure children from parents, friends from friends, and even some lovers from lovers. There will be more people he can captivate than those he can't." She met Gyfree's bleak gaze with one of her own. "How far ahead of us are they?"

"Much farther than they should be," he answered. "They're hours away from the nearest town. And at this rate, we won't catch up for at least two days."

"How is that possible?" Timi gasped.

"I don't know," Gyfree replied. "But they were only a few hours ahead of us when we started. Perhaps there are other talents your Figment possesses."

This time when Timi shook her head, she looked like a small child who had been asked to answer a question outside the realm of her simple understanding. "Not that I know of."

"Well," Gyfree grumbled, squeezing Drew's hand so tightly that she winced, "there's nothing we can do but follow, and hope that he doesn't do more damage than we can cope with."

Without another word, the three set off in the wake of the Figment's passing. Before long, however, all signs that anyone had traveled this way completely and abruptly vanished. The surrounding trees whispered to Gyfree that the path they followed was the path they sought, but there was no evidence other than the voice of the land to convince them that they weren't chasing insubstantial phantoms. It wasn't that someone had left a trail and then painstakingly covered any incriminating tracks. Gyfree knew every trick that Mischa knew; there simply were no tracks to cover up. No tracks at all. The others had passed this way, passed with incredible speed, and left no mark of their presence on the land, although the land had still marked their presence.

It was far into the night when the weary trackers finally stumbled to a halt. They had long ago broken free from the forest, and had spent the last hours wading through knee-high grasses that whispered soothingly to them as they staggered on. The sky had filled with a creamy yellow moon that indeed looked like a wedge of cheese suspended above, and its mellow glow had led them on until their legs could no longer support them. Beneath the yellow moon they had collapsed, and the long grasses had bent beneath them to cushion them from the hard ground, and had folded over them to cloak them against the chill of the air. They were too tired to even speak, and Drew hoped, too tired to dream. She snuggled into the silky grass and, with her hand tucked snugly into Gyfree's for the night, immediately fell asleep.

Forgotten in the backseat of a car, she watched as her parents sped through a misty countryside over an old brick road. Her heart clenched, for she knew this dream, had suffered through it innumerable times before, although she had not felt its grip for several years. Her parents were there, in the front seat, but they were too far away to touch, and growing farther away every second. Their eyes were on the road, on some unseen destination known only to them, some objective into which she did not figure. The car around her grew insubstantial, and despite the certain outcome, she tried desperately to find something to hold, groping around until suddenly there was no car beyond the front seat in which her parents still sat, their eyes fixed firmly ahead, never looking back as she fell to the pavement, never even realizing that she was gone. She sprawled where they had left her, watching them vanish as they had not watched her, and then they were gone, and she knew they were never coming back, for they never came back, and she would always be alone in this strange place, alone with no idea what to do.

"It doesn't have to be so bleak," a voice sounded behind her.

In a blink she was up on her feet and turning to face the source of the voice. A man stood before her, a man with twinkling blue eyes and a crooked smile, dark hair curling down his neck, hands deep in his pockets as he gazed down at her. "What doesn't have to be so bleak?" she questioned.

"This dream," he answered. "So what if they're gone? You never really needed them anyway; even when you were small you were quite independent. And you certainly don't need them now. For all you know, the reason they never look back is because you can't remember their faces."

Her eyes narrowed as she studied his friendly expression. "Who are you?" she asked. "And where am I?" *In a dream, but what dream?*

"Name's Sevor," he responded, the grin spreading across his face until she was certain his chin would fall away. "And you're here with me."

"Am I dreaming?" *Still her childhood nightmare, or a new dream, or perhaps a dream within the first dream?*

"Yes and no."

"What is that supposed to mean?" *Waiting to wake up, or just dreaming that it was possible to wake up when the only possible reality was just another dream?*

He shifted his weight from foot to foot and shrugged his shoulders. "A dream brought you here. But you're not asleep or dreaming anymore."

"Where's Gyfree?" *Not just a dream, please, not just a dream.*

"Looking for you. He should be here soon."

"What about Timi?" *Lost because of one dream, but maybe that was always how it started.*

"She needed a little nudging. And some help. But she'll get here eventually."

Drew stomped a foot for emphasis as she demanded, "And just where is here?" *And where was the other world, the dream world that seemed so real, that she wanted so desperately to be real?*

The slap of hurried footsteps on rough pavement pulled away Sevor's attention before he could answer, but Drew had already turned her face in the direction of the sound and didn't notice. Running down the road directly toward her was Gyfree, his rusty hair more disheveled than ever, his eyes black holes in his face, and his mouth a thin, hard line. He ran straight to her, grabbing her by the arms and pulling her close so that she could feel the trembling in his limbs. "You disappeared on me again," he mumbled into her hair. "How many times before I can't find you? Before you disappear completely?" His lips pressed into hers, and for a moment, this strange unidentified world fell away and they clung together, bodies so close they seemed like a single being dreaming a solitary dream.

Then a throat cleared nearby, and a friendly voice apologized, "Just thought I ought to remind you that you're not alone this time."

Gyfree raised his eyes to glare at the other man. "Where in the worlds are we?" he growled.

Sevor grinned even more broadly than before. "I've never been good at answering a lot of questions, so why don't we wait for the last of you to arrive so I can explain all at once?"

There was a shimmering in the air nearby, and then Timi was standing there, her skin translucent and her eyes awed. "I dreamed that I needed to find you," she whispered. "Am I really here? And where is here?"

Before anyone could respond, Sevor stepped forward and slapped Timi sharply across one cheek. Where his hand struck, her skin turned bright red, the outline of his fingers vivid on her flickering face. Like the poison from a Figment bite, the red laced through her skin, streaking out from each finger of color and spreading rapidly down her body until she glowed hotly from head to toe. Then as quickly as it had blossomed, the red receded, and Timi was left standing there as solidly as the rest of them, her skin a healthy and definitely opaque pink. "Sorry," apologized Sevor, "but you needed something to snap you awake and bring you fully here. There's just nothing like a good slap to bring someone to themselves."

"You still haven't explained where here is," Drew snapped impatiently. "Or who you are, for that matter."

"Told you, name's Sevor. You're in my world now. And I'm here to help you. Might even say I'm here to save the day."

"Did you bring us here?" Gyfree demanded.

"No, that's not in my power," Sevor answered, the grin still splitting his face as if he was barely containing his glee. "I just knew that Drew would dream herself here, and that you would follow. I had to nudge Timi so she would dream herself here after you, but each of you got here on your own."

"How did you know I would dream myself here? And how do you know who we are?" Drew questioned, frowning at Sevor from within the circle of Gyfree's arm.

"I'm a Dreamer in this world," Sevor answered, "but that means something different here. In my world, Dreamers don't dream something into reality; they dream of realities that already exist. Or that are on the verge of existing. And our strongest Dreamers sometimes dream of the realities that are unfolding in other worlds. I'm a very strong Dreamer, so I have dreamed often of all of you. I have seen you in my dreams, learned your names and watched your lives each night as I slept. And tonight when I dreamed, I saw you arriving here, so I woke myself up and rushed here to meet you. Because in my dream, I knew I must. You see, in my world, Dreamers never dream about themselves, but tonight I did, so I knew that after a lifetime filled with dreams of you, your reality would finally be mine as well."

Timi at last spoke up, "Are we fully here, or are we here in just a dream?"

"You're here all right. At least as best as I can tell. When Drew heard me speak, she pulled herself out of her dream and ended up here. When her hand vanished from his, Gyfree woke up and dreamed himself after her. And when I slipped into your dream, you dreamed yourself partially here. When I slapped you, your sleeping body followed your dreaming body and mind."

"How did you slip inside my mind?" Timi asked.

"I didn't really, but what happened is outside my normal experience, and I'm not really sure how best to explain it. I dreamed of you dreaming, and in my dream I saw that you would never find your way here unless you had help. Then in my dream I was suddenly beside you, shaking you by the shoulder and telling you what to do. I knew in my dream that you had somehow understood, and that your arrival had become as sure a reality as Drew's or Gyfree's. Yet no one from my world has ever influenced reality before, so I'm not sure how I helped dream you here, but I am sure that tonight my dreams showed me a new reality. A reality in which a Dreamer from my world could actually take part."

A crease folded Drew's forehead as she puzzled through Sevor's tangled string of words. "So Dreamers in your world only see things, but never take part in any of the things they dream?" she queried.

"That's right," Sevor confirmed.

"So how do you explain the fact that you, a Dreamer, are taking part in something you've dreamed?" Drew inquired.

Sevor's smile broadened. "Now that is the question, isn't it? Well, my answer, since I have had a little time to consider it, is that one of you dreamed me into your lives because I am the solution to a problem that has been nagging you all day. You didn't dream of me personally, or at least I don't believe you did. But you did dream that there would be some way to detach Mischa from the Figment. And here I am."

"How are you going to destroy the Figment's influence over her?" Gyfree demanded.

"You can't just destroy the Figment," Timi added. "If you do, you might kill Mischa, and any other people he's enslaved. If they are too enmeshed, they will die with him, simply because they have lost the will to live without him."

"I know," Sevor replied, and for the first time since they had encountered him, the smile faded slowly from his face. "As much as I would like to wring the Figment's neck, it just won't do any good. Back when you first asked Gyfree for help, it was still possible to destroy the Figment without real harm, but it's too late for such rough-and-ready action now. He has entangled Mischa so completely that for now she can't live without him. But the others he has enslaved since he left you should hopefully be a simpler matter. Since Mischa has filled most of his needs, his hold on them may not be as demanding. And even for Mischa, there's still a hope, a hope that I was surprised to see in my dreams."

"You haven't answered my question," Gyfree stated tersely. "How are you going to remove Mischa from the Figment?"

"There is only one thing that can save her," Sevor responded, his eyes suddenly as dark as Gyfree's. "She must form an attachment to another person strong enough to break the Figment's hold." He smiled again, but this time his face filled with pain and self-deprecation. "I have dreamed of Mischa for years now. I know her almost as well as I know myself. And I have loved her for a very long time. If I can make her love me back, then the Figment will lose his control. It may not be much of a hope, but it's the only one you have. And the only one, however impossible it has always seemed, that has lightened my entire life. That's why one of you dreamed me into your reality. I'm the one person with the will and the desire to win Mischa back from the Figment; the one person who will do whatever it takes. You might say I am exactly what the Dreamer ordered."

The fangs on her neck burned through the ice, sinking through layer after layer until the heat of their touch was against her skin and her blood was spurting into his mouth. On the surface she melted, groaning as his forked tongue slid across her skin, then slithered into her ear and across the delicate nerves at the base of her skull. His tongue and his fangs explored her face, licking away the ice from her eyes, gnawing the ice from her lips; then he was plunging into her open mouth like a diver indifferent to the threat of drowning. Like the sea she welcomed him, enfolding him within her coolness, sliding along his skin, clouding his eyes, filling his nose, threatening to steal the air hidden in his lungs. Yet just as she drew him in, he also drew her. The taste of smoke filled her mouth, its texture rich on her tongue, and careless of consequences, she slipped her icy tongue through his razor teeth so she might sate herself on the flavor. As their tongues entangled, fire and ice together, he too groaned, amorous flames bursting from his skin as her icy nails slid across his shoulders and trailed glacial paths down his sides to rest against his powerful hips. In urgency his claws scattered slivers of ice as he raked them down her back to clutch her buttocks and pull her against him so that she might feel the burning and throbbing need that drove him. Sliding a thigh between his two, she deliberately drew up her knee, pressing her frosty flesh against the spot where he burned the hottest, until his entire body erupted into new and brilliant flames. Then his massive arms were swinging her off the ground and flames were caressing her as he held her high, his tongue thawing the snowy crevice between her breasts, his fangs grazing the chilly slopes.

She had him now, had pushed him beyond the point of caution. She wrapped her arms around his stooped neck, running her fingers through the flames sprouting from his head, her body arching in his hold. Then they were both plunging through the writhing swirls of gray, his body heavy and pressing down, his thighs demanding, her thighs wrapping around his heaving hips. It was this moment she had waited for, this moment when she must hold to the inner ice, this moment when she must watch her prey closely so she might know when to pounce.

His lips closed on hers, his fangs pressing down as fiercely as his body, his breath filling her mouth with sparks, his need everything she had ever desired. As he took her she clung desperately to the ice buried deep inside, her inner fingers scrambling urgently to maintain their hold. His need, and her own suppressed needs, almost swept her away, but her most secret ice froze to her slipping fingers, and when at last he groaned and fell limply against her, she knew that she had won. But there would be little time before he would return fully to himself, little time to take full advantage of her victory, so she must act quickly.

Even as she lay beneath him, she cast her invisible self forward, not through the void or into some distant world, but into and through the mind and being of her sated lover. It would now be an easy task to find and seize hold of his most inner flame, to capture it, to take everything that made him who and what he was, and to make it her own, so that she could be everything that she had always been, and everything that he had been as well, so that she could become more than she had ever been before, could finally become even more than him. Changeable whenever she chose, unalterable whenever she chose, from now on she would have no limits, would be anything and everything she had ever wanted to be. Ice and fire. It was hard to resist either, but impossible to resist both. And from this time forward no one and nothing would be able to resist or withstand her again.

She plunged through the inner flames, but something seemed wrong. It wasn't as easy as it should have been. She had been here before, the last time he had taken her, for even though she had then allowed herself to be carried away, she had returned before he had. So she had delved within his being, not with anything specific in mind, but out of simple curiosity. And in the quiet before his return, she had found the heart of the fire, had seen it and recognized it for what it could do. She had been mesmerized by its heat, by its enduring hunger, and she had forgotten everything in that moment, forgotten to slip back into her own body and shift her face back to the icy one he expected, and not the hideous one that her passion had exposed. His howl of anger had brought her back to herself, but too late, for he knew at last that she had tricked him, knew that she wasn't his icy counterpart, the frozen version of his immutable fiery self as she had claimed, and his anger had been more violent than any she could have envisioned, violent enough to make even her shiver.

It had seemed as if it was too late for her then, too late to hold on to the lover she would always desire, and far too late to claim that glorious hidden fire that was more precious than even his most ardent embrace. Yet she had been patient, working her way slowly back into his attention, tempting him with the icy beauty he still craved, watching and waiting for the perfect opportunity to take him, everything that was him, and make it her own. And she had succeeded; he had fallen silent against her, his passion spent, and she had returned to claim what she had earned. But it was wrong, all wrong. There was smoke everywhere, blinding her vision, and flames rioting out of control. There was no clear path as there had been before, but instead a maze of burning tunnels that turned her around, confusing her even more than the smoke.

It only took a moment for her to realize that she was lost, that she was trapped, before she felt his claws digging into her body's arms, and then from an insurmountable distance she could see his eyes burning down into her vacant ones, could hear him growl, "So that was what you wanted. I knew not to trust you, but you forgot to distrust me." Something within her body stirred, and she realized that he had not sated himself after all; he had waited, as patiently as she had always waited, holding his own passion in rein so that he could lay a clever trap for her. He moved now, moved against her, and she was too far from her own core of ice to take hold. This time he carried her body as far as it could go and there was nothing she could do to stop him; he carried her inner self to the heart of his hidden fire and dropped her there, and as both her selves thrashed in delight, he reached in and seized everything that made her who and what she was. And made it his own.

Chapter 9

There was no need to wonder which of them had dreamed Sevor into their company; it didn't really matter, for he was with them now, and the real question was how all of them would proceed from here, wherever here might be. Yet while the others pondered their next step, Drew wandered to the rough brick road that she had seen so many times in her dreams. There had once been a road like this that she had touched as a child, and not, she was almost certain, in a dream. It had been outside her great-grandmother's house, a house that she associated with nightmares because they had always visited her in great number the few times she had visited there. It was a house heavy with history, and for her, heavy with ghosts. A house where she was never alone, even if the corners of the room were sprayed by sunlight and seemingly empty of life. When she had looked into the fading eyes of her great-grandmother, she felt as if they alone shared the same vision of this house. The old woman's eyes were full of phantoms, her gaze far away as she wandered through a world that only she could see, and only her visiting great-granddaughter could share. Looking back over the years, Drew finally realized that the old woman, swaying forlornly in her rocking chair, oblivious of her surroundings, was not the senile fool that the other adults whispered her to be. She was a Dreamer, just like her great-granddaughter, a Dreamer who had populated her house with the wisps and fragments of her dreams, a Dreamer who had lived so many years in a world that never felt like home, a Dreamer who was living out her dwindling days wandering wherever her last dreams might lead.

Yet there were more dreams haunting that house than could be accounted for by one old Dreamer's presence. Perhaps there had been other Dreamers who had lived and died in that old house; perhaps slave women who had climbed the narrow, winding back stairs with their hands full of laundry or balancing a tray of food and their eyes full of green meadows or of themselves balancing gracefully in the deep curtsey reserved for the indolent Southern belles. Perhaps there had even been other Dreamers in her family, women who had chafed beneath their petticoats and rehearsed manners, chafed for another world that existed only in their dreams. And like her great-grandmother, all of them, slave and belle alike, had never known escape, had never slipped beyond the house and run free down the rough brick road to see where it might lead. Instead they had filled the house with the ghosts of everything that had eluded them in life, and had left these bits and pieces of longing to haunt any future Dreamer who might pass this way. They had haunted her great-grandmother, and while Drew had slept beneath the same roof that had once sheltered them, they had haunted her as well, slipping into her dreams, wailing softly, chasing her to the edge of a cliff and waiting for her to plunge off. And she had always snapped awake crying, tangled in blankets on the floor by her bed, her eyes darting into the now darkened corners for the movement of a graceful hand or the turn of a gently curving cheek.

Her dreams in that house had been especially vivid, and had followed her throughout the years of her childhood, but the most common of these dreams had always ended with the rough brick road looming before her, its weathered face watchful, as if it was waiting for her parents to desert her so she could finally walk its surface unhindered. And as the uneven pavement stretched before her now, she understood what had haunted her dreams while she slept in that house with the old woman whose eyes were infinitely sad and distant, and she knew why she had cried each time she had opened her own eyes and found herself on the cold, hard floor. All of those Dreamers had wanted to escape, had wanted to slip away into the worlds they dreamed, but they had failed, each and every one. So they had waited, or at least the bits of themselves they had dreamed into life and then left behind waited, and they had watched for other Dreamers, for a Dreamer like her who might one day step from the safety of the cliff and plummet not to death, but into a dream that did not end on the floor beside the bed. And she had cried because she had wanted it as badly for herself as they had wanted it for her, had even jumped from the cliff willingly as they stood by and watched, and had been heartbroken when she had opened her eyes on the same walls and shadows that had bound them, and bound them still.

So little had changed since those childhood dreams, although the house had passed from the hands of her family when the old woman had died, and the brick road had been torn up to make room for a flat gray strand; so little had changed, for she still wanted to escape, and more than anything, she feared opening her eyes to find herself tangled in blankets beside her empty bed. So little had changed, except for the fact that this time, her parents a distant memory even before they drove away, she was ready to see where the lonely road might lead.

She felt Gyfree as he stepped up beside her, felt him even before he slipped his fingers through hers. It was not, however, his voice that sounded.

"You know, that road was never here before," Sevor announced as he stepped forward to stand at her other side.

Drew raised her eyes from the road to glance up at his face. "I dreamed it here?" she asked, although the answer was already in not just his eyes, but also her own.

"It's your dream, so who else could have done it?"

"Have you dreamed of what lies at the end of this road?"

He shrugged his shoulders, but his eyes glinted as mischievously as Mischa's had when Drew had first seen her. "Not yet."

"Let's find out," Drew insisted, setting a foot upon the road.

"We don't have time," Timi protested frantically. "We have to get back to our world as quickly as possible if we want to stop my Figment."

Drew looked at the other woman, and at the sight of the age-old phantoms flitting through the Dreamer's eyes, Timi grew silent. "This road has always been in my dreams so that it could one day take me where I most wanted to go," whispered Drew.

"Where is that?" Gyfree asked, an anxious edge to his voice, his fingers tight on hers.

"Your world," Drew murmured, her eyes afloat with all those bits and pieces of the dreams of dead women.

"But Gyfree is still connected to our world," Timi said softly, her eyes uncertain. "He can carry us all back in a flash, just as he claims he did when you found my Figment."

"Back to where we started," Drew breathed. "But this road was dreamed to take me wherever I wanted to go. Wherever I was brave enough to go. And this time that means straight to the Figment, wherever he might be." A ghostly smile drifted across her face, the same smile she had once seen flit over her great-grandmother's lips. "We all came here, leaving nothing of ourselves behind. It would be such a waste to go backward instead of forward." The cliff awaits, sighed the dead women. And this time when she jumped, she intended to land exactly where she dreamed.

Without another word, Drew placed her second foot onto the road, its surface warm and inviting even through the soles of her shoes. One by one the others followed, Gyfree walking at Drew's side while Sevor and Timi trailed a few steps behind, the road stretching before them full of a promise that, after untold lifetimes, would finally be kept.

She had always arrived in a swirl of silver flecks, her exquisite face emerging as if conjured by some wonderful magic, her perfect form stepping from the mist like a dream come to life. Not a nightmare come to life, like him, but a beautiful, heart-stopping dream. Now the silver motes danced across the ground like wayward dust, dissipating slowly into the endless gray until there was no silver left to be seen, and no beauty to disappear with it into the void. Her body had dissolved into those silver flecks, so at last he knew the silver, like the ice he had found deep within her, had not been her invention. Even the beautiful face, the one he had so mistrusted, had been real. It was the one she had been created with, and the other face, the hideous one that had driven him away, was the mask she had gained over time. The mask provided a face of passion for one who had been born free from all passions, a face of greed for one born too cold for its taint, a face that spoke of betrayal only because she had herself been so often betrayed. He knew now, as he had never suspected before, that she had begun in innocence, just as he had begun in innocence, and that they both had understood too late that they had been born not from love or need, but from fear. It had driven them to hatred; it had consumed them with the need to destroy those who feared them long before they were something to fear.

Long ago she had sought him out and seduced him with the promise that they were two of a kind, and despite the shifting features that had revealed her deception, she had been right. He now knew that even when she had tried to deceive, every lie she had used had been based on truth, whether she knew it or not. They had indeed been kindred, the two most powerful Figments created by one world's most powerful Dreamers. They belonged together, for together they would be stronger than either could be alone. Only together could they accomplish their goals; only together could they kill their Dreamers and break free from the limits that thwarted them. She had wanted to bring them together, and had resorted at last to the one thing she thought would successfully combine their powers into one. And she had been right. He knew she had been right, for he held her inside himself now, held all of her memories, her thoughts, her desires, her fears, and most of all, her power. Everything that had once been hers, had once been her, was now his. The two of them were together almost exactly as she had envisioned. The only thing she had failed to envision was that together they would wear his face and speak with his voice and live in his body, that he would be her master whether she agreed or not, for without him, she would never see, or speak, or feel again.

Fire and ice sparked in his eyes, and at last he could see through both. The fire was an old friend, and he had seen its view of things many times before. But the ice was new, and it showed him things he had never suspected, taught him things he had never imagined. Everything she had ever known, he now knew, so he knew why she had needed his help to slip into the world harboring his Dreamer, for it had for years harbored her Dreamer as well, and just like him, she had watched and waited for an opportunity to slay the being who had dreamed her to life and then kept her at a distance much greater than arms' length. He could see it all now, see it just as she had seen it, could see it all unfold in her memory with the fuzzy overcast of a cheap home video. He could even see her as she sprang to life, a small ice maiden with a finely sculpted face, could see the rusty-haired wide-eyed child screaming in a room full of other children, could see the lights flashing on to chase the icy young vision away. He could see her wandering through the worlds of dream and void, lost and without purpose, until the one day she had been found by a Figment with slathering jaws and wild eyes. This Figment had befriended her, had told her they were two of a kind, had kept her company as they wandered together, had taught her about the worlds of waking, of dreaming, had taught her the ways of the void. Then he had begged her to help him kill the Dreamer who had brought him to life, to slip her exquisite face into the Dreamer's dream, and to entice him into her cold arms. Then, the Figment told her, he would emerge for the kill, but it could not be until then because if the Dreamer detected his presence too soon, he would awaken from the dream.

The thought of killing a Dreamer was new to her, but she agreed readily enough simply because her friend had asked, and she had slipped into the Dreamer's dream, and had stood there, her breathtaking face touched by a smile, her tiny arms open. The Dreamer had been bewitched, had not been able to tear his dream eyes from her perfect face, had reached out dreaming and taken her in his arms. But the other Figment had not appeared as he had promised, and she was left alone in the strange Dreamer's dream, his suddenly cold and lifeless body stiffening in her arms. The dream faded around her, and she found herself in the waking world, standing by the bedside of a dead man with blue skin, his arms frozen as if something precious lay in his embrace. She had freed the Figment, freed him without knowing that she would be the one to kill, freed him and then never seen him again, for she had served the sole purpose for which he had befriended her.

Yet she had learned from him, and most importantly, had learned that a Dreamer could be killed. She had watched her Dreamer before, watched him with longing and even with love, but now her watching began to change. He had made her beautiful, but he had also made her deadly, and if her beauty was not enough to win his love, then perhaps her deadliness would win his life. It was true that she had not enjoyed killing, and that the thought of killing him was still more than she could tolerate, but now as she watched, and now as she waited, she began to think of the unthinkable a little more each day.

Other Figments befriended her as she waited and watched, but these were no different than the first, and in time she realized that for everyone who saw her she had one purpose only: to seduce with her beauty and to slay with her touch. For them she killed, and killed often, because she hated being alone, yet after each killing she was more alone than before, for each killing set her apart, and it wasn't long before she was a Figment feared by others. In time, she would be feared by all others except one, all except him. He knew now why she had deceived him, for she had learned that it was the only sure way to get what she wanted. And she had wanted him, had wanted him almost as much as she had wanted her Dreamer, and she had played every trick she had learned simply so he would take her in his arms, take her and burn her, take her and not feel the cold that her Dreamer had created in her core.

But it was long before she and he had met, long after she had decided that the unthinkable was thinkable after all. So many had died in her arms, that one more would seem like nothing, even if that one more was the Dreamer she both adored and abhorred. She would stand before him and risk everything. If he smiled she would disappear, unwilling to harm him. But if he frowned, if he turned to run, she would pursue him until he had been wrapped in her lethal arms. She still waited, still watched, but now with a purpose in mind, and for the perfect opportunity. She didn't want one of his nightmares, for if she slipped into one of those he would already be predisposed to flee; she wanted one of his rare pleasant dreams so that the test would be fair. And at last such a dream unfolded, and she slipped into its folds slowly so he wouldn't startle as she suddenly took shape. She had approached so carefully, the smile on her face gentle and pleading, her eyes and her hair and her skin shimmering with bright silver flecks, and he had looked at her through dream eyes filled with horror, and he had run. There had been a moment when she almost crept away in defeat, but then she remembered the look in his eyes, the look that acknowledged nothing of her beauty, and she chased him just as she had promised herself she would.

Never before had she been required to run after her prey, and she realized almost immediately that he was better at fleeing than she was at chasing, but now that she had taken the first step, she refused to stop until she had finished the last. She chased him all through his dream, breaking through walls that sprang

up between them, never losing sight of her prey. She chased
him until out of the grayness that marked both dream and void
there appeared a bright point of light. Her Dreamer dashed for
the light, his small form swallowed by a flash of brilliance as he
dived into its corona. Wherever he had gone, she was determined
to follow, so she too dove through the light.

The landscape of a dream vanished, and she found herself in
the teeming streets of a waking town. People were milling wildly
about as if something unprecedented had just happened and they
were uncertain whether to be excited or terrified. A particularly
noisy group swarmed at the edge of the growing crowd, and
there in their midst stood a small, rusty-haired boy with darkly
frightened eyes attached to her exquisite face. As they stood there
and faced each other in the dawning light of a young day, and
she saw more clearly than ever before the fear and revulsion in
his eyes, something deep inside of her shifted, like two blocks
of ice slipping against each other, and her entire body quaked.
Let him fear her, she decided. Let him really fear her, and have
good reason for his fear.

Without even removing her eyes from his stricken face, she
reached out and seized the person nearest her, touching a pounding heart with her little lethal hands. Like a whirlwind of ice
she tore through the crowd, touching and killing all in her path,
littering the street with ice-cold corpses as she worked her way
in his direction. All around her the people scrambled to escape,
trying to break through the bodies pressing in from all sides,
knocking against each other in their frenzy to flee the beautiful
and merciless specter of death in their midst. She gloried in her
newfound power, gloried in the frantic fear that she had brought
to this sunny world, and she even laughed as the people ran each
other down in their haste to escape. Those who had been trampled
by their fellows fell victim to her as she moved toward where the
boy still waited as if spellbound, for she deliberately stepped on
them with her icy little feet until they were colder and harder
than the ground to which they had tumbled. No longer was it a
chore to kill, an unpleasant task that she had learned to merely
tolerate; killing was an unexpected joy, a thrill that shivered down
her icy spine. Death was far sweeter than she had realized before,
far sweeter than anything else she had ever tasted.

She was upon him now, standing face to face, and she raised

her hand slowly, relishing the moment in advance, raised it and held it just a fraction above the space where his heart raged wildly in his chest. The eyes that looked into hers were no longer frightened, but sad, so oppressively sad, that she faltered, and in that moment she lost him. With a suddenness and ferocity that threw her to the ground, the land beneath her feet heaved and bucked like an animal that feels the claws of a predator piercing its hide. She was thrown back to the spot where she had started, thrown over the layer of dead bodies that shrouded the ground to land in a heap in the dirt, ice flaking from her skin to drift to the ground like new-fallen snow. How long she sprawled there stunned she had no idea, but when she scrambled back to her feet and again raised her eyes toward the spot where she could feel him still standing, there was a man looming at his back, a man with tears rolling unchecked down his cheeks as he held the lifeless body of a boy in his arms.

"Enough!" boomed the man, and in his voice it seemed she could hear the very ground beneath her feet and the sky above her head crying out, could hear the shriek of distant trees and the rumble of mountains. "There will be no more killing! No more deaths like the death of my son! The land has chosen me as its Keeper, has chosen me to expel you, and with the help of the land, that is exactly what I intend to do." Laying the dead body gently on the ground, he crouched for a second, tears spilling from his face to the still one at his feet, and then, head still bowed, he lifted his hands toward her, palms facing out, and a storm of green slammed into her body, pushing her relentlessly back step by step until she could feel the light slipping past her skin and the darkness of her Dreamer's deserted dream reaching out to pull her back.

She plummeted through the layers of the dream, falling forever through the endless gray, but she did not fall alone. Somewhere behind her she could feel her Dreamer falling too, could feel that he had been banished just as had she, and she exulted for he had not escaped her after all. She knew what she must next do, and even as she fell she carefully laid her plans. When she landed at the beginning of his dream, she didn't stay. She was done with the usual watching and waiting. With all her strength she flung herself into the nearby waking world and leaned over the drab metal-framed bed where his small body tossed and turned, and taking a deep breath of the air that hung heavy with his scent, she placed her hand on his thumping heart. As her hand brushed against him, his eyes flew open, and there in the dark, in a room lined with other dingy little beds, they stared at the ice in each other's eyes. And then he was gone, the bed beneath her empty, and she could feel him as he fled through the gray, single in body and mind, back toward that distant light.

Despite the Keeper who would assuredly be waiting beyond that light, she plunged after her Dreamer, and this time she knew she had the advantage, for she was accustomed to traversing the realms of dream and void, and he had never been here before other than when dreaming. Yet even now he was not as power-less as he seemed, for each time she thought she had him within her grasp, her hands were slapped away by something unseen, as if he carried a phantom guardian strapped across his back. Even awake, he was a vivid Dreamer, and able to dream her at bay. She was kept an icy breath away as he sped once more toward the light, and this time when they burst together into the other world, the Keeper was waiting, tears still streaking his face, his mouth compressed as grimly as an executioner's.

The Dreamer scurried forward to cower behind the Keeper's back, but she stood defiantly facing him, ice streaming from her eyes and her lips more grimly frozen than his. Again he raised his hands, and again the green slammed into her, but this time she was prepared, and as the green met the ice it parted and fell lifelessly to the ground. Another wave of green swept over her, but it too was repelled and nullified by the ice. Again the Keeper struck at her, and again, but each onslaught was easier to ignore than the one before. After a while, she stepped forward, a smile creeping coldly up her face, her own hands lifting as silver flecks flew from her fingers in a miniature blizzard. She knew that she could kill this Keeper, this man new to his power, and that her Dreamer would have nowhere left to run. Her fingers curled in anticipation and shards of blue crashed through her eyes as she moved ever closer to the man who stood motionless before her, green light outlining his fingers and shining in his tears. She had almost reached him, almost tasted his death on her tongue, when the Dreamer stepped from behind his back and took the man's hand in his own.

The boy faced her, his chin lifted high, his eyes like stone. He looked directly into her eyes, looked at her as if he understood her at last, looked at her as if she was everything that he most despised, and suddenly she was frozen in place by those young, implacable eyes. The clasped hands of the Dreamer and Keeper lifted together, and this time a stream of ice-laced green slammed into her, and it was colder and more piercing than even she could bear. Somehow he was using her own nature against her, using a cold more cruel than she had ever been to slice through her icy shield so the power of the land could drive her backward, step by unwilling step, and try as she might, there was nothing she could do to counter the force her Dreamer had brought against her. Ice squeezed through her pores as she fought him, but it was hopeless, and she knew it was hopeless. Soon she was back to the light, its glow filling her eyes and its presence roaring in her ears, and then she was alone in the gray of either the void or a dream; at that moment she didn't quite know which, nor did she care, for in the end they were much alike to a Figment hurt and alone.

For a long time she wandered forlornly through the gray, and for a while she could still sense her Dreamer on the other side of the Barrier that enclosed his new world, could even sense the strange course his life had taken. She knew that the Keeper had adopted him as his son, could sense that he finally had found a home, and that though there were many in that world who feared him, there were also many who loved and admired him. Unlike her, he was far from alone. Solitary, perhaps, but not completely alone. He was not fully happy, but he was not fully unhappy either, and much of the pain that had shaped his dreams and brought her to life was gone. Most importantly, however, she could sense the memory of her held strongly in his mind, so strongly that whenever she neared the Barrier the force of his awareness turned against her to thrust her away again. She waited, but her presence within his mind only strengthened over time, and the moment came when she was closed off from him completely, when she could no longer sense anything of him at all. It was then, and only then, that she turned back into the populated pockets of the void. And it was then that she finally met her future lover, finally met a Figment more terrifying than she had yet been, finally met someone or something worthy of her desire.

He knew now how deeply she had wanted him, just as he

had always deeply wanted her. And they had each other at last, had each other in a way that neither had suspected when her icy eyes had first met his fiery ones, when her frigid skin had first steamed against his. He could feel her now, feel her stirring deep within, moved by the very memories that he had probed so closely. She was gone from his embrace, would never return to his arms, but she was as alive and aware as she had ever been. Her voice whispered within him, no longer seductive or deceptive, for it seemed too late for passion, and she would never again be able to keep anything secret from him. So she whispered instead an idea, and as she whispered, he too knew exactly what must be done. They would have their Dreamers, would use all of the power and deceit that they now shared, and would finally bring their Dreamers to death. Given the new strength he and she had gained together, they could easily conquer any world without their Dreamers stopping them, but this had never been simply about power, never been solely about escaping limitations. This was about death, about revenge, about hatred. This was about tearing out the hearts of those who had failed to love them, about punishing them for every disappointment that existence had dealt their creations. This was about the joy of killing, a joy they had each known apart, and the only real joy they had left to share.

The brick road was rough underfoot, and it curved ahead as far as the eye could follow. In the waking world it would have eventually circled back over itself, but it was a dream road and its tendency to veer continually to the left did not keep it from carrying them perpetually forward. It had always curved in Drew's dreams, and so it curved here, yet at the same time it carried them straight toward their destination, just as it had always carried her parents straight away from her. Down this road she walked, Gyfree by her side and Timi and Sevor a few steps behind. Soon the stately trees lining the road faded away and the ground to the sides vanished until it seemed as if they were traveling through a heavy, gray fog that no light could ever penetrate. To the sides and above there was nothing but swirling eddies of gray, yet the road still stretched ahead as clearly as before, its bend to the left as marked now as it had been the moment they had set forward.

Timi and Sevor stared wide-eyed out into the gray as if they expected something monstrous to lunge at them and swallow them whole, and then in unspoken agreement edged closer to the two Dreamers in the lead. Around them the gray twisted into shapes that would one moment seem hauntingly familiar, but would then dissipate before a name could be given to whatever had seemed to lurk there. None of the elusive shapes ever evoked the sense that they were something either comforting or welcome, but since no hint of gray ever intruded upon the road itself, in time even Timi grew accustomed to the gray forms dancing in the corners of her eyes.

No one was certain how much time had passed when the ghostly shapes of trees began to emerge once more from the gray, and pale brown earth again materialized beside the ruddy bricks. The four walked on without speaking, but the sound of their footsteps striking the rough pavement grew louder and quicker, and soon the trees began to solidify and the ground to burgeon with the green of living things. A pink-streaked sky broke through from above, pushing the gray aside like a visitor who had overstayed his welcome, and as the companions glanced up, they could see the sun just beginning to peek over the tops of the trees. A cool finger of breeze slipped through the leafy branches to caress their faces, and on the breeze was the perfume of woodsmoke and cooking food. The road veered left into a thick copse of trees directly ahead, and as the four entered the shadowy thicket, they suddenly found soft earth beneath their feet. When Drew glanced over her shoulder, the brick road that had carried them here was nowhere to be seen.

"There's a town just beyond these trees," Gyfree announced as the last wisps of a dream seemed to fade from his eyes. "We'll find both Mischa and the Figment there."

The eager light that blazed in Sevor's eyes at the mention of Mischa's name was extinguished with the introduction of the Figment. His mouth set in determination, he snapped, "What are we waiting for? We have things to do here, and little enough time to do them."

Without another word, the four companions moved from the shelter of the trees and out onto the open path. There before them was a small cluster of homes that made Drew pause in the midst of a step, and blink as if she needed to loosen the sleep from her eyes. The houses scattered before her were both hauntingly familiar and disturbingly foreign. They reminded her of the many houses that she had lived in as a child, always different yet always the same, as if each wore a slightly varying mask over the exact same face. As she had grown older she had reached the conclusion that it mattered little where she lived, for the entire country she had spent her life in was filled with one endless string of uniform tract homes that only pretended to be individual and apart. Whatever the mask, underneath it was always the same: same dusty living room, same constricting bedrooms, same dimly lit bathrooms, same cramped kitchen, same barren feeling as if no one had ever lived there before, and no one really lived there yet. To her the houses she inhabited were just like the people she encountered: vaguely dissimilar on the outside, disturbingly similar on the inside, and somehow, in the end, vaguely unreal. The only real house was the one in which her great-grandmother lived, and the only real person was the dreaming old woman with the faraway eyes.

Even the streets each house had occupied had been much the same, lined with the occasional scraggly tree and the same threadbare lawns, with the same cars crouched in the same driveways beneath their own facades of uniqueness. The only real street had been the one paved with rough red brick, and that was a street that had never been built for cars even though cars were known to trespass often. And that was what felt so disturbingly unfamiliar here. The houses were the same as all the houses she had ever known, but the street was not the same street at all. No cars parked there, in driveways or next to sidewalks, for there were no driveways, no sidewalks, no pavement at all. Each house had been set down in the middle of green grass, grass more green and full than the faded and overmowed lawns of her memory, and each was surrounded by towering trees that seemed to hold their branches over the roofs as if protecting those within from any chance elements. The houses were also spaced much farther apart than those she had known, but at the same time they seemed much closer, for their porches formed the sides of a large semicircle and their front doors all angled outward as if trying to keep in touch with each other; there was a distinct feeling that they all belonged together, had chosen somehow to share this space, and had not been thrown up one on top of the other by some impersonal force that was indifferent to the prospects of strangers listening to each other fight and love, shout and cry and sometimes whisper, in a house that truly was right next door.

Out of one of these familiar yet alien houses a gray-haired man rushed, his hands outstretched, a tiny, beaming woman on his heels. "Gyfree, lad!" boomed the man. "We were expecting your father, not you. The trees have been whispering since before the sun came up that the Keeper was on his way, and I must say, we certainly need some help here. The strangest things have been happening ever since Mischa and that young man showed up yesterday."

The round-faced woman pushed the man aside and threw her arms around Gyfree's waist, giving him a quick hug and smiling up into his face. "It's not often we get visits from you and your father, at least not anymore, like we did when you were just a little lad. Are you traveling together? Have you come on ahead to tell us he was on his way? You should know that the trees would be so excited that we couldn't help but hear their news."

Gyfree returned the woman's hug, but there was no smile on his face and his eyes were like dark pits of quicksand in his face. "My father is dead," he announced sharply. "Killed by two Figments."

The color washed from the man's face and his hands trembled, but the surrounding trees only sighed. "But the trees . . ." the man faltered.

"The trees were telling you that I was coming. The land has chosen me as the new Keeper," Gyfree finished for him.

The woman lifted a hand to gently cup the face scowling above her. "Poor lad," she murmured. "So much pain to bear, and then such a large burden on top of it."

"Aren't you worried about my selection as Keeper?" Gyfree snarled. "Mischa certainly was."

"Of course not!" the man exclaimed, his eyes equally filled with sorrow and surprise. "We know you, lad. We feel your connection to this land. In our opinion, you were the only and obvious choice to replace your father once he was gone. We are saddened by the loss of our old, dear friend, but there is nothing to cause us concern."

"Actually, there is much to cause you concern," Gyfree retorted, but the hard edge had left his voice and his eyes had lightened to their usual luminous brown.

"Let's discuss whatever we need to discuss inside," the woman interrupted. "I have a feeling you're all in need of breakfast and a chance to get off your feet. And you can introduce us to your friends once you're all comfortable and warm."

Gyfree actually smiled, and so did the sunny little woman as she slyly watched his fingers close over Drew's.

"Excuse me," Timi interrupted, "but where is Mischa and the ... man she's with? We need to find them as soon as possible."

The woman turned her sly smile to Timi. "Don't worry, child," she replied gently. "They will be right at your fingertips as soon as you get a little rest."

"Where are they?" insisted Timi.

"Why, they're locked in the back room of our house," answered the man. "Along with several young people from this town and those two giant creatures who flew them here."

"Giant creatures?" echoed Gyfree and Drew.

"Call themselves hummeybees," the man explained.

"They're big," exclaimed Drew, "but I wouldn't describe them as giant!"

"Well, young lady, I don't know how big something has to be before you can call it giant, but those things are pretty darn close. At least they were when they arrived. They were as big as me, after all, and although I'm no giant, I'm also not some strange creature flying through the skies and carrying a person between my legs. After they got here, they shrank back down to about the size of my fist, but I still can't help seeing them like they were the first time I set eyes on them."

Gyfree and Drew exchanged worried frowns. "Mischa isn't a Dreamer, is she?" asked Drew.

Gyfree simply shook his head.

"Her ... companion couldn't dream something into reality, could he?" Drew pursued.

"No," Gyfree answered firmly, although his eyes churned with uncertainty. "But we know almost nothing about the hummeybees: what they are, what powers they possess, what harm they are truly capable of doing. All we know is that they seem to be completely loyal to the ... Mischa's friend."

"Enough!" briskly chided the woman, directing a mock frown at the entire group. "Inside now, all of you! Mischa and her man and those hummeybee things are going nowhere, so let's move along and get you some food. And don't tell me you're not hungry, because you have to be. What you're doing wandering around without a single pack amongst you is a mystery to me."

With a look of shocked dismay, Gyfree glanced over his shoulder, only to find that he was in fact carrying nothing at all.

Sevor politely cleared his throat. "Since you all came to my world dreaming, you weren't exactly paying attention to the more mundane details of life," he clarified.

The couple's eyes widened, but the smiles on their faces remained welcoming. "Inside, now, all of you," the woman scolded, and like obedient children they allowed themselves to be steered in the direction of the house and through the door.

As she passed over the threshold, the floor seemed to suddenly shift beneath Drew's feet and she reached instinctively for something to grab onto and steady herself. Yet the moment she faltered, or perhaps even the moment before, Gyfree was there, a strong arm wrapping around her waist to keep her on her feet. She leaned against him as if he was the only solid reality in her world, as if her own continued existence relied on him holding her near. She was only vaguely aware that the others had passed farther into the house, and that she and Gyfree stood completely alone in the entryway, was only vaguely aware that the others were even alive. There was Gyfree, and there was her, and there were the fluctuating corridors of a dream house crisscrossing before her. Then there were lips, warm and pulsing with life, and they were parting hers, and there was breath, his breath, steaming in her mouth, and a sweet flavor, his flavor, tingling on her tongue. She closed her eyes as his mouth plunged farther into hers, and then his mouth was gone, and she opened her eyes to the golden brown alive in his. A faint smile ghosted over Gyfree's mouth, and she noticed that his lips were as flushed as hers felt. "Sorry," he mumbled, "but I know what effect these houses have on me, and I was hoping a little distraction would help both of us adjust."

With difficulty, Drew moved her lips and tongue in a way that had nothing to do with a kiss. "Shouldn't we be joining the others?" she asked hoarsely.

"In a minute," he answered, his lips hovering just above hers, his breath warming her cheeks. "Our hosts know how I react every time I visit, so they expect me to take a while before I make it all the way inside." His lips brushed hers again, and her own responded as if this was the real purpose for which they had been created, and the only purpose worth serving. The two Dreamers clung together, neither feeling the walls swaying around them nor the floor shivering beneath their feet, alone in a world that felt like a dream even though they were not necessarily dreaming, as a room full of others ate and chatted nearby. After some time, Gyfree again lifted his head, his breath speeding now across her cheeks, his eyes a bit wild and his hair far more disheveled than usual. "I think we should probably join everyone before they decide to come find us," he whispered.

Drew lifted a finger and trailed it around his lips. "Not that I have the slightest objection to your solution, but what is the problem with this place that there was the need to resort to such rough-and-ready action?"

Gyfree nipped playfully at her finger before answering. "I don't know exactly why, but buildings this close to the Barrier have always felt tenuous and unreal, at least to me. They've never had that effect on anyone else, at least not until now."

Drew nodded in understanding. "It feels almost like stepping into someone else's dream. It's a bit unsettling." She clung to him as another wave of dizziness shook her. "Does it ever go away?"

"No, but you'll get used to it," he assured her.

A voice called from somewhere within the house. "Gyfree! Young lady! Where are you? You've had plenty of time to adjust!"

Gyfree grimaced as he once more clasped Drew's fingers firmly in his own. "We're coming," he called as he led her down the snaking hallway and into a room that seemed alternately huge and tiny, its walls receding and then closing in as if some giant heart pulsed around the people gathered there.

"There you are," the woman announced with a twinkle as she jumped up to herd the two Dreamers to a table that blinked in and out of existence beneath Drew's eyes. "Now sit and eat. Timi and Sevor have very politely introduced themselves, and have been amazing us with the story of what all of you young people have been up to."

Drew gulped at the bucking and rippling chairs circling the table, then squeezing her eyes shut as Gyfree squeezed her hand, slid into a chair that felt far more solid than it appeared. When she finally squinted her eyes open again, she carefully focused on the faces surrounding her rather than on the pulsating walls of the room. After a few minutes staring into Gyfree's smiling eyes, she was even able to accept the savory roll and fresh juice that she had been offered.

As the last crumb vanished from Drew's plate, the woman smiled warmly and patted the Dreamer on the head. "Now it's time to decide what to do with all the people locked in my back room," she declared.

"How did everyone end up in your house?" Gyfree inquired.

The man cleared his throat, his cheeks flushing with embarrassment as he explained, "Our son, Peyr, brought them here, supposedly because Mischa's handsome friend needed to rest; at least that's what he told us. But Peyr didn't really seem like himself, and when we saw how strangely everyone else was behaving too, well, we just decided to lock the door behind them. Especially after they all crowded into the same room as if their lives depended on it. Peyr included, even though he has a perfectly nice room of his own."

"We knew help would be on the way soon, and we didn't know what else to do," his wife added, an anxious note creeping into her voice. "If we had known what trouble Mischa and her companions would bring when they first arrived, we would have tried to do something sooner. But despite those hummeybee things, they seemed harmless enough. And when they asked Peyr to take them into the town, we saw no reason to object."

"It wasn't until they came back with so many others that we started to wonder just what was going on," continued the man. "And when they all scrambled into our back room behind Mischa's man, well like we already told you, we decided to just lock the door and wait for help."

"Just how many people do you have locked up here?" Timi asked, a worried frown creasing her face.

"Counting Mischa and that gorgeous young man, about twenty," answered the woman. "Maybe even more. They kept milling around that young man so much it was difficult to keep track."

Groaning, Timi dropped her head into her hands. "Now what?" she wailed plaintively.

Sevor wrapped a reassuring arm around her stooped shoulders. "It's really quite simple," he told her. "We go get Mischa and the Figment and leave as quickly as we can. Once the Figment is gone, the others should all return to themselves."

Timi raised clouded eyes to Sevor's face. "It might be that simple, but it might not. Now there may be others who are so ensnared that separation from the Figment could kill them too. How can we be certain whom may be safely left behind and whom may not?"

The question hung heavily in the air, so heavily that, for Gyfree and Drew, the quivering walls and table suddenly seemed too weighted to move. Everything was finally still, and for the moment everyone was frozen in place, immobilized by their uncertainty and fear, so that Drew once again felt as if she and Gyfree were completely alone, not in the room beneath the stairs, and not in the entryway of this dreaming house, but alone in the midst of a group of breathing statues, so alone that she could almost feel the insistent pressure of his lips on hers, could almost taste him on her tongue, could almost feel his heart thrumming with her own. And she could clearly see in the dark pools of his eyes that he felt as she felt. They had known each other for only a blink of time, had come closest in the world of dreams, and yet he was the only person she had ever met who was as real to her as she was to herself. If she closed her eyes she knew she would still see him just as clearly, would probably even feel him with the same intensity he had felt her all those times she had slipped away dreaming. With that thought she suddenly realized that she had felt him intensely from the beginning, had felt him outside the door before he entered the room beneath the stairs, had felt his frantic heartbeat as he ran down the brick road in her direction, had even felt that spark that gave him life, and by holding it in her dreams and breathing her own fire into it, had kept him alive when death should have quenched it. He had done nothing to coerce her feelings, no more than she had done anything to coerce his, but his hold on her was as sure as the Figment's hold on Mischa.

Drew's eyes widened as they stared into Gyfree's, and she saw the answer she had reached reflected in the dark core of his eyes. A smile trembled on her lips as she again felt the phantom presence of his kiss. "We must wait until they're all asleep," she murmured, her voice sending ripples through the stillness of the room. "Then we'll be able to remove Mischa and the Figment, although we must do so quietly and carefully. If anyone wakes up immediately because they can feel the Figment leave, then we must take them with us as well. Those whose sleep is undisturbed should be safe."

"What can we do if the Figment has snared someone other than Mischa? Sevor is our only chance to free Mischa. Who will free any others?" Timi asked anxiously.

"Maybe one of you'll dream up another solution," Sevor quipped, although his eyes were solemn and dark above his smiling lips.

"We have no choice," Gyfree announced, his eyes still entangled in Drew's. "We must keep an eye on the Figment, and we must do our best to free anyone in his grasp. And right now that simply means keeping him and his victims with us at all times. What that means later, not even Sevor's dreams may tell."

The sound of a throat clearing drew everyone's attention toward the corner where the middle-aged couple huddled, standing side by side as if only together could they remain on their feet, their fingers intertwined and faces pale reflections of each other. "If it's any help," the man informed them, the lines in his face suddenly etched as deeply as the fear in his eyes, "I think they're sleeping now. Things were pretty rowdy there for a while, but shortly before you showed up, it quieted down. There hasn't been a peep from that room for a couple hours now. Just a buzzing sound and a lot of slow, heavy breathing."

"Please," added the woman, her pupils mere pinpricks of panic, "Peyr is all we have. You have to get him away from the Figment anyway you can. If we'd known it was a Figment Mischa had with her, we would never have opened our door. Please, whatever it takes, please get Peyr back."

"We'll do whatever we can," Timi reassured them. "But try not to worry too much. Peyr might be fine."

If anything, Peyr's parents looked even more concerned. "They're all this way," said the man, moving toward a door that pulsed as wildly as Drew's heart as she turned her eyes in its direction. Her hand reached instinctively for Gyfree's; gripping his fingers and squinting her eyes she followed the man, woman, and her companions down a slithering hallway and stopped with them outside a rippling door. As the man had reported, there was no sound from beyond the door other than the snuffling sound of people sleeping and a steady, rumbling buzz.

"The hummeybees!" exclaimed Timi, her face awash with sudden consternation. "What are we supposed to do about the hummeybees? They certainly aren't going to allow us to meddle with the Figment in any way."

Once again Gyfree and Drew locked gazes, and as a message seemed to pass between them, flecks of blue as hard as steel shot through the brown of Gyfree's eyes. "It will work," Drew said, a note of apology creeping through her voice. "It may not be something you welcome at the moment, but it will work."

"What will work?" questioned Sevor, his eager eyes intent upon the door, impatience lending an uncharacteristic edge to his words.

"Ice," whispered the two Dreamers, their locked eyes flooding completely blue as they summoned a small sliver of the dream they had shared once before, a dream not unlike the one that had long ago given birth to the Figment who had pursued Gyfree to this world. Ice flowed from their dreaming minds, ice slithered down their arms and fused their hands together, ice glistened in the air around them, marking with brilliant crystals the boundaries of a world that was theirs and theirs alone. Yet beneath the ice where their fingers joined, and beneath the silvery blue that coated their skin and engulfed their eyes, they were bound by a warmth that no one else could see.

"Open the door, Timi," Gyfree finally whispered through stiff lips, and as the door swung inward, he and Drew stepped through together, bringing a fragment of winter in their wake. Across the room the two hummeybees stirred as if only they could feel the treacherous blast of cold, but as their wings shimmered into motion and their stingers shivered in alarm, the Dreamers exhaled a breath of ice that stopped their wings in midbeat, arresting the delicate membranes like flower petals startled by an early frost. Caught in an icy web as intricate as a snowflake, their fuzzy bodies hung suspended in the air a few inches above the Figment's perfect face, black and yellow stripes wan in the gripping cold. And as the hummeybees dangled above him, the Figment opened groggy eyes and blinked in confusion.

With a lethal swiftness belied by his wry smile and easy manner, Sevor darted past the fog of cold emanating from the Dreamers, through the tangle of sleeping bodies toward the shining hub around which they all seemed to radiate like the spokes of a wheel, and forcefully stuffed one of their hosts' colorful napkins into the Figment's mouth, binding it firmly in place with another. Then, without a single pause, he threw the Figment over his shoulder and hurried from the room. As he passed the couple still huddled in the doorway, he smiled disarmingly. "Sorry about your napkins," he stated softly. "Didn't dream I would need something to keep this one quiet, but decided it might be a good idea anyway."

Timi had scurried in behind Sevor to kneel at the side of Mischa as she slept, body curled tightly against the Figment, dirty tear tracks smudging her face. Yet once Sevor had disappeared into the farthest recesses of the house, Mischa was not the first of his victims to stir. A young man slumped next to the door, head buried in his knees, suddenly jerked awake and scrambled to his feet, eyes clouded by more than just panic. "Mustn't sleep," he muttered disjointedly. "Must protect him. Must always protect him."

A whimper sounded from the doorway. "Peyr," whispered the woman, reaching out an unsteady hand to take him by the arm. "Just go back to sleep."

The young man shook off his mother's restraining hand and tried to push his way through the door, clearly intent on following the path that had carried the Figment away from him. His father stepped in front of him, face grim, as clearly intent on holding his son in place as his son was intent on escaping.

Gyfree's voice was still cold and brittle from the ice shrouding him and Drew. "Let him go," he insisted. "I don't want anyone hurt, and in his condition, he will try to hurt you. And forcing him to stay will cause him far more harm than good."

The man's face hardened and darkened, but he stepped aside as instructed, and watched with eyes as haunted as any Dreamer's as his son dashed past without a glance at his parents' tortured faces.

"Follow him," Gyfree ordered. "Sevor may need your help if he becomes violent."

The man's face darkened even more, and his eyes flashed, but without a word he turned to follow his son, and face as pale as his was dark, eyes as dull as his were flaming, his wife turned to follow him.

A whimper slipped through the surrounding murmurs of exhausted sleep, and then a wail, and the Dreamers turned to see Mischa thrashing in Timi's arms, her eyes wild with fear and her face bruised with a pain buried deep within her skin. "Where is he?" she cried. "I need him, I need him." Tears streaked from her eyes to glisten against the dried paths on her cheeks, as if her face held the furrows of numerous dusty riverbeds that had suddenly been flooded by a long expected rain. "He needs more than me, so much more. I'm not enough, I'll never be enough, but I still need him. I need him, I need him," she sobbed.

"Shhh," Timi soothed, her pale face luminously soft, her own eyes spilling tears. "He's waiting for you. He wants you to come to him right now. Let me take you to him."

Mischa fell silent as Timi helped her to her feet, but the tears still coursed down the paths on her cheeks, and the overflowing pools in her eyes reflected the dark pain in her face. With Timi a step behind, Mischa followed unerringly in the path of the Figment whose heart kept hers beating, whose lungs kept her breathing, whose smile kept her lost, whose needs kept her ignorant of her own.

From amid the tangle of bodies another head lifted, a snarl of dark hair framing two bleary eyes. "What's all the noise?" a woman's voice asked drowsily as several others nearby tossed restlessly and grumbled in their sleep. "What's going on?"

"Just go back to sleep," Drew murmured, her voice as heavy as a dream, and the young woman's eyes slid shut as she settled back to the floor, and around her several others also stilled as sleep carried them farther and farther away from the Figment's hold.

Alone amidst a room full of sleepers who did not know what it meant to dream, the two Dreamers sighed, hard ice melting from their eyes, breath evaporating the ice from each other's faces, fingers stirring against palms. "What do we do with the hummeybees?" Drew asked with a smile that freed the last shards of ice from deep behind Gyfree's eyes.

"We certainly can't leave them here," Gyfree responded with a smile of his own. "They will thaw out eventually if we don't keep an eye on them, and Peyr's parents have more than enough to worry about already."

Drew reached out her free hand to touch the frozen creatures, tracing with one finger the motionless wings that still shimmered with a rainbow of color as if even now they took flight. "They're so beautiful," she murmured, "and so dangerous. Just like a dream. Do you think they'll be safe to thaw out at some point?"

"I don't know," admitted Gyfree, reaching out his own finger to gingerly touch the sharp point of one ice-hard beak. "But I do know they are too cold for us to carry." His eyes darted around the room until they settled on a crumpled blanket thrown haphazardly over a few half-naked torsos. Without making a sound he moved across the room and whisked the blanket away, returning to wrap it around the hummeybees. Throwing his improvised bag over his shoulder, he smiled crookedly at Drew and announced, "We'd better go help the others. They're certain to have their hands full."

Without a backward glance, the two Dreamers left the room, quietly closing the door behind them so that the sleepers clustered on the floor could rest undisturbed by anything close to a dream.

Chapter 10

Deep inside of him she shivered, a sliver of impenetrable ice held fast within a seething inferno. Deep inside she whispered, for despite the loss of her body, her eyes still saw clearly, and there was much to explain. Deep inside she thrilled, for she knew that there was much she could accomplish now that had seemed impossible before. Deep inside she remembered and she mused. She had wanted him, not like this, but this had its advantages. She had wanted him, wanted to be like him, wanted to share in his strength, his ferocity, his cruelty, and now she was him, just as he was somehow her. And she saw all too clearly how truly indomitable they could be, for nothing and no one could withstand both fire and ice. But first, before all else, she saw the surest way of killing her Dreamer and his, and this time, keeping them dead. And deep inside of him, she shivered, she whispered, she thrilled. And close, so close there was no easy way to determine where she ended and he began, he responded. He shivered. He listened. He thrilled.

With the rustling voice of ice in his head and cutting shards of blue in his eyes, he reached through the void, claws raking through all the realms of gray to gather every Figment sheltered there. Many tried to flee when they felt the breath of fire blistering their bodies and the stab of ice piercing their spines, many tried to burrow into the farthest reaches of the void while others tried to lose themselves in the fleeting refuge of some fragmentary dream, but the immense and merciless hands with claws that burned and froze could not be escaped. With her in his head he harvested Figments as if they were as rooted as stalks of wheat, tearing them from whatever illusory soil nourished them and gathering them in his invisible arms. The more he amassed, the more his arms swelled to hold them all, until his arms were brimming with every phantom being that called the void home, every Figment that had ever called him master, and every Figment that had carefully evaded his rule. Only then did he draw in his arms, dropping his bounty of Figments at his feet, then erecting a wall of fire and ice to pen them in as they tried to scramble free.

Through his eyes she watched as the Figments milled in panic, the stronger ones trampling the weaker ones as all tried to flee both the wall and the fiery demon who towered above them, his face contorting as flames frolicked across his skin, and his eyes casting daggers of ice. Spread at his feet was every conceivable shape ever born of a nightmare, each with a face that flickered in and out of focus, one moment emerging as something soft and almost human, the next moment reemerging as a monster more hideous than any ever created by an adult mind trying to elicit screams and shudders for the latest horror movie. Among these nightmare creatures were other Figments, their forms as distant and diffused as stars in a cloudy sky, flickering in and out of existence, as enigmatic as the dreams that had given them life. The full spectrum was there, from the merest wisp of a fleeting fear to a fully fleshed nightmare. And there, in their midst, was a familiar one with wild eyes and a slathering jaw, slashing and tearing at those who bumped him in their frenzy to hide from those burning, ice-cold eyes that watched from above.

"That one," she whispered. "Let's start with that one."

He looked as she looked, saw as she saw, and remembered just as she remembered, her memory alive in his memory. He knew why she had chosen that Figment, chosen the first of her kind who had ever taught her the lessons of deceit and betrayal, and he relished the thought, just as she relished the thought, of betraying this one in return. A smile both blazing and chilling split his face, and those below who saw it groveled, blood spurting from their very pores as they tried to hide among the feet of the mob, faces pressed in taloned hands, bodies curling into the eddies of the void. Across them he reached, his claws piercing the rough hide of his quarry as he lifted the flailing body high so all could see.

"Watch and learn," he whispered, and the sound of his voice drove the breath from each and every creature below, and sent the ones still standing reeling to the ground. Yet every wavering face turned up, and even those without faces held still to watch in whatever way they could, as he slit the Figment open from chin to groin and exhaled smoke and frost into the gaping belly. The Figment screamed, the sound as piercing as a drill splintering teeth and striking bone, but then the demon sank his fangs through the other's leathery neck, and there was no sound beyond a faint gurgle and the steady drip of blood.

Lifting his blood-filled mouth, the demon smiled again, and even those without blood of their own writhed in pain as the sharpness of his glance ripped through them. "This one will not die," he whispered, bringing even greater agony to those who must survive not only his smile, but also his voice, "no matter how welcome death might seem. There will be pain, relentless pain, until I choose to end it. If I choose to end it. And what I have done to this one is less than nothing. There will be far greater pain for any who hesitate, however slightly, to do my bidding. There will be everlasting pain for any who do not bow down to me now."

There was no hesitation. As one the captive Figments bowed their heads, and even those Figments too nebulous to possess anything resembling a head prostrated their wavering forms until they almost appeared as nothing more than another feature of the swirling gray ground. With heads or entire forms bowed, all were spared his next smile, although not the shredding onslaught of his voice. "If you are wise, you will always serve me this promptly."

A soft gurgle sounded in the silence that trailed his voice, and a faint voice begged. "Let me serve you too, master. Please."

Through the demon's eyes she looked down into a face with a jaw that no longer slathered, for it had been torn away. Once-wild eyes were now not only tamed, but beaten, and from their dull depths the Figment pled for a reprieve from the unbearable pain, even conceded that no price would be too high. Glancing down his pain-wracked body, she watched tiny flames lick his intestines while slivers of crystalline ice pierced his lungs and heart, and then she watched as the fire and ice changed places, the flames sealing the gashes left by the ice before scorching the exposed tissues, and the ice soothing blisters before tearing new holes in the quivering gut. "Let him see me," she whispered so only her demon could hear. "Please, just for a moment, let him know it's not just you holding him in your claws."

He heard her whisper, as he now always heard her whisper. He understood her desire, as he now always understood her desire. And he knew, as she knew, that there were other ways this Figment could suffer, and ways this Figment should still suffer. Deep inside she felt herself lifted, as if she was soaring toward the very eyes she could see through but not touch. Then she was seeping through the fire of his skin, and cascading over the furnace of his face, and she could feel, since he could feel, her own perfect features sculpting themselves from layer upon layer of ice across the seething surface. The eyes she looked through were still his eyes, but the smile that abruptly silenced the whimpering Figment was her smile, cold and brittle and full of malice, and it was her beauty that brought new fear to the Figment's face and a shattering recognition to the once-wild eyes. And it was her voice that whispered, "You should never have betrayed me," as his claws released the Figment to plunge alone through the void, eternal fire and ice weaving through his belly in an agonizing waltz. Then, like a glacier that had perched atop an erupting volcano, the layers of ice melted away, and she felt herself seeping back through his skin, plunging through smoke and fire, and settling back into the inviolable sliver of ice nestled within his inferno.

From deep within once more she watched through his eyes, but he had let her show herself, had even let her taste the blood of the doomed Figment as her lips shaped themselves above his lips, had let her voice sound for all the gathered Figments to hear. He had taken everything from her, but when there had been something she desperately wanted, he had given it to her with as little hesitation as his captives had given him their allegiance. She was part of him now, a valuable part, a part as lethal as his own mind, and although this was not what she had wanted, for this moment, and the even bloodier moments to come, it was enough.

There was no twinkle in Sevor's intense blue eyes as he and Peyr's father struggled to pin the thrashing young man to the ground, but Drew somehow knew that the grimness that had replaced his usual wry smile had more to do with the way Mischa shivered and groveled on the floor, her eyes beseeching as she stared across the room at the Figment, than with anything else. On either side of the prostrate Mischa knelt Timi and Peyr's mother, but their ineffectual attempts to comfort her only hardened the lines around Sevor's mouth and intensified the murderous look in his eyes as they rested on the bound and gagged Figment. Sevor certainly wasn't focusing enough of his attention on Peyr, who suddenly thrashed free from the arms holding him down, breaking away from Sevor's grip and knocking his father over as he scrambled to his feet and assumed a defensive posture in front of the object of an obsession he felt but could probably not explain.

"Enough!" boomed Gyfree, and even Drew turned startled eyes in his direction, for in his voice she heard wind pelting restlessly through tall grasses, the groan of rock sliding against rock, the roar of water tumbling toward the sea. In his eyes she saw reflected the impatience of a burgeoning seed, the implacability of a mountain soaring to impossible heights, the strength of a massive tree whose roots could never be dislodged from the unbelievable depths to which they had delved. It was Gyfree who spoke, but it was also more than Gyfree, and for the first time everyone saw clearly the new Keeper of this world.

From where she sprawled on the floor, Mischa raised overcast eyes to the Keeper's face. A glimmer of recognition drifted across her tearstained face. "Gyfree?" she asked. "Why are you here? What do you want?"

The Keeper answered softly, the hum of a summer evening in his voice and the light of dawn streaking his eyes, "I want you and your friends to come with me."

"Why?"

"Because you are needed."

For a fraction of a second the old Mischa looked through her laughing eyes, and Sevor jerked a step nearer to where she knelt, but then something luminous surged through the Figment's eyes, and the old Mischa vanished as quickly as she had appeared. "You will hurt him," she mumbled. "You will send him away."

"No," replied the Keeper. "Not unless you tell me to."

"Never," asserted Mischa, although there was a fleeting flicker of doubt behind her eyes.

"So you will come," stated the Keeper.

Tears welled in Mischa's eyes and traced the dirty tracks on her cheeks. "Ask him," she mumbled. "Don't ask me."

The glow of countless sunrises and sunsets seemed to follow Gyfree as he stepped across the room to confront a glowering Peyr. "I must protect him," insisted the young man, squaring his shoulders and raising his chin defiantly.

"I will not hurt him," promised the Keeper. "I only wish to speak with him."

Peyr's forehead creased with uncertainty, but he turned to meet the Figment's eyes, and whatever he saw there caused him to quietly step aside.

With a motion so swift it seemed to spring from a dream, Gyfree whisked the gag from the Figment's mouth. "Will you come with us willingly?" he asked.

The Figment's eyes darted across the faces of those gathered in the room. "Where are all of the others? They must come too."

"No," replied the Keeper. "We have far to go and cannot be slowed down by so many. The two here who follow you will have to be enough."

The Figment stared up with eyes as hurt and perplexed as a small child faced with the death of someone loved. "But I need more."

A sob broke from Mischa as she burrowed her face into the floor.

The Figment looked at the weeping woman, his expression puzzled. "She was so colorful, so bright, so alive. It is because of her. She made me want more."

"There will be no more," insisted the Keeper, his voice as unyielding as a storm.

The Figment blinked, his eyes sweeping the room once more. "Where are the hummeybees?" he asked. "I cannot leave without them. They have been with me forever."

Gyfree tossed the blanket slung over his shoulder to the ground and out skittered the motionless hummeybees, their silent bodies sliding across the floor like chunks of scattered ice.

"What have you done?" gasped the Figment.

"I have frozen them," answered the Keeper. "I will thaw them only if you agree to come with us, and if you promise to meet all my terms."

"What must I promise?"

"That you will not seek any others to follow you. That you will not try to escape again. That you will not have your followers interfere with the rest of us in any way. And that you will not allow the hummeybees to harm a single person here. If you violate any of these conditions, I will destroy the hummeybees. I assure you, it is within my power."

The Figment turned anguished eyes to where the hummeybees had come to rest, their fuzzy bodies tipped with blue, their wings as still as glass. "Very well," he whispered, "I promise. So please, bring them back."

The Keeper's face filled with light as if the sun was rising in his eyes, and from where she stood nearby, Drew could feel the heat radiating from his body, could even see the air shimmer in waves off his skin as it traveled across the room to where the hummeybees lay unmoving on a floor that continued to shudder in Drew's eyes. As the heat washed over the creatures, the blue streaks on their bodies were flicked away by fingers of yellow and black, and their stingers quivered like guitar strings plucked by invisible hands. A buzz vibrated through the air as the hummeybees stirred to life, their wings blurring into motion and casting rainbows across the faces of all who watched. In a blink they were high in the air, razor beaks and barbed stingers pointing unerringly toward the faces of the two Dreamers who had encased them in ice. Yet something seemed to hold them back, and although their eyes and weapons stayed focused on the Dreamers, their pulsing wings carried them back to the Figment's shoulders and away from where Gyfree and Drew both stood unflinching, shards of uncompromising ice again glittering in their eyes.

The Figment's glance was as soft and distant as the world that had once held him as the two hummeybees settled to his shoulders, their hums reverberating through his ears as his eyes slid slowly shut. In the momentary lull, Sevor edged closer to the spot where Mischa hunched on the floor; kneeling beside her, he stroked the back of her golden head with a shaking hand. "You're far too beautiful to hide your face against the floor," he chided playfully, although his eyes were like two open wounds marring his smiling face.

Mischa raised her tear-ravaged face and blinked uncertainly at the man with the wry smile. "Who are you?" she whispered, curiosity chasing the tears from her eyes like a wind blowing clouds across the sky.

"Sevor," he answered, his eyes filling with light as hers returned to their customary blue.

"Why are you here?"

"To be with you."

Her brow puckered, but she didn't look away. "Do I know you?"

"Not yet. But I've known you most of your life."

Mischa lifted a hand to wipe the wetness from her cheeks, her eyes still fixed on the man who smiled down at her as if she was the only other person in the room. "That doesn't make sense," she stated.

"It will in time," replied Sevor. Reaching out a hand to grasp her tear-dampened one, he added, "Here, let me help you up. You really don't belong on the floor."

Mischa allowed herself to be pulled to her feet, and a smile even flitted across her mouth as Sevor stepped a fraction closer, but then across the room the Figment's eyes burst open and the light instantly drained from her face, darkening her expression more dramatically than a nightmare ever darkened a Dreamer's sleep. As if some unseen force had caught hold of her, she inched back step by step until she had reached the Figment's side and collapsed to the floor beside him. With a growing distance overshadowing her once vibrant eyes, she carefully untied the Figment's wrists, and as she finished, he reached out an arm to wrap around her shoulders and pull her close, his eyes suddenly hard and ugly as he glared across at the impudently grinning Sevor. And although she was again lost in the circle of the Figment's hold, there was a flicker of new life in Mischa's face as she stared across at the man with eyes that were once again as smiling as his lips. A man impervious to the Figment's powers.

A quick look passed between Timi and Drew as Gyfree turned to Peyr's mother, who stood wringing her hands. "I hate to ask anything else of you," he apologized, "but we have no packs. We have a long way to travel, and we will need supplies."

The woman lifted wet eyes to his face. "What of my son, Gyfree?"

"I'm sorry, but he must come with us."

"Why?" demanded the man, stepping forward to encircle his wife's shoulders in a comforting embrace. "If he stays here with us, won't he recover on his own?"

"He'll die," Timi interjected with unaccustomed authority. "He's too ensnared to survive on his own."

"And just how do you expect to free him?" wailed the woman.

Timi's eyes drifted to where the tall, muscular young man stood, feet apart and chin lifted as if daring anyone to approach the Figment. As she watched, Sevor took a single step in Mischa's direction, and Peyr snapped, "You are the one he trusts the least. You will stay away. Or else."

Sevor only laughed and tweaked an eyebrow toward Mischa, and as she turned back to Peyr's parents, Timi murmured so softly that no one could hear, "I don't. Not even in my dreams."

The last shrill scream of their agonized victim permeated the heavy air with a stench that gagged the horde of cowering Figments and choked their minds with fear. She watched as he watched, through eyes that no creature dared meet, and she waited as he waited, with a patience as cold as a glacier and enduring as hell. Time slipped into eternity and still the scream echoed through the void, and still they waited, patiently waited for fear to drive every Figment to the edge of desperate and unthinking violence. And as they waited they watched, her eyes moving where his eyes led, together probing each prone figure, looking for something they would see with more than any set of eyes. When they found what they were seeking, found first one and then another, he reached into the trembling mass and extracted two writhing Figments whose features filled with a horror more vivid than any found in a nightmare.

The first creature wavered between two faces, one a shimmering ghost and the other a stocky woman with empty eyes, but it was the human face rather than the phantom that rendered it monstrous. The second fluctuated back and forth between the smiling faces of different men, women, and children, always returning after each face to a snarling dog, and unlike the first Figment, this one's menace clearly lurked behind fangs and slitted eyes. The demon brought them close to his own changeless face, but he stayed his claws from shredding their hides and stayed his fangs from ripping their throats. "Will you serve me?" he rumbled, drawing blood from their open mouths.

"Yes, master," both gurgled, blood dripping from their jaws.

In the depths she stirred, and when he spoke again it was with her voice, a voice that froze the dripping blood and cooled the panic in the Figments' eyes. "You have been chosen for a special task. Do you know why?"

The face of the dead-eyed woman turned upward, and a voice as flat as the eyes answered, "We were dreamed by the same Dreamer."

"No," whined the dog, "the master was not created by the one who dreamed me."

"But me," the cold one whispered through his fiery lips, "don't you know me? Don't just look. Listen."

The dog yelped, its hackles rising before its face shifted away to that of a sniveling boy. "The ice queen," whimpered the boy, sprouting fangs and a muzzle. "You I know, but you and the master are far greater than me."

"Yes," she whispered, "we are. But we have much to do, many worlds to conquer, and we want you to perform a task, a simple task, but one that consumes valuable time. We are tired of wasting time on this task, but your time is of no importance, so you will do it for us from this moment on."

"Yes," sniveled the dog as the ghost shifting back to woman nodded a tongueless head. "Just tell us what we must do."

"You will watch both our Dreamers ceaselessly so that we too can see," the demon growled in his harshest voice, and as they opened their mouths to shriek their unspeakable pain, he pierced their skulls, stabbing through their brains with talons that dripped fire, slicing away their hidden thoughts with daggers of ice. As they dangled from his claws, he breathed into their gaping mouths, spilling fire and ice into their lungs until the fragile sacs burst and volatile air ignited the blood coursing through their veins to shatter their hearts. He had taken other creatures like this before, taken them far away from her prying eyes, but now he took them as she watched avidly, took them and made them his own, made them her own, melded them to the single purpose he and she now shared. He fused them to himself and to her, fused them until their shapes were as unchangeable as fire, as permanently frozen as she had always wanted to be. Then he returned them to those tattered remnants of self they still possessed, and set them before the now lifeless screen where he had always watched his Dreamer as she stumbled sleepily through the waking world and sprang fully to life in the world of dreams. "You will watch from here," he murmured in their ears, carving the words like bloody graffiti into their brains, "and everything you see, we shall see. Do not forget. The moment either of you close your eyes, we will know. And the moment we know, we will be here. And the moment we are here, you will both die. Not just once, but many times. Over and over again, each time in a new and dreadful way, until we grow bored. And when it comes to killing, we never grow bored."

He loosened his claws from their skin and slowly, and for them quite painfully, pulled away. As he withdrew, the numbfaced woman stumbled, her legs quaking beneath her as she sank toward the gray eddies hiding her feet and the dog's paws. With a growl the dog sank sharp fangs into her hand, his jaw snapping shut with the sound of crunching bones as the woman jerked upright and turned her dead eyes upon him. With her hand held deep in his throat, he snarled, "I will not be punished because of your weakness. You will watch, as I will watch, if I must gnaw on your hand forever."

The woman remained completely still as she stared back at the dog, and it seemed to the snarling creature that no lungs had ever expanded in her chest, that no heart had ever pumped blood to warm her clammy flesh, that she had known death long before she had ever tasted birth. The dog shriveled in her gaze, but held firmly to her hand even when her arm followed her fingers down his throat and she seized hold of the lungs that filled his chest, and pinched the heart that directed his blood. She held in her hand his shrinking lungs, held his quivering heart, but she did not tighten her grip. "Very well," she stated flatly. "You will hold my hand to keep me awake. I will hold your air and your blood to keep your attention. We will forevermore be as one."

Watching through his slitted demon eyes, the ice queen smiled as he smiled, satisfied that these long-deserted Figments, these Figments long ignored, would serve their purpose well. No longer would he or she be blind to their Dreamers; they would be watching through these eyes, these eyes that were now theirs although not their own, and they would see more clearly than they had seen in years, for once again they would be seeing with eyes that were new, at least to them. Even now the emptiness was dissipating; the screen was filling as if a hidden projectionist had snapped awake, and out of nothing she could see the face of her Dreamer coalescing as if from frozen dust, just as he could see his Dreamer flaming back to life like a match igniting in the darkness. What the watchers watched they too saw, and would continue to see wherever they might be, whatever they might be doing. From this moment on there would always be a constant, unfolding drama played in the back of their shared mind. A drama they were determined to bring to a bloody end.

At his feet and below their joined eyes the mass of Figments still groveled, the skin on the backs of those with skin crawling, the muscles of those solid enough to possess muscles writhing, the combined breaths of both substantial and insubstantial hissing loudly and harshly as they all waited in growing trepidation for whatever violence would next befall them. And watching both them and the drama unfolding far from their eyes, he and she waited as well, waited for the fever of unthinking terror to seize them completely and transform them once and for always into mindlessly grateful slaves.

Although her life in fact revolved around something quite different, Drew felt as if she had blundered into a group of lost planets caught in the gravity of the Figment's sun, and that like the rest of them, she had no choice but to circle endlessly around his bright core. As they traveled through space he remained in the center, the hummeybees orbiting him closely as if that was their only chance to keep warm. Next and directly behind him came Mischa, caught as firmly in his gravity as the closest of planets is caught by a sun, her face alight whenever he smiled upon her and darker than night the moment he looked away. Beyond Mischa ranged Peyr, eyes glazed as if he had stared too long at the light, his feet helpless satellites that the Figment could pull between Sevor and Mischa. For of all those not truly caught by the Figment, Sevor remained the nearest, his eyes dark when Mischa's were light and light when Mischa's were dark, his feet weaving a path through separate orbits as he first tried to intercept Mischa, and then stepped aside for Peyr. Beyond Sevor was Gyfree, his eyes darting constantly back toward the Figment, flecks of ice leaping to his fingers whenever the hummeybees drifted too far from the center, and a mere step behind Gyfree walked Drew, not so much as if she orbited the Figment, but as if she orbited Gyfree, and so had no other choice but to follow the path he followed. Beside Drew walked Timi, as far from her creation as she could be, yet not truly free to wander off on her own or escape the sphere of the Figment's influence.

On they moved, even after the sun in the darkening sky had lost its hold on them, long after its face had faded into the distant hills, for the light in their center had not faded and his hold had not weakened, and as long as he moved, so did they. Through the deepest of the night they traveled, and they might have traveled until that world's sun once more lifted its head and captured them with its luminous smile, but at last Gyfree stopped, and the entire group stumbled to a halt. As she gazed back to see the Figment's wan face reflected in the moonlight, Drew suddenly realized that he had never been the center that moved them after all, that in fact it had been Gyfree, the Keeper, leading the way and pulling the others behind him, like a comet trailing a tail of debris. Within that cloud of debris the Figment was just another fragment, large enough to draw smaller particles into the small sphere of his gravity, but no more able to control and direct than any other speck of stellar dust.

"We'll rest here until morning," announced Gyfree, dropping his heavy pack to the ground. "We've covered more than enough distance despite our late start."

The sigh of his followers was echoed by the sigh of the wind, as if the very earth beneath their feet was weary and as badly in need of rest as the most weary of the small creatures stumbling over its vast back. Copying Gyfree's example, all those with packs dropped their heavy burdens to the ground and, rolling their necks and flexing their shoulders, tried to ease their aching muscles. When Gyfree settled to the grass, so did they, nestling down into the welcoming softness, snuggling beneath invisible blankets of warm air. Drowsily Drew wondered if someone should at least remain awake to keep an eye on the Figment and his followers, when she felt the grass rustle as if something surprisingly huge moved through the dark. In the stillness that followed there came an unnatural hush, as if the grass and the air and the people were all expectantly waiting. Then humming through the grass like sound through a telephone wire came the Figment's coaxing murmur, followed by the crackle of Mischa's equally joyful and agonized whimper. The grass thrashed and the air whirled as Sevor stirred, his limbs convulsing as he felt Mischa succumb to the deadening embrace, his sudden pain and longing blasting through the night like an exploded bomb.

"You will all sleep," ordered Gyfree harshly, but the fingers he slipped through Drew's were gentle and warm, and the eyes that caught hers shimmered with a dream. "Sleep," he whispered, "let's dream them to sleep."

Drew's eyes filled with the grit of countless mornings, filled until the heavy sand spilled from between her open lashes to swirl away in a miniature dust storm, tiny twisters angling into every open eye, corkscrewing downward until even the most anchored minds were caught in the calm center of the storm, caught and carried into the peaceful quiet of sleep. Yet as the last grain of sand drifted away from her, she realized her own eyes were wide open and clear, untouched by the sleep that had held her before she and Gyfree had summoned the dream.

"I can guard them," she whispered. "I'm not tired anymore."

The breath on her face was as warm as his laughter. "They won't need guarding," he murmured, his lips hovering above hers, his taste already alive on her tongue. "They will sleep until we dream them awake again."

Lips brushed her lips as gently as a dream, and his embrace was the welcome embrace of sleep. Holding her in his arms, her head nestled into his pulsing neck, he whispered, "Sleep, but don't dream yourself away from me. Just sleep."

The flames within him writhed around her, but the sliver of ice that was her remained untouched, and in fact provided enough coolness to hold the violent eruption of his impatience in check. Sprawled at his feet and spread beneath their shared eyes was a multitude of Figments, faces still pressed to the ground as if they could remain unseen if they themselves could not see. Fear had made them grovel, fear had long held them in debased subjection, but fear had not yet fired them, had not yet gnawed away enough of their minds to drive them into the frenzy he and she desired. So he waited, and she waited with him, but his patience was burning away, and only her presence, her icy whisper drifting through his mind, kept him from reaching out his claws and rending his conscripts to shreds.

Then finally, when even her coolness could no longer assuage his fiery fury, a massive Figment reared its head from the ground and roared, sharp fangs glinting as it turned its face upward, eyes black as if something darker than the darkest night moved through its mind. In a motion too swift to anticipate, it turned on its nearest neighbor, a Figment that had tried to hide itself against the other's impressive bulk, and sank its fangs through the back of the exposed skull, piercing bone as easily as if it had been decaying flesh. Raising its head again, blood dripping from its jutting jaw, it thundered, "Let me kill for you, master! Whoever and whatever you hate, I will kill! Just let me kill!"

The mob erupted, Figment turning upon Figment, those with claws and fangs ripping into others, tearing through flesh as well as through more elusive matter, while those with less substance sizzled like lightning as they bolted their way through the grappling bodies, leaving a plume of smoke and the stench of seared flesh wherever they struck. Within moments blood and strips of tattered skin were everywhere, and the sundered scraps of countless phantom Figments drifted through the melee like wisps of stray fog.

"Enough!" he boomed, the cutting edge of his voice inflicting more damage on the warring multitude than they had inflicted on each other. As one the Figments fell to their knees, but this time they all faced him, eyes or whatever passed for eyes lifted, blood dripping from innumerable wounds, shredded phantoms shivering as their lost pieces wafted between bodies like lost children trying to find their way home. "You will all kill for me," he whispered, and a shudder of both unbearable pain and intensely sensual pleasure rippled through the kneeling creatures. "You are mine now, my nightmare army, and nothing can stop you."

A ragged cheer broke from the gathered masses, only to be strangled at the moment of birth as he reached out a hand and a wave of icy flames engulfed them. In a flash they no longer existed, not even to themselves, as more than burning agony and freezing pain. Everything that made them what they were was peeled away so that the acid fire could course through their frames and the merciless ice could freeze it forever in place. Their wounds were healed: jagged gashes closed, burns sloughed away, lost wisps reattached to shivering forms. Yet they were also injured in ways they could not even comprehend as the fire and ice crackled through their minds, reducing their old selves to ashes but sculpting them new selves from the frozen soot. When the fire and ice finally withdrew, they were left standing, spines straighter yet more jagged, eyes brighter yet more insane, purpose decided yet unexplained. There were no more wavering forms, and even those that had once been only insubstantial mists stood solid, eyes in actual faces seeing for the first time as others saw. And what they saw, what they all saw, was the demon looming over them, fire and ice storming through his eyes.

"There will be enough killing for all of you," he rumbled, "but not until I say." Whipping out a hand with flaming fingers and icy claws, he separated more than a dozen Figments from his eager army. "These will face the enemy first. They will fight the first skirmish. They will start the war. There are many worlds to conquer, many battles to win, and they will be the first to taste combat. They will face the Barrier's Keeper. For when the Barrier world falls, all other worlds will follow."

This time when the Figments cheered, he did not stop them. Towering above them he smiled, and so completely were they his creatures now that they didn't even wince at the devastating sight.

She watched as he watched, and thrilled as he thrilled, and whispered finally words only he could hear. "Do you see our Dreamers?"

They were one in thought now, one in intent, but still the hidden whisper of her voice seared him with pleasure, and simply to feel her response, he answered, "They are sleeping."

"Yes, sleeping but not dreaming," she sighed, knowing why he had answered in the same way he had known why she had asked, and aching as he ached for the sensual intensity of their silent exchange.

"A shame, since dreams are their life," he moaned.

"Yes, a shame."

"Perhaps we can help. Let's bring them a nightmare."

Chapter 11

Dreamlessly asleep, only half aware of the arms that encircled her, Drew was still startled awake when those arms hastily withdrew. She didn't need Gyfree frantically shaking her shoulders to fully return her to his waking world, although her heart would not have quickened with the same alarm if he had only tried to whisper her awake. Her eyes were sharply clear as she opened them on his hovering face, and she recognized immediately that the shadows flitting across his cheeks were the shadows of distant trees thrashing their branches in alarm, and that the wounded darkness in his eyes leapt from a pain that was not human.

"Figments have broken through the Barrier," he whispered, his voice rough and rasping, as if something unbearably heavy was stepping down upon his throat. "I must stop them before they do more damage. I cannot spare the time to bring the others with me." A haunted darkness that was not the land's entered his eyes. "I must leave you here with them. There is no one else with the ability to hold them here, hold them asleep. There is no one else I can trust to keep control. You must guard them. They won't be able to cause any trouble as long as you keep them asleep."

"What if I need to awaken them?" she asked, his urgency echoed in her voice and eyes.

"You dreamed them asleep with me, so you have the same powers to wake them that I do. But there should be no reason. I'll be back as soon as possible." His lips pressed into hers for a single breath, and then he was gone, dashing away through the dwindling night, spurred on by a need far greater than his own. She watched him until the distance consumed him as completely as that impersonal yet somehow personal need. Then she pulled her legs into the circle of her arms, nestled her chin between her knees, and waited for the coming day to banish the intruding darkness back beyond the barrier of the distant horizon, beyond the barrier hidden by the very dark that had broken through the night before, and that would be back however many times it might be driven away.

The watchers watched, dog fangs clacking together through a fleshy arm, jaws gnawing on bone. The watchers watched, woman fingers pulsing in rhythm with a captured heart, fist opening and closing with gasping lungs. The watchers watched, and what they saw so did those who could not watch. The watchers watched, watched what they were intended to watch, watched without thought, watched despite the searing pressure behind their eyes, watched despite the icy pangs that shivered down their spines, watched because the penalty for not watching would bring much greater pain, more pain than they could bear.

As the others watched through the watchers' eyes, they saw all they wanted to see, all but the watchers themselves. They saw all they had hoped to see, all they had intended to see. They saw and they schemed and the watchers watched.

"Now?" whispered the ice queen watching through demon eyes.

"Now," replied the demon watching as the watchers watched.

The dark still held sway in the sky when Drew was startled by the sound of Sevor moaning loudly in his sleep. Turning her eyes to where he sprawled in the grass, she saw his mouth twist as if he was trying to unleash a scream. Beneath her startled eyes his arms and legs flinched, muscles bunching as if some invisible hand held him back from running. He groaned again, head thrashing from side to side as if in denial, or as if he was trying to throw off the heavy yoke of sleep that she and Gyfree had placed around his neck. Crawling to his side, Drew placed a hand to the heart thumping wildly in his chest, and into her eyes drifted a dream of bright mornings and busy stirrings. Sevor moaned again, but the sound was choked off before it was finished, and his eyes popped open, as alert and keen as Drew's.

"You were having a bad dream," she murmured soothingly, but as the meaning of her own words pierced her understanding, she gasped, eyes widening in alarm. "What did you dream? What is going to happen?"

"There are Figments coming toward us," he blurted, scrambling to his feet. "We must flee!"

"Gyfree has gone to deal with the Figments," Drew responded, relief warring in her face with the greatest fear of all. "He will be back, won't he?"

"I don't know," admitted Sevor, reaching down to haul her unceremoniously to her feet, his words racing to be heard. "I dreamed that he had gone, and I dreamed of the Figments he had gone to face. I did not dream of the outcome of that confrontation, although I could see him facing the Figments as clearly as I can see you. I don't know what will happen with him, but I do know that the Figments he will face are not the same Figments I dreamed were coming our way. We have Figments of our own to deal with and Gyfree cannot help us."

The blood drained from Drew's face more rapidly than the dark could ever drain from the sky. For a moment she stood helpless, as if frozen by a nightmare she could never hope to escape, watching from an impassable distance as Sevor futilely tried to shake Mischa awake. Now that she knew they were coming, she could feel the approach of the Figments like an itch in the center of her back, an itch that would be impossible to soothe even if she could reach it. She had felt this way before, but only in the darkest dreams, had felt the dreaded approach of something vicious, something that could not be confronted but must be escaped at all costs. Looking out into the distance, beyond the range of her eyes but not her dream-laden mind, she could even see the grotesque shapes of the stalking monsters outlined by the first hint of light in the sky. Many times she had seen similar shapes in her dreams, had even felt them menace the companions whose faces never solidified in her eyes, but whose danger was as great as her own, and whose lives hinged upon her actions. In dreams, one dream in particular, she always saved them. She took them to the house that always waited, not to hide within its walls, but to slip completely away.

She was rocked with a shock of recognition. The house. A large rambling house with rooms that merged together, like a maze with no ordinary way out but countless ways in. She had dreamed that house more times than she could remember, and would dream it again now. And this time she would not only dream it, but make it real.

Across from her a frantic Sevor continued to shake the unresponsive Mischa, and from where Drew stood, dreams within dreams pouring from her eyes and over the murmuring ground, she felt Mischa stir and blink in wonder and surprise at the man who held her. "You were calling me," whispered Mischa, but Drew had no time to ponder how Mischa had heard, for now she felt her dream of waking take Timi and Peyr, felt the Figment and the hummeybees regain themselves. From within her dreaming she could hear Sevor explaining their danger, could sense the fear that deadened even the hummeybees' buzz, but as had happened in innumerable dreams before, she felt as if she had stepped outside herself and was watching her own dream unfold from a quiet, hidden refuge where no nightmare could harm her. From her refuge she saw herself open her mouth, heard familiar words fall from her lips. "We will be safe if you follow me to the house."

From afar she watched as Timi seized her by the arms and shouted, "What's the matter with you, Drew? What house? There is no house near here."

"She's dreaming," Sevor observed, pushing Timi aside and looking far into Drew's eyes as Drew watched him from where she stood invisible, watched him peer into the wells of her eyes, watched him look for her in the one place she could not be found. "She's trying to save us."

"Follow me," the Drew dreamed by Drew said, turning to run down a hill that hadn't been there a moment before, but that had to be there now because the house was always nestled at the foot of a hill. Without a word they followed, and from her refuge Drew watched the Figment charge ahead of the others, the hummeybees on his shoulders but everyone else forgotten in his mad rush to save himself. As his hold on them loosened, Peyr and Mischa stumbled and fell, unable in that moment to comprehend that their lives held any value apart from the Figment and that they had good reason to try to stay alive. Sprawled on the ground, they watched with confused yet wounded eyes as the

Figment deserted them, and then Sevor was sweeping Mischa into his arms and cradling her against his body as he hurried down the hill, and Timi was trying to pull Peyr to his feet. At first he resisted, but then his eyes moved from the retreating figure of the Figment and he blinked up at the pale woman above him as if he was truly seeing her for the very first time. For a second they stared into each other's faces, and then a strange recognition widened his eyes, and he staggered to his feet. Hand in hand, he and Timi scampered down the hill.

Ahead they could all now see the house unfolding its wings at the base of the hill, its myriad multifaceted windows and glass-inlaid doors all glittering like insect eyes. Drew watched herself as she halted outside the first of many doors and pushed it open, watched as the Figment shoved his way through the gaping mouth, as Sevor disappeared with Mischa over the lip, as Timi led Peyr into the rumbling belly of the house. And she watched as she stepped through the door, just as she had stepped through all those times before, and shuddered as she found herself back behind her eyes.

The others stood huddled in a group nearby, the Figment cowering with his back to a wall, the hummeybees buzzing dangerously as they hovered above his stricken face. Everyone else, even Mischa and Peyr, had turned stunned eyes onto the innumerable windows, for each window displayed a different view, all familiar to Drew, but alien to those who had not spent their lives in dreams. Shrouded city streets like the ones that had brought her to this world, twisted gray hallways leading into the far recesses of some other shadowy house, the brick road that had carried many of them from Sevor's world, empty gray land that stretched desolate as far as any eye could see, and the secret room beneath the stairs, glowing now as it never had before: these and more were outside the windows. And there, through the largest window of all, was the hill. Drew already knew what she would see on its crest; there was no reason to look, except that she always looked. She lifted her eyes and there loomed the hill. The hill where the Figments stood outlined against the gray sky, the hill that was the same distant hill where they had stood when she had first seen them, but now was also the hill overlooking the house, for that was how she always dreamed this dream.

Behind her Timi gasped, and then gasped even more sharply as the door shimmered and vanished into the wall. "We're trapped!" she cried.

"No," responded Drew, "because I have always dreamed the only way out. Follow me. They will be here soon, and as long as they choose another door, the house will open for them as readily as it opened for us." Turning on her heel, she headed into the dark center of the house, the walls pulsing around her with every step the Figments took down the slope of the hill. As the pulsing grew ever louder, she twisted a path through the recesses of the house, following the curve of a hallway that could not be seen or touched, and then in the middle of nothing she stopped. There seemed no particular reason to stop, no sign that there was something to help them here, but this was the place she always stopped, and she knew its feel as clearly as she had dreamed its secret. Dropping to her knees, she slipped her hands unerringly into an invisible groove in the floor and lifted a weightless door. "No arguments," she told the others as they stared at the black maw in the floor, faces filling with dread as a breath of musty air wafted from the hole like the exhalation of some giant, lurking beast. "There's no time. This is the way we must go."

For a fraction of time no one moved, and then Timi stepped forward, her hand pulling Peyr behind her, and together they plunged into the black throat, instantly vanishing from view. Without hesitation Sevor followed, dropping Mischa in before jumping after her. The Figment, however, only backed away when Drew looked up to meet his eyes, the hummeybees buzzing furiously as they whirred around his head. There was no way and no time to reach through the fear in the Figment's eyes, so instead Drew focused on the pinpoint glare of the hummeybees. "He will die if you stay," she said flatly. "Either you must all go now or I will go without you."

As if testifying to the truth of Drew's words, the house shuddered as the crash of a huge door slamming open echoed through its invisible halls, and then the floor shook with the approach of monstrous steps. Drew glanced quickly over her shoulder, knowing that if anything other than darkness met her eyes, it would be too late for even the most potent dream to save her. Her eyes met nothing, but the floor bucked wildly, and she turned back toward the Figment, her own eyes spilling fear. Fear became shock when she saw the two hummeybees, swollen to incredible size, their burred feet clutching the Figment's shoulders as they carried him over the gaping darkness and dropped his thrashing body into the inky depths. Then with a swiftness as startling as the pulsing of their wings, the hummeybees returned to their usual size and plummeted from sight.

From closer than she had ever heard in any other dream something growled, and then the floor beneath her heaved, tossing her into the waiting hole. She had no idea how she managed not to lose hold of the secret door, but her hands continued to grip it as if they had minds of their own, minds that understood the danger that would follow if the door was not in place; as she slid into the darkness, arms stretched over her head, the door clicked home above her, and only then did her hands agree to let go. And just as she had dreamed so many times before, she was sliding through complete darkness, speeding through a tunnel that curved about her but that could not be seen. The tunnel twisted and turned, and as she plunged endlessly downward through its coils, she lost all sense of time. Yet she could feel the others plunging through darkness just ahead of her, could feel the frantic thrumming of their hearts, could feel the sobbing of their lungs, could even feel the vibration of the hummeybees' throbbing wings. And she could feel the trapped creatures crashing through the house above, could feel their claws tearing futilely at the unyielding walls, could feel their fangs gnashing in hunger, could even feel them ultimately turn upon each other with claws and fangs, slashing and rending with a success that they could never know against the house itself.

On through the tunnel she plunged, and then she knew her ride through the dark would be over soon, not because her speed had slowed or because a hint of light could be seen faintly outlining her feet, but because no matter how many times she dreamed this dream, she always knew. She knew, yet she still felt a jolt as the tunnel opened before her and she rocketed out, feet landing firmly on the ground as if she had never sailed through the darkness of space. Around her the others lay strewn across the ground like discarded rags, but she knew that they had survived just as her dream companions always survived, although this time their faces would resolve and when the dream ended she would still remember who they were and why she had needed to save them. Even now one of the faces turned toward her, and she could see with startling clarity bright blue eyes above a wry smile. "That was quite an experience," dryly remarked Sevor.

Another face with pale eyes surrounded by a halo of ashen hair came into focus. "Where exactly are we?" questioned Timi.

"In the tunnels beneath the house," answered Drew.

"Are we lost?" Timi asked, her eyes on the featureless walls curving over their heads.

"No. I've dreamed my way through these tunnels before and I know the way out."

A whining buzz erupted from one of the others still sprawled on the ground, and as the perfect face of the Figment lifted into view, the two hummeybees darted out from beneath him.

"How could you?" whimpered the Figment, his eyes full of an injury darker than the twisted bowels of the house.

"It waz nezezzary," droned the larger hummeybee, its eyes on the Figment, its wings a blur of agitation. "We had to zave you."

"Yez," continued the smaller hummeybee. "You are too pre-ziouz to die."

The Figment shuddered as violently as the house shuddered each time monsters crossed its sensitive threshold, and in response the hummeybees settled on his shoulders, trembling wings brush-ing his face and casting rainbow hues across his cheeks. As they buzzed soothingly in his ears, his trembling slowly abated, until soon his eyelids drooped heavily and a sensual smile drifted across his lips.

Beside Sevor another face lifted, and Mischa turned expectant eyes toward the Figment, but when no silent summons forced her to his side, her eyes darkened with bewilderment rather than pain. And when a strong arm encircled her, and then pulled her close, she turned her eyes to a different face. "You saved me," she murmured.

"Now that you mention it, I suppose I did," Sevor replied, his voice warm and his eyes teasing.

"Why?" she asked with a perplexity that was more haunting than the plaintive cries of a child trying to shake loose the cling-ing tendrils of a nightmare.

"Because I care about you," answered Sevor, eyes turning as dim as the light in the surrounding tunnel.

"How can you care? He doesn't."

"I care because you're special."

Mischa gently shook her head as silent tears slid down her cheeks. "He said I was special too. But I am clearly not special enough."

As Sevor and Mischa continued to whisper back and forth, the last face materialized, and Peyr gazed up at Timi as if she was the solution to a puzzle that had long teased his mind. "You're like him," he murmured. "I can see it in your face."

Timi startled backward as if he had raised a fist to strike her. "Like who?" she blurted.

"Like him," answered Peyr, gesturing toward the Figment as if he was the only possible answer to her question. "There's something about you too. Something powerful. Something enthralling. I can feel it in you, feel it just as strongly as I feel it in him."

Timi recoiled as if he had in fact punched her in the face. Turning toward Drew, she snapped, "Why are we still here? Are we waiting for something? Perhaps for one of those Figments to find its way down?"

Far overhead a solitary pair of feet scraped back and forth across the hidden door, the sound reverberating through Drew's dreaming mind like a scream bouncing off the walls of an empty theater. The vague shape of something monstrous crept through her eyes. "There is always one," she murmured.

"One what?" demanded Timi, her voice tight with a fear that was only in part the house and the dark and the creatures that stalked them.

"One will find the door and follow. We must go."

From far away a door shrieked open, and a shock of cold air erupted from the twisting tunnel that had dropped them all there only minutes or maybe hours ago.

"We must go," repeated Drew, her words jolting the Figment from his reverie and spurring the hummeybees into flight.

"I need," moaned the Figment as he stumbled to his feet, his voice drawing both Mischa and Peyr like the bait in a trap, and his eyes snaring them before they could feel the steel jaws slamming shut on their ankles. At the first sound of his voice, Mischa jerked free from Sevor's arm and Peyr tore his eyes from Timi's flushed face. There was a long moment as they stood poised, not fully recaptured yet still not free, and then something seemed to blast into them and their bodies crumpled. Shoulders slumped and heads bowed, they both limped to his side, limbs twitching clumsily as if their ownership was in contention and they were struggling either to surrender completely or resume possession of themselves. Peyr halted just before he reached the Figment and swivelled around to face the others, his stance once more challenging, although his eyes were gently questioning as he again focused on Timi's face. Mischa, however, did not stop until she was tucked beneath the Figment's arm, but instead of nestling against him as she had in the past, she shivered, and the eyes that had once been completely absorbed by his face gazed outward with a yearning that had nothing to do with desire.

Without another word, Drew turned toward a dark, narrow opening in the tunnel wall, and plunged forward. She could feel the others falling in behind her, just as she could always feel those who involuntarily shared this dream, and just as she could feel the monstrous predator plummeting through the darkness that was the only exit from the house.

And the watchers watched, teeth gnawing through arm and hand clutching both heart and lungs while the watchers watched their Dreamers move farther and farther apart. Together the watchers watched, but separately as well, for what they watched was not the same. Intent on watching what he must watch, the dog still felt the grip on his heart loosen, felt his lungs suddenly expand without interference, and he growled a warning and a reminder of what failure in this task would mean.

"I am sorry," whispered the woman, "but there is something about my Dreamer that pushes my eyes away. It is so very hard to watch when in her dreams I've never truly seen her."

"How is that possible?" snarled the dog, his own fear turning his growl to a whine.

"I am the mother of her nightmares. The one who never looks at her except to kill her, and even then doesn't truly see her. And since her real mother never paid much attention to her, I have never completely escaped her thoughts and memories. And those thoughts and memories continue to insist that I don't notice her. I am trying, and I will not stop trying, but you must bite harder, for this is arduous."

The dog's teeth clamped down until the taste of withered flesh was bitter on his tongue. Even more intent on his task, he watched, but this time while he watched his Dreamer he watched the other watcher as well.

And those who watched through the watchers' eyes still saw everything except the watchers.

Gyfree ran through the night, ran through trees that shuddered with a distant pain, ran over ground that trembled with the strain of bearing too much weight. Gyfree ran through the night and toward the first gray smears of dawn, toward trees that thrashed in unspeakable agony, toward ground that sank beneath the pressure of so many monstrous feet. Gyfree ran directly into a nightmare rather than away from it, but he knew he was not running quickly enough, that just as he ran so did the Figments, their giant strides carrying them farther than he could match and farther than the land could withstand. He was the Keeper, and no one could stop the Figments other than himself, but first he must reach them, and he was going far too slowly.

As the world grayed around him, Gyfree felt as if he was running through a dream, his limbs leaden with exhaustion, the air in his lungs as trapped as a scream. Yet this wasn't a dream, for a dream would have brought the monsters to him shortly after he felt their presence. A dream would never have placed so much distance between him and the menace that threatened. A dream would have carried him farther and faster than he could ever carry himself. With that thought, Gyfree's feet faltered and the gray touching the sky and marking the trees filled his eyes. A dream. He needed a dream; needed to dream a dream. A dream that spanned distances, a dream that rocketed through the grayness, a dream that could transport a Dreamer across any world.

The seeds of gray in his eyes blossomed within his mind, and now when he ran there was nothing beneath his feet and nothing to mark the course of his passage, and more importantly, nothing to slow him or to keep him from his destination. He ran with all the speed of a dream winging its way through the night, with the urgency of a Dreamer trying to awaken from a nightmare. And then with the disjointed abruptness that characterized the most restless of dreams, he was there, feet back on firm ground, the dream spilling from his eyes like muddy tears, more than a dozen Figments rushing toward him.

Suddenly confronted by the Keeper, the lead Figment skidded to a halt, clawed feet tearing deep gashes in the skin of the land. Behind him came others, each as solid as the shivering trees and as present as Gyfree himself. There was not a single misty phantom or fluctuating figure. Each Figment wore a face twisted and torn from some unbearable nightmare, but no other faces emerged from beneath the deformed masks, and the only rippling Gyfree could see was the rippling of muscles beneath grainy skin or slimy scales. The Figments stood before him, massive and hideous, their exhaled breaths rancid with the reek of death. And the most massive and hideous was the one that stood before the rest.

"You must leave," boomed the Keeper, voice echoing in the still air as if bounding and rebounding from cavern walls buried deep within the earth.

"You must die," rumbled the giant Figment in response, voice as fathomless and vast as the void, eyes agleam with malicious laughter.

The Keeper's eyes squinted as if he was trying to focus on something far away while the sun shone fully into his face, and then flitting across his features there came the vague shapes of leafs, the shadows that marked time passing across the ridges of a mountainside, the fluid outline of a waterfall dancing its way down from incredible heights. As if of their own volition, his hands spread open, palms toward the emerging sky, and all the verdant greens and rich browns of fertile earth, all the elusive blues and trapped rainbows of water and sky, all the riotous colors that heralded spring, burst through his skin and ignited the air.

"You must leave," boomed the Keeper, his voice the rumble of nearby thunder that warns that lightning can strike anywhere at any time.

This time the Figment did not offer a response, but instead stepped forward, the earth sinking beneath its feet. All of the light and color ablaze in the Keeper's hands exploded outward to strike the creature directly in the chest, but the Figment swiped it aside with one immense paw as if swatting at an annoying bug. Closer it came, and icy waves from the Keeper's hands pounded against the creature as if it was a rocky shore that time and the elements could patiently erode away. Yet still closer came the living nightmare, and the waves shimmered with the heavy heat of a summer afternoon, a heat that always coaxed the very trees and rocks to lose themselves in drowsy fantasies, but even that did not slow the approaching monstrosity. Instead of hesitating as the waves crashed into it, the Figment cupped its paws to its chest, so that all the light and color, all the numbing cold of deep winter and all the sapping heat of high summer, the very essence of the land itself, cascaded from the grimy palms and splashed upward into the black hole of the Figment's gaping mouth.

As if seized by a gravity greater than any world's, the force spilling through the Keeper was sucked into the Figment's maw and drawn down its throat. The Keeper shuddered and gasped, and across his face now flitted the shadowy smudges of dust-filled clouds stirred by a hot, dry wind from arid land where nothing lives and nothing grows. He tried to close his hands, to hold back the surge of life and power that came from the land, but it seemed as if some force greater than his own pried his fingers open each time they curled shut. With unappeased hunger the Figment continued to swallow the stream of brightness flowing from the Keeper's hands, continued to swallow it even after the colors faded and the light dimmed, and long after all of the surrounding land had visibly started to fade, the trees and the grass, the sky and the soil, now all empty and wan. Only when the knees of the Keeper buckled, and his hands fell to the brittle grass, did the Figment close its massive jaws. Then, with scraps of green and blue and brown hanging from its fangs, it smiled, and to Gyfree it seemed as if death itself stood smiling over him. He could hear the mob of Figments laughing derisively, as if from far away, could hear the giant Figment laughing above all the others. And resounding through his mind he could hear the sighs and whispers of death as his world teetered on the edge of the waiting darkness.

He was the Keeper, the one chosen to defend this world, and he had failed. He was the Keeper, and he was dying, just as his world was dying. He could feel countless withered trees trembling in unison with his own feeble limbs, could feel every river and stream turn to sludge with the blood in his veins, could feel the dense and gritty air settling in his lungs and across the land with the heaviness of cement. He was the Keeper, and he would never again walk through tall grass or along the paths of a dream, would never hold Drew in either his waking or dreaming arms, for there would be no world or dreams left in which to hold her.

He was the Keeper. The world stirred within him, and the sighs and whispers changed from mourning to admonishment.

He was the Keeper, but he had been chosen for a reason. He had been chosen because he was different. He had been chosen because he was a Dreamer. A Dreamer before all else, a Dreamer before he was the Keeper. A Dreamer first, a Dreamer always, for only as a Dreamer could the Keeper hope to prevail against enemies more numerous and powerful than any this world had ever faced before.

He was the Keeper. The world stirred within him, and the sighs and whispers changed from admonishment to advice. He was the Keeper, but no ordinary Keeper, for he had the power to dream. Even now a dream was streaming through his eyes, and in his dream he was no longer crouched in the crumbling grass with heavy dust deadening his lungs; instead he was adrift in a sun-speckled clearing among trees as green as Drew's eyes. Here the air was vibrant, crackling with all the pent-up energy of undischarged electricity, and he was the outlet it had chosen. Lightning thrilled through him, sparking from his fingers, forking from the soles of his feet, and when he laughed his was the voice of thunder, this time warning that the lightning had indeed arrived, and that it was now too late to seek shelter.

Spread below in his dream were the tiny figures of more than a dozen Figments floundering in a flood of gray, distant faces turned upward as if gulping for air, but he was in the air, and into their gaping mouths he rained lightning. At first the Figments all seemed to possess the same unquenchable appetite as the largest one, the capacity to consume anything and everything, but then their forms began to bulge as if hundreds of snakes were tunneling beneath their skin, and forks of light poked from their eyes and from beneath the claws of their splayed paws like reptilian tongues testing the air. The light licked their faces and wrapped around their arms and legs, and then sank its own bright fangs into their bulky torsos, closing its jaws until they were swallowed whole. Then the light slithered its way across the gray ground and, with a flick of its sinuous tail, vanished.

The Dreamer still dreamed, suspended in the electric air, for below remained one Figment, the largest of them all, its leering mouth crammed with greens and browns and blues too dense for any light to penetrate. The Dreamer dreamed, for in this place, dreams were power, but the creature beneath had power of its own, and locked away behind the bars of its fangs it held the Dreamer's world hostage. The Keeper might despair; in fact, the Keeper had despaired, but the Dreamer still dreamed, and through him the land now too had the power to dream. And together the Dreamer and the land dreamed of trees that grew and grew to enormous heights, scraping the stars from the sky with their swaying branches; of mountains orbiting beyond the trees to pierce through the velvet fabric of space; of waterfalls leaping from the tips of the mountains to extinguish distant suns; of a world too galactic to be contained.

Now so far below that it seemed no more than a mote of dust, the figure lost its leer, but the Dreamer that was the Keeper and the Dreamer that was the land were too immersed in their dream to notice. The figure swelled, but the Dreamer and the dreaming land were too wide-ranging to mark so minuscule a change. The figure continued to swell, and the Dreamers continued to dream, for in their dream was forgotten the distant pangs of a dying and parched world. But when the figure finally burst, and the greens and browns and blues, and all the other countless colors of life, flooded back through the Keeper to shower every dreaming particle of land, the Keeper's eyes refocused on a world once more vibrant and alive. A world in which not a single Figment could be seen.

The Keeper who was a Dreamer climbed slowly to his feet, still dreaming with the land, but now dreaming of a land that was content to shrink back within the limiting boundaries of its world. Within his mind the world then stirred, its sighs and whispers filled with relief. And then, with a jolt that dispelled the last clinging tendrils of the dream, he felt something else rip through the Barrier. Something far from where he now stood. Something large and dangerous. Something rushing directly toward Drew.

Still the watchers watched, watched because they had no choice, watched because they were the ones who could watch. Yet watching was not an easy thing. The dog had watched long and faithfully, but as he watched so many Figments die, his tail pulled between his legs, and a trickle of urine sizzled into the gray. The hand around his heart and lungs squeezed tightly, and the dead-faced woman, the nightmare mother, leaned over him, her eyes darting briefly away from her own Dreamer. "Is the poor puppy frightened?" she hissed.

The dog bit harder on the tattered arm and growled deep in his throat. "At least I have no trouble watching."

Ragged nails pinched the fitful heart and palsied lungs. "Perhaps my Dreamer is more powerful."

Before he could stop it, a whimper slipped up the woman's arm. "My Dreamer just killed all of the Figments sent against him."

"So you are frightened," she mocked.

"There is reason," snarled the dog.

"Why? Is he the type to kill a stray dog?"

A whine reverberated deep in the dog's chest. "In his dreams, I was always the one to turn on him. He was hurt so many times that he dreamed me, and in his dreams I became every thing and every person ever to give him pain. To him I was always more than a stray dog; I was the teeth that hid behind a friendly face to snap and rend, and he would have no reason not to kill me."

Again the nightmare mother's eyes slid off of her Dreamer like rain off of an umbrella.

The jaws snapped shut.

The fingers curled into a tight fist.

The watchers shuddered, but still the watchers watched. And as they watched they could feel the piercing heat of the demon eyes watching through their eyes, could feel the blistering cold of the ice queen watching through the demon eyes, could feel both watching as if they were one. Two watching as one through watchers who had been chosen as one but who watched as two. Two watchers who watched two Dreamers who had learned to dream as one. Two in one body. Two watchers with one task. Two Dreamers who even apart were slowly becoming one.

"Two in one," murmured the woman, her eyes slipping again.

"You must always watch!" barked the dog.

"I will watch if you will watch."

"I am watching."

"We are one in this task. Two in one. Two interchangeable parts of a single whole. Just like those we watch. Just like those for whom we watch."

"What are you talking about?" growled the dog, his teeth crunching bone as his tail thrashed through the gray.

"You must watch my Dreamer. I must watch yours. Then I will always be able to see. And you will always be able to remain unseen, not to mention unpunished."

"It's impossible to watch another's Dreamer."

The woman continued as if the dog had never interrupted. "We are connected now. Two in one. Even now I can feel your Dreamer, just as I can feel you chewing on my arm. If I can feel, I can also watch."

The dog's jaws stopped gnawing and his ears cocked as if he was listening for that high-pitched whistle that only dogs could hear. Then he yelped and scampered from paw to paw. "You are right," he barked. "I can feel your Dreamer. I can feel her through the fingers you have wrapped around my lungs and heart."

"Watch her," whispered the nightmare mother as her eyes glided to something new.

"Watch him," whined the dog as he cringed away from the friend he had bitten far too often.

The watchers watched, and those who watched through the watchers watched. And the watchers were satisfied, for now it was easy to watch, and there was so much to learn. There was much to learn from the Dreamers, and much to learn from the touch of those other feverish yet chilling eyes. And those who watched through the watchers' eyes also saw much, and also learned much. But they still did not learn anything about the watchers.

Chapter 12

Twisting and turning through the tunnels that headed away from the house and out of the dream, Drew led the way as if she could see the path clearly, as if she had cat eyes that could penetrate the absolute darkness enclosing them, a darkness that could only be found deep in caverns beneath the earth and in dreams. Here there was the darkness of both, and through it the others stumbled, their hands trailing the feathery dry walls, their feet scraping across the ground as if they would lose the only anchor that held them to this place if they dared lift their feet for even the briefest of seconds. Drew knew they moved too slowly, but they moved slowly in her dreams as well, and despite the stabbing pressure in her spine that imparted all too clearly that the Figment would soon catch up with them, she knew they would still somehow manage to break free from the tunnel before any fatal encounter.

There was no gradual brightening of the tunnel to indicate that the end was drawing near, but suddenly Drew was stumbling through the opening and into the gray light of either a dawning or a dreaming day. The others stumbled out behind her, blinking their eyes and gasping in wonder, but Drew already knew what her eyes would see. They were back on the crest of the hill overlooking the house. They had plummeted to a depth far beneath the ground, and in all their windings through the tunnel they had never climbed, but this was a dream, and in this dream, Drew always found herself and her companions back on the crest of the hill as if they had never left. The mouth of the tunnel that had a moment before spit them all out had immediately closed, and then vanished from sight. Yet not all things were exactly the same as they had been before the plunge down the hill. Spread below them the house's windows gleamed blood red, and the sound of something thick and heavy dripping leaked through its walls and surged all the way up to where they stood gathered. Stepping up beside her, wide eyes glued to the uncanny house, Sevor gulped. "Are they all dead?" he questioned.

"All but one," Drew coolly replied.

Halfway down the hill the ground abruptly bulged, as if something immense was shouldering it aside. Earth rained upward and then hailed back down, showering a huge head as it broke through dirt and rock with the ease of a swimmer breaking water. Two massive paws followed the head, grabbing hold of the crumbling edges of the giant hole to lift the creature's shoulders and torso into the gray light. A face smeared with blood and filth leered up at the transfixed companions, and then the Figment continued to wriggle its way free from the clinging darkness of the tunnel below.

"What do we do now?" demanded Timi, her hand closing convulsively on Drew's arm.

"I don't know," Drew admitted, fear tinging her voice for the first time since she had summoned the dream. "I've never had a creature break free from the tunnel before. Before that could happen, I've always woken up."

"What?" shrieked Timi as the Figment pulled one bulging knee onto the ground.

"Run," answered Drew, shoving Timi away. "All of you, run as far and as fast as you can."

Timi's Figment and the hummeybees required no further urging. As had happened before, the hummeybees swelled to incredible size in less than a heartbeat of time, and swooping down upon the Figment, seized him by the shoulders and darted away with a speed so astonishing that they disappeared almost immediately from view. Deserted once again, Mischa blinked as if clearing something gritty from beneath her lids, and then turned away from the empty space that had seemingly swallowed the Figment whole. "He left me again," she stated flatly, her eyes seeking and finding Sevor's.

"But I haven't," Sevor responded with a wry smile that didn't even waver when the creature pursuing them pulled free its other knee.

"Timi, follow your Figment. Keep him away from others. Now go!" ordered Drew.

Timi turned quickly to seize Peyr's hand, only to discover that his eyes were already sharply focused on her face. "Come with me," she demanded, and without a word he fell in beside her as she sped unerringly along the path of the Figment.

The hillside quaked as the creature lurched to its feet.

"Sevor, take Mischa and run!" cried Drew.

Sevor grabbed Mischa's hand and pulled her in the direction that Timi and Peyr were running, but after a short while, when the sound of other feet failed to chase their own, Mischa jerked to a stop and tore her hand free, abruptly turning her face back toward where Drew stood alone in the distance, a tiny speck face to face with the towering Figment. "No," she protested as Sevor tried to regain his hold on her hand, "we cannot leave Drew to face this danger alone. I won't desert her!"

Sevor dropped his hand and a crooked smile accented the rueful gleam in his eyes. "You've certainly picked an interesting time to start returning to yourself," he remarked dryly.

A puzzled frown creased Mischa's brow, but there was no time to waste on questions, and without another word she hurried back toward Drew, Sevor directly on her heels.

At the crest of the hill Drew waited for the Figment, not because she had dreamed this meeting before, but because there was no other way she could think of to dream the others to safety. So she stood and watched as the Figment shook the clinging debris from its skin like a mammoth dog sloughing water, and not even when it crested the hill and loomed over her did she step backward. Nor did she flinch when the Figment's voice rumbled out with all the force of an earthquake, "So, pretty little Dreamer, what do you plan to do now?"

"I don't know," Drew responded. Or perhaps she did. There were so many dreams. So many ways to slip from dream to dream.

The Figment threw back its head and laughed, the raucous sound rebounding off the countless walls of the house. "I have come to kill you, pretty little Dreamer. Perhaps you should have run away with all your friends."

"Perhaps, but it is too late now."

The Figment fixed her in its wild eyes. "Do you intend to fight me? You can try, if you choose, but you are not my Dreamer, and you have no real power over me. Not even my own Dreamer had the power to withstand me."

"I have no intention to fight. But before you kill me, I would like to ask a few questions."

Again the Figment laughed, and again the sound bounced back and forth off the distant walls, this time even shaking the house. "Ask away, pretty little Dreamer."

"Did he send you?"

The laughter in its face died more quickly than the Figment could kill. "Enough questions," it growled. "Time to die."

"Why did he send you?" persisted Drew imperturbably.

The Figment leaned over her until its face was only inches from her own, and she could smell the blood on its breath. "Because, pretty little Dreamer, he is bringing an army, and more than an army, to conquer this world. We were sent to get rid of you, just as others were sent to get rid of the Keeper. With both of you gone, this world will fall without resistance. And then world after world will follow. And it all starts with you."

A huge paw with claws fully extended swept out toward the Dreamer's head, but before it could strike her, she was gone. For a fraction of time the Figment stood still, and then it threw back its massive head and howled, howled until the ground shook so violently that Mischa and Sevor, who had skidded to a stop nearby just as Drew blinked out of existence, were hurled off their feet.

"I will find you!" roared the Figment, swiping its claws through the air. "I know what games a pretty little Dreamer like you can play. I know you're still here."

The Figment had not noticed the dream flowing through her eyes, so intent had it been on gloating. But the dream had been there, and the moment she could see her death reflected in the Figment's eyes, that dream had carried her into invisibility. She had fallen immediately to her knees and darted through the creature's legs, and from there she would have fled far beyond its reach, but as she turned her back on the beast and prepared to run, she was arrested by the sight of Mischa and Sevor tumbling to the ground. Within seconds she was beside them, whispering urgently in their ears, "I told you to run for a reason. Now run, quickly, before it's too late."

Sevor and Mischa scrambled to their feet, but it was already too late. With a roar of triumph, the Figment lunged over to them, grabbing each with one giant paw and lifting them off their feet. "I have your friends, pretty little Dreamer!" it thundered. "If you don't show yourself, I will rip out their throats and bathe in their blood."

There was a shimmer in the air and then Drew blinked back into existence as abruptly as she had blinked out. With a growl the Figment tossed its two captives to the ground, and with a swiftness completely belied by its incomprehensible size, seized Drew by the throat and lifted her high above its head. Sharp talons pricked her neck and blood trickled down the sides of its fist. "I will enjoy watching you die, pretty little Dreamer," it rumbled. "So die, Dreamer, die."

Mischa pulled herself off of the ground and charged toward the Figment from one side just as Sevor, who had rolled quickly to his own feet, charged from the other. Yet their effort was wasted, for with a single swipe of one vast paw, the Figment sent them both crashing back to earth. If Drew had been able to turn her eyes their way, she would have seen their noses dripping blood and their eyes blinking dazedly, but her eyes had filled with a darkness that had nothing to do with dreaming, and much to do with nothing.

Gyfree was already racing through his own summoned dream when he felt Drew slip into hers, and felt her pull all the others in with her. In his mind he could even see the house of her dream, straddling the bottom of a hill, its multifaceted eyes agleam, its stillness the stillness of a preying insect camouflaged against the bark of a tree. Then his dream merged into the edges of her dream, and he was running toward the same house that had already opened its door to her. Dream folding into dream, he was carried quickly to the crest of the hill, and from there he watched the last few Figments vanish through an open door. And without thought for what he followed, he too tumbled down the hill and headed directly for the same door. Yet by the time he reached it, the door had crashed shut like a giant mouth closing on a rare delicacy. He banged his fists against the door, heedless of everything but his need to reach Drew, but the house remained as impervious to his needs as those locked inside remained unaware of his presence. Beyond the door he could hear the growls and shrieks of the Figments as they first tried to attack the house, and then finally tore each other apart in their frenzy, but however fiercely he shouted, nothing and no one seemed to hear him. His fists were bruised and his voice was battered when silence at last seized the house, and then finally, the door cracked open.

Gyfree pushed open the door and almost fell as he placed one foot in a puddle of blood. Looking through the door, he could see blood everywhere, more blood than he could have ever dreamed. The walls and floors and even the ceiling were completely coated with blood, and the stench was so overwhelming he gagged. If he hadn't already felt Drew pass through these rooms, hadn't felt her slip away through a concealed door and plunge down into some hidden place beneath the house, he would have never been able to budge his second foot over the threshold, but his need to reach Drew was far greater than his abhorrence of so much death. And even when the door shimmered and vanished behind him, his only thought was still that he must find Drew.

Without hesitation Gyfree waded into the blood-filled room, but even as he slogged forward, he could see the blood seeping into the floor, could see it soaking into the walls and ceiling, as if the house was slowly lapping it up. But more importantly, he could see the heavy footprints tracking through the blood and following the same path that Drew had followed. Footprints that led directly through the unexpected twists and turns of the house to a black hole in the floor where a door had been torn from its hinges and tossed aside. This was the way Drew had gone, the way a Figment had followed, and the way he now plunged. As if it possessed a gravity of its own, the tunnel seized him and pulled him down through the darkness, hurling him through space as if he was a meteorite rocketing toward an alien world. It was cold in this strange space he traversed, icy cold, and it was empty, for there was nothing here except for the darkness and him, although somewhere far beneath there was the sensation of warmth and life that was Drew.

He could not guess how much time he had spent hurtling through the space beneath the house, but suddenly he was standing in the center of a gray chamber surrounded by several black passages. He didn't need the bloody footprints of the Figment to tell him which tunnel Drew had taken, for he could feel it, just as he could feel her breaking free at the other end somewhere in the world above. And just as he could feel how closely danger trailed her. Fear gripped him with talons more merciless than any Figment as he rushed into the tunnel after her. The trace of Drew was so strong here that, despite the total absence of light, he ran as heedlessly as if every curve and bend were exposed beneath the noonday sun, speeding unerringly onward as if he could see Drew racing ahead only a few steps away, her smoky hair bouncing as she ran, her eyes filling with laughter as she tossed a glance over her shoulder to make sure he was there. He could feel the gap between them closing with every thump of his feet on the invisible ground, for she had finally stopped moving, but he could also feel the dream of invisibility wrapping around her, and he knew that danger had caught her. With a gasp that ricocheted off the enclosing walls he spurred himself forward, but he had only covered a short distance when he saw light spilling into the tunnel directly ahead, shining down from a giant hole to illuminate a large pile of stone and earth. And rumbling down from above he could hear the voice of the Figment telling Drew to die.

Gyfree scrambled frantically up the mound of debris, and as he grasped desperately for a hold, the land he touched fused back together, grass sprouting roots to hold together rocks and dirt, rocks and dirt forming ledges so that the Keeper could quickly reach his objective, an objective the land itself recognized and shared, for the land had come to value the other true Dreamer just as had the Keeper, and was equally ready to fight for her life. So there was no need for the Keeper to call upon the land; all the powers blatant in a driving wind or hidden in a waiting seed, all the land had to offer, was already pouring from the Keeper's hands and slamming into the back of the Figment before Gyfree's feet had fully returned to the ground above.

When the full force of the land crashed into it, the Figment pitched to its knees, and as it instinctively threw out its paws to catch itself, it flung Drew's body to the ground. In the barest instant the Figment was lunging back to its legs, its eyes full of death and its claws raking the air, so there was no time for the Keeper to turn his eyes to the body that lay still and silent beyond his reach. But to Gyfree it seemed suddenly as if he and the

Keeper were two separate beings, and even as the Keeper turned his complete attention to the maddened creature hurtling in his direction, Gyfree could see nothing but Drew, her blood seeping sluggishly from her neck, her smoky hair obscuring eyes that might be drained of all dreams, and her limbs lying motionless and twisted as if they had never been attached to a living being. The Keeper might fight, but in that moment Gyfree knew only despair, and even as the land lashed out in defiance and hatred, the Dreamer refused to stir. He faced the Figment but all he could see was Drew, her blood, her hair, her quiet limbs, and finally, the barely perceptible rise and fall of her chest. Then, with the realization that she was still alive, the Keeper and the Dreamer were one again, one in purpose and one in desire, one with the land that now dreamed with the Dreamer, dreamed this time of its own deeply buried frictions and tensions, and in dreaming surged through the Keeper's outstretched hands to open a chasm beneath the Figment's charging feet, dreaming itself splitting apart, dreaming itself cracking open to its core, and then dreaming itself whole again. As the ground violently quaked, the Keeper who was one with the land, and the Dreamer who dreamed with the land, alone stood firm, as if he was rooted in the soil and could not be shaken loose. And when the tremors of the dreaming land settled into a drowsy peace, the Figment was gone, entombed and crushed deep within the unyielding ground.

Gyfree did not wait for the last of the land's trembling to pass before he scurried to Drew's side, his hands folding over the gashes in her neck and a new dream filling his eyes even before he had settled to the ground beside her. And again his world dreamed with him, dreamed quietly this time, dreamed of all the healing powers that spring brought to the face of the land. Beneath his hands Drew stirred as if she was dreaming of something far-away, and then her eyes fluttered open and she blinked up at the rusty-haired man leaning over her, the shadow of a living world dreaming behind his eyes. Then a faint smile quirked her lips and she murmured, "I had a terrible nightmare."

"You did?" Gyfree responded with a weak smile of his own.

"Yes, but it ended well. You came to save me."

"Are you sure it was me?"

"I'm sure. It was you, but you weren't alone. There was an entire world standing with you." Tears suddenly leaked from the corners of her eyes as if she had finally lost the power to check them. "I never thought I'd see you again."

Roughly Gyfree pulled her into his arms, one hand stroking her tousled hair as he whispered the same words that had been whispered to every child who had ever felt the touch of a nightmare. "It's over now. It was just a bad dream."

Drew lifted her face to Gyfree's, and what he saw in her eyes stilled the words on his lips. "No, it's far from over," she told him huskily. "My Figment sent all of those others, and he will be sending more. He will keep sending more until we are both dead and this world has fallen. It's not over at all; it's just begun."

The Dreamers were both still alive, just as they had expected them to be, for death was not yet what he and she had in mind. It was no longer their intention to share their Dreamers' deaths with anyone other than each other; in fact, they had even been gripped by a strange fear when each Dreamer had escaped death so narrowly. No, all they had wanted for the time being was to test their Dreamers, to tamper with their minds, to prepare the way for the true assault, an assault that hid itself within the army he had raised with her help, but had little to do with the army itself. After all, their victories were also something he and she had never planned to share; the Figments that waited restlessly now were as expendable as those that had gone before. They had been shaped to serve a purpose, a definite purpose, but they had not been shaped to exhale death with every breath. They had not been shaped for any additional deadliness at all, yet still they would serve their purpose, just as the others had already served theirs, and if the Dreamers failed to destroy them all before they were themselves destroyed, then he and she would have no compunction in completing the task. In fact, they would enjoy it, although not as much as they would enjoy killing the Dreamers who had brought them to life and then refused in turn to die.

Inside the demon's eyes the ice queen glittered and it was her smile that froze on his lips, but where she nestled within, flames licked across her mind and would have melted her limbs if she still had limbs. More than ever before, she was one with her lover, wrapped in an embrace that never ended, wrapped in a pleasure that heightened with each passing heartbeat as they felt each other with a growing intensity that made his face writhe in ecstasy and made her squirm for release. No longer was she buried deep within his farthest recesses, for he thrilled at the sensation of her presence, and had slowly brought her closer and closer to the surface, so that now she shivered in delight just beneath his skin while the heat that had once been in his loins spread over and through her until they were both left shuddering and gasping and yearning to feel more than they had ever felt before. They had already shared more than even she could have imagined, but their sharing could not be complete until they had shared their Dreamers' deaths, had forever banished the dreams from their Dreamers' eyes and left their bodies in tatters. Their desire for death was as unquenchable as their desire to feel each other with an intensity that surpassed every moment of intensity that had come before. And like their desire, their power was unstoppable, and just as they had ultimately conquered each other, they would now conquer worlds. Beginning with the world that most truly mattered, and then continuing with the world that had spawned so many Dreamers, although none greater than their own.

Images of their Dreamers flashed without interruption through their joined minds, for as the watchers watched so did they, but unlike the watchers, they were not limited to watching. Even now he was stalking through the army of Figments, lashing out with talons that burned and froze whenever a Figment moved too slowly from his path. And she shivered below his skin, reveling in the fear and pain she wielded with him, unseen herself but seeing and feeling all. In the midst of the army he stopped, and around him all Figments dropped to their knees, faces not pressed into the gray, but lifted as he had demanded, eyes not squeezed tight, but open and watching with both anticipation and dread. He swept his eyes across the gathered throng, and her eyes swept with his, and then he spoke, her voice cooling the heat that burst veins, and the Figments lapped up the words as thirstily as he had lapped up his Dreamer's blood when she had held it in her icy hands, when she had still possessed icy hands. "The Figments I sent have failed to kill either the Barrier's Keeper or the Dreamer who helps him."

As one the kneeling Figments growled, their own lust for blood throbbing through the sound.

"Yet they came close to succeeding," he rumbled, his voice carving through them until all they knew was the insatiable hunger in their guts. "They had their prey at the verge of death and only failed at the last moment when their victims each received unexpected help. Figments only a fraction stronger would have succeeded, and I did not send the strongest Figments. For I did not send all of you."

The roar that ripped through the mob thundered through every remote corner of the void, echoing and reechoing through the vast emptiness before returning to this sole concentration of life. Yet the echoes faded away when the demon raised his hand as if they too knew better than to disobey. "The time is not yet," he boomed. "But it will be soon. And when the moment is right, I will go too."

He waded through the cheering throng, too intent on her seductive whisper and arousing presence to even kick aside the Figments who could not avoid his path. Over the tumult his groans went unnoticed, but she heard him just as he heard her, their groans merging and quickening until they reached another new peak that would now only need to be surpassed.

And not so far away, the watchers still watched. They watched the Dreamers wrapped in each other's arms and immersed in each other's dreams. And they felt the watchers who watched through them, felt the burning yet frigid eyes of the two wrapped in one body and immersed in one need. They watched and they endured, but they did not watch in silence.

"Very impressive," murmured the woman with dead eyes. "Your Dreamer is very impressive indeed."

The dog whimpered and cringed, but his bark when it came was just as cutting as his bite. "Your Dreamer would have won if those others had not interfered. That house she dreamed is the most lethal thing I've ever seen."

"Yes, they are both dangerous Dreamers. I can see why our masters want them destroyed."

"The Dreamers have no chance," whined the dog. "Nothing can withstand the masters."

"We will see."

"Yes, we will see."

"And we will learn."

"What will we learn?"

"We will learn the strengths of the weakest and the weaknesses of the strongest."

"And what will we gain?"

"Ah," sighed the woman, her smile as dead as her eyes. "We will see."

So the watchers watched, and the watchers saw, and the watchers learned, but still no one watched or saw or learned anything about the watchers.

Drew could taste the salt of her own tears as Gyfree's lips brushed against hers, but before the salt could burn on her tongue or trickle down her throat, a nearby moan parted their lips from each other and dragged their eyes toward the disheveled and dirty woman hauling herself to her knees. Turning bleary yet teasing eyes their way, Mischa commented, "Well, Dreamer, I thought you were dead. How did you survive?"

"Gyfree saved me and healed me."

"Very thoughtful of him," Mischa responded with a wince. Then, lifting a shaking hand to her brow, she added plaintively, "Gyfree, old friend, I don't suppose you could dream away this splitting headache of mine?"

Gyfree's eyes widened as he stared at her. "Mischa, are you all right?" he blurted.

"Well, my head hurts as if that nasty Figment must have been stomping on it, and my nose is still bleeding. I feel as if I have bruises in places I didn't even know could be bruised, and you want to know if I'm all right?" snapped Mischa.

Gyfree laughed weakly, but before Mischa could berate him, another moan diverted everyone's attention to where Sevor was sitting up, eyes glazed and a hand lifted to his brow as if he and Mischa were mirror images.

"Sevor!" cried Mischa, her own injuries temporarily forgotten as she threw herself against him, with the unfortunate effect of knocking him back down. "Are you all right?"

"Well," Sevor gasped, "my head must be cracked in two to hurt this badly, I have blood all over my face, my entire body is splitting apart, and I am flat on my back looking up at you. I do believe I've never been better."

Impulsively Mischa leaned over and kissed him, and before she could retreat, his arms wrapped around her, pulling her close against his body. "I take that back," he gasped a few minutes later. "I'm even better now than I was before."

Gyfree laughed again as Drew's head rested on his shoulder. "I must admit, Sevor, I didn't think you could do it, and certainly not so quickly."

"Do what?" asked Mischa, lifting her head to frown in Gyfree's direction.

Sevor struggled to a sitting position, wrapping his arm around Mischa just as Gyfree's was wrapped around Drew. "To break the Figment's hold on you," he explained solemnly. "Timi's Figment has the power to attach people to himself, but since I've always wanted you, I set out to attach you to me instead." He smiled ruefully as he added, "Of course, I don't know how much of breaking you free from the Figment had to do with me, and how much had to do with the Figment loosening his own hold every time he felt endangered."

"How could you have always wanted me when you'd never seen me before?" Mischa demanded suspiciously, her rallying tone barely hiding the sudden fear in her eyes.

"I'm a Dreamer from a world other than Gyfree's and Drew's," he explained quickly, his own eyes brimming with the painful awareness that everything he had hoped to gain still hung in the balance. "But not one whose dreams change things. Where I come from, all Dreamers do is see things that have recently happened, things that are currently happening, and things that will happen soon. Most of my dreams took me to other worlds, and I have spent the bulk of my life watching you in my dreams. And wishing that I could be with you here."

For a long moment Mischa weighed everything she had heard and felt, and the balance between acceptance and rejection teetered delicately back and forth. Then Sevor whispered, "Please," and she relaxed back into his arms.

"I'm not sure about this," she admitted softly, "but at the moment, I'm willing to suspend judgment and to just see how everything works out. It doesn't make sense, but then, what does lately?"

"It makes more sense than you realize," Sevor responded, his eyes suddenly mysterious. "Given all the things that can and do happen in so many worlds, what is happening to us is simple and straightforward."

"But it's all coming so fast. I've spent years wondering why there wasn't more excitement and romance in my life. And now that both are here, I'm not sure I trust what's happening. How could you make me feel so much for you so quickly? That sort of thing may happen to Dreamers like Drew and Gyfree, but not to someone ordinary like me."

"You're not ordinary," chided Sevor.

"You know what I mean. It seems perfectly natural for Drew and Gyfree to have found each other so quickly, but that sort of thing doesn't happen to someone who not only has never made a dream come true, but who doesn't even dream."

"Just think of this as a dream that can come true without the help of a Dreamer," he whispered back, his eyes brimming with teasing laughter.

For another long moment, a moment in which everyone could simply breathe, there was silence, and then Mischa sighed reproachfully, "Gyfree, my head really does still hurt. And I'm sure Sevor's must too. The least you can do, considering the fact that we did not desert Drew, is fix our poor cracked skulls."

When Gyfree had withdrawn his hands from both her and Sevor's heads, Mischa sighed again, and her eyes grew distant, as if she was looking back to her earliest moments and trying to remember what it had felt like to be small and helpless and needy. "It was the strangest thing I have ever experienced," she finally whispered, shuddering within the comforting circle of Sevor's arms. "From the moment I first saw the Figment I felt as if I was no longer myself, or at least not exactly. As if I was still in my body, but at the same time watching myself from outside, watching from a place where I no longer had control. I could see everything, but it was all disjointed and fuzzy. Muted. As if I was seeing things happening in the air above me as I looked up through a pool of water. And I could feel things happening, feel the Figment touching me, but at the same time I always felt as if I was really watching him touch someone else. The only thing that seemed real was this overwhelming need I felt to make the Figment happy, and this even more overwhelming need to be everything he could ever want. Yet at the same time, it felt as if someone was trying to convince me that I needed these things, when I didn't really need them at all. It was uncanny. Like nothing I've ever known. I just don't know how to explain it."

"It was like a dream," Gyfree and Drew replied in unison, the shadows in Mischa's eyes reflected in their own.

"Is that how dreaming feels?" asked Mischa. "As if you're

powerless, and you accept your powerlessness as a natural thing? As something inevitable?"

"Sometimes," answered Drew. "Especially when you're young and alone, and everything around you seems to exist only to hurt you. It changes when you grow older, but sometimes even then, you can find yourself back in those old dreams, facing the same nightmares with no better ideas how to defeat them than you ever had before. That's how I felt when that last Figment caught me. I would have simply run away if I could, for I didn't know what else to do."

"And because we came back, you couldn't run," Mischa stated contritely. "We should have run away just like Timi's Figment."

As if he had just been rudely jolted awake, Gyfree jumped, and casting his eyes from side to side, realized at last not only what he saw, but also what he failed to see. "Where is the Figment?" he demanded. "And where are Timi and Peyr?"

The last wisps of dreaming were blown from Drew's eyes as her spine stiffened. "The hummeybees whisked the Figment away from the danger," she blurted. "And Timi chased after them with Peyr."

"With Peyr and the hummeybees ranged against her, Timi doesn't have a chance to stop the Figment. We'd better hurry," declared Gyfree as he scrambled to his feet, pulling Drew up after him.

It took almost no time for the four to retrieve the packs that were still piled in the spot that had sheltered them the night before, and then they were hurrying in the direction the Figment had fled, not knowing if they would catch him in time; not even knowing if in this world there was enough time left to make a difference.

Chapter 13

Timi and Peyr ran until their hearts seemed to leap into their throats, blocking what little air whistled through their lungs, until their eyes clouded with either sweat or fatigue, and they were beyond knowing or even caring which, until their legs buckled beneath them and all they could do was stumble forward rather than truly run. They ran until they collapsed retching to the ground, and Timi would have struggled to her feet to run again if Peyr had not reached out a shaking hand to stop her.

Sobbing to catch his breath, he gasped, "We'll never reach him if we kill ourselves."

"You don't understand," Timi gasped and sobbed in turn, but she allowed herself to be pulled back to the ground, to lie whimpering as her sides heaved and her legs shook. They sprawled side by side until their breathing slowly quieted and their hearts finally opted to not break through their ribs. "We must go on," Timi eventually whispered, once more battling to rise.

"Why?"

"Because I'm responsible," Timi replied with a whimper.

"I know."

"What do you mean? What do you know?" gasped Timi breathlessly.

"I told you before. You're like him. I can see it, feel it. I have felt it all along, although at first I thought you were less than him, and I don't think so now. I thought he was stronger, but he's not. You are."

"I don't know what you're talking about," Timi responded defensively.

"You do nothing to draw notice; you go out of your way to go unheeded. Yet you have the same ability to draw, to attract, to make people need you. You hide your charms. He doesn't. He's like a child wandering lost, in need of someone to watch over him, doing everything in his power so he'll get the attention he thinks he needs."

"He has far more power than any child."

"But he's a child nonetheless. A very needy child who forgets everything and everyone else when he's frightened. A child who sees no needs other than his own. And somehow I know you're the adult. So you're responsible for him."

This time when Timi sobbed, it had little to do with exhaustion. "If he's just a child, how did he gain so much control over you?"

A puzzled frown creased Peyr's brow. "Somehow he let me know that he needed someone like me. Not to love him. Just to look after him. I will admit his needs overwhelmed me at first. But that's not true anymore. Ever since we left my home, his hold on me has slowly faded. So slowly I don't think I noticed at first. But almost from the first there was another force countering his, whether it was being used intentionally or not. There was something I could feel pulling at me, drawing me away despite all his efforts to hold me; something so strong that his hold on me had been almost completely destroyed even before he ran away. And that something was you."

"What are you saying?" gasped Timi.

"His need for me to protect him was strong. Almost too strong to resist. But my need to be with you is stronger."

Timi flinched away as if she was frightened by whatever she saw in his face. "I've done nothing to captivate you. Nothing to make you need me."

Peyr's lips quirked into a sad smile. "I know. You have not drawn me against my will as he did. Yet you have still drawn me. You see, there was something I recognized in him, something I responded to from the beginning, but it was really you I was feeling and responding to, the part of him that somehow is also a part of you. That is why, even at its height, his hold on me was only on my compassion, on my willingness to protect. That was all he could ask, for he wasn't and couldn't be everything to me. He could only be a poor substitute for the real thing. And he could only be that because he tried so desperately when you didn't try at all."

"I never wanted to draw you like he does. I never wanted to do that to anyone. I'm not like that," Timi insisted tearfully.

"Why are you so busy hiding? What is it about yourself that frightens you so?"

"You still don't understand."

Peyr reached out a trembling hand and brushed the tears from her cheek, and although she winced, she didn't pull away. "So explain it to me," he whispered.

A shudder passed through Timi as if something as icy as Gyfree's Figment stood face to face with her again. Her teeth began to chatter and the hair prickled on her arms even after Peyr pulled her gently into the circle of his warmth. She shivered uncontrollably against his body as if she had always been cold and would always be cold, but then finally she murmured, "I always told myself that I was less vivid, less real than other people. That there was nothing in me that could attract another. Then I dreamed him. I dreamed him into existence although I had never dreamed before, and have never dreamed in the same way since. And I realized he had all the ability to attract that I lacked, that he was everything I wasn't."

"Yet that isn't true," Peyr breathed into her hair.

"I convinced myself that it was, but since I first saw you, I've been less sure."

"Why?"

Instead of answering directly, Timi continued in a voice that shivered with cold. "I have spent a lot of time with Dreamers now, and from watching them, and from my own limited experience, I have come to believe that there are different reasons people dream strongly. Sometimes dreams spring from things we desire for ourselves, or things we desire to be. That's what I convinced myself had happened when I dreamed. But more often dreams spring from the things we fear, the things that won't let go of our most secret thoughts. And sometimes our dreams spring not from what we fear from unseen things outside ourselves, from others or the world, but from what we fear in ourselves. That is really why I dreamed him. He wasn't what I secretly wanted to be; he was what I secretly feared in myself."

Peyr's arms tightened around her, pulling her even closer, until finally his warmth began to seep through like the sun thawing frost-hardened ground, and her shivering slowly subsided. "There's really nothing to fear," he whispered into her hair. "You may possess the ability to attract, but unless you choose to use it as he does, you'll never hurt people or force them to do anything against their will. Because you fear what you might do, you'll always control it. You don't even have to try; it's already what you do."

She stiffened in his hold, then twisted around to meet his eyes. "But that's where you're wrong," she said urgently, the tears that had dried once more springing to her eyes. "When I saw you, I wanted you. And now here you are. As simple as that. I really am no better than he is."

"No, that's where you're wrong," Peyr retorted, his eyes delving down through all the layers of her fear and self-doubt. "When he wanted my protection it felt as if he had closed a giant hand around me. I couldn't move unless he wanted me to move. As if I was still in my body but at the same time watching myself being moved around like a child's toy. You have never used any of your powers against me. If you had, I would have been your puppet more completely than I ever was his, and he would never have been able to exert control over me at all. Trust me, I know the feel of someone using this particular talent. You may have wanted me, and in fact, I hope you did and that you still do, but you have never coerced me."

"I must have," Timi cried, "or you wouldn't feel as you do."

This time when Peyr smiled there was nothing sad in his expression, and his eyes were filled with a hope bordering on joy. "Didn't it ever occur to you that someone might respond freely to all those things you keep so carefully hidden, and that they would want you because you were exactly what they had always wanted? That someone like me could see in you everything I've ever desired?" Without waiting for an answer, he lowered his mouth to hers, parting her lips insistently, urgently, as if everything he wanted and needed in life could be found within that kiss.

"How can you feel that way?" Timi gasped when she could

finally surface for air, her breathing quick and her heart hammering as if she had never stopped running. "If I'm like him at all you should shun me. The power in him is in me. It's not something to desire. It's something to fear. Something to hate."

"There is something in him desirable, something worth loving and caring for. The same thing that makes you so desirable and lovable. In the end, that is one of the things that makes him so powerful. He's not a monster, and despite what he did to me, I couldn't hate him for it. He didn't act from cruelty or maliciousness, but from simple childish need. I said he was a child, and I meant it. A selfish, misguided child in need of some direction, some unsolicited attention, and some real, uncoerced love."

"For someone who seemed at first to be the strong and silent type, you certainly know what to say when the need arises."

"And what to do when the need arises, even though I'm sure I seemed more like the strong and stupid type the first time you saw me," Peyr replied with a smile that wiped everything else from Timi's mind. "And what we need to do now is stop him before he reaches someone else."

"My Figment!" exclaimed Timi, breaking free from Peyr's embrace and stumbling to her feet. "We have to go!"

Once again Peyr reached up a restraining hand to keep her from bolting away. "We need to stop him," he agreed, "but we'll never do it by dashing around madly. The hummeybees will carry him farther and faster than we could ever run. We need to find another way."

"What other way?" Timi cried.

Peyr rose to his feet and towered above her, his eyes reflecting back her face as she had never seen it before, or perhaps as she had always feared to see it: full of color and life and a mysterious magnetism. "You said you dreamed him."

"Yes. He's a Figment."

"Then don't you have any power over him? The ability to make him stop? Can't you dream him somewhere quiet and empty, so that we can catch him?"

The old Timi would have balked at such a suggestion, but the new Timi, the real Timi, the Timi that had hidden beneath the pale mask of the old Timi, slowly nodded her head. "I can try. At this point, we have nothing to lose other than a few extra minutes of futile running."

Settling back to the ground with her hands clasped firmly in Peyr's, Timi cast herself into a dream, the one dream she had avoided for so long, avoided from the moment she had first awakened to the realization that she was no longer whole. She dreamed of the Figment, of his perfect features, but in her dream she could now see his winsome smile, could see the loneliness deep in his beautiful eyes. Dreaming, she soared through space until she was with him, and invisible she flew by his side as he sailed into a thicket of trees, the hummeybees buzzing in her ears as well as his as they wove a path through the high branches, their wings spraying rainbow light across her eyes. There was no way to slow the hummeybees, for they were not hers to control, and she was afraid to slip into the Figment's thoughts, afraid of what she might find there, afraid of what she would become if she came too close. It might be in her power to make him want to stop, to make him insist that the hummeybees return him to the ground so that he might rest, but maybe it was also possible that when she tried, she would find herself inside him, one with him, wanting what he wanted, needing what he needed, so that instead of stopping him, she would become him. That was not a risk she was willing to take. But she had dreamed him into being, had dreamed him not only as a living entity, but also as a perfectly sculpted form, and that was something she could change, and change without risk. So in dreaming she wrapped herself around his slender body and dreamed of weight, of an incredible heaviness that seeped through the skin, of limbs with the density of lead, of a body with the concentrated mass of a mountain, of a head dragged down by forces even weightier than sleep. Heavy, so heavy, too heavy, she dreamed him far too heavy for the hummeybees to carry; their wings were throbbing desperately now, and still they were foundering, were being pulled from the sky by so much weight, and there was nothing they could do but lower his dense body to the ground so that he could rest as one with the other rocks, solid and heavy and inert.

A smile chased the dream from Timi's eyes, and her smile grew even brighter when she saw the brightness of her reflection in Peyr's eyes. "Let's go," she told him. "He's waiting for us, so there's no need to run. But I still don't want to leave him alone for too long."

"Fine with me," countered Peyr, "but there's one thing I need to do first." Without further preamble he took her in his arms again, his mouth devouring hers with the unquenchable thirst of a man who has gone too long without water and, finally finding a deep, cool stream, cannot be satisfied with just one sip. When he eventually raised his lips from hers, he teased huskily, "I can't wait to take you home. My parents are going to love you."

The soft bemusement in Timi's face was dispelled, and she looked back at him with sudden dread. "What makes you think so?"

"Well, all you have to do is try a little, and they really won't have a choice."

The color drained from Timi's face until she saw in his eyes the same pale reflection of herself that she had seen countless times before. Stricken, she quickly glanced away. With a strength she knew he possessed, but that she had not yet felt, he tilted her chin back up so that her face was trapped in the light of his eyes. "You need to learn to trust yourself," he admonished. "Until you do, you'll never be everything you could be."

"But I don't want to be everything I could be, because then I'll be just like him!"

"I don't think so. You share those qualities that make him attractive, but you are not him. You'll never be him. What you could be is so much more than you let yourself be, but far less than what you fear. Trust yourself. And until you're ready to trust yourself, at least trust me."

Timi shook her head. "And what if you're wrong? What if I can't trust you? What if he regains his hold on you the moment we reach him?"

"It won't happen," Peyr chuckled. "I've never wanted to kiss him, after all, and I can't stop thinking about kissing you."

The color slowly rose in Timi's cheeks and sparked her eyes to life again.

"We'd better be going," Peyr stated grudgingly. "Your charge is waiting. And if I kiss you again, I might not be able to stop."

Without another word they set off hand in hand in the direction Timi could sense the stranded Figment, Peyr's eyes full of Timi, and Timi's eyes full of both doubt and determination.

It was wearing to keep up the strenuous pace that they all realized was necessary, for they had been through much recently, and two of them had even looked directly into the eyes of death.

Yet they all knew there was no choice. They must keep moving, steadily moving in the direction whispered into Gyfree's mind from the watching land, moving in the direction of Timi and her Figment. The danger this Figment represented might be nothing compared to the danger that would soon be visited upon this world, but at present it was the only danger they had the ability to address. So on they trudged, the packs on their backs as heavy as their eyes and as cumbersome as their legs. On they trudged, until in a weariness that she couldn't dream away, Drew stumbled and fell. And when Gyfree stooped over to help her to her feet, his own legs crumpled beneath him, so that he too tumbled to the ground.

"That's it," gasped Mischa, collapsing in turn to the ground. "Like it or not, our bodies are demanding that we rest. And I for one am going to comply."

Throwing himself down beside her, Sevor groaned, "If I had ever dreamed that I could be this tired, I would have been tempted to stay home in bed, and not to come venturing into this world."

"Is that so?" quipped Mischa.

"No," grinned Sevor, "but it sure sounds good right now."

"We've got to keep going," Gyfree insisted, "or we'll never catch the Figment in time."

"We're never going to catch him in time regardless," sighed Mischa. "Isn't there another way?"

"What are you talking about?" snapped Gyfree.

Mischa's eyes twinkled with all the glee of a child pointing out a parent's mistake. "You are the Keeper, aren't you? So can't you call on the land for a little help? Perhaps a few trees could be convinced to catch him as he flies by and entangle him in their branches."

Gyfree blinked, his expression stunned, and then slowly his cheeks flushed with embarrassment. "Why didn't you say something sooner?"

"Well, in truth I had forgotten about your promotion until just now. It was wiped from my mind by everything else I've been through lately. What's your excuse?"

"I am new to this," he scowled. "And I've been dealing with a fair amount myself lately."

"Now that I have reminded you, what are you waiting for?" Mischa asked slyly, eliciting a quick laugh from Sevor.

Gyfree frowned angrily, but his eyes immediately sparked as if something dormant had leapt to life inside, and then his frown faded away as his gaze grew distant. Accustomed to working with the last Keeper, and well aware that these things took time, Mischa settled back with her head on Sevor's chest to enjoy a much needed rest. The last thing she expected was Gyfree's sudden exclamation of surprise.

Opening one eye and glaring at the new Keeper, Mischa griped, "Why all the noise?"

"Because for some reason the Figment has stopped moving. And according to the land directly beneath him, he couldn't move even if he wanted to. He weighs so much that the land is actually complaining."

"Timi?" Drew queried in surprise.

"Timi," agreed Gyfree, "has been busily dreaming."

For the first time since he had entered this new, colorful world, he found himself perched on a rock, basking in the sun, and since there was nothing else to do at the moment, he let his mind drift aimlessly through the trees as his eyes inched shut. Spread out below his mind's eye were all the sharp lines and bright hues that he had found here, the bold brushstrokes of the trees a deep emerald green, the distant ground a splash of rich brown speckled with flecks of every color imaginable, as if some giant hand had dropped a palette full of paint to splatter across the land in every direction. Everything was so crisp, so clear, so full of life that it brought tears trickling from the corners of his eyes, and spurred the hummeybees on his shoulders into anxious buzzing. There were birds as bright and distinct as the rest of the scene darting from tree to tree, but there were no other hummeybees here, no other creatures he could trust. Only the hummeybees who had accompanied him here were loyal; only they had proven themselves to care about him and only him.

He had thought at first that he had finally found the world he had waited for, and although it was as full and rich as he had always envisioned, it had failed to bring him the joy he had once expected. For a brief time it had brought him a woman, and he had certainly enjoyed touching her, holding her, listening to the music in her voice. But she had grown strange and distant, and almost as indistinct and hazy as the world he had left, and she had done nothing to protect him when he needed protection the most. There had also been others for a while, but except for the man he had chosen above all others to protect him, they had not followed him as they should have followed. And even his protector had seemed distracted for most of the time, needing constant reminders that his job was to protect rather than to watch the pale Dreamer as if she was more important than anything else.

For all its vivid beauty, this world, so promising at first, had not brought him all he had wanted. It had brought him disappointment and even discomfort, and now it had allowed his Dreamer to reach out and pull him from the sky, to imprison him on this rock in the sun, to trap him more securely than the burning wall had imprisoned him in his old world. And now it was bringing his Dreamer to him, as well as his protector, for he could see them as his mind floated above, striding toward him with a purpose that rendered them as vivid and striking as the canvas of life that surrounded him, the beautiful canvas brimming with color and texture and cruelty.

Eyes still shut, he watched them enter the sun-drenched clearing where he sat immobile on a rock, watched them enter hand in hand, and with his mind he pulled at his protector, tried to pull him away and back to the spot where he belonged. When his protector failed to respond, his eyes inched open again and slowly filled with tears as pure and lovely as his face. On his shoulders the hummeybees buzzed fiercely, but he was tired, too tired and sad to ask for their help, at least not yet.

"I am losing them all," he whispered, his eyes shifting from his erstwhile protector and settling on his Dreamer's face. His Dreamer's newly colorful and surprisingly lovely face. "You have taken my protector away from me just as that other man has taken the woman. You have left me with nothing but the hummeybees, and I need more. So much more. Why won't you let me find more? You never wanted me, but others will if you only let me go."

Timi stepped forward, relieved and stunned that Peyr's hand still gripped her own. "I can't allow you to find any others. You make people do things they would never do if given a choice."

"But they want to do things for me. It makes them happy."

"Perhaps at first. But when you care for a person, it helps if they care for you too. You made people love you and need you, but you never loved them back."

"But I needed them. I still need them."

"Yes, but all you have ever cared about was what they could do for you. You never considered what they needed."

The Figment shook his head like the petulant child Peyr had claimed him to be. "I don't understand," he complained. "Why couldn't they be happy by making me happy? Shouldn't that be enough?"

Timi's eyes widened in comprehension as Peyr gently squeezed her hand. "You really don't understand, do you?" she asked softly.

The Figment scowled and the hummeybees lifted from his shoulders, buzzing with menace. "I understand that you never cared about me. You were the one who brought me life, but then you sent me away. You left me alone, and you never came to get me, and when someone else brought me here you were unhappy. You wanted to send me back. You wanted to hurt me. You still want to hurt me. You're the one who should have loved me and needed me, but you never did."

As Peyr squeezed her hand again, all his words came back to Timi, and somehow she finally understood what she needed to do, what she had needed to do from the beginning but could never have faced until now. Carefully pulling her hand free from Peyr's hold she stepped forward alone, her eyes never leaving the Figment's flushed face. She could feel Peyr behind her, but she could also feel that he too understood what must be done, and she smiled with the realization that he had known long before she had, and had done everything in his power to help her understand.

As she neared the Figment the hummeybees buzzed a distinct warning, but with her eyes still on her creation's face, she said soothingly, "I promise not to hurt you," and the hummeybees immediately subsided. Stepping even closer, close enough to feel the Figment's warm breath wafting across her cheeks, she raised trembling hands and gently cupped his face. "I never wanted to hurt you," she whispered. "How could I hurt someone so beautiful, so wonderful?"

The crystalline tears adorning his face like rare jewels suddenly ceased. "You think I'm beautiful? Wonderful?"

"Isn't that how I created you? As someone who would always be loved."

"My protector doesn't love me anymore," he sulked, his eyes shifting to the quietly attentive Peyr.

"Of course he does," consoled Timi. "And so does Mischa. They both love you very much, but it also hurts them to love you so much. They feel more love than they can bear."

"How is that possible?" he pouted.

"You are so wonderful that people want to give you all their love. More than all their love. More love than they can contain within their bodies. So much love that they forget everything else. But people aren't made to hold so much love. We are weak things compared to you, too weak to give you as much love as you deserve."

"The hummeybees love me that much."

"That is why they are special. Their capacity for love is worthy of you."

Tears leaked from his eyes again and he whimpered. "It's still not enough."

"I know. And you deserve more."

For a long moment he stared back at her, and the only sound in the clearing was the now pensive buzz of the hummeybees. At last he asked, "Do you love me?"

Tears as beautiful and precious as his slid down her face. "Yes. Very much."

"Will you give yourself to me?"

Timi shook her head gently. "No. It still would not be enough. You would still need more. You will always need more."

"Then what can I do?" he cried plaintively. "Who will take care of me?"

"I will take care of you," Timi answered, her voice brushing across him in a comforting caress. "I will hold you as you need to be held, and I will never let you go. I will watch over you and protect you and make sure all your needs are met."

"How will you do these things if you don't belong to me?"

"There is another way. A way that will be enough."

"What way?" he wept, with all the sorrow and trust of a child who seeks an answer, and both fears and knows that the answer exists.

Timi leaned closer, her lips a breath away from his lips. "You are mine," she whispered huskily. "You have always been mine. You are part of me. I need you. I want you. I need you to come back." With the last word her lips folded over his, and she kissed him with all the love and pain and fearful hope with which a mother kisses her child, knowing all the beauty and hurt life can bring, and knowing that she could no more bestow enough of the joy than she could completely exclude all the anguish.

Beneath her hands and lips her Figment shivered, and she could taste his tears as they coursed down his face, their flavor sweet and pure. Dropping her hands from his face, she wrapped her arms about his body and pulled him close, lifting her face and sheltering his head in the crook of her neck. She hugged him tightly and he shivered again, shivered until it seemed that he would shake apart. "Trust yourself," she heard Peyr whisper at her back, or perhaps in her memory, but it no longer mattered which. Beneath closed lids her eyes filled with the one true dream, the dream that had changed her life, the dream that was cradled in her arms. This time she held nothing back as she wrapped her dreaming self around him, wrapped her entire self around him. And dreaming she soaked into his mind, sponging up all his needs and wants and desires, all the needs and wants and desires that she had given him, and absorbed them back into herself. She was no longer afraid of losing herself to him; she was, after all, the stronger. Nor was he afraid of being destroyed, for he had never felt so loved. This was what he needed. This was what she needed. To become one. To become whole.

Within her arms the Figment shivered one last time, and then he slowly dissolved into breathtaking particles of shimmering light that briefly swirled and basked in the sunshine before filtering through his Dreamer's glowing skin. And when Timi's eyes blinked open, and she saw the vibrant colors surrounding her, saw in her mind's eye the richness and wonder of this world, she knew he wasn't truly gone. He was simply back where he belonged.

A hush held the clearing in thrall, a hush so intense that not even the hummeybees seemed capable of sound. A hush held them all, a hush full of things that could never be said because there were no words to say them. And then Timi turned and smiled at Peyr, and the silence released them.

A loud buzz split the air. "He'z gone," droned the larger hummeybee.

The smaller hummeybee swept across the clearing to linger above Timi's face. "Not gone. Changed. Zhe will command uz now."

Timi gazed up at the hovering hummeybees, their wings a blur of rainbow-lit motion, their fuzzy bodies pulsing with life as stunning as the throbbing of their wings. They were so beautiful, so incredible, that her heart clenched and she would have forgotten to breathe if her body hadn't proceeded without her. And she looked into the eyes that were prepared to surrender to her as completely as they had surrendered to her Figment. "No," she told them softly, "I will never command you. You may stay or you may leave, but what you do from this moment forward is entirely up to you."

Two strong arms folded around her waist and pulled her close to a warm body, and then an even warmer voice whispered in her ear. "I told you that you could trust yourself."

Timi leaned her head back against Peyr's shoulder and allowed her eyes to inch shut. "How did you know?" she murmured.

"I could just feel it. From the first I knew he truly did need someone to take care of him, that for all his willfulness and power he was just a little lost boy in search of something he could feel was missing, although he didn't seem to know what it might be. And then I could also feel in you that there was something missing, as if you had long denied an important part of yourself, a part you could never completely be yourself without. When I realized who both of you were, the rest seemed fairly obvious."

Timi turned in his arms, her eyes suddenly intent on his face. "What do you see when you look at me now?" she demanded.

A smile lit Peyr's eyes and tightened the corners of his mouth. "The woman of my dreams," he answered.

"But you don't have dreams," Timi protested with a frown.

"But I do have an imagination, and I've spent all my life imagining a woman just like you. And my imaginings came true. So perhaps imagination is a bit like dreaming, with a special power of its own."

Peyr's lips lowered to hers, but just as his mouth parted hers, she jumped and shrieked. A sudden buzzing filled her ears as an unexpected weight settled onto each of her shoulders. "Don't worry," buzzed the heavier hummeybee, and she was almost certain that his buzz reverberated with laughter, "but thiz iz our choize."

"We know we are free," buzzed the lighter weight. "But thiz iz not our world, and for the time being, it zeemz bezt to ztay with you."

As he looked at the expression of consternation on Timi's face, Peyr undutifully threw back his head and laughed. And knowing that her Figment would have never allowed such a reaction, Timi felt safe enough to laugh as well.

Curiosity drove them forward even after the land had whispered to the Keeper that something had changed, or was changing, and they would not be urgently needed after all. Curiosity even continued to drive them when the land sighed with relief that the great weight of the Figment had been lifted from the grumbling rock. And curiosity kept them poised on their feet when their eyes spotted two figures emerge from the horizon and gradually transform into Peyr and Timi. And stunned incredulity held them in place when the two approaching figures had grown large enough and clear enough for the hummeybees perched on Timi's shoulders to resolve themselves as more than misleading shadows. Then as if to break the spell that held them all in check, the hummeybees sprang from Timi's shoulders and hurdled directly toward Drew, speeding far ahead of their traveling companions to whir around her head in boundless excitement.

"Yez, we remember now," the larger one buzzed. "It'z her, it'z her."

"Free, we are free," buzzed the smaller one, "the other zet uz free zo we could remember."

At first Drew ducked her head beneath the hummeybees seeming assault, but almost immediately she lifted her face toward their hovering bodies as if she was seeing them for the very first time, and as their rainbow wings scattered light across her cheeks, her eyes slowly widened. "This must be a dream," she breathed.

Gyfree flinched as if something invisible had reached out and slapped him across the face. "What are you talking about?" he blurted.

"The hummeybees," murmured Drew, so entranced that she failed to notice the color draining from Gyfree's face and the light draining from his eyes. "They're a dream. My dream. Earlier I said they seemed like something from a dream, but not until this moment did I recognize the truth."

"Yez, yez," proclaimed the large hummeybee. "Zhe iz the one. Zhe made uz, all of uz. All the hummeybeez in our world."

"There was a dream," Drew sighed, "a dream I had often,

although when I remember, it doesn't seem like a dream at all. There were bees, countless bees, all at least as big as a man's fist and sometimes bigger, and they all swarmed around me. They seemed so fierce, so formidable, as if nothing could ever really harm them, that at first I was frightened, but they never did sting me. They would just fly so close and buzz in my ears until I seemed to see them and hear them inside my head." She blinked as if awakening from that long forgotten dream, her eyes losing their distance as she focused on the living, soaring hummeybees. "They always lived in a forest. A beautiful forest that looked like the watercolor my great-grandmother had hanging on the wall above the rocking chair where she spent all her days. Soft colors running into other colors, as muted and hazy as a dream."

"Yez," agreed the smaller hummeybee. "Our world. You zaw it. You were there."

"Yes, I saw it. I was there. But I was there many times before. In my dreams."

Slowly her knees buckled beneath her, and she would have fallen if Gyfree hadn't caught her and lowered her gently to the ground. "I visited their world," she whispered to him, frightened eyes on his bleak face, "and then I woke up in my bed. In my world. From dream to dream. That's how I've lived my life. And in the end, I'm always back home in my bed, whether I choose to be or not."

Without a word, Gyfree pulled her into his arms, but the eyes that looked over her head were shaken by the approach of a nightmare that he feared could not be averted.

The hummeybees droned soothingly, but it was the sound of Sevor clearing his throat that broke through the nightmare fear that had seized both Drew and Gyfree. "It's not that simple," he remarked almost apologetically.

Drew turned her eyes up to his crookedly smiling face. "What's not simple?"

"You never visited the hummeybees' world."

"I remember it clearly from my dreams. Now that I've taken the time to think about it, I know it's the same world I saw when Gyfree and I found the Figment," objected Drew.

"True enough."

"So how is that not simple?"

Sevor squatted down, looking deeply into Drew's eyes, then

just as deeply into Gyfree's. Then looking back at Drew, he said so softly that only she and Gyfree could clearly hear, "You never visited the hummeybees. Not the way you are visiting here, your body and mind exploring a completely new world, a world that was shaped long before you discovered it. It was different with the hummeybees. You did more than just visit in all those dreams. You see, you dreamed their world into existence."

"What?" exclaimed Gyfree and Drew in unison.

"You dreamed the hummeybees into life, and then you dreamed them a world of their own. I dreamed of you doing it, and I must admit, it was rather impressive."

"Are you saying it's possible for a Dreamer to actually dream an entire world into existence?" demanded Gyfree.

"It's very rare, but it has happened at least once or twice."

"So the hummeybees are Figments?" queried Drew.

"I said it's not that simple. When a Dreamer like you dreams a world for the creatures she dreams, she gives those creatures a new reality. The hummeybees' world is as real as this one, as real as mine, as real as your old one. And they are as real as anyone or anything that inhabits any other world."

"But I thought Figments were real as well," Drew protested with a confused frown.

"They are real," he agreed, "but they are not alive in the same way as you or Gyfree, Mischa or me, Timi or Peyr, or even the hummeybees are alive. They change constantly in a way we could never change, but they don't really age or grow in the same way we do. They may have physical relationships, but they don't reproduce. And even though they can be destroyed, in the normal course of things, they don't really die. They are real. But they aren't bound by the same rules that apply to us, or to creatures born from a dream but then anchored to a world of their own."

At that moment Mischa leaned over and tugged frantically on Sevor's arm. "You can finish your explanation later," she hissed. "In the meantime, you need to look at this."

Four pairs of eyes turned to watch the arrival of Timi and Peyr, and four pairs of eyes were suddenly riveted to Timi's face. The pale phantom of a woman was gone, and in her place stood another woman brimming with color and life. Her hair was no longer limp and faded, but was instead thick and full and shimmering golden like the sun. Cheeks once waxen were flushed, and lips once thin and colorless were as swollen and blushing as a bud in bloom. Yet it was her eyes that were the most remarkable. Eyes still gray, but no longer the gray of a cool and distant mist. Eyes now the intense gray of a stormy sky so beautiful that even the most cautious of weather watchers would be willing to risk a soaking if they could only capture and remember the wonder of such a sight.

Hand in hand with Peyr, Timi stepped forward, her own eyes riveted to just one stunned face. "Mischa?" she asked tentatively.

"Yes?" croaked Mischa.

"Are you all right?"

With a laugh Sevor scrambled to his feet and wrapped an arm around Mischa. "She's more than all right," he answered. "You might say she's herself again."

"Timi?" asked Mischa uncertainly.

"Yes?" responded Timi with a shaky smile.

"Are you all right?"

This time Peyr laughed and wrapped an arm around Timi's slender shoulders. "She's more than all right too," he announced proudly. "You might say she's her entire self again."

"Where's the Figment?" Gyfree asked sharply.

"Not gone. Changed," droned a hummeybee.

Before Gyfree could explode, Timi answered with a mysterious smile. "I finally understood him and accepted him, and gave him what he needed."

"What?" demanded Gyfree.

"It's a long story," Timi admitted ruefully.

"Well, since we're all in need of some rest," Mischa interjected decisively, "now might be a good time to sit down and hear it."

"Mischa," Timi remarked softly, "it's nice to have you back."

"Timi," replied Mischa with a twinkle in her eye, "it's nice to meet you."

Chapter 14

Looming above him was a creature unlike anything he had ever seen, a creature whose face writhed beneath a sheet of flames that licked but never seemed to consume his features. Even his red-slitted eyes and the fangs that sliced through his mouth were ringed in flame, but in the very center of his eyes, just within the bottomless slit, was a fine, cutting sliver of deep blue ice. And when he opened his mouth to howl out his demands, his forked tongue was tipped with daggers of the same mind-numbing ice.

In every direction, as far as he could see, there knelt other creatures, some large and hideous, some small but with eyes remarkably vicious, some with cruel faces surprisingly human, some no more than wraiths somehow caught in a flash of light and endowed with a permanent shape and substance. And dangling from the flaming, ice-tipped claws of their obvious leader was the mangled and bloody body of one large creature.

"Any more questions?" hissed the massive creature in the center, and as he listened he did not know whether he was burning to death in horrible agony, or whether his body had been plunged into suffocating ice.

There was no response to the dangerous question other than absolute quiet; not even the sound of a single breath or frantic heartbeat disturbed the silence.

"Then you know my commands. Now go!" boomed the creature, and even in his invisible watching he writhed, his body on fire and his mind gripped by ice. Around him the creatures stampeded as if in that moment their minds had been completely stripped away and their bodies had thrashed out of control. There was no sense of order, no discipline, as larger creatures crushed smaller ones in their frenzied charge, and smaller ones ripped at the larger ones' throats as the flood of bodies washed over them. Riding the crest of this monstrous wave were those less substantial creatures, but even as they sailed toward whatever shore awaited, sharp claws surfaced from below like sharks seeking prey, and dragged the expressionless wraiths back into the bloody depths.

Yet despite the seeming chaos, the wave of creatures flowed steadily forward, the creature of fire and ice wading in the center of the advancing tide. And caught up like a piece of flotsam, he too was carried helplessly along, carried until at last he could glimpse whatever end awaited the creatures, whatever end their fiery yet glacial leader had chosen. Ahead was a barrier rising like a cliff, but he could clearly see the light-filled fracture snaking up the stark bluff, as if years of erosion had worn the underlying foundation away, and a single crash of one giant wave could topple it completely. A wave that was fast approaching.

The wave struck with tremendous force, and with a single shudder, the barrier split fully open, and the creatures poured through the resulting gap, mouths frothing like foam on a breaking sea. From his place in the center, the creature of fire and ice roared as if in sudden and uncheckable hunger, and his giant paws swept out, lethal claws extended to swipe aside all those in his path. Forward he rushed, trampling and slashing, his eyes on something above and beyond the encroaching wave, his precipitous surge pulling along countless others in his wake. Including the single piece of helpless flotsam who saw it all and could do nothing more than float along. Powerless to stop, powerless to do anything other than watch, he now flowed through the gap directly behind the maddened creature, only to find himself tossed into a world that was disturbingly familiar, a world that would have stolen his breath away if he hadn't long ago lost it beneath the swelling waves.

Ahead he could see the bellowing creature advance on two lone figures standing hand in hand, but then all around him the rest of the wave broke upon the land and he could see nothing but the creatures pouring through the gap and spreading out in every direction. He was caught in the flood once again, but this time he found himself riding the crest that would soon crash down upon the land below. Against this unstoppable tide there stood only a handful of men and women, and as he was swept toward those doomed few, he saw himself, face set and feet braced as if that alone could keep him from drowning. And standing beside him was Mischa, the love he had waited for all his life only to lose so soon.

Sevor awoke with a terrified cry, bolting up so quickly that Mischa's head, which had been pillowed on his shoulder, was knocked to the ground with a thud. So intense was his fear, he didn't even notice or respond to her startled gasp, but he was still enough himself to change his panicked outcry into a coherent warning. "They intend to break through the Barrier at the Source itself!" he shouted. "We're running out of time!"

Around him everyone jolted awake with an abruptness that dispelled even the lingering memory of sleep. Five pairs of eyes snapped open as if they had never closed, but before anyone else could expostulate, Drew, who already had good reason to trust the reliability of Sevor's dreams, demanded urgently, "Is it happening yet?"

Sevor's eyes turned inward as he surveyed time unfolding in a way only he could see. "Not yet," he finally murmured, "but soon. Sooner than we can possibly get there. Although somehow we will get there."

"What is that supposed to mean?" Gyfree asked anxiously.

"I dreamed of us there, so that means we will be there, each and every one of us. The city itself seemed deserted, so not only will we somehow arrive in time, but we'll arrive in time for the townspeople to have the chance to evacuate. I just don't know how we're supposed to get there, because that helpful bit of information wasn't in my dream," Sevor explained with a sardonic smile, although his eyes were mournfully haunted.

"You definitely dreamed that they will breach the Source rather than any other section of the Barrier? You're sure it wasn't the weakened area where Drew broke through?" persisted Gyfree.

"I may not be from here, but I know your world relatively well. In some ways better than you do. There is only one place in this world where a city juxtaposes the Barrier."

"Does everything you dream always come true?" Gyfree questioned.

"As far as I know," Sevor admitted unhappily.

"What exactly did you see?" Mischa asked intently, her hand instinctively reaching out to give his a reassuring squeeze.

Sevor shuddered, and his eyes grew even more haunted and distant. "There were more Figments than I could count. Thousands upon thousands of them. In their center was a Figment larger than the rest, a Figment with burning skin. When the first wave of Figments broke through the Barrier, he suddenly charged forward, rushing to the front. And once he broke through the gap opened by the others, he rocketed directly toward Gyfree and Drew."

There was an uncomfortable silence, the silence of those who don't want to hear unpleasant yet unavoidable news. Then Gyfree inquired roughly, "Did you see a beautiful woman? A woman carved from ice?"

"No, but there was ice in the eyes of the fiery Figment, and ice tipping his tongue and curving from the ends of his claws. On the outside he burned, but deep inside, he seemed made of solid ice."

Drew shivered as if touched by the ice in her Figment's eyes. "He must have defeated her," she stated bleakly.

"No!" blurted Timi as something deep within her stirred, something new that whispered of other possibilities. "Don't assume anything. Gyfree's Figment was ice, just as Drew's is fire. If the Figment Sevor dreamed was both fire and ice, then there may be more here than we can easily understand."

Timi's words fell with a weight that pulled at them all, dragging them into another dark silence which was finally broken when Peyr quietly asked, "What else did you see?"

"I saw us standing there as the Figments charged. Then I woke up."

The same question was in all of their minds, but only Mischa had the courage to whisper, "Did you see any of us die?"

"No."

"Then I suppose we have a chance even if we don't know what that chance may be," Mischa stated flatly. "But I'd still like to know how we're supposed to get from here to there."

A buzz that sounded suspiciously like laughter suggested, "Perhapz you are forgetting uz?"

In surprise all eyes turned toward the two hummeybees who had quietly perched overhead on the lowest branch of a tree. "But there are only two of you and six of us," Mischa expostulated. "You cannot carry us all."

"There are only two of uz here," buzzed the smaller hummeybee, "but there are far more than two of uz."

"But there's only one way to reach your world," protested Gyfree, "and that is through the nightmare that stretches across its path."

Sevor cleared his throat before the hummeybees could buzz out a reply. "I already told you that Drew dreamed that world, but what I didn't tell you before is that she dreamed that nightmare as well. And since she is connected to it in a way that no one else can ever be, she has always been able to survive it."

Drew flinched as if she suddenly felt a blast of unbearable heat, and wrapping his arm around her, Gyfree declared, "I don't care where the nightmare came from; she's not going back through that hell again. There must be another way."

"There iz another way to reach our world," droned the larger hummeybee, its sharp black eyes drilling into Drew, "at leazt for you, Dreamer. You choze the hard way before. But there iz an eazy way too. The way you uzually vizited when you were zmall."

"But I don't remember that way," Drew whispered.

Sevor leaned close, his eyes intent on Drew's stricken face, his own nightmare momentarily forgotten. "When you dreamed the hummeybee's world into existence, it became your refuge from the nightmare, a refuge you sought so often that you left the two forever connected to one another. For you, and you alone, that world exists as the only way to escape the nightmare, and even now your connection to it is so strong that all you must do is dream you are there. Just dream of the world you created, and you'll slip through the heat without feeling a trace of its touch."

"Yez," the large hummeybee buzzed excitedly, "that iz the eazy way. And you muzt go there again both for uz and for your-zelf."

"You gave uz a choize. We chooze to ztay here, in thiz world. But we would prefer not to ztay alone. Bring uz otherz, and we will help you. We will carry you. We will fight with you. We will give you the chanze you need," finished the other hummeybee.

✧　✧　✧

In this place each tree bloomed with every single shade of flower, the colors soft and almost translucent, blossoms hanging in the branches with the same ethereal glow as a rainbow arching hazily in the sky. It was a world of muted colors, with shadows as velvety as the petals that drifted like a summer snow from the trees. A world that had never known autumn, and had only recently, for one brief moment, felt the icy touch of winter. Spring melted into summer here, and summer melted back into spring, so there was always something blooming, and always something preparing to bloom. And always something winging from blossom to blossom, buzzing with busy delight.

In a dream Drew walked once more beneath the brimming trees, and around her swarmed a hive of excited hummeybees, droning as one, "It'z her, it'z her." And dreaming she showed them another world, a larger world, a world with many flowers, but more scattered, a world with many colors, and not all of them pastel. A world of not just spring and summer, and not just hummeybees.

"Will you come help us? Will you join the other two?" asked the dream Drew.

Many of the hummeybees buzzed away, their wings scattering rainbow light that melted into the trees. But some of the hummeybees stayed, and some of these even buzzed, "Yez, we will come. It iz time for a change, zo we will come." And wrapping her dream arms around them, and pulling them into herself until their buzzing filled her mind and their black and yellow stripes pressed against the backs of her eyes, she soared back on the wings of her dream, and on waking set them free.

Surprisingly it was Mischa and only Mischa who balked at the thought of being flown by the hummeybees. She stood defiantly, hands on hips and feet far apart, but a shadow of memory that reminded Drew of a nightmare drained her eyes and washed the color from her face. "I can't do it," she pleaded. "I just can't."

"But you did it before," protested Timi, "didn't you? Isn't that how you got to Peyr's so quickly?"

Mischa shuddered and the shadow darkened in her eyes. "It was horrible," she whispered. "He didn't even warn me, but there was this strange smile on his face as he looked out into the distance, and then suddenly this giant hummeybee swooped down and grabbed me by the shoulders. I wanted to kick and scream, but I couldn't because somehow I knew he would be unhappy if I did. So I hung from the hummeybee like a bemused Dreamer, and we soared higher into the air, far from the ground, but not above the trees. We swerved wildly through the trees, and branches lashed across my face as we sped by. I couldn't see where I was or where I was going because everything was a blur. I've never felt so helpless or so lost."

"It doez not need to be that way," buzzed a dainty hummeybee as it flitted back and forth across Mischa's vision. "If two are carrying you inztead of one, it will be eazy to fly above the treez. It iz a pleazure to fly zo high. It iz beautiful to zee the land zpread out below, to zee all the bright colorz dotting the land like rainbow ztars in a green zea."

"Nizely zpoken," droned the larger of the two original hummeybees with a sound that sounded suspiciously like a seductive purr. "Your wordz are az lovely az your wingz."

A surprised and delighted laugh escaped Timi as she watched the two hummeybees circle each other before disappearing into the branches of the nearby trees. "Amorous little things," she murmured. "I had no idea. What exactly were you up to, Drew, when you created them?"

Drew flushed, but before she could answer, Sevor interjected with a wry smile, "She was simply up to creating actual life. The hummeybees may have started as Figments, but when Drew connected them to a real world, they became average, mortal creatures. And to survive, mortal creatures have to procreate." Then wrapping an arm around Mischa's tense shoulders, he droned in his own seductive purr, "Perhaps we can soar together too."

"Not now!" snapped Mischa irritably.

"Well, you may be right about that. We can't do anything until our ardent escorts return."

Turning in the curve of his arm, Mischa scowled dangerously up into Sevor's teasing face. "What are you talking about?" she growled.

"When we leave, just wrap your arms around my waist and hide your face against my back. There's no reason the hummeybees carrying me and those carrying you can't fly that close to each other. They have remarkable maneuverability in flight."

"Yez, we do!" buzzed another hummeybee as it performed a triple somersault in midair.

Mischa moaned, then closed her eyes as if that alone kept her from being violently sick. "Very well," she sighed, "I'll give it a try. But I'm warning you now. I don't care if it does make you unhappy. I'm reserving the right to kick and scream to my heart's content."

"I wouldn't want it any other way," Sevor replied with his usual crooked grin.

Spread out below was a colorful and brilliant world that reminded Drew forcibly of an illustration in a children's picture book. Tiny towns dotted the crayon green land, the buildings small blocks of primary colors outlined in what appeared from so high above to be bold black lines, each house or store painstakingly shaded as if by a child's tireless hand. Around these boxes of startling hue were specks of people circulating, each one like a pinpoint of color dabbed on to a page with the tip of a Magic Marker and then somehow set free to wander about. At first these bright drawings of towns seemed few and far apart, with nothing but construction paper slabs of green, blue, and brown in between, but the farther Drew and the others flew in the grasp of the swollen hummeybees, the more of these towns appeared, and the larger they became. Soon there were curling ribbons of brown swirling gracefully from town to town, as if the artistic child had grown playful when completing a book of connect-the-dots. And if anything, the colors grew even more intense and even appeared waxy, as if that same child had worked each crayon down to a stub coloring and recoloring the same small blocks.

It was a beautiful land, and one that truly did feel untouched and undefiled, just as if some innocent child had indeed brought the many colors and shapes to life. The only exception Drew had seen had been the house she herself had brought to this place, for when they had passed over it ages ago, it had appeared like a dark blot in the midst of so much color, oppressive and even sinister, and as far from the creative hands of a clear-eyed child as possible. Yet for all its nightmare horror it had saved her as it always saved her, and it had saved all the others as well. And staring down at the loathsome stain she had brought to this unsuspecting world, she had finally understood that the house was the way it was because it was exactly what she had always dreamed it to be; it wasn't something that had long haunted her dreams, but something she had brought to the dreams that haunted her. It was dark because its darkness blocked all eyes but hers, oppressive because its bulk weighed heavily on all spirits but hers, sinister because its job had always been to trap and destroy whatever creatures pursued her so that she would not be required to face or destroy them herself. So she would not have to kill, or risk being killed. She had not dreamed it infallible, but even the one Figment who always managed to elude the house and follow through the tunnels had been defeated every time before, for at the very least the house had always bought her the time to wake up. Perhaps that was what rendered the house so dark and oppressive now; in this world there would be no waking up from the house itself, and no escaping from whatever nightmares the house could not hold. And the darkest and most sinister thing of all was that this brightly colored land was about to change, had in fact already felt the first twinges of change, and from here on might actually need the house just as she had always needed the house.

Drew's thoughts remained as dark as the house even as she sped over the brightly patterned land, and when her eyes moved from the once again dwindling number of towns below her dangling feet, she saw that Gyfree's face, suspended between the legs of two giant hummeybees flying side by side with those carrying her, was as dark as her own. At the sight of his blindly staring eyes, her stomach clenched and her heart faltered, for she could clearly recognize that he was desperately holding a nightmare at bay. But there was no keeping this nightmare at bay; they were flying directly into it, flying into it knowing in advance that it might swallow them whole. Knowing that if they failed to dream their way out of it, it would sap all the brightness from this world. And knowing that even if they could dream their way free, they still might awake in two different worlds, one on either side of the waiting Source.

With a jolt the hummeybees holding her began to spiral downward toward the town directly beneath her feet, their wings beating with a furious hum as they slowed their descent, their bodies corkscrewing through the air so that they wouldn't lower her too quickly to the ground. Her eyes were filled with the flashing iridescence of their vibrating wings, and her ears were filled with high-pitched thrumming, and then her feet were touching the warm pavement of a street and she was blinking up at buildings that seen up close reminded her even more forcibly of storybook illustrations. Behind her she could feel Gyfree land, but she could also feel that his attention was drawn by something far different than what had drawn hers. Turning around, she let her eyes follow the path his had already taken down the street and through the town, passing by other brightly colored buildings, and stopping abruptly where the street ended, or perhaps began. There was no barrier she could see as she had seen the shimmering hot Barrier that had imprisoned Timi's Figment, yet there at the end or beginning of the road was a bright blue sky touching the ground, the intense blue rising directly from the earth and arcing far overhead to curve over this world like a giant bowl. Beyond that depthless blue there was nothing, not even a distant cloud, for there was no distance. There was sky, just like the sky where she had entered this world, but here there was a difference, for hanging in the sky with the same two-dimensionality of a child's drawing was a fat white streak that also held nothing. The Source.

Dreams within dreams within dreams, and she had moved from one to another and then always back to the dream of this world. Yet this was the place where all the dreams might come to an end, where at least this dream was supposed to come to an end. And if she somehow lived but this really was still the end, and not perhaps another beginning, for her there might still be dreaming, but her dreams would never be the same, and would never again bring her to a world worth awakening in.

The watchers watched, and what they saw the others who used their eyes saw as well, but what they learned they still learned alone. Their eyes never wavered from the two Dreamers, for those other eyes would notice even the slightest lapse, but they watched more than the others cared to note, so what they saw, and what they heard, was far more. They watched the hummeybees, and they learned why these creatures had escaped the limitations that held them bound, that even held their masters bound, and they learned what they would need to also be free. A world. A world of their own. A world to anchor them firmly in place so they too might truly live, and when they grew weary of living, truly die. And since they would never be gifted a world, perhaps they could steal one. But for now they must still watch, and they must still learn.

So the watchers watched as the Dreamers were carried far through the sky, and they watched as they touched feet to the ground again. And without blinking they watched as their Dreamers turned their eyes warily upon the white slash that marked the Barrier's most vulnerable yet strongest point. Most vulnerable because it was the easiest to break through from the other side. Strongest because it was the most difficult to move beyond. Then the eyes that watched through the watchers' eyes sharpened, and then those other eyes thrilled, and the watchers knew that their watching would soon be over. At least their watching for those other eyes. And in their own avid watching the dog's heart fluttered and the woman's arm trembled until the shaking that consumed them both had assumed a single rhythm that bound them not just in watching and not just in learning but also in waiting.

As the watchers saw the Dreamers turn toward the Source, so did the demon and his epidermal ice queen, and the sensual shiver that seized them both nearly buckled his knees. It was time, finally and irrevocably the time they had anticipated with a yearning even greater than their craving for each other. All of their deceptions had succeeded. They had deceived all existing Figments into sacrificing themselves in the mistaken belief that they would share in the conquering of countless worlds. They had deceived their Dreamers into believing that an army was being sent against them, when in actuality the army was only there to break through a Barrier held impassable against him and her, and to rush through in a deluge too overwhelming for the Source to pull back. Even if the entire army was destroyed in the first assault, they would already have served their true purpose simply by shielding his body in their midst, by closing around and hiding him just as his fist had closed around and hidden her when she set out to kill her Dreamer, by sheltering him and her in a nightmare so vast and overwhelming that together he and she could not merely enter this world, but also reach and kill their Dreamers before the Dreamers fully realized what danger they faced. And finally, they had even deceived their Dreamers into believing that they were more vulnerable when apart, for both had nearly died when they had separated before. Little did the Dreamers realize that at this point he and she wanted them together, wanted to share in their simultaneous deaths not just for the thrill of one equally intense sensation, but because they wanted nothing to disturb the delicate balance of their arousing union; the death of either Dreamer before the other was a risk they were now unwilling to take, for neither of them any longer desired to overwhelm the other with a flood of power that might leave one of them alone in his skin, wandering through the void as just fire or ice, but never again knowing the exhilarating sensation of both.

There was fire licking across her breasts and fire plunging deep into her body even though her body was no longer there. Yet fulfillment would have to wait. There was ice racing up his spine and across his loins, and although she was inside him, just inside his skin, with no hands of her own, he could feel icy fingers squeezing his buttocks and pressing sharp nails into his shoulders. Yet fulfillment would have to wait. They had shared much, but for the pleasure to come, the pleasure they wanted now, the greatest pleasure they still had left to share, they would have to wait for the anticipated kill.

Stepping into the center of the eagerly milling throng, he boomed in a voice that made his army shiver in the incredible cold and gasp in the unbearable heat, "It is time. Together we will take this world!"

A burly Figment stepped forward, its eyes mad with a ravenous carelessness. "What reward will I receive if I kill the Dreamer or the Keeper?" it demanded.

A massive paw filled with fire and tipped with daggers of ice swept the Figment from its feet and shredded its body with one swift contraction. "Any more questions?" he hissed.

There was no response to the dangerous question other than absolute quiet; not even the sound of a single breath or frantic heartbeat disturbed the silence.

"Then you know my commands. Now go!"

And just as they had in Sevor's dream, the Figments stampeded.

Drew's eyes were riveted to the white slash in the sky, and she could almost feel it drawing her forward, down the road and into that gash of aching emptiness. She even started to move toward it, but a strong hand suddenly closed around her arm, and Gyfree spun her around to meet his anguished eyes. "Don't leave," he whispered so no one else could hear. "Please don't leave."

Eyes locked with Gyfree's, for a moment Drew felt as if they were alone, back in the room beneath the stairs, where no one else could ever find them and nothing could separate them. Then the moment was lost as people began to pour from the buildings, clustering around the visitors who had arrived in such startling fashion. Most of these people gathered around Gyfree, calling out his name and asking him questions that rang out and then vanished in the growing swell of noisy chatter. Bodies jostled against Drew as more people shouldered their way through the crowd, but even as she was pushed helplessly from side to side, Gyfree's hand never loosened on her arm. She felt as if she had suddenly been caught up in a dream that she had long avoided but never forgotten, a dream of drowning, yet it was not water rushing over her head and stealing the breath from her lungs, but a flood of people, and the only thing that kept her from sinking forever beneath the crowd was that hand painfully gripping her arm. Even now that hand was reeling her in, pulling her up out of the depths, and dropping her at the top of a broad stairway overlooking the upturned and wondering faces of the townspeople below.

"Quiet!" shouted Gyfree. "If you value your lives, you must be quiet!"

The noise of the crowd ebbed, but the suspiration of whispers and murmured questions still washed up the steps like the voice of a distant sea.

"I said quiet!" roared Gyfree.

A stout man with a flushed face shoved his way to the front of the crowd and portentously cleared his throat. "Gyfree, what are you doing here? What are those things that brought you here? And where is your father?" he demanded.

"My father is dead," announced Gyfree baldly, but the bleakness in his eyes had nothing to do with his father, and nothing to do with death, but much to do with the one thing he most feared to lose now.

The tide of noise withdrew so suddenly and completely that it felt as if the waves on that distant sea had frozen in midcurl.

"My father is dead," repeated Gyfree, "and the land has chosen me as the new Keeper. I know this may make some of you uneasy, but you will need to save your feelings for another time. If there is another time. I have already destroyed more than a dozen Figments who have invaded our world, and this woman, Drew, a powerful Dreamer from my old world, has destroyed just as many as I have."

"Did you say destroyed?" croaked the stout man.

"Yes. We have destroyed Figments, not banished them. But now there is an entire army of Figments headed directly toward this town. They will be breaking through the Source soon. If you are not prepared to stand against them, you must flee. There is time for you to all escape if you move now, but there is no time to waste."

Far away a wave of infinite darkness flowed toward the land, but here the tide receded, people turning and rushing away from the town, people gathering more people as they moved along, people spilling from homes and workplaces, people pouring over the edges of the road and across green fields as they streamed away. And side by side with Gyfree, his fingers bruising her arm, Drew watched them vanish as if into a dream. Or perhaps from one dream into another.

"I don't know how much time we have," Sevor announced tersely, approaching the Dreamers hand in hand with Mischa, Peyr and Timi directly behind, and a swarm of hummeybees hovering overhead. "But I don't think there's much."

"Then you should run now," Gyfree answered shortly.

"What?" snapped Mischa. "You expect us to just leave you here to face the danger alone?"

"I'm the Keeper. Stopping the Figments is my responsibility, not yours. I'm not even sure why I let you come this far."

"You let us come because you couldn't have stopped us," Mischa retorted with a gleam in her eyes. "And because the moment you knew you finally had no other choice but to come here, you were so worried about what would happen to Drew when she reached the Source that you were completely unable to focus on anything else."

The hand on Drew's arm tightened convulsively. "Well, I'm focused now, and I want the rest of you to run as far and as fast as you can. Take Drew with you. If I can stop the Figments here, and if I survive, then we can worry about what should happen next."

"I'm not leaving," Drew said flatly, although her eyes were far away. "This is my danger to face as much as yours. It is my Figment who leads the attack, my Figment who must be stopped above all others."

"I'm not leaving, either," stated Timi, voice as flat as Drew's and eyes far more keen. "I came on this adventure because I felt that I had an important part to play, and despite everything else that's happened, I don't feel as if my part has been finished yet."

"And I'm not leaving if Timi is staying," Peyr announced. "Nor would I want her to go. I also believe she still has an important part to play, and I believe just as strongly that she'll need me to help her."

"There you have it," Sevor interjected wryly. "We're all staying, and since I dreamed of myself here, I would never have it otherwise. But we are limited to time, so we need to prepare. Gyfree, you and Drew need to stay where you are, but the rest of us are supposed to wait on that hill over there," he explained, pointing off toward a spot just beyond the town. "That's where I dreamed us, so that's where we need to be."

"And what if we're not there?" demanded Timi. "How do we know that what you dreamed for us is the best choice?"

Sevor shrugged his shoulders and smiled helplessly. "I don't know," he admitted. "I've never been a part of anything I've dreamed until I dreamed of all of you coming to my world. I suppose I would be uncomfortable trying to deviate from a dream when everything I've ever dreamed in my life has unfolded exactly as I expected. When I have dreamed of something happening in my world, my dreams have always been right. Always. It hasn't always been possible to verify my dreams of other worlds, but since all of you are exactly as I dreamed you, I would say my dreams have been amazingly accurate. That may not mean anything now, and it certainly may not mean that what I dreamed is the best thing possible for all of us, but I can't help but trust my dream."

"I'm just not sure that there isn't a better strategy than standing out in the open," Timi objected, "whatever you may have dreamed."

A frown creased Sevor's brow as he answered slowly, "When I dreamed of the last group of Figments coming to attack us, my dream was a warning, and that warning was enough to save us. Yet when I dreamed of the upcoming attack, the dream did more than just warn me that the Figments would attack, and more than show me where. It showed me each and every one of us, and all in specific places. If there was no reason for that, my dream should have ended as soon as I recognized this town. That would have been all the warning we needed. But my dream didn't end there because it was trying to not just warn us; it was trying to guide us. Just like the dream that guided me to all of you."

"That's enough for me," Drew stated softly, dreams rushing in and out of her eyes. Dream people pouring from houses then vanishing into the surrounding hills. The world of her dreams marred by a white gash that was like the harsh light slashing through her eyes when she first woke up every morning. The dream of a room beneath the stairs where strong arms and warm lips waited. Dreams within dreams until she couldn't quite recall what was real. But she could still feel what she thought felt real. Or at least she still dreamed she could feel the difference. "We have nothing left to trust in other than our dreams."

"And in uz," buzzed a familiar voice, and the companions all looked up at the larger of the original hummeybees. "If the man'z dream waz true, he zhould have zeen uz. We have come through a dream to help zave you. Where zhould we wait?"

Sevor's eyes grew distant, until once more he could see the wave of creatures crashing against the land and the pitiful handful of people waiting on a hill, and the lonely couple standing hand in hand in the shadow of a building, and this time, now that he had paused to recall every last detail, he could see the tiny dots of black and yellow flitting across the empty sky that stretched between the Source and the hill.

"You must wait in the sky overhead, between us and the Barrier," Sevor told the hummeybees. "And you must make yourselves as small as possible."

The hummeybee buzzed a distinct laugh. "We will wait az you zay, but you need not tell uz how bezt to fight. When we are zmall, we are quick. When we are unnotized, we ztrike without warning. We know how to fight."

A dream of a watercolor world floated through Drew's eyes. "In your world, you never had reason to fight," she murmured drowsily, and Gyfree's hand tightened its hold as if he was afraid that any moment she might slip from his grasp.

"Yez, but zometimez you dreamed uz fierze, juzt az zometimez you dreamed uz huge. Zo we have the power to be gentle or fierze, zmall or huge. You gave uz a choize, even then," droned the hummeybee fondly, its wings brushing fingers of air across her face in a tender caress. "Juzt az you may give yourzelf a choize zoon." Without another word, the hummeybee soared high into the empty sky, and with an excited buzz, all the other hummeybees followed.

"I think that's our cue," Sevor said tensely. "Places, everyone."

The others were barely out of earshot when Gyfree reached out his other hand and roughly turned Drew around to face him. "Stay with me, Drew," he implored, voice harsh with the same pain that darkened his eyes. "Don't let yourself be pulled away."

Drew blinked dreamily, then blinked again, her eyes once more sharply focused on Gyfree's face. "I feel so strange," she whispered, "as if I really have been caught up in nothing but a dream. You seem so real to me, but I'm not sure. Maybe you're just the best and most wonderful dream I've ever had."

"It's the Source," Gyfree explained urgently. "That's what it does. It pulls Dreamers back to their waking world. And it's trying to pull you away from me now."

"It feels like the morning light, telling me it's time to wake up. Time to wake up before the beautiful dream turns into another nightmare," murmured Drew.

"But it hasn't all been like a dream," insisted Gyfree, "and it hasn't all been beautiful. Remember the death of my father. Remember the Figments you fought and killed. Remember my Figment killing me. Remember the Figment that caught and nearly killed you. Remember all the pain and death, and you'll know this has been more than just a marvelous dream."

Drew gazed up into the intense golden brown eyes and lifted a hand to touch Gyfree's disheveled, rusty hair. "Help me," she cried. "I don't want to wake up. Even if it has just been a dream, even if the nightmare is about to take us all, I want to stay here with you."

Gyfree's mouth crashed down, his lips pressing hers open to steal her breath in exchange for his own, and caught tightly against his body she could feel his heart racing against hers, could feel her heart quicken to keep pace, could feel both hearts running as if they would never stop, running not away from something feared, but toward something desired.

Then a shudder ran through the ground beneath their feet, and their lips fell apart as their eyes were pulled toward the white crack in the sky that was suddenly spilling something viscous and black.

✦　　✦　　✦

Timi and Peyr rushed hand in hand toward the waiting hill and scampered up its bank to stand panting side by side, eyes on the white scar of the Source. Once they had caught their breaths, Peyr wrapped an arm around Timi and pulled her into the crook of his shoulder. Then, leaning close, he whispered, "I know what you need to do."

Tearing her eyes free from the ominous Source, Timi blinked up at him. "What are you talking about?"

"You need to trust yourself," answered Peyr enigmatically.

Timi blinked again. "Now I'm truly confused. How is trusting myself going to make a difference here and now?"

Peyr turned her around to face him, gripping her by the shoulders just as Gyfree was gripping Drew, and said with an urgency that also matched his, "When you absorbed your Figment, you regained all the powers you had detached from yourself. You know that, and so you've been very careful to rein in all your seductive powers, all your ability to entice and capture. You need to unleash those powers now and use them against the Figments."

The bewilderment in Timi's face was whisked away by an expression of horror. "I can't," she gasped. "What if I lose control? What if I can't rein myself back in? Then I'll be no better than my Figment was, and you'll be no more than just another helpless slave."

"Trust yourself," insisted Peyr. "I trust you because I know all those things you fear will never happen. But there has to be a reason you possess the powers you do, just as there has to be a reason you felt compelled to stay here. Don't you see? That reason is because you have the power to make a difference if you only trust yourself first."

Timi stared up at Peyr, but she no longer saw his strong and earnest face; instead she saw the perfect features of the Figment, his golden hair curling over his forehead, his blue eyes filled with all the glory of a summer sky, an alluring, irresistible smile curling across his face, and a horde of faceless, helpless people groveling at his feet. Then his face melted into her face, and a kneeling man looked up at her with hungry, slavish eyes, his features no longer anonymous, but the same as the man who only moments ago had looked down at her as he held her by the arms. Tears surged through her eyes to wash away the appalling vision, and she was again staring up at Peyr's strong, freed face. "I can't," she whispered.

There was no time for further urging, for at that moment the ground shook, and they turned their eyes to see a thick black flood gush from the Source.

Mischa didn't even wait to reach their destination before she pulled a knife from a sheath wrapped around the calf of her leg and handed it to Sevor hilt first. "I want you to have this. Just in case," she said with a twisted smile. "If we're fighting Figments, it might be better to at least have something to fight with."

Sevor replied with his own twisted grin, and handed her another knife from a sheath strapped across his chest beneath his shirt. "And I'd like you to have this. Just in case. Dreamers from my world don't believe in going anywhere unprepared, especially into battle."

"They sound very wise, the Dreamers from your world," Mischa remarked with a lightness that could only be forced.

"Mostly very foolish, actually," Sevor tried to tease in return, "since most of them don't go anywhere, prepared or otherwise."

As they reached the crest of the hill, Mischa turned to face him. Over his shoulder, she could see Timi and Peyr standing side by side, Peyr's eyes intent on Timi's upturned ones, their voices intense and hushed, and she quickly averted her eyes so that all she could see was the smile twisting Sevor's lips and the hopelessness in his eyes. "What is it like, your world?" she asked softly, and without even the shadow of an attempted smile.

"Dull, at least for a Dreamer like me. True Dreamers are as rare in my world as they are in Drew's, and although we dream differently in my world, our lives are also centered on our dreams. Even the weakest Dreamers prefer living through their dreams because it seems so much simpler than living themselves. And all the weak ones dream of are ordinary people living ordinary lives. Worst of all are the strongest Dreamers, for their dreams are filled with the richer lives of extraordinary people, people from worlds like yours who live each moment fully. Dreamers like that, Dreamers like me, can barely tolerate waking up because the worlds we dream are the only worlds we want to see, and the only people we can bear to touch are those we love in our dreams."

Mischa reached up her free hand to twine her fingers through the hair that curled at the back of his neck. "So instead of just dreaming, you found your way to me. I've never really thanked you for that. For coming here to save me."

Sevor caught her hand in his and held it tight. "You never needed to thank me. I came not just to save you, but to save myself. I've never lived as fully as I have in the short time I've spent with you."

"But now you may die," Mischa whispered, her eyes reflecting the nightmare vision that still haunted his. "Living may be better than dreaming, but dreaming must be better than dying."

Gently Sevor wrapped her in his arms, as careful to avoid the knife she held as he was careful not to nick her with the blade in his hand. "To a Dreamer like me, every awakening is death, and in my world I felt the pain of death every day of my life."

"Yet dying is more absolute than the pain of death."

There was no laughter in Sevor's eyes, but there was no longer complete despair either. "I've never feared dying. What's dying to me other than just another sleep, a sleep that doesn't bring the torment of unfulfilled yearnings in its wake? And what is death to you other than just another dreamless sleep? I would rather live, and live with you, but if death awaits us, then perhaps we will still be together in a quiet sleep untouched by the painful longings that are inseparable from both life and dreams."

Sevor lowered his head to kiss her, but there was no more time. The ground trembled, and they felt as if their eyes had been seized by the white gash in the sky as it bled poisoned darkness.

Sevor tightened his grip on the knife Mischa had given him, and growled, "There are things worse than unrealized dreams or dying. And here they come."

Chapter 15

Forgotten in their dark corner of the void, the watchers watched, but no longer did they watch because it was too dangerous to close their eyes. Their eyes were theirs alone now, their eyes had served well, and although there would be no reward for the watchers' service, there was actually a chance there would be no punishment if they disappeared before they could be remembered. Yet they did not disappear, and they did not turn their eyes away. They watched still, not out of fear or constraint or even habit, but because they could not help themselves. Watching had given them new identity, new purpose, and they wanted to watch. So on the screen created by the demon they watched the Dreamers prepare for the expected attack, but they also watched through those eyes that had recently watched through theirs, watched through the same eyes that had watched all that they had watched, but had then forgotten whose eyes were attached to whose.

Now the watchers truly saw everything, saw more than they had ever seen before. For at last they could see beyond the fire burning in the demon's eyes, could see beyond the fog that billowed off the ice queen's ice, and they could see that those they had called master were too blind to see for themselves. Yet for all their blindness, the watchers knew their masters were still formidable, perhaps even more formidable for their lack of sight, and unquestionably more dangerous, far more dangerous than the watchers who could see, but who lacked the power to do. They were certainly more than formidable and dangerous enough to deal with the pitiful group of people who stood waiting, and the two Dreamers who clung together without seeming to understand the powers they themselves possessed.

Arm between fangs, heart and lung between fingers, the watchers watched as one, and the dog gnawed bone not because he needed to keep the woman alert, and the woman squeezed in rhythm with the pulsing heart and quivering lungs not because she needed to keep the dog on a leash, but because this was what had made them one and each was simply carrying out the task they had been given: the dog chewed and the woman pinched, and together they kept the joint body that was the watchers alive.

Together they watched the scene unfold before them, watched the Dreamers grip hands in fear, and at the same time watched through the fire and ice within the demon's eyes as the stream of ravening Figments rushed forward, unwittingly concealing their leader in their midst so that he and the invisible companion he carried could sneak into the one world that had been closed to both of them. And they watched as the alien light of this world broke into the demon's shared eyes, watched as he and his queen blinked to see so much color and life, and watched the fire and ice explode behind their eyes when they finally caught sight of the two small figures waiting in the center of the town.

Then the watchers could only watch from afar, from their small corner of the void, for they could not see beyond the towering flames and sheer walls of ice that suddenly filled their masters' eyes, could not see past the madness that had seized not only him, but also her. Yet the watchers still watched, for not only was watching still their purpose and identity, but there was something worth watching, something they would have been compelled to watch even if they had watched nothing of what had come before. As they watched, they could see the Figments break like a wave against a rocky shore, parting ways so they could charge in various directions across the smooth green surface of the land; they could see the demon towering above the others, wading brutally through the bodies that blocked his way so he might quickly reach the two Dreamers; they could see a darkness spread rapidly and irrevocably across the land until there was nothing else to see, and for the first time since they had started watching, all the watchers could do was wait, dog gnawing bone, woman pinching heart and lungs, and both sets of eyes intent on the darkened and uncommunicative screen.

The tide of Figments that surged through the gash was so heavy and unceasing that even Sevor, who had known what to expect, knew a moment of overwhelming despair. He clutched his knife convulsively, wondering what he would have seen if his dream had continued, wondering if he would have seen his knife plunging into a slathering Figment, wondering how much blood and carnage would have preceded his own death, wondering if he would have seen Mischa and the others fall before him, or whether he would have seen himself fall first. And most of all wondering if he still had a chance to wake up from this nightmare, wake up and find Mischa folded in his arms, wake up and know for the first time in his life that a dream could just be a dream and didn't have to mean anything else at all.

He and the others stood as if they had no choice but to stand and wait, and then suddenly Peyr was dashing down the hill, waving empty hands above his head and bellowing wordlessly as if sound alone was the most deadly weapon imaginable. There was a moment of stunned silence on the hill, as if the three remaining people had unexpectedly found themselves in a soundproof bubble that could not be penetrated by the stampeding feet and piercing shrieks of the innumerable charging Figments, and then the bubble was burst from within as Timi screamed, "Peyr! No!"

Despite the seeming futility of any effort, Sevor charged down the hill, Mischa's knife clutched over his head, his eyes on the blood red eyes and dripping fangs of the closing enemy, Mischa directly on his heels. As he ran he could smell the stench of the swarming creatures, could even feel their muddy breaths drizzling stickily across his face, but just as he saw his own certain death reflected in the nearest slitted eyes, something impossibly strange stayed his headlong plunge. He wavered expectantly at the base of the hill with Mischa to one side and Peyr on the other, while a long straggling line of glassy-eyed Figments swayed unsteadily in place only a few feet away, their faces filled with unthinking adoration as they gazed longingly at the lone figure of Timi poised on the crest of the hill. Then, as the next wave of crazed Figments crashed into the stalled attackers, a cluster of diving hummeybees plunged into the packed mob, barbed stingers stabbing into the backs of unprotected necks so that the Figments reeled senseless to the ground.

Peyr and Mischa tumbled immediately into the melee, Peyr throttling unresisting Figments with his bare hands, Mischa calmly slitting exposed throats, but for a second Sevor paused, his eyes on the distant figure of Timi. She stood outlined against a graying sky, but even from here her eyes shone more intensely gray, and her hair glowed more golden than the lowering sun. There was an aura about her, as if all the heat and light in the world radiated from her slim form, and not from that distant yellow ball, and Sevor could even feel the pull of her ensnaring gravity slip over and past him and seize the next wave of Figments. Then his eyes were back on his own personal sun, and he was plunging into battle after Mischa, her knife ready in his hand. Resistless the Figments fell before him until he felt sickened by his own savagery, but he knew better than anyone that they were followed by an endless deluge of more Figments, and he doubted that Timi could hold them all. So like Peyr and Mischa and the fiercely buzzing hummeybees, he struck over and over again, sending Figment after Figment collapsing to the ground, where they either groaned and wallowed in their blood and in the blood of countless others, or sprawled unconscious.

As he waded forward through fallen bodies to reach those still standing, Sevor's arm grew weary and his vision blurred, but still he struck, not killing, for these creatures could not be killed by such as him, but removing them effectively from the battle, at least for the time being. On he moved, until he was covered in thick, oily blood, and the knife he wielded was almost too slick to hold. And still he pressed forward. It was an endless, consuming task, but at last there was a pause, for an inbound wave of Figments had halted abruptly just within the Barrier, and in the lull Sevor glanced back over the innumerable felled bodies toward where Timi still stood, on top of a hill now covered completely with those Figments who had somehow evaded not only the dangerous hummeybees, but also him and his two fellow fighters. He caught his breath in sudden fear, but as one the Figments knelt before her, their eyes tilted upward in abject devotion, and as he watched in amazement, he could see her place her hands atop two of the bowed heads at her sides and lift her shining eyes toward where Peyr, standing in the midst of his senseless victims, smiled up at her.

Drew felt caught in a dream as the first wave of Figments burst through the crack in the sky, and she watched helplessly as the scene unfolded before her with all the inevitability and distorted aloofness that came whenever she dreamed herself a spectator in her own nightmare. A dark coil of creatures unwound over the land, blotting out all traces of green as they rolled inexorably toward the foot of the hill where even now three small specks rushed down as if to lose themselves in the innundation of darkness. Yet another mass of creatures churned over the road and into the paths of the town, crashing against empty buildings and howling for blood, their driving need blinding them to the two motionless Dreamers hiding hand in hand within the shadows. It seemed as if she and Gyfree floated above the devouring flood, watching and waiting as the creatures swirled madly below, watching and waiting for some faraway dam to completely burst and disgorge a tidal wave of darkness so immense it would wash them away.

Drew perched above the roiling creatures, and then her ears were shattered by the roar of the explosion she had unwillingly awaited, a roar of crushing madness; raising her eyes once more to the gushing crack, she saw him looming over her just as he had once loomed over her child-size bed, his eyes filled with the promise of her death. Even now she could remember that first moment so clearly, could still see him as she had seen him then, his face on fire and his eyes aglow with all the other flames that raged within him. He had opened his lips, not as if he wished to speak, but as if he had wanted to suck her into the furnace of his mouth, and his forked tongue had flickered out like the tongue of a snake smelling fear in the air. Cowering in her bed, she had met his eyes, and had recognized that he was laying claim to her, that he had already marked her as his own just as her parents had warned he would, and then he had smiled, his fangs glinting in the glow of his flames, smiled because he knew that she had recognized his possession. She had screamed then, and he had fled, but she had seen him once again, and felt his presence stalking her as she grew from child to teen, from teen to adult, felt him waiting to collect what he had laid stake to all those years ago.

Now he had returned, just as she had always secretly feared he would, and the years seemed to fall away, leaving her as helpless as a child again. Watching him plow through the swarming

Figments, blood in his wake, she was more afraid than she had ever been before, for she realized that he had grown more dangerous, more merciless, than she had once dreamed him. That was, in the end, the only change she had dreamed possible for him. His fiery features hadn't changed in the least since that first time, but he had grown infinitely larger, just as she had dreamed he would, for she had dreamed that over time all those flames that he held inside would grow, and that he would be forced to grow with them, would need to keep growing so that he could contain all his pent-up hatred and rage. All the hatred and rage that he had saved for her.

Yet as he drew ever closer she realized that there was something about him that had changed after all, something that she had never dreamed possible. His eyes flamed, but intermixed with the flames were shards of glittering ice. Flames licked across his face, but at the heart of each flame was a sliver of ice. And when he opened his mouth to loose another insane roar, his fiery tongue was forked with ice, and his fangs glinted more silvery blue than burning red. Something incredibly cold snaked down Drew's spine, and with a shudder she squeezed the hand that convulsively gripped her own, knowing that Gyfree had seen the ice long before she had, and that he had felt its touch all his life. Timi had been right; there was more here than could be easily understood.

Rushing in with the thought of Timi came the memory of her explanation of what exactly had become of her Figment, and rushing in behind that memory came an idea that rocked Drew to her core. She knew what she and Gyfree needed to do now, not without a doubt, for there was no way not to have doubt, but still she knew that of all possible choices, there was now one that might be the best. And once that choice was made, there would be no time to change, since they were already nearly out of time, already in danger of not having enough time, for now she could feel both the heat washing over her face and the chill radiating from Gyfree's body. With a gasp she blurted her idea into Gyfree's ear, and then the demon was upon them, towering directly above, his eyes both aflame with hunger and cool with anticipation.

A dream erupted in Drew's eyes, a dream she had dreamed only once, and had feared to dream again. The dream itself had been born of fear, born from all the dire warnings and threats that her parents had bombarded her with, all the mad ravings of the robed man they had dragged her to hear, and in the dream she was surrounded by flames, and the flames formed a creature who always burned, a creature whose laughter crackled as he reached out to make her burn with him. He had seemed so real, so full of life, so full of fire, that when she forced open her eyes, he was standing there, flames licking across her bed but scorching nothing other than her mind. And now she dreamed him again, and saw him again, saw him not as he towered above her, but as he had stood at the foot of her bed, and this time across the chasm of years she saw that what glowed in his face was need, and that what burned on his tongue was a plea, and that the eyes marking her recognized that she was the one who owned him, that he was hers to love or hate, embrace or spurn, need or reject, and whatever her choice, forever hers to possess. Finally she could see him clearly, see him as no more than a child himself, and seeing him new and vulnerable she understood that when she had turned from him in fear, she had turned him into something to fear.

Drew's blurted words had pierced through the cold that held Gyfree in its grip, and just as she had flung herself into her dream, he had flung himself into one of his own, flung himself with complete abandon into the one dream that had so haunted him as a child that it had chased him into another world. Plunging into the dream he could even recall, as if it was an integral part of the dream itself, how he had shivered in the freezing cold, a small boy dragged through a snowstorm, teeth chattering as some cheery adult voice pointed out that a little snow never hurt anyone, and then the same voice, less cheery, questioned why he didn't recognize the beauty in the snow-gowned land, and at last icily hostile, as all adult voices ultimately were, the faceless voice snapped that he needed to stop feeling sorry for himself. Still shivering uncontrollably in his dream, he watched the snow swirling above the ground, silvery flecks dancing as if in a playful wind, then whirling madly through the tops of the snow-laden trees and dislodging icicles that then joined the dance of silvery flakes. Like a tiny tornado of ice and snow, the silvery flecks whirled and spun around him, catching at his clothes and then twirling him helplessly through deep drifts of snow before tossing him to the frozen ground. Through tears that froze as soon as they trickled from his eyes, he stared up at the silver ice storm as it hovered above him, and stared as the silvery flecks coalesced and solidified into an exquisitely lovely little girl, a little girl more beautiful than the snow-gowned land, a little girl who reached out to touch him with hands of solid ice, reached out to freeze him so that he would never be warm again.

This was the moment, as a boy, that he had shuddered awake, and teeth chattering with a cold that had to do with much more than just his dream, saw the exquisite little ice maiden reaching out her hand. He had screamed then, and she had fled, only to return later, more beautiful and far more deadly, and it had been his turn to flee. He started to shiver even now, started to turn away from the beautiful girl of ice and snow, but then he paused, for he wasn't a child anymore, and his hand was gripped in the warmest of clasps, and he had not faced this dream again only to let it frighten him away. So he turned back toward the beautiful creature sculpted from ice, and as he turned he saw the pleading in eyes where tears were permanently frozen in place, saw the trembling of arms that were extended not because they wanted to touch, but because they longed to be touched, saw the shivering of the tiny hand that wanted, just like his, to be held in a warm clasp.

Standing eye to eye with his beautiful creation, Gyfree noticed as if from a great distance that the silvery blue was draining from the suddenly paralyzed figure towering above, that the ice was melting from the fiery eyes, seeping through the flaming skin, shivering away from the searing claws, and that there in the space before him, where the girl he had dreamed long ago and finally dreamed again stood wavering, the silver drifting down from above swirled and danced, sinking through her transparent skin, filtering through her translucent eyes, until she was once more as substantial and chilling as she had been the first time she had reached out her tiny hand to touch him. And this time when she reached out, her eyes full of crystal tears, he did not flinch, but he still did not move to take the hand she extended. Yet he paused not from uncertainty, or even from fear, but because the fiery creature looming over them all was dissolving into a whirl-wind of sparks that rained down upon the shimmery form of a much smaller, although equally fiery creature poised expectantly, flaming eyes on Drew.

Hand in hand the Dreamers stood, and as they watched, their Figments reached out to each other, icy fingers slipping into a fiery paw, and although the frigid eyes that gazed back at Gyfree were the same eyes that had watched him with longing, and the fiery eyes that burned into Drew were the same eyes that had first marked her, both pairs of eyes were also the eyes that remembered everything. And those eyes were filled with demands that must be answered, needs that must be fulfilled, and the consequences that would be delivered if this time was to be no different from the time that had gone before. Gyfree saw the icy warning, just as Drew saw the fiery menace, but they both saw the fear behind the threat, saw the shadows of infinite hurt that neither Figment could bear to endure again, and this time when the ice maiden extended a shimmering hand, and the demon's forked tongue slipped between his parted lips, the two Dreamers stepped forward hand in hand, and Gyfree wrapped his free fingers around the tiny frigid hand, while Drew reached up her empty palm to cup the demon's fiery cheek.

A shudder shook the Figments, and shook the ground beneath their feet more violently than the swarming army of Figments shook the world beneath theirs. Together the Dreamers stepped forward again, until their bodies almost touched the bodies of their creations, and Gyfree could feel the wintry chill that radiated from the glistening sheen of the ice maiden's skin, while Drew could feel the burning heat that leapt from the demon's pores. Then, looking deep beneath the ice-coated eyes, beneath all the layers of ice she had built around herself, Gyfree met the gaze of the small shivering creature that needed warmth, needed love, needed him, and he pulled her gently by the hand and tucked her into the space beneath his shoulder, holding her as closely as she had always wanted to be held. She shivered against him, but where her body touched his, he felt only warmth, and when she sighed, there was no cloud of frost hanging in the air.

Beside Gyfree, Drew stroked the flaming cheek beneath her palm, but even though flames erupted between her fingers, she felt no pain, only a comforting warmth. Looking up into the pits of fire that were her demon's eyes, and gazing deep into the heart of the flames, she could see the truths concealed within, the secrets of fire itself, but she could also see that these were not the secrets she had always thought them to be. There was no ecstasy in burning, only a gnawing hunger that could never be assuaged; no eagerness to destroy, only an empty yearning to find something that would not disappear, and that could never be devoured. And there was no drive, no great desire, to consume the very thing that had granted life, but there was a need, a burning need, to be gathered in and sheltered, to be contained, to be granted the freedom to leap and dance with no need to find food and no fear of being extinguished. Without hesitation, and without the smallest trace of fear, Drew pulled down the demon's head to nestle on her shoulder and wrapped her arm around him, holding him close, and where his body touched hers, the flames flickered and subsided until his skin glowed like hot embers that needed only a nudge to spark back to life.

Together the Dreamers and their creations stood, pressed so close that from afar they seemed to form a single whole, and then Gyfree lowered his head to kiss the quivering lips of his ice maiden, and Drew turned her head to kiss the blazing lips of her demon, and into their kisses they dreamed all the words they had never said but should have, all the comfort they had denied but should have provided, all the love and acceptance they had withheld but now gave freely, and a promise that should have been made years ago, but was still not too late to keep. And in the embrace of their Dreamers, the two Figments shuddered, and their forms wavered and flickered, and with a sigh that seemed to tremble throughout their bodies, they dissolved into the air, flecks of silver and red swirling together as one, climbing high into the sky in a joyous explosion of color and light, and then floating back down and drifting apart to stream into the bodies and dreaming minds that would finally, or perhaps once more, be their homes.

Alone in the shadows, although never truly alone again, the two Dreamers stood hand in hand, and while the hand Gyfree held felt deliciously warm, the hand Drew held was soothingly cool.

All around her were creatures who desired only to serve her, creatures who would do anything just to satisfy her slightest whim. And there were more creatures than these, just beyond the Barrier, more who would just as readily, just as eagerly, bow down to her. At first she had only had the power to attract a few, but then her strength and confidence had grown, and she had added more and more to the growing number of creatures who groveled before her, had added more and more until only one creature who had entered this world was left untouched. It was intoxicating, this sense of overweening power, but it was also strangely empty. She was adored, even worshiped, but what she truly wanted was something different, something more. What she wanted couldn't be found in these groveling creatures, or in the ones sprawled senseless, or even in the ones still to blunder into her trap; instead, everything she wanted, everything she had always wanted, was in the smile of the one man gazing back at her, his eyes neither reverent nor submissive, but filled with love and pride and even a hint of laughter.

Timi smiled back at Peyr, but she did not release the multitude she held in thrall, for there was a reason she held them, and that reason was as pressing now as it had been the moment she had unleashed all those powers she had kept carefully restrained inside. She had not wanted to loose her powers, for she had not truly trusted her ability to rein them back in when the time came; she had feared that she would crave more, just as her Figment had always craved more, that once she had tasted conquest, she would never be satiated. Peyr had known her fears, had told her to trust herself, but her terror of what she might become had been so great that she would have preferred to die rather than risk becoming a monster. But she hadn't been willing to watch him die, and he had known that too. He had not been able to convince her, so instead he had compelled her to act, compelled her to save his life the only way she could. And since he had compelled her, perhaps his power over her was as great as any power she might wield over him. With that thought she was able to release her last nagging doubt; whatever his feelings, and whatever her attraction, she had not ensnared him. She was capable of so much, but she didn't need to be afraid anymore; she knew now that she could trust herself, just as he had wanted her to trust herself.

Across the space that divided them, Peyr smiled again, and Timi knew he understood everything she had felt, and everything she had learned. But she also knew he was waiting, for she still had a job to complete, and it was time to begin. Lifting her eyes from his face, and summoning a smile that was her own private weapon, Timi turned to the Figments surrounding her, and asked softly, "Who will serve me?"

"I will!" resounded a chorus of voices, and the sound was echoed all the way down the hill, across the land and to the Source itself. It even penetrated into the town, where from the corner of her eye Timi could no longer see the monstrous creature who had rushed toward the place where she had last seen Drew and Gyfree, and where now she could detect nothing but shadows. A moment of hopelessness seized her, for if Drew and Gyfree had not survived, all her efforts would be futile; there had been something in that massive Figment that, she had sensed from even here, would be beyond her ability to control. But that Figment was nowhere to be seen, and she shook the hopelessness aside, for she had no choice but to try, even if she was destined to fail, and with a strength she had never known she possessed, she threw herself fully into her task.

"Will you do anything I ask of you?" she crooned seductively.

"Yes! Anything!" cried the Figments.

"Will you leave this world and never return?"

There was abject pain in the eyes that gazed back at her, but there was only one answer the Figments could give. "Yes," they whispered, "we will leave." Then beneath her hand, one creature shivered, its imploring eyes fixed to her face. "I will leave if you wish, but I would rather stay and serve you," it whimpered, and all around Timi the Figments shivered, and their eyes begged for her to reconsider.

Panic rushed through Timi, and for a brief moment she doubted her ability to simultaneously hold the Figments and send them away, for it seemed impossible that she could still exert control at the same moment she was spurning them. But then she saw that the eyes on hers were begging not just to stay, not just to be allowed to adore her, but to be cared for in return, and she armed her smile with a gentleness that could not be dodged. "Every Figment who has come here before you is dead," she related. "Not one has survived. This is a dangerous world for all of you, a world so dangerous that I fear for your safety. I want you to leave, but only because I can't bear the thought of harm coming to you."

The Figments nearest her shivered again, but one with a bloody gash across its throat whined, "But you let those three people hurt many of us. They are covered with our blood, and the ground is covered with those of us who are injured."

"Yet they did not kill any of you. They only stopped you before the dangers of this world could find you. I had to let them hurt you so I could save you."

A sigh rippled through the gathered Figments, and in their eyes she could see how desperately they needed to believe that she cared. "Will you come with us?" begged one raspy voice, and then another, and another, until the plea was left trembling in the air.

"No, for I cannot live where you live. If I left here it would mean my death."

As one the Figments quaked, for the thought of her death was more intolerable than the thought of never seeing her again. "Then we must leave," rumbled a voice from somewhere within the mob.

"Please, before it is too late," urged Timi, tears actually springing to her eyes as she felt the power of their feelings wash over her. "And help those who do not yet have the strength."

First one, and then another, and then countless others turned from Timi, blood red tears streaming down their forlorn faces, and with heavy steps they walked back toward the white gouge in the sky, some battered creatures stumbling alone, but most trudging arm in arm with those who had somehow gone unscathed. Even from the farthest recesses of the town they poured, as if Timi's voice had tracked them down wherever they had ventured, and lured them back to the road that led away from not only a town, but also a world. They left far more slowly than they had arrived, and there were many backward glances cast at the lone figure standing silhouetted on the crest of the hill, but as they neared the Source, an invisible hand seemed to reach out and wrest them away, and finally, as the sun tilted in the sky to light the hill on fire, the last Figment vanished into the white slash that stood out even more starkly in the darkening sky.

How long the Dreamers stood hand in hand dreaming they could not guess, but they could see as if from a fathomless distance the dark tide of Figments that continued to roll past them into the town, and that slowly covered the distant hill. From afar they could hear the land wailing beneath the onslaught of a terrible pain, and then for an uncharted time a roaring drowned all other noise, until finally the roar subsided and they could hear a seductive voice rippling through the Figments like a strong current. From their far-off dreaming they could even sense the reluctant departure of the surprisingly gentled Figments, but this too was just something to note in passing, for what held their attention above all else were the scattered memories and lingering sensations that had filled their Figments' lives, and which they now absorbed dreaming just as they had absorbed the Figments themselves.

Roaring through Drew with the fury of a wildfire were all the searing sensations of pain that had shaped her Figment, and all the cruel delight he had eventually felt bringing that pain to others. She watched in her dreaming as so many others writhed beneath his burning touch, watched as he ripped them apart and made them his, and the heat of his remembered pleasure drove through and scorched her most cherished dreams. Everything beautiful that had ever graced her dreaming mind was consumed in the blaze of his presence, and she knew that if she could not control the fire, she would be lost. Yet as quickly as it had flared out of control, the fire he had brought abated, cooled by all those dreams she had only moments before feared lost, and her own memories and self fell back into place, so that once more she could watch and fully understand as she had promised.

Flickering through her dreaming mind were now other images, and although these too were fueled by an incredible heat, their glow was soft and seductive, and in them she could see Gyfree's Figment, could see the desire the two Figments had shared, the pain they had given even in passion because pain was all they had ever known; she could even feel the intensity of their need to almost completely consume each other. She watched as her Figment took his lover deep within himself, watched as she filled him as if he was empty rather than brimming with fire, and was shaken as she felt how their need for each other had even then flared out of control. And as she once more felt in danger of losing herself, the flames again carefully receded, until at last she watched herself through his eyes, watched herself grow and change and wander aimlessly through her world, living with intensity only in her dreams. She watched just as he had always watched, watched every movement and every moment he had ever watched, watched herself thwart him again and again, and at long last watched as she finally and miraculously opened her eyes to him, then opened her arms, then opened herself. With this final vision the flames subsided, content for the moment to smolder quietly in the recesses she had provided, fueled by her presence and her power. And there was a warmth in her smile greater than any she had known before when she realized the gift he had unintentionally given her.

Gripped by a cold more intense than any he had ever felt before, a cold more intense than he had even felt when his Figment had placed her hand over his heart to steal his life, Gyfree stood frozen beside Drew as he too watched all his Figment needed him to watch and felt all she had yearned for him to feel. He wandered lost with her as she had wandered lost, and he held in his dreaming arms all the victims she had held, and he was left as cold and hardened by their deaths as she had been. He was filled with the coldness of so much death that his mind was numbed and he doubted that he would ever feel again, even wondered if he had ever felt before at all. But then the ice that filled him cracked, and he saw himself, a scruffy boy with dream-filled eyes, and he did feel again, feel with a sharpness as cutting as a dagger of ice. He felt the yearning she had felt for him, felt the despair his final rejection had brought, and for the first time felt the joy of killing she had found when she pursued him, a joy that was icy but joy nonetheless, and deep within he knew that he would rather never feel again than to feel all of this.

Gyfree recoiled from the cruelty of the cold, and he knew that he was lost now, as lost as his Figment had once been, lost to wander in the darkness and the cold that he now held within, but suddenly he felt a flash of warmth, and there in his dreaming mind was Drew's Figment, his fiery figure promising release just as a sweltering sun promised release from the grasp of winter. And then the release came, came when it was least expected, and he felt himself dragged away from his body just as she had been dragged away, felt himself enfolded with her in a dark that was filled with heat, a heat that penetrated to the very core of the ice without melting it. He was wrapped as she was wrapped in a sensual heat, and as the heat intensified the dark receded until he was looking with her through the demon's eyes and feeling with her through the demon's skin. And then he was watching himself standing before her, ready to turn away as he had always turned away, but then unexpectedly turning back and seeing her truly for the very first time, and he dreamed with her as she remembered the promise she had made so many years ago, the promise that if he would just see her and smile, see her and not run, she would leave him in peace, and the cold drifted as silently as snow down into his farthest recesses, to be wrapped in a warmth that would lull rather than arouse her needs.

As their Figments settled, Drew and Gyfree awoke to the sight of Peyr rushing up a hill to catch Timi in his arms and swing her exuberantly through the air. They blinked to see Sevor and Mischa wrapped in each other's arms despite the oily blood that coated them both. And then Drew was turning her head toward the white gash that now pulsed in the sky as if a giant artery pressed against it from behind, and with a new dream filling her eyes, she was stepping in its direction. Yet even as she succumbed to the pull of the Source, a sharp tug on her arm pulled her in the opposite direction.

"Drew, no!" Gyfree's voice rasped harshly in her ear. "I can't lose you. We'll have the hummeybees fly us away from here, and you'll be fine. Just close your eyes and come with me."

Drew met the pleading darkness in his eyes, but instead of following the pull of his hand away from the Source, she stood firmly in place. "I can't just leave," she whispered. "It's calling me, and if you let yourself listen, you will hear it calling you too."

The Dreamers stood poised in the lengthening shadows of the town, Drew pulled toward the Source, while Gyfree tried to pull her away, until finally Gyfree's shoulders sagged and his body slumped in defeat. Then a wry smile twisted his lips, and he whispered, "I can't stay here without you. So if you must go, I'll go too. This world will have to find a new Keeper for itself. Perhaps Timi might accept the job."

A smile ghosted over Drew's face in response, but the dream filling her eyes could not be frightened away. Without another word, she turned back toward the Source, and with his hand in hers, led him away from the town and away from his world. From somewhere far behind them, they could hear a cry of protest, but their feet were on the road and were being hauled forward by something they could no more control than they could control their need to dream. They didn't feel themselves moving; instead it seemed as if the Source rushed toward them, or as if the intervening space had been an illusion that had been erased as soon as their feet had touched the road. They didn't know how they had reached the Source so quickly; all they knew for certain was that they were caught in the hold of something larger and far more powerful than they were, and that it was towering above them, an immense white that filled the entire field of their vision. Yet the white did not reach out to engulf them as Gyfree had expected; rather it receded before them, drawing their eyes but not their bodies into its unknown depths, revealing a distant gray that briefly swirled with the hazy forms of the last retreating creatures, and then closing against the gray so that once more there was nothing but an empty white that split apart the sky.

Pulled into Drew's dream, Gyfree felt his hand lifted in hers and then watched in detached surprise as their joined hands were plunged into the barren white. Suddenly his hand felt turned to ice, fingers wrapped in Drew's fingers of pure fire, and his eyes were stunned by the sight of ice-filled flames pouring into the gaping trap, filling the emptiness with heat and cold that first expanded then contracted the white in a wild pulse that threatened to shatter the whole. Like a giant and frantic heart the Source beat in and out, but even caught up in the frenzied throbbing, Gyfree realized that each outward thrust was being driven back by a wall of flames that had spread to the very edges of the white, and that each inward pulse constricted tighter and tighter around a thin silver vein of ice that ran through the center of the white as if offering permanent refuge from the blistering heat. Ever farther inward the white contracted, freezing to the ice in layers as the Source strained more and more toward the coolness and away from the heat, until at last all that remained was a solid core of glittering ice surrounded by flames. Then, just beyond where his fingers still twined through Drew's, the fire and the ice reached out long fingers to seize hold of each other, wrapping around and twisting together until they were once more completely intertwined, with every flame flickering around a chunk of ice at its center, and every chunk of ice fueling a silver-tipped flame.

There was nothing now except the fire and ice that had poured through the clasped hands of the Dreamers, and as Gyfree continued to watch with the detached surprise of a dream, the flames shrank back into the palms of their hands, and once more he could feel the cold soaking through his skin just as he could sense the heat seeping through Drew's. Then with a surprise that was no longer detached he realized that his eyes were filled with a smooth, pristine blue, and that this unmarred blue curved gracefully over him and the woman who still stood at his side, a dream slowly fading from her eyes, her warm hand clasped in his cool one.

"What just happened?" he asked her hoarsely.

A faint smile flickered over Drew's lips. "There was something my Figment gave me with his memories," she replied. "Something that gave me the courage to listen to the call of the Source, and to trust my own response."

"What could that have possibly been?" Gyfree asked faintly.

The smile that blazed across her face was reflected in eyes as clear as the sky arcing overhead. "The knowledge that I am here, completely here just as you are here, and not asleep in another world."

There was nothing tenuous in the pressure of their lips, and nothing tentative in the way their bodies curved together beneath the dark blue sky curving over them.

Chapter 16

Since no one had yet had the courage to venture back to ascertain what had become of their homes, for the time being the six companions and the hummeybees had the town completely to themselves. The hummeybees had discovered a delightfully well-stocked garden in the center of town and were busily buzzing from blossom to blossom before settling into the nearby treetops for the night, while the people, after helping themselves to the stores of an equally well-stocked kitchen, were lounging at their ease in front of their unwitting host's fireplace.

"So," Peyr laughingly finished his account of the day's events, "once Timi released all restraints on her perilous charm, the Figments had no choice but to do exactly as they were bid and take themselves back home."

"Their tails between their legs," joked Mischa. "At least those that had tails."

"And you're telling us that these abilities were in Timi before she ever dreamed the Figment?" questioned Gyfree.

"I think they had to be," Timi herself admitted softly. "Now that I look back at myself honestly, I always seemed to have the talent of drawing people to me. I think it frightened me, frightened me so much that I went out of my way to go unnoticed, to try to push people away from me, to convince myself that I was somehow less than what I was. Then when I dreamed the Figment, I was less." A flush rose in her cheeks, and the old fear shone in her eyes. "But I will also admit that any power I might have possessed before I dreamed my Figment was nothing compared to the power I possess now that I have reabsorbed him. I dreamed him far, far more powerful than I had ever been, and now all that increased power is inside me. I even have powers and abilities that I never had before, simply because I dreamed those things as part of him. Just as the power of your Figments is now within the two of you."

Peyr gave Timi a reassuring squeeze, and smiled as she turned her eyes in his direction. "You've already proven that you can be trusted with those powers."

"And us?" queried Gyfree. "Do the rest of you still trust Drew and me?"

"Trust really shouldn't be an issue here," stated Peyr. "Whatever powers you've gained should be well within your ability to control."

"What makes you so sure?" persisted Gyfree.

"You both already had so much power," Timi replied, "what difference can the power added by your Figments really make? And I for one believe that you two will always use whatever powers you possess for the best of this world. Despite, Gyfree, what you inadvertently did to me when you turned me into a Dreamer."

"Which, you will note, ended up being of great benefit to this world," Peyr interjected dryly.

"It certainly saved our lives," Sevor declared, pulling Mischa close as the memory of the horde of Figments flashed through his eyes.

"The one thing I still don't understand," Timi commented after a lengthy and thoughtful pause, her brow creasing in a delicate frown, "is what happened to the Source. What happened to your Figments is easy to understand—"

"At least for you," irrepressibly interrupted Mischa.

Timi glared at the other woman but continued on as if she had never been cut off. "But I'm still not sure how sticking your hands into the Source made it disappear."

"To tell the truth, neither am I," Gyfree admitted.

Staring drowsily, but not dreamily, into the flames that tamely crackled and flickered in the fireplace, Drew thought of the fire that glowed deep within her, and of all the things she had seen in the light of those wild flames. She had learned much, had even learned much about herself, but there were still things she didn't understand, things that hovered in shadow, things she was still trying to grasp. "It's hard to explain," she murmured, trying through words to find understanding not just for the others, but for herself, "but although there was something about the Source that made me think at first of a giant wound that needed healing, I somehow knew there was more to it than that. The closer I came to it, the more it seemed like a door that had been opened so quickly and violently that it had been torn off its hinges, a door that could not be repaired until someone with the correct tools came along. A door that desperately needed to be repaired." Drew shook her head, as if the ideas she was grasping had jumbled her thoughts. "Yet it was also more than just a damaged door, for it seemed not so much as if the Barrier had been ripped open there, but as if the Barrier had itself been built around that gaping portal. And somehow I knew that in our hands Gyfree and I finally had the tools to fix it, then close it, and even lock it so it could never be opened again."

"I'm sorry to say this, Drew," Timi sighed, "but the more you explain, the more confused I become. You're not making any sense at all."

"I wouldn't say that," Sevor remarked cryptically.

"Wouldn't say what?" demanded Peyr.

"That she doesn't make sense. Because, in fact, she makes perfect sense," Sevor answered with a mysterious smile.

"Well, if you understand what I'm trying to explain, I wish you'd clarify it for me too!" Drew snapped.

"Be glad to. I guess now that everything's been finished, there's no harm."

Mischa growled playfully, baring her teeth at him. "Now!"

Sevor grinned impudently at Mischa, but then the smile slowly faded and his eyes sought out the fire as if his explanation, like Drew's, could be found in its flames. "When I first met you I told you that I had been dreaming about you for years. I meant it. I was a young man when I first dreamed of Mischa, and Timi didn't enter my dreams until the night Gyfree changed her, but I've witnessed from very early on almost everything important that has happened to Gyfree and Drew. That's how I knew about Drew and the hummeybees, even though she had almost completely forgotten. And how I know things that Gyfree has himself carefully forgotten, assuming he ever understood them at all."

Gyfree leaned forward, the arm he had wrapped around Drew's shoulders pulling her forward as well. "Such as?" he demanded.

Despite the insistence in Gyfree's voice, Sevor's eyes never wavered from the fire, and it was several minutes before he continued. "It's a funny thing about fire," he mused when he finally spoke again. "Sometimes it springs into existence in a single moment, like when a bolt of lightning strikes a dead tree, but other times it takes a number of things to create a fire. Take our fire here for instance. I collected the wood from a shed outside. Mischa piled it in the fireplace. Peyr opened the flue so there would be enough air to sustain the flames. And Drew, in a fashion I'd rather not think about, sparked it to life with a touch of her hand. In other words, it was a group effort, with several of us contributing to the creation of the final product."

"And I thought Drew was confusing," snapped Timi.

"Be patient," Sevor returned, another smile kinking the corners of his lips. "I promise, at some point it will hopefully all make sense."

Peyr quipped, "Let's hope that point is sooner rather than later."

Sevor grimaced, but continued, "There are more worlds in existence than mine, or Drew's old one, or the hummeybees' home, or the one beneath us now. And most of these worlds are like the fire in this fireplace. They were created not by one thing, but by many. They are the products of a collective effort. To be specific, they are the outcome of collective dreams."

Drew gasped, "What are you trying to say?"

"You should have learned by now the power inherent in dreams," Sevor answered softly. "So you shouldn't be so surprised. Dreams that are strong enough create worlds of their own, but at the start these are no more than feeble mists floating somewhere between the void and the solid, waking worlds. To take this a step further, you might say these misty places exist in a universe of dreams that is separate and distinct, but not completely apart, from the universe of the void and the universe of waking. This is the universe visited by Dreamers whenever they dream. And there are places in this universe returned to time and again, places visited by not just one Dreamer but many, places that once created, however tenuously, slowly take on a life of their own. A real life that can move them from outside the universe of dreaming into the universe of waking worlds. These are the worlds created, slowly over time, by the power of collective dreams. Most worlds, whether or not you accept it, were brought into existence as collective dreams."

"But what of the people who live in a world like yours, or this one, or my old one?" Drew questioned.

"When you dream, don't you people your dreams?" responded Sevor. When both Gyfree and Drew silently nodded, he added. "Like the misty places they first occupy, these dream people are insubstantial and vague, but as the world they occupy solidifies, so do they. And when the world slips free from the dream universe, so do the people who only started as wisps of dream themselves."

"Are you saying that the worlds we know are all populated by Figments?" demanded Mischa.

Sevor shook his head. "Remember the hummeybees?" he chided. "If you anchor your dream creations to a real world, they take on a new life different from the existence of a Figment. And some of these onetime Figments even start to dream real dreams themselves. Dreams that over time may contribute to the creation of other new worlds."

"What of my Figment, then?" demanded Timi. "Wasn't he anchored to the same world as the hummeybees?"

"No," answered Sevor with a shake of his head. "He never belonged there, not even in his own mind. Given the time, he might have been able to anchor himself to this world, but fortunately that didn't happen."

Timi questioned, "And if he had?"

"It would have been nearly impossible to expel him. And impossible for you to reabsorb him. Yet his powers over people would have been the same."

"So why don't all Figments become as solid and living as the hummeybees?" asked Peyr. "Or do they, over time?"

"Only if they are connected strongly enough to a dream world that becomes real. Many Figments aren't even linked to any specific dream world, for they are neither dreamed repeatedly in the same dream setting, like Drew's hummeybees, nor dreamed somewhere so decisively that they can't break free. And just as it takes truly strong dreaming to create a Figment in the first place, and even stronger dreaming to connect a Figment to a world, it also takes a lot of truly powerful dreaming before a world can slip from dreaming to waking. Most dream worlds never move beyond the realm of dreams," answered Sevor. "Many are created, only to slowly fade away, just like a fire deprived of fuel. Any Figments brought to existence in these dreams slip into the void. They may easily visit any of the worlds within the dream universe whenever they choose, and the very strongest may even slip into a waking world, but the void is their home, and as long as they live there, they can never be anything other than Figments."

"Yet if that's true," commented Drew, "there should be far more Figments than there are people, and in my old world alone, there are a lot of people."

Sevor's eyes gleamed wickedly. "Figments don't reproduce, remember? People, on the other hand, are quite proficient in that area."

A thoughtful frown settled over Gyfree's face as he observed, "Earlier you said that Figments aren't bound by the same rules that bind people like us. They don't age, and in the normal course of things, they never die. So how do you explain the fact that my Figment had aged, just as I have aged, in the time since I first dreamed her?"

"She chose to age, to change in the same way she could feel you change. Figments don't age naturally, but they are usually able to change at will. There have only been two exceptions to that rule, at least as far as I know," Sevor responded.

"My Figment," stated Drew.

And Timi added, "And mine."

There was a long moment of silence, a long moment when all eyes delved deeply into the fire, and then Gyfree asked, "So what does any of this have to do with me? Or with what Drew and I did to the Source? Isn't that where this explanation started?"

Sevor again nodded. "Remember what I said about the fire? That sometimes creating a fire is a group effort, and sometimes a single thing can bring it into being? Well, it's the same with worlds. Drew dreamed the hummeybees' world into existence without any help at all. And you did the exact same thing."

"Now what are you talking about?" Gyfree demanded.

"This world, of course. This world that has chosen you as its Keeper. This world that has been your home since you were a child. It was never here until you dreamed it into existence."

Every previous silence had been thoughtful, even uneasy, but the silence that followed this announcement was stunned. Then finally, in a voice that would have been faint even for her old self, Timi asked, "So everyone on this world was once just a Figment?"

"Everyone on every other world I know of was once just a Figment," replied Sevor, "or the descendant of a onetime Figment. But you were all a bit different. Most worlds start as dreams, and these dreams are peopled by Figments, and if these worlds and Figments move out of the dream universe, it only happens gradually. Gyfree's dream of this world was so powerful that the world itself never existed as just a dream. This world sprang to life, full life, with people and all, from one powerful dream. Perhaps that is why dreams have so much power here, because this world was created by perhaps the most powerful dream ever dreamed. You, Timi, just like Peyr and Mischa, were born of people who were as living and breathing as no Figment has ever been, because that was what Gyfree dreamed: a real world filled with real people. A world he could escape to. A world that wouldn't hurt him the way his own world did. And just as importantly, a world where there were no dreams other than his own, for already he had seen the power in dreams, and he feared what dreams could do even more than he feared people. In his young mind, everyone had the same powers dreaming that he had. It wasn't in his power to stop his own dreams, but it was in his power to stop all others, so that at least here he would have no dreams to fear other than his own."

"But this world was already here when my Figment chased me here," Gyfree protested. "It was here before I ever knew it existed!"

"It was here because you had already dreamed it here. You dreamed it to be here whenever you needed it, and when you did need it, it was waiting, shining through the void to lead you home."

"So that's what the Source was!" Drew suddenly exclaimed.

Sevor smiled wryly in her direction. "Very good. You've impressed me once again."

"Well, I'm glad you're impressed," snapped Mischa, "but my head is reeling, and I'm feeling quite befuddled. If someone says one more thing that I can't understand, I'm going to scream."

Drew leaned forward despite Gyfree's convulsive grasp and laid a comforting hand on the other woman's shoulder. "I think it's more simple than you realize," she said soothingly. Then, with a quick smile at Sevor, she added, "Just correct me if I'm wrong."

"Certainly," agreed Sevor.

"It's just like the fire again . . ." began Drew.

Mischa groaned, "Please, not the fire again."

"Trust me," comforted Drew. "A fire always has to start with a single spark. Something ignites it with one single flash. However large that fire might grow, it still begins with just that first spark. And that's how Gyfree created this world. It had to start somewhere. Like a fire, every dream has a beginning, a starting place. And for this world, that place was the Source. The place where the dream of this world began. The place where this world itself began. The Source was never a break in the Barrier. It was where Gyfree began his dream, and then began his life in the world he had dreamed into reality."

Gyfree disagreed, "It's not just like I decided to show up one day, and here I was. And in fact, the first time I showed up, I was sent away again. Against my will."

"But you hadn't fully dreamed yourself here. You were still sleeping in a bed, away in the other world, so you had to return so you could wrest yourself away completely."

"But I felt myself break through the Barrier," Gyfree persisted.

"But if you created this world, you also created the Barrier around it," insisted Drew. "And I would suspect that you didn't do that until you found yourself pursued to the world that you had dreamed as a safe refuge. You were dreaming the first time you were chased here, so in your dream you created a Barrier to keep your Figment out. But you left a door in the Barrier so you could still get in. You left a door in the very spot the world began for you. Right at the Source."

"Very, very good," murmured Sevor.

Gyfree shook his head, his eyes a puzzle that demanded solving. "It just doesn't make sense to me. Even with everything I've seen and experienced, this world is far too alive to simply be one of my dreams. Especially since I would have had to dream it while I was still in a world where dreams are severely limited in power."

"Where your dream of this world started is irrelevant; where it ended is all that matters. Dreams in your old world are limited, but only within that world itself," Sevor informed him, "and only because most of them don't have the power to take hold and stay once they have been realized. That has nothing to do with their power in realms in which dreams can take hold, especially when dreams originate from a Dreamer as powerful as you."

"Why is our old world so limited?" questioned Drew. "Why are dreams there so weak?"

"Because that is how it was dreamed into existence. Yet there are many worlds out there, many worlds besides this one, where dreams don't immediately vanish into the dream world or the void, where dreams are part of reality, where dreams can shape reality. Worlds like the hummeybees'; even worlds like mine. After all, Drew did dream a road into my world. The power of dreams may be strongest here, but their power has never been limited to just this one world. Even in your old world there are dreams that cling, dreams that stay like ghosts to haunt the waking. These dreams might not be as powerful as they could be here, but they are not completely without power either."

"What are you trying to say now?" demanded Mischa.

Sevor's smile was even more wry than usual. "That Gyfree and Drew can dream their way into more worlds than just this one if they ever choose to, and change more worlds as well. They are only limited by whatever limits they set themselves in their own dreams."

"This is going way beyond me," complained Gyfree. "I can't accept that I created this world, and now you're trying to claim that there are no limits to what Drew and I could do."

Sevor shook his head. "There are always limits. Look around you, and you will see that this world is everything you dreamed it to be, but that your dream was controlled by definite limits."

Another piece of the puzzle clicked together in Drew's eyes. Looking up into his face she insisted, "If you really think about it, Gyfree, think about it as if it has nothing to do with you, you'll see there are so many strange things about this world that make sense only if you understand that they sprang originally from a dream."

"Such as?"

"This storybook town, to begin with. It reminded me of an illustration in a picture book from the moment I set eyes on it. If you dreamed it, you would have dreamed it as an ideal, and the only ideal you could have envisioned as a child would have been from a favorite movie or a treasured book. I doubt, from all you've hinted, that your childhood held many movies or even television shows."

"But there was a book," Gyfree conceded. "It was the one thing that was mine, the one thing I cherished. The one thing in my life that felt real and permanent."

"And then there are those other houses, the ones nearest the Barrier," Drew pressed. "The ones farthest from where your dream first took shape. The ones that had such an unpleasant effect on both of us. They looked just like the average house I grew up in, the average house that seemed to cover the part of the world I grew up in. If you ever lived in such a house, however fleetingly, you could have easily dreamed it and its duplicates into this world."

"I seem to remember a house or two. Maybe even more, although what I remember most was a large barren room full of children. But they all seem distant and unreal. Not like the pictures I recall from my book."

"Isn't distant and unreal a good way to describe how those houses still feel, at least to Dreamers like us? People who are sensitive to the peculiarities of things that spring from a dream? Is there anyone or anything other than a Dreamer who could create such houses, and make them feel that way?"

"But why would I dream something like those houses instead of more like the ones here, in this town?" Gyfree questioned.

"Haven't you ever had something unexpected slip into a dream?" Drew questioned. "It's like me and the hummeybees again. When Sevor first told me that I had dreamed their world as a refuge, I couldn't understand how such frightening creatures could have ever been a part of such a dream. Yet when I thought about it, I realized that, of all the hiding places I ever dreamed, only one never posed a threat of its own." Color flooded her cheeks as she thought of her hidden room beneath the stairs, and as sudden light flared in his eyes, she knew that his thoughts had followed hers as unerringly as he had always followed her himself. Leaning forward, the color in her cheeks even brighter, she continued, "I guess it wasn't in my nature to dream a perfect world, and it probably wasn't in your nature either. Just because your dream started as something desirable doesn't mean it would continue that way until the end. You began with a dream that was special to you, and then the dream turned and you found yourself in a place that was hauntingly familiar and uncomfortable, and then it stretched away into empty land, the sort of land that always springs up in my dreams when I'm feeling helpless and lost, and then the dream ended. At the edges of this dream you later erected a Barrier in fear of what nightmares might spill into your world, but where the dream started, at the Source, you left a perfect town against the Barrier itself because that was where you had first dreamed it into being. But even despite the success of your dream, you still were afraid to close the one opening in the Barrier, because at the time you thought this world was nothing more than just another dream, and that it could still transform into a nightmare like dreams often do. You may have dreamed your fears away over time, but you also dreamed away your memory of what the Source truly was. But you didn't dream the truth completely away, for the truth is still there, hidden in the Source's name. A source, after all, is where something begins, and not an exit as you always claimed yours to be."

"Very, very, very good," breathed Sevor, his eyes finally as wide with surprise as everyone else's.

"So if the Source was really just a door to this world, what happened to it today?" Peyr inquired after another uneasy pause. "And why have Dreamers always slipped through the Barrier itself instead? After all, the Source was the one place that could always be relied upon to take Dreamers back to their own world. How could it have ever been the way in when it has always been the surest way out?"

"That's a lot of questions all at once," Sevor responded with a laugh, "but I'll do my best to answer them all. The Source was a door, just as Drew surmised earlier, but something strange happened after Gyfree tore through it so violently, and after he and the Keeper had thrust his Figment back through. Despite the fact that he had finally gained his dream world, Gyfree never even thought of trying to close that gaping door. Because his earlier life experiences had indeed made him distrustful, he wanted it to stay open in case he ever needed to escape this world too. Yet his Figment was still there, on the other side, held at bay by the

Barrier he had dreamed to keep her out, but quite capable of slipping back in through that open door. He wanted that door open, but at the same time, he would only be safe if it was closed. So he dreamed that it led outward only, led irresistibly out of this world. And from that moment on, the Source always provided a sure way out, but only someone or something extraordinarily powerful could force a way in."

"Such as my Figment and his army," stated Drew.

"Right. Since the Source was the one open place in the Barrier, it was the easiest to enter, but since Gyfree had dreamed it leading inexorably away, it was the most difficult to move beyond. It took the strength of Drew's Figment, combined with the strength of his immense army, to move beyond the threshold of that door."

"You haven't really answered all my questions. What about the weakness of the Barrier itself?" Peyr interjected.

"That's right," added Mischa. "If Gyfree had the power to dream this world into existence, why couldn't he dream of a more substantial Barrier? A Barrier capable of keeping more than just his own Figment out?"

"Several reasons. First, once a world slips from dreaming to waking and becomes, for lack of a better word, real, it is no longer limited by the dream or dreams that brought it into existence. Just as Figments change when they become bound to a world, so do the worlds to which they are bound. And something like a Barrier can, and in fact will, change over time."

"And second?" wondered Timi.

"The same reason you are what you are," Sevor replied enigmatically.

Timi drawled, "A clearer explanation would be appreciated."

"This world was safe for Gyfree, but it was lonely. That was why, in a moment of weakness, he changed you with a single dream. And it's why he dreamed a Barrier that an occasional Dreamer could slip through. To be exact, an occasional Dreamer from a specific world. You see, without thinking about it, he was waiting, but he wasn't waiting for just anyone. He was waiting for Drew, and he needed to make sure she had a way to get in when she arrived."

"Are you saying he was somehow expecting Drew from the very beginning?" questioned Mischa, eyes wide and expression stunned. "Expecting her from the time he was just a little boy?"

"Yes," answered Sevor. "He could feel her shortly after he arrived here, could actually feel her from the moment she was born, could feel her long before he was old enough for his dreams of her to even take shape. Without truly understanding what he was feeling, or what the future would bring, he dreamed that the Barrier would be weak enough to someday let her in, yet strong enough to afford her whatever protection it could. And that's why, once she was here, her Figment couldn't find her, at least at first. The Barrier was shielding her because that was one of the most important things it had been dreamed to do."

Gyfree's arm tightened around Drew with a strength that stole her breath. But before she could protest, Peyr remarked, "Well, you've managed to answer all of my questions except for the first one I asked. The same question that started this whole thing. What exactly happened to the Source today?"

"Maybe I can answer that now," Gyfree murmured, his earliest dreams flitting through his eyes with his most recent ones. "If the Source was a door, it really was a door torn off its hinges. And where that door had been, there was nothing left, nothing to fill the empty space left behind. That's what Drew and I did. We dreamed a new door, gave it form and substance, and then we closed it so that it could never be opened again."

A worried frown settled over Mischa's face. "So what happens to the next strong Dreamer who arrives? We have had to rely on the Source a few times before."

"If a Dreamer is meant to leave, at some point, even if it takes a long time, that Dreamer will leave. But any Dreamer powerful enough to stay will be able to stay," Sevor told her gently.

"How many truly powerful Dreamers can this world survive?" Mischa insisted.

Sevor quirked an eyebrow, but his eyes reflected the concern in hers. "At least two."

"Maybe the Keeper can stop . . ." Mischa blurted before her eyes widened and she turned to Gyfree, consternation darkening her face.

"That's right," Sevor reminded her, "Gyfree is now the Keeper."

"This does get a bit tangled," remarked Peyr. "If this world has a Keeper, it's because Gyfree dreamed a Keeper for this world. Would that be right?"

"Absolutely. Gyfree dreamed a world that had the power to take care of him. A world he could trust even when he could trust no one else. But he needed more than the comfort or care that trees and rocks could supply. So he created a world that was conscious and alive, but that also invested its powers in a single person. A person who could then, along with the world, take care of him."

"So how could Gyfree dream a Keeper for this world, then become that Keeper himself?" Peyr continued.

"I'm not a small boy anymore," Gyfree answered for himself. "I don't want or need to be taken care of. For a long time now, I've wanted to take care of this world and its people. There's no one else I would trust with this task as I trust myself. I have the powers and the desire to keep this world safe."

"So did you choose to become Keeper, or did the land choose you?" Mischa pursued.

"I don't know," admitted Gyfree.

"Does it matter?" asked Timi. "For whatever reason, Gyfree is still as dedicated and as effective a Keeper as this world could have. In the last few days, he has accomplished more than his father could have ever accomplished. We don't need him despite the fact that he's a Dreamer, but because of it. And if he's now the Keeper of the world he created simply because he created it, well, who's better qualified? I've said I trust him, and I meant it. I for one am willing to trust him completely with the well-being of this world."

"And are you willing to trust him even when it comes to Drew? Willing to trust that he will serve the best interests of this world even if that means she cannot stay?" Mischa inquired, her eyes filled with an apology as great as her hidden fears as she looked at Gyfree and Drew.

"If there is a consensus that Drew must leave, then I will leave with her," Gyfree confessed. "I haven't waited all my life for her to appear just so I could watch her disappear. I feel nothing from the land other than its own desire for her to remain, but if you can't trust me in this, I will go with her."

"You would desert this world?" Mischa rasped sharply.

"I don't want to, but I will if that is my only choice. Although with the Source gone, I'm not sure how."

"With a dream," Drew whispered sadly. "You heard Sevor. You know as well as I do now that dreams really can take us anywhere."

Timi exclaimed, "This is absurd! Since her arrival, Drew has done as much to help this world as Gyfree has. From all I've seen, Gyfree needs her so he can be the best possible Keeper, and this world needs her because Gyfree alone may no longer be enough. This world is changing. It has been for some time. Didn't you hear what Sevor told us? Once a world has been truly established, it will grow and change just as we do. And just as we do, a world can die. Somehow I know that, for all the dangers behind us, there are still dangers ahead. And I would rather face them with Gyfree and Drew than alone."

Her own eyes shadowed by the dreams that still haunted her, Drew murmured, "I don't blame Mischa. I did bring an army of Figments on my trail. And I opened up the way for Gyfree's Figment to finally break through."

An ominous stillness followed, and the only sound was the snarling of the fire, a snarling that echoed deep within Drew. Then out of the stillness Mischa's voice finally crackled, "There were Dreamers who came before you, and many have been followed by Figments. You may have been the strongest, but not all have been weak, and not all of the Figments have been easy to expel. The fact that you were followed no longer matters, for the things that followed you have been defeated or expelled. What matters now is what effect you would have on this world if you stayed. What matters is whether there would be more harm in your staying than there would be in your leaving."

Sevor stated quietly, "I know this isn't my world, and the decision isn't mine. The decision may not even belong to those in this room, but to the rest of the people in this world. But I do feel compelled to say that I have dreamed of worlds other than yours, and of dangers you have yet to face, and I would not be hasty exiling Dreamers with not only the power but also the character of Gyfree and Drew. If it was my world I wouldn't ask them to stay, I'd beg them."

"Isn't this your world now?" Mischa questioned with a shy smile.

"I hope so. In which case, I'm begging for them to stay."

"Me too," Peyr and Timi echoed in unison.

Mischa tore her eyes from Sevor's smiling ones and looked deep into Drew's, so deep that Drew was almost certain that the other woman could see all the dreams that had chased her throughout her life, all the nightmares that had somehow herded her here. "Well, Dreamer," she murmured, "what are your dreams now?"

"To stay in the first place that has ever felt real to me, real enough that I don't need to dream of something better, real enough to live for. And to wake up to the man of my dreams even when I'm done dreaming," whispered Drew.

Mischa nodded, but her eyes probed even deeper, to Drew's very core, where a dream of fire, for the moment, peacefully glowed. "There's so much I'm still trying to absorb. So much I'm trying to understand. So just answer me one more question," she requested.

"I will if I can."

"What is a dream, and what is reality?"

Drew smiled, and seeing the birth of a different fire in her eyes, Mischa smiled back. In a voice that made the flames in the fireplace leap high, she replied, "Reality is whatever we dream it to be."

The fire had died down, as all fires denied an endless supply of fuel inevitably must, and the six companions had tactfully split apart to seek their own rooms for the night. Timi and Peyr, then Sevor and Mischa, had disappeared up the stairs, but Gyfree and Drew had lingered behind, his arms wrapped about her waist and his face immersed in her hair as she watched the soft glow of the dying embers. Then as the last of the firelight faded, she twisted in his arms and lifted her face toward his, her lips as warm and inviting as the fire had been, far too warm and inviting to resist. His breath was cool as his mouth plunged down, and her tongue felt like fire, but as their lips parted against each other, her breath heated his just as his tongue cooled hers, until all they shared was a deliciously arousing warmth. When at long last he raised his head, he commented hoarsely, "Time to turn in."

Swinging her up into his arms, he headed toward the stairs, but instead of setting his foot upon the bottom step, he continued on, pausing outside a narrow door nestled beneath the stairs. With a flick of one hand, he flung the door open, and together they peered into the cramped and gloomy space cluttered with mops and brooms. Then a dream brightened their eyes, a dream they had shared and would always share, and the closet before them stretched back farther than their eyes could follow. Unlike the shadowy room Drew had once dreamed alone, this one was well-lit, and instead of the narrow bed that had sheltered her in her lonely dreaming, there was a spacious one stacked with welcoming pillows and thick blankets. Kicking the door closed behind them, Gyfree carried her across the room and laid her gently among the pillows. As she opened her arms to him, he lowered his body slowly over hers, until his entire length pressed against her, his body trembling just as she was trembling. Lips hovering directly above hers, once more waiting to crash down, he whispered, "Except for the room, we're not dreaming this time."

"So what's the difference?" she whispered back, her eyes alight with mischief and desire.

"Let me show you," he answered.

Alone in their secret corner of the void, the watchers still watched. They had watched through the darkness, fangs gnawing anxiously on bone, fingers flexing nervously around heart and lungs, dog and mother waiting for the darkness to pass. And then, when the brittle bone seemed sure to snap, and the quivering heart and lungs sure to collapse, they could once more see through the eyes that had for a time seen through theirs. Before them stood the Dreamers, so small and vulnerable, like children holding hands, and then the Dreamers looked up, pinning them in place, pinning their masters in place, and as they watched through their masters' eyes, they knew they and their masters were the ones as helpless as children, that their masters were once again as vulnerable as they had been in the moment of their creation, and they were grateful that they were the ones simply watching, that they could still hide in the dark where they could not be seen as their masters had been seen, or understood as their masters had been understood, or accepted as they could not have borne being accepted. Their masters had been imprisoned by those dreaming eyes, but they at least were still free.

And still they watched the Dreamers, watched through eyes that were just their own, watched because they could see clearly now that the darkness had receded. They watched, and they listened, and they learned about the world beneath the Dreamers' feet, and they learned about the ways of dreaming. They learned more and saw more than their masters had ever taken the time to learn or see. And still they watched, fangs gently gnawing bone, fingers softly massaging heart and lungs, watched because they had been granted the power to watch, watched because they felt the need to watch, there in their hidden corner of the void.

On they watched, until finally the dog grew restless, and his fangs again grew sharp, and as the woman's fingers pierced his heart and scraped raw his lungs, he growled, "Why are we still watching?"

"We're not," hissed the nightmare mother. "We're planning."